Third Starlighter

Third Starlighter

TALES OF STARLIGHT SERIES

LIVING
INK
BOOKS
Writing Worth Reading

Bryan Davis

Third Starlighter
Volume 2 in the Tales of Starlight® series

Copyright © 2011 by Bryan Davis

Published by Living Ink Books, an imprint of
AMG Publishers, Inc.
6815 Shallowford Rd.
Chattanooga, Tennessee 37421

This is a work of fiction. Names, characters, places, and incidents either are the
product of the author's imagination or are used fictitiously. Any resemblance to
actual persons, either living or dead, events, or locales, is entirely coincidental.

Print Edition:	ISBN 13: 978-0-89957-885-9	ISBN 10: 0-89957-885-3
EPUB Edition	ISBN 13: 978-1-61715-116-3	ISBN 10: 1-61715-116-5
Mobi Edition	ISBN 13: 978-1-61715-218-4	ISBN 10: 1-61715-218-8
PDF Edition	ISBN 13: 978-1-61715-219-1	ISBN 10: 1-61715-219-6

First Printing—September 2011

TALES OF STARLIGHT is a registered trademark of AMG Publishers.

Cover designed by Daryle Beam at Bright Boy Design,
Chattanooga, TN.

Interior design and typesetting by Reider Publishing Services, West Holly-
wood, California.

Edited and proofread by Susie Davis, Sharon Neal, and Rick Steele.

Printed in the United States of America
15 14 13 12 11 10 –BP– 6 5 4 3 2 1

Third Starlighter, published by AMG/Living Ink, is the second book in Tales of Starlight, a series for adults that acts as a companion series to Dragons of Starlight, a series for young adults published by Zondervan.

How to Read the Series:

You can fully enjoy the Tales of Starlight series without reading the companion series, Dragons of Starlight. If you read both series, however, you will enjoy a fuller understanding of the story world.

If you intend to read both series, here is my suggested reading order:

1. Starlighter (Dragons of Starlight book #1)
2. Masters & Slayers (Tales of Starlight book #1)
3. Warrior (Dragons of Starlight book #2)
4. Third Starlighter (Tales of Starlight book #2)
5. Diviner (Dragons of Starlight book #3)
6. Liberator (Dragons of Starlight book #4)
7. Exodus Rising (Tales of Starlight book #3)

You may switch the reading order for entries 1 and 2 on the above list without any problem, and you may also switch the order for entries 4 and 5.

Parents' Guide:

Although *Third Starlighter* is designed for adults, it can be read by teenagers, especially those who have enjoyed *Starlighter* and *Warrior*, the first two books in the Dragons of Starlight series. The adult designation is due to the fact that the story follows the adventures of adult characters instead of teenagers.

The good-versus-evil violence in this book is similar to that of the young adult series. It is no more graphic or gory. There are no sexual scenes and no profanity or sexually provocative language.

ONE

DARKNESS is a robe that cloaks an eerie choir, and sleepless is the protector of the innocent. Adrian sat against a wide cypress trunk, listening to the swamp's chorus—the clacking of branches tossed by a wet breeze, the trilling of crickets nestled under rotting logs, and the stirring of marsh water that veiled serpents and other nocturnal predators, restless at the presence of a human intruder.

As a faint splash sounded, he tightened his grip on the hilt of his sword, his usual response. No matter how many times he reminded himself that countless frogs and bugs hopped from place to place, the slightest noise raised a reflexive twitch, an instinctive call to protect the girls in his care.

Penelope and Shellinda lay in his embrace. Their weight had stiffened his arms, creating a buzzing numbness and making it difficult to hold a sword as well as two girls. Discomfort was a minor sacrifice. After their harrowing escape, the fugitive slave girls needed as much rest as they could get, and their slumber provided a chance to pause and plan. Not only that, their gentle breathing added a soothing background hum to the choir's never-ending song. At least they were able to sleep peacefully, unaware of the surrounding peril and unconcerned about their draconic slave masters' relentless pursuit.

Near Adrian's feet, Marcelle lay quietly, still showing no signs of conscious thought. Only an occasional blink interrupted her wide-eyed stare. The spirited sword maiden who once animated that sinewy frame seemed to be lost within, unable to surface. The torturous ordeal she had suffered while chained to the Reflections Crystal had accomplished what no battle opponent ever could—it had vanquished her fighting spirit. His childhood friend needed someone to lead her out of the fog, but who could grasp the hand of a phantom wandering in a sightless world?

Biting his lip, Adrian looked toward the sky, barely visible through the web of overhanging branches. A cloud bank obscured Starlight's triple moons, allowing the swampy floor just a faint glow to dress its murky pools. If only the Creator could shed at least that much light on Marcelle's path, maybe she could find her way home.

Adrian gazed at the girls' dirty faces, their slack muscles showing no hint of anxiety. For many children, darkness equals fear. The shadows of the unknown conceal lurking predators, especially the contorted shadows cast by the gnarled branches of wind-battered trees. Not so for children running from a whip. For them, darkness provides a blanket of protection—a hideaway, a cloaked corner of this blood- and tear-stained world where the dragons' piercing eyes could not reach.

Glancing again at the dark sky, Adrian relaxed his muscles. No dragon had shown a leathered wing for hours. Their patrol had apparently veered toward a more habitable portion of the forest, thinking no escapees in their right mind would dare venture into the snake-infested marshes that spread across the wilderness in the dragon realm. Yet, those on the run had little choice, hemmed in by the forest's natural borders—an impassable mountain range to the south and dangerous swamps to the west. Any other direction would take an escaping human out into an open plateau where he would be easy prey for the winged hunters. Even if he could elude the dragons under the cover of darkness, he would eventually run into an insurmountable barrier wall encompassing most of the region.

Adrian firmed his jaw. They still had one hope—to find Frederick, his older brother. He had indicated in a video message that he would try to help the Lost Ones, but searching for him in the dragons' domain had been fruitless. Every human slave agreed that the wilderness remained the only possible refuge for the would-be emancipator.

No sign of Frederick had appeared, though that was no big surprise considering the darkness, the swiftness of their flight, and the worsening terrain. After trudging into these lowlands, it had taken hours to find high ground where they could sit in relative dryness and try to get a little sleep. With dawn approaching, their refuge would soon lose its protective shield, and they would have to find an area with a denser population of trees, though the protection would come at a painful cost—wet trousers and biting insects.

A louder splash reached Adrian's ears. Holding his breath, he stared into the blackness. Something moved out there, something creeping closer, then stopping, then drawing closer again. He took in a long draw of the moldy air. A new scent spiced the breeze, a bestial odor that raised images of the mountain bears back on Major Four, yet fouler, like wet goat's hair that had soured in the sun.

"We have to go," he whispered in a calm tone. A slow-and-easy exit would likely keep the girls composed and the beast at bay. Maybe it drew near to investigate the new arrivals, and startling it might put it in a defensive mode.

He rose to his feet, his arms loosening around the girls as he propped them up. "Stay close while I get Marcelle."

"Okay," Shellinda said, her whispered voice rattling, a sign of exposure to the cool, damp air. She still wore a makeshift tunic she had fashioned out of a sheet, far too big for her undersized body, but better than what she had worn at the cattle camp—short, ratty trousers and no shirt at all. "Do you need help?"

"Just hold this a second." Adrian pushed the sword hilt into Shellinda's hand and hoisted Marcelle over his shoulder. She struggled, flailing her arms and kicking, though she said nothing. "Shhh ..." He let the shushing sound fade slowly. Soon, Marcelle relaxed, though one hand clutched the back of his shirt tightly, her nails digging into his skin.

After taking the sword again, he guided the girls together. Although dimness shaded their faces, they were easy to tell apart. Penelope, a former dragon-cave servant, stood a foot taller than the younger, malnourished Shellinda, a recent escapee from the cattle camp. "It's pretty dark," he said, "but we can find our way back without a problem. Just look for the branches I broke. Since we know it's safe the way we came, I'll guard our rear. Okay?"

"That's okay with me." Penelope peeked around him. "Is something out there?"

"I think so, but if it's hungry, it probably would've attacked by now. Let's just move out of its sniffing range." He pointed with his sword. "March slowly and as quietly as possible."

Taking Shellinda's hand, Penelope walked away from the tree and into shallow water, her progress slow as her head shifted, apparently in search of the branches Adrian had sliced to mark their trail. He stayed close, glancing back every few seconds while trying to listen for the slightest sounds, though the noise they made themselves threatened to drown out the stealthy creature that skulked behind them.

A slight breeze wafted in their faces, providing no help in detecting the beast's approach. Instead, it sent their own odor, a blend of sweat from their recent run and blood from the various scratches and bug bites, back to the potential predator. If it relished the aroma of stinking, wounded humans, it was probably getting enough to whet its appetite.

"Now that we can travel more slowly," Adrian said, forcing a confident tone, "we can look for signs of my brother."

"What signs?" Shellinda asked without looking back.

"Wood smoke in the air. Stumps with no fallen trees. Bushes that ought to have berries this time of year but don't. And once the sun gets high enough, if there are no dragons around, we can look for footprints out in open areas."

"I hope they didn't catch Scott," Penelope said.

"He's fine. Since he got us to the wilderness safely, I'm sure he could stay away from the dragons on his way back to the village. It's a lot easier to hide when you're alone."

The girls marched on, their forms becoming clearer in the glow of dawn. Marcelle squirmed, grunting whenever Adrian took a harder step. "Hang in there," he whispered. "I'll get you home, and we'll find a doctor. As long as you're alive, there's hope."

A new odor filtered into his nostrils, the distinctive scent of urine, and wetness spread across his shoulder. Wrinkling his nose, he didn't miss a step. "It's okay. I know you don't have control. When we stop, I'll ask the girls to clean you up, and we'll get you some more water." As he spoke, it seemed at times that her fingers tightened around his shirt in response. Yet, the movements could also have been instinctive reactions to the jostling. Although she drank water readily, no amount of coaxing could get her to chew and swallow food. He would need to find liquid nutrients for her before too much longer.

Adrian glanced back again. The sound of sloshing water, perhaps a dozen steps behind, had definitely increased, now slow and rhythmic, as if the predator intentionally matched their pace. A slight rumble joined the rising din, a growl that could be from the throat of a big cat or the empty stomach of a bear. Whatever it was, the cadence of the splashes gave evidence of a four-legged beast.

As rays of dawn filtered through the canopy, Adrian touched Penelope's shoulder. "The sun's coming up. I think we can move a little faster now."

"I smell smoke," Shellinda said. "That's a good sign, right?"

"I hope so." Adrian sniffed the air. With all his attention diverted to the sounds, he had neglected the other senses. Indeed, the aroma of burning wood rode the breeze—new wood, freshly cut. With dry ground only a few paces ahead, maybe they were approaching Frederick's refuge. It made sense that he would stay close to the swamp, a source of water and a place to hide. "I smell it, too. Veer a little bit to the right and—"

A loud splash erupted. Adrian spun. A huge, catlike beast lunged, claws extended and teeth bared. With another spin, he heaved Marcelle toward the girls, shouting, "Take her!" and swung back toward the beast, both hands now on the hilt as he hacked with his sword. The flat of the blade crashed against the cat's skull, barely raising a spray of blood as its hairy body barreled into him and knocked him flat.

His sword flew out of his hands. The girls screamed. The cat's teeth sank into Adrian's shoulder. Its claws dug into his scalp. Then, it fell limp.

Lying under its crushing weight, Adrian pushed with both arms. With a final heave, he rolled out from under its smelly body and jumped to his feet. The cat lay motionless, its head separated from its shoulders. Less than two paces away, Penelope and Shellinda stood as if frozen, their mouths agape. Next to them, Marcelle wobbled on her feet, Adrian's sword in hand. Her eyes wide, she dropped it and backed away.

"Marcelle!" Adrian leaped to a run. As he reached out to grab her, she fell to her knees.

Blinking, she whispered, "Adrian," then collapsed.

Before she could fall into the mud, he scooped her into his arms. Without looking back at the cat, he marched away from the swamp, the mud thick on his boots. "Let's go, girls! Penelope, get my sword."

Penelope snatched up the sword and scrambled to the front, slashing ferns and fronds with the blade.

"Don't get too far ahead!" Adrian called.

Shellinda half walked, half jogged at his side, her tunic slipping down her rail-thin shoulders. "Is Marcelle okay?"

"She's breathing. And her instinctive response to danger is a good sign."

"I suppose so." Shellinda let out a quiet sigh. "I'll keep praying for her."

As Adrian hurried to keep Penelope in sight, Shellinda's words reverberated in his mind. *I'll keep praying for her.* This girl had suffered so much at the whips and claws of cruel beasts, yet her faith survived. Did others still cling to hope? Or had most given up? It seemed that desperation, at least in Shellinda's case, was fertile ground for seeds of faith.

The aroma of burning wood came and went, as if teasing, first leading one direction, then another. After about an hour, Penelope called, "The smell is getting stronger!"

Adrian took in a deep draught. Yes, the distinctive odor had thickened. They wouldn't lose it again.

Soon, the ground sloped upward. Penelope halted at the top of the rise and waited, her eyes wide as a smile grew on her face. When Adrian arrived with Marcelle and Shellinda, he stopped and surveyed the area. Nestled in the center of a dense stand of trees, a primitive cabin stood, undetectable if not for a worn path weaving through the trees to the front door. With a roof of huge leaves and intertwined vines, and walls of stacked logs cemented with mud, it appeared to be something from a storybook, a primitive squatter's cabin from Mesolantrum's early settlement days.

"That has to be Frederick's refuge." Adrian hiked Marcelle higher into his arms. "Let's go!"

Marcelle thrashed, forcing Adrian to set her on her feet. She crouched low and hid her face between her knees, breathing rapidly.

"Everything's fine," Adrian whispered. "This is the place we were looking for." Grasping her arm, he pulled her up. As he steadied her, her legs trembled. "Would you like to try to walk?"

Her eyes darted all around, but she said nothing. He guided her forward, taking slow, easy steps to avoid the trees and brambles. As she wobbled and swayed, he held her arm more firmly. This exercise would be good for her. She needed to strengthen her muscles. Maybe more blood flow would heal her brain as well.

When they drew within a dozen paces of the door, three boys and three girls emerged from the cabin, their stares fixed on their visitors. One boy stood taller than the others. Perhaps twelve or so, he wore a hardened face—skeptical beyond his years. His muscles bulged under his thin clothes, apparently swelled by slave labor. Although clean from head to toe, all six wore ragged knee-length trousers and hole-infested shirts. One also wore a hat made of black feathers woven together with green ivy that bloomed with tiny white flowers. Since she was young, thin, and apparently bald, if not for the feminine hat, guessing her gender would have been impossible. With spotty blemishes on her face, she gazed aimlessly, as if blind.

A man appeared from around the cabin, pushing a one-wheeled cart between two trees. When he noticed the arrivals, his eyes bulged, and he dropped the cart. Blinking rapidly, he smoothed out his clothes and hurried to join the children, his fingers tight around a sword hilt at his hip. His uniform and dark handlebar mustache gave away his identity, though both appeared damp and drooping, as if he had been caught in a rainstorm.

"Drexel?" Adrian said. "What are you doing here?"

"Hoping to help you." Drexel bowed toward Marcelle, then toward Adrian. "You look like you have been through a battle."

Adrian touched the bite mark on his scalp. It oozed blood, but it wasn't too bad. "I've been through my share of tussles, but I'm okay."

"That's good, but it seems that Marcelle has not fared as well. She appears to be quite ill."

Adrian glanced at her. With her mouth partially open and her eyes wide and glazed, she seemed to be lost in her dream world again. "She is ill. She suffered a lot at the hands of the dragons."

"Wicked beasts!" Drexel scowled for a moment before letting his face relax. "Shall we prepare a place for her to lie down?"

Adrian eyed Drexel. As the head of the palace sentries, he held an influential position in the Underground Gateway. He had always been able to switch facial expressions quickly, aiding the cause to rescue the slaves at one moment and licking the governor's boots the next. "Thank you. That would be very helpful."

Drexel waved a hand toward the door. "Take her inside. The children will help you."

"She needs to be cleaned up. She's not ... well ... not in control of her faculties."

"I understand. Perhaps your female companions can take her in, and Cassandra"—he patted one of the three girls on her head, pressing down her tangled dark hair—"will help with the bedding and cleanup. In fact, all three girls can help, and I will send the boys away, then we can discuss my presence here privately."

Adrian nodded. "That will be fine."

Penelope gave Adrian his sword, then, led by the other girls, she and Shellinda guided Marcelle through the door. When all six faded from sight, Drexel tousled the hair of the tallest boy, but he ducked away, a scowl on his face.

"Orlan," Drexel said, apparently unaffected by the boy's rebuff, "find Frederick. He'll want to know that his brother is here."

"His brother?" Orlan stared at Adrian. "He *does* look like Frederick."

"Of course he does. Go on now, and take the other boys with you. There is safety in numbers."

The two younger boys looked at each other, fear in their eyes, but they stayed quiet.

"Did Frederick say where he was going?" Orlan asked. "He must have gotten up before dawn."

Drexel nodded. "He said he was going to check his traps."

"He checks them in the evening," one of the younger boys said, "so the birds won't pick them clean during the night."

"Perhaps I misheard him. He might be trying to catch some fish for breakfast, so look for him at the stream."

Orlan shook his head. "His fishing gear is still behind the cabin."

"Very well. Then look for him at the hunting stand. If he isn't there, then check the stream."

"He's not hunting." Orlan pointed over his shoulder with his thumb. "His bow and arrows are still here, too."

"Since you're so well-informed," Drexel said through clenched teeth, "search for him wherever you wish. If you're frightened, take the bow and arrows. Just go."

Orlan shot a glance at Adrian and at his sword, then scampered around the cabin with the other two boys. Seconds later, they appeared at the corner where Drexel had left the cart and ran deeper into the woods, Orlan with a bow in his hand and the two boys clutching arrows. Soon, the pounding of their bare feet faded.

Adrian continued listening. Could there be other big cats prowling the woods, or were they confined to the marsh? The two smaller boys seemed pensive, frightened. Their slave mentalities, however, wouldn't allow them to appeal. "I would like to go with them." He lifted his sword, displaying a smear of blood on the blade. "We killed a big catlike creature on the way here. They wouldn't stand a chance against one."

"They're long gone," Drexel said. "We could never catch up."

"I'm sure I can track them. Let's talk on the way."

Drexel glanced at the cabin. "Who will guard the girls?"

"The door's closed. They should be fine." Adrian marched along the path the boys had taken, eyeing the broken twigs and flattened foliage they had left behind. His heart pounded with every footfall. After all these long months, he and Frederick would soon be reunited.

"I take it you found the dragon's portal," Drexel said from a few steps back.

A chill ran up Adrian's spine. Walking in front of Drexel was unnerving. "I did find the portal, but in an unexpected way. I can explain everything when Frederick comes."

"Of course. Retelling stories can be tedious."

"I know what you mean." Adrian used his blade to push a broken fern out of the way. "But do you mind telling me how you got here?"

"I found the portal Uriel Blackstone used." Drexel pulled on Adrian's sleeve, stopping him. In his hand, he held a small book. "This is his journal. I happened upon it in Governor Prescott's room when we were searching for evidence. You see, shortly after you left, someone murdered the good governor, so I—"

"Murdered?"

"Yes, a tragedy, to be sure." Drexel averted his gaze, apparently looking in the cabin's direction. "Of course, with this portal information in hand, I decided to come here. I hoped to bring proof of Dracon's existence back to Mesolantrum so I could muster an army to rescue the Lost Ones. I thought bringing a malnourished child home would be sufficient to embolden the hearts of our people against the dragons."

"I see," Adrian said, nodding. "An emotional hook. Since you have children now, are you going back soon?"

Drexel shook his head. "It seems that the journal lacks instructions on how to open the portal from this side, so I am trapped here. Since I was fortunate enough to find Frederick, I assume the Creator is guiding me on my path, and I expected, knowing your reputation as a superb tracker, that you would eventually find both of us here. Since you have arrived, it seems that my supposition has been confirmed. Now the three of us will find a way home with these children in tow."

"Maybe more than three. My father is in a place called the Northlands, and a dragon told me Jason is trying to get there."

"A dragon told you Jason is here?" Drexel's scowl returned. "And you believed the lying beast?"

Adrian cocked his head, pondering Drexel's sudden outburst. Was this real anger or another one of his calculated shifts in mood? "I spoke to Arxad, the dragon priest. He mentioned Jason's name before I did, so they must have met."

"Not necessarily." Drexel shifted his weight from foot to foot, again averting his eyes. "I have long suspected that the dragons have been communicating with Governor Prescott about a possible trade to obtain extane from our world. Perhaps Arxad heard your brother's name from him."

"Not likely. I think Arxad wants the Lost Ones to leave. He has no reason to lie."

Drexel's eyes focused on Adrian, his brow bending. "A naïve conclusion. I doubt his sympathy and his words. Jason had no way to get here. Uriel Blackstone's portal required a genetic key that Jason was unable to obtain."

"A genetic key? How did you get it?"

"I can explain at another time. For now, we need to decide how many adults will be returning to Major Four. Someone will have to stay with the children, and perhaps Marcelle will not be well enough to join us." He glanced toward the cabin. "What did the dragons do to her?"

"Again, allow me to explain when we find Frederick." Adrian refocused on the path. Soon the signs would be more difficult to discern. "We'd better hurry before the boys get too far—"

Something rustled in the woods, and a low growl followed. Adrian lifted his sword and searched for the source, but the dense forest gave away nothing. "Did you hear that?"

"I heard." Drexel drew his own sword. "I have been here only since last night, so I am not familiar with the beasts that lurk in these woods."

"It sounded just like the cat creature."

Drexel nodded in the direction the boys had gone. "Then by all means, make haste!"

Adrian ran ahead, again following the trampled undergrowth. The terrain sloped downward and grew moister. Maybe the boys had gone toward the stream after all. He glanced back, but Drexel was nowhere in sight. Obviously he had no intention of keeping up.

Soon, the sound of running water reached his ears. In the distance, the three boys stood at the edge of a shallow stream, staring at the water. He hustled down a vine-covered slope and halted behind them. "What are you looking at?"

Orlan pointed at the stream. "Frederick's sword." He shifted his finger. "And it looks like someone climbed out at the other side."

Adrian ran into the ankle-deep water and snatched up the sword from the stream's rocky bed. Yes, it was Frederick's. The miniature family crest engraved in the hilt gave it away. He scanned the slope at the opposite bank, a mixture of grass and mud that led upward to a ledge overlooking the stream from about five feet up.

Deep gouges in the turf verified Orlan's guess that someone had crawled out.

He leaped up to the ledge and scanned the grass beyond. Dried drops of blood dotted a trail leading away from the stream with a wide gap between each drop. The person or animal was either running or bleeding slowly, perhaps both.

Following the trail for several steps, he studied the flattened grass. The pattern definitely matched that of a running human, most likely an adult. Yet, an odd narrow depression ran down the middle of the trail, consistent in width and depth, like a wheel bearing a heavy load.

He turned back to the boys. "Did you see anyone? Hear anything?"

Orlan shook his head. "Just you when you came up behind us."

"No rustling sounds? No animal noises?"

"Nothing."

"I heard some birds," one of the younger boys said. "And the water."

Adrian leaped back to the stream and splashed across it. Showing the boys Frederick's sword, he ran a finger along the blade. "There's no blood, obviously, because of the water, but there's a nick here. I know my brother. He hones any flaw in his blade, so this has to be fresh."

Orlan touched the nick. "Could he have been battling Drexel and lost his sword?"

"Battling Drexel?" Adrian cocked his head at Orlan. "Why would you ask that?"

"Well ..." Orlan averted his eyes. "I just don't trust Drexel."

"I don't blame you. But don't worry about Frederick. He could best Drexel with a dull stick." Adrian looked at the stream again. "Maybe he fell, and the blade got nicked on the rocks."

"Then why would he leave the sword behind?" Orlan asked.

Adrian glanced between the stream and the ledge. "That puzzles me. Unless my brother was severely dazed by the fall, he would've picked it up."

"So what are you going to do?"

"Follow the trail." He extended Frederick's sword to Orlan. "Can you handle a blade?"

"No." Orlan raised the bow. "I can't even use this. These two can shoot it, though."

Adrian gazed at the two younger boys, likely no older than six or seven, but if they were once cattle children, their growth might have been stunted by malnutrition. "I heard something prowling on my way here, so maybe you should come with me. Drexel's back there somewhere, but I can't count on him to protect you. He might have headed to the cabin."

Orlan took the sword. "Maybe you should go alone, and I'll take these two home."

"Why?"

Orlan looked toward the cabin, though it wasn't in sight. "The truth? Nothing held back?"

"Of course."

Half closing an eye, Orlan stared at Adrian for several seconds. "I think I can trust you."

"I just gave you a sword. That should tell you something."

"True." Orlan focused on the blade. "Like I said, I don't trust Drexel, especially around the girls."

"Why? What do you think he would do?"

"I don't know. Back at the mine where I work, a lot of people died after he showed up and killed a dragon."

"Drexel killed a dragon?" Adrian let out a whistle. "That's impressive."

"I know, but I still don't trust him." He looked Adrian in the eye again. "The only reason I took off to find Frederick was because I think you're an honest man. He wouldn't do anything to the girls while you're around."

Adrian looked at the trail of blood. Frederick was in obvious trouble, while Marcelle and the girls were likely fine, in danger only in Orlan's imagination. Apparently Drexel had done them no harm to this point, and this boy was obviously strong and smart, so with a sword in hand, he could get to the cabin safely, allowing a faster search for Frederick. The cat creature hadn't bothered them so far. "Okay. Take the boys. I'll be back as soon as I can."

"Just watch out for the deer trap," one of the smaller boys said, pointing across the stream. "It's in that direction."

"A trap?" Adrian pointed at the ground. "Is it a pit?"

The boy nodded. "With spikes at the bottom."

"Thanks for the warning. I'll watch out for it."

Orlan ran up the vine-covered slope, herding the boys, one at each side. Adrian leaped across the stream in two bounds and then up the embankment. Clutching his sword, he sprinted through the grass and into the forest, dodging low branches and jumping over exposed roots. The trail stayed clear, and the blood splotches grew bigger and closer together.

Finally, he reached a glade surrounded by pine trees. Their needles covered the ground with a copper-colored blanket, making the red trail a bit harder to see, but it was still evident. As long as he stayed on the path Frederick had followed, he wouldn't fall into a pit.

Slowing to a jog, he continued, glancing left and right for any other sign of—

The ground collapsed. As Adrian toppled forward, he rammed his sword into the dirt on the far side and held on. Now dangling, he looked at the pit's floor. Sharpened stakes protruded about ten feet below. A man lay face down, apparently impaled, but the sun's angle didn't allow much light to reach the bottom. The man had to be Frederick, but it was impossible to tell how badly he was hurt.

As the loose dirt gave way, the sword bent. Only seconds remained before it would pry free from the wall. Adrian lunged and reached for the lip of the pit, but his hands fell short. Clawing and scrabbling, he slid down the side, bringing a miniature avalanche and the sword down with him.

He bent his body and thrust out his arms, trying to avoid the sword and the stakes, but when he landed, one stake pierced the heel of his hand and passed through, leaving at least three inches visible on the other side.

Biting his lip to keep from yelling, he grabbed the sword and chopped the base of the stake, freeing himself. With pine needles and green leaves raining from above, he edged around to the opposite side of the pit and examined the prostrate man. It seemed that his body broke some stakes, but one had rammed through his leg and now protruded from his calf.

Adrian squinted at the man's profile. His scruffy beard and shaggy hair covered all but his nose and part of his cheek. Still, his identity was clear. "Frederick! Can you hear me?"

Frederick neither moved nor answered. Adrian set his ear against Frederick's back. His heart beat steadily, but his breaths were shallow and labored.

Using the sword again, he chopped off the stake piercing Frederick's leg and slowly turned him on his side. Three stakes under his body lay fragmented on the dirt, though one section pierced his belt and stomach.

Adrian felt the entry point. It appeared to be embedded only an inch or so. With pain ripping through his impaled hand, he eased the stake out of Frederick's stomach and pressed his fingers over the hole. Blood oozed slowly—a minor wound.

Running his fingers through Frederick's hair, Adrian found a hefty lump. Apparently someone clubbed him and threw him down, then covered the hole and sprinkled blood on top to make it look safe to cross.

Through clenched teeth, Adrian muttered, "Drexel!" That scoundrel did this. Wasn't he pushing a one-wheeled cart earlier? And his damp clothes indicated that he had perspired profusely. Apparently he had committed this crime only moments before they arrived at the cabin.

Adrian's biceps flexed. So now he had to get back to the cabin. Who could tell what Drexel might do next? But he couldn't leave his brother here.

Turning to Frederick's leg, Adrian felt the bone. It shifted, evidence of a break. Frederick gasped, his eyes clenching. When the pain eased, he relaxed, but stayed unconscious. A shiver ran across his body, but it soon eased as well.

Adrian touched Frederick's thin sleeve. In the video, hadn't he worn an outer tunic? When he traveled, he always wore at least two layers. Maybe he had given one to the children to keep them warm at night.

Looking up, Adrian scanned their trap, a circular pit about ten feet deep. Frederick likely chose this spot because the dirt was so loose, allowing for easy digging. If not for the stakes, a victim could claw at the sides until it caved in enough to allow for crawling out.

He glared at the stake still embedded in his hand. If he took it out, blood loss might make him too weak to carry Frederick, but if it stayed, it might make digging impossible, and it wouldn't take long for infection to set in.

Heaving a deep sigh, Adrian shifted to the opposite side of the pit and began clawing at the dirt. One way or another, he would get his brother the help he needed. The first step, though, would be to get back to Marcelle and the children. Drexel had to be stopped.

TWO

MARCELLE wrapped her arms around herself and shivered. So far, perpetual cold was the worst part about being a bloodless pseudohuman. It had taken a while to become accustomed to having no heartbeat, but the upwelling surges of bitter chills felt like fountains of inner ice, relentless and numbing.

She pushed through a stand of withered cornstalks and marched on the well-worn path of hardened dirt that led to the governor's palace. Even though she looked like a walking corpse, it seemed best to go about her business as if nothing were unusual. Sneaking around would only double suspicion, and as long as she acted in a casual manner, she could explain her pallid face easily. Lots of people grew pale because of sickness. That excuse would have to do.

Squaring her shoulders and holding her head high, she strode ahead. Checking on her father was the highest priority. They had parted on reasonably good terms, so he would likely welcome her return, but one worry remained. It had become clear that someone in the palace had been slowly poisoning him. Had he kept his promise to watch for a poisoned goblet? Whoever the villain was, he had to be in the employ of the governor, and the governor likely had commissioned the slow execution in an effort to stop her father from investigating the extane mining company. As royal banker, it was her father's duty to audit companies doing business with the governor, but his poison-induced illness had rendered him incapable of doing anything more than watching over palace funds. If the governor was involved in shady deals, a sick banker would never uncover the corruption.

Relaxing her muscles, Marcelle kept her eyes fixed straight ahead. No use getting furious now. Too much was at stake. The second priority was vital as well, to muster an army and charge into the dragon world. Convincing the populace of the truth would be the most difficult task, and every minute taken to prove the slaves' plight could mean another dead slave and another minute Adrian would have to fend for himself against the dragons. Even when convinced, would the men of the land march? The heroes of the past had proven their valor in years gone by, but the courage of the younger men had not yet been tested.

As she walked, the farmland gave way to a commerce district—shops and service providers lined up on each side of the road, now a path of cobblestones. A stocky man wearing a bloodstained white apron swept the entryway to a butcher shop on the left, not bothering to glance her way. On the right, a willowy young woman, her hair tied in a bandanna, poured sudsy water from a basin and let it splash aimlessly on the road. Splatters flew back, dappling her ankle-length taupe skirt with tiny soap bubbles. She, too, paid no attention to Marcelle, apparently too busy preparing her store for customers.

A girl exited the store. Wearing a dark gray cloak that swept the walk with its hem and covered her arms with baggy sleeves, she stopped in front of the woman and curtsied.

Marcelle paused to watch and listen.

"Thank you for the cloak, Mrs. Longley," the girl said, tear tracks evident on her cheeks. "I'll go to the home now."

"You're quite welcome." Mrs. Longley set the basin down and pulled the cloak's hood over the girl's head. "Remember, orphans hide their faces in public until they are adopted. When you get to the home, you can take it off."

"Yes'm." The girl pinched the hood closed in front of her face. "I hope you will visit me."

"Of course, of course." Mrs. Longley patted the girl's head and looked at Marcelle, her eyes narrowing. "Now run along. They'll be waiting for you."

As the girl trotted down the street toward the palace, Mrs. Longley kept her stare on Marcelle. "Aren't you the banker's daughter?"

Marcelle glanced up at the shop's sign—Miriam Longley-Royal Seamstress—then gave her a half bow. "I am."

"You should see a physician." Mrs. Longley scooped up the basin. "You're paler than a corpse."

"I'm not feeling my usual self this morning," Marcelle said, laying a hand on her cheek. "Thank you for the advice."

"If you will endure a bit more advice." Her smile obviously forced, Mrs. Longley gestured toward her shop's door. "I'm sure I can find a dress that will look lovely on you. With your physique, a size that would fit your shoulders would require that I taper the waist, but I am willing to do that at no extra charge."

"Thank you." Marcelle glanced at her battle garb—leather boots, black trousers, and tunic with a sword belt cinching the middle, though no scabbard or sword dressed her hip. Everything looked passable, though half-naked without a weapon. "These are better for my purposes."

"If your purposes are to keep suitors away." The smile flatted to a horizontal line. "Good day, Miss Stafford." Without another glance, Mrs. Longley strode into her shop and closed the door.

Marcelle whispered to herself, mimicking the frosty tone. "And good day to you, Mrs. Longley."

Shaking off the chill again, she continued along the road. With every few steps, it seemed that the cobblestones evened out, and the shops became larger and more varied, the wares transforming from necessities to luxuries—silks, beads, feathered hats, extane lanterns, and multicolored candies.

Soon, the palace came into view over its bordering trees and shrubs. Marcelle paused and took in the sight. As always, its ivory columns and stairs, sculptures of lions and wolves, and carved oaken doors stood in all their ostentatious splendor. Not long ago, to a younger, starry-eyed Marcelle, the stately ornamentations were like a purple satin robe dressing a dignified queen, but now they were nothing more than filthy rags around rotting bones. Hypocrisy had stripped the governor and his ilk of all their pretense. No amount of hot-air statesmanship could disguise what they really were—self-seeking, power-hungry charlatans.

Breaking again into a confident stride, she stepped away from the road and followed the grassy path leading around the palace's east side. She crossed the rear courtyard's Enforcement Zone, passing the familiar torture devices—the gallows with its ever-present hangman's noose; the pillories that now sat empty atop the red-stone floor; and the burning stake, a six-foot-tall column of charred manna wood.

As she passed by the stake, a muffled cry reached her ears. She stepped across the blackened stones and paused near the block of wood upon which the victim stood. Was it her imagination? A memory of a past execution? Although she had heard about dozens of supposed traitors and witches being burned here, she had witnessed only one—Madam Halstead, the poor widow Counselor Orion had persecuted for years. After finally collecting enough witnesses willing to testify concerning her "magical" feats, which amounted to little more than accurately predicting events and perceiving what people were thinking, he had her condemned as a Diviner and cruelly torched.

Marcelle twisted the toe of her boot over a scorch mark, her ears still alert for another call. Maybe in this semiphysical state she was able to hear beyond the mortal veil. Perhaps even now Madam Halstead's soul cried out for justice. What was it like to stand on that block, elevated a few feet above the crowd, watching wide-eyed torture lust as the voyeurs became drunk with agony? Which was worse, the flames that melted flesh and charred bone, or the darkness of dying without an advocate, surrounded by gawkers who hoped to tell a morbid tale? While shedding sham tears, they would recount her screams and terror-filled eyes, and they would mutter epithets against the brutality, but would they draw a sword and oppose the oppressors?

Clenching a fist, Marcelle shook her head. The men of this land were a vacillating lot. While ready to march together to battle a foreign adversary, when faced with an enemy from within, they cowered in the shadows, fearing to speak their minds, afraid that a word against the powers that be would find its way to the ears of the ambitious and then to purveyors of persecution. A man often swears alone against the oppressors of the land, but the echoes reach only his own ears, a mollifying sound, yet futile when drowned out by the crackling flames.

Pumping new energy into her gait, she ran from the Enforcement Zone, then slowed her pace as she ascended the back stairs toward the palace doorway. Gregor, the guard who normally watched the dungeon entrance, leaned his hefty frame against a marble column. She took in a deep breath, a strange sensation. To this point, she hadn't breathed except to speak with Cassabrie in the forest and with Mrs. Longley at the clothing shop. It seemed that respiration was optional for this new body, and taking breaths required deliberate thought.

As she mounted the final step, Gregor snapped to attention, nodding as he opened one of the twin doors. "Good morning, Marcelle. I didn't expect to see you here."

"Nor did I expect to see you." She stopped and looked him in the eye, trying to ignore the deep pockmarks that ravaged his cheeks. "Why did they transfer you from the dungeon?"

"The governor freed all the prisoners." Gregor shrugged. "There wasn't anyone to guard."

"Why would Prescott do that? He never grants clemency to anyone."

"I think you'd better get some rest." He tilted his head. "You look awfully pale."

She squinted at him. "What has that got to do with anything?"

"Well, you're either sick, or you're the only person in the kingdom who doesn't know that Counselor Orion took Prescott's place."

"Took his place! What happened to Prescott?"

"He was murdered by his new bodyguard, Jason Masters."

"What!" Marcelle shook her head hard. "That's impossible!"

"Oh, he was murdered to be sure. I saw his body myself. A bloody mess."

"I mean Jason Masters as the murderer. You know Jason would never do that."

"Well, unless Drexel's lying—"

"He's lying. Drexel would lie to his own reflection." Marcelle reached for Gregor's scabbard and began unfastening it from his belt. "I need a weapon."

Gregor lifted his arms. "What do you think you're doing? I'm a palace guard now. You can't—"

"Since I am head of the training school, we are of equal rank." With a grunt, she jerked the scabbard's harness from his belt. "If you want to report me, feel free to do so."

"But what's a guard to do without a sword? There are dangerous criminals about."

"I believe that, especially since Orion emptied the dungeon." She strapped the scabbard to her belt and fastened it in place. "I'm sure you can find an extra one in the weapons cache."

"But—"

"No buts." She set her hand on the hilt. "Any rumblings from the Underground Gateway?"

"Nothing since the most recent newsletter. Why?"

"I have a bulletin for the next issue, a story the readers will never forget."

"Is that so?" Gregor leaned back on the column again. "Fill me in. I have plenty of time."

"Well, I don't." She pointed at him. "Do you know who the editor is?"

He shook his head. "A mystery man. If his identity slipped out, Prescott would have had his head."

"That's what I thought." She strode into the palace's rear vestibule, calling back, "If I see a patrol guard, I'll tell him to get you a sword."

Trying to ignore Gregor's fading grumbles, she turned left into the palace's residence area and climbed the spiral staircase leading to her family's quarters. Her legs seemed squishy as they took on the extra burden, as if her muscles were little more than bricks of cheese. She paused and massaged her thighs. So cold! Everything was cold, from her toes to her nose. And rubbing didn't help. How could she aid circulation without any blood circulating?

Taking in an unnecessary breath, she pressed on up the stairs. Would her father be in their room? Would he be ill? If he had avoided the poison, might he have had to go into hiding to do so? Yet, Gregor would have mentioned that, so maybe all was well.

At the top of the stairs, she hurried along a corridor to the left, her hand brushing the railing between her and the foyer below as she bypassed the portraits and sketches on the opposite wall. When she reached her suite, she touched the nameplate on the door—*Stafford*—spelled out in gold letters. Unlike many surnames, this one was common among peasants and nobles alike, allowing her father to transition into nobility without raising too many eyebrows.

She grasped the brass doorknob and leaned close, listening. No sound emanated from the front room, the place where Daddy slept. Although he was usually up and around by this time of morning, he could still be sleeping if he had suffered another bout of nausea during the night.

Slowly turning the knob, she pushed the door open a crack and peered in. At the far wall, his covers lay scattered across the bed, as if pulled askew during a nightmare. An open window allowed a breeze to push sheer white curtains in a lazy wave, coloring the bed with a shifting shadow.

A slow clopping sound rose from behind her. She spun and scanned the palace's lower level. A man dressed in satin finery strode toward the stairwell, looking at Marcelle, his reddish eyebrows bending and his clean-shaven chin twitching as he chewed on something that made his cheek bulge. His hair, stark red and bushy, covered his ears and swept down to the nape of his neck.

He stopped at the bottom of the stairs and continued his watchful pose, staring with piercing green eyes and saying nothing. Although wearing what appeared to be the garb of a high-level official, the colors—black with orange trim—didn't match any of the uniforms she had come to know.

Marcelle gave him a nod but nothing more. Since this was a new official, he likely didn't recognize her, especially considering her appearance. She had to act as if she owned the place.

She strode in and scanned the room, calling in a hushed voice. "Daddy?"

No one answered.

She ran to the adjoining room and scanned the small confines—empty except for her bed and dresser. Her covers had also been thrown to the floor, and every drawer had been pulled open.

Ransacked? She leaped to the dresser and tossed away a tunic that draped the top. Underneath lay a hairbrush and a mirror—her manna mirror. She snapped it up and caressed it in both hands.

The glass had been smudged but not broken or scratched. She turned it over and read the message burned into the manna wood frame on the back. *Your heart is reflected by the light you shine. How great is your light when you sacrifice all you have for those who have nothing to give.*

She breathed a relieved sigh. No harm had been done. Her heirloom from Mother was intact. Maybe leaving it here was a mistake. With spies in the palace, who could tell what might become of her family's irreplaceable possessions?

As she gazed into the mirror, old thoughts drifted in. It seemed that Mother's face took the place of her own as Mother sang a lullaby. Her soft, gentle lips moved in time with the lyrics, painting the portrait of so many dreams of late. Whenever danger rose to a peak, the dream always returned the following night, featuring Mother's voice as she showed a young version of Marcelle this very mirror.

"When you look into this glass, remember my face and these words I speak, for we are reflections of one another. You are part of me, and I am part of you. Your heart beats in my bosom, and mine in yours. As long as you keep this manna mirror close, you will remember my love, and love will protect you—my love, your father's love, and most of all, the Creator's love. When you're frightened, never forget that love is what makes your protector cover you with his shield."

Marcelle clasped the mirror tightly against her chest. Leaving it here was stupid. Maybe that's why she was wandering around as a collection of dirt and dust, a wraith without a heartbeat. Forgetting about love had made her vulnerable.

She slid the mirror into her tunic's inner pocket, then hurried back to her father's room. She sat on the far edge of the mattress and looked out the window overlooking the palace's east side. The village stretched out before her, dozens of citizens now milling about, likely going to their jobs. No one seemed dressed for Cathedral, so it had to be a normal workday. Daddy wouldn't be among them. Ever since his illness, he never ventured beyond the palace doors.

She closed the window and set her fists on her hips, again scanning the room. If something had happened to Daddy, wouldn't Gregor have told her, especially after her display of ignorance about Prescott's death?

Her gaze fell on her father's desk situated against the adjacent wall. Papers lay strewn across it, and the rolling chair had been pulled back. Daddy would never leave his work area in such a condition. He was a stickler for order.

She picked up a sheet of paper lying on top of a haphazard stack, a memo from Governor Orion, and read it, whispering out loud. "All royal officers are required to attend a meeting in the commons court one hour after dawn. I apologize for the short notice, but recent circumstances have raised the need for urgent action."

Marcelle dropped the memo back to the desk. Apparently one item on the meeting agenda was to search the rooms while they were vacant. Someone had already been in here rifling through the desk and bed. Maybe Orion was searching for a way to break into the royal bank accounts without permission. He might have learned that Father's safeguards against stealing applied even to the governor.

She hustled out of the room and down the stairs. Running seemed so odd now, no breathing, no racing heartbeat, no muscle strain, no sweat—almost like running in a dream, as if at any moment she might awaken to a different reality.

When her feet landed at the bottom of the stairs, she stopped and gazed at the wide corridor leading back to the vestibule. The palace official dressed in orange and black was nowhere in sight, yet it seemed that a phantom stood at her side, watching, waiting. Might all this really be a dream? No dream had ever felt this real, had it? How many times had she dreamed, thinking her imagined world the real one, only to learn the truth at the break of dawn?

She pinched her wrist. Her skin crumbled at the pressure point. As she stared at the bloodless gash, a thin stream of dust from the stairwell banister swirled toward her arm, gathering at the site until it patched the wound. After a few seconds, her skin appeared as it did before, whole, yet ghostly pale and still cold, very cold.

Marcelle shuddered. What could this mean? Maybe it proved she really was dreaming, that she lay unconscious somewhere, the victim of Magnar's cooking stake. Had she conjured the journey to the Northlands with Arxad and Cassabrie? The idea that she could fashion from the soil a body that didn't have a heartbeat, and weave clothes with such precise detail, was really hard to believe. And now regenerating it by mere thought seemed impossible.

Closing her eyes, she tried to focus on another reality, a sleeping version of herself, perhaps still cooking at the loathsome stake. Was there pain? Thirst? Any other sensation she could connect with?

After a few seconds, a hazy vision entered her mind—the sense of bobbing, pressure on her stomach, intense pain in her head, and a fistful of material in her clenched hand. Water appeared, dark murky water, barely visible as it came closer and withdrew again in a consistent rhythm. Then, the water twisted and flew away. Arms caught her, fragile arms that pushed her to her feet. Now Adrian stood in view, his feet set as a beast lunged from a marsh and knocked him to the ground.

Marcelle drew her sword and slashed at the creature, slicing through its neck, decapitating it. She gasped, her heart pounding. Adrian rolled out from under the beast, climbed to his feet, and ran toward her, shouting, "Marcelle!"

The sharp word shook the vision. As the scene dimmed, she whispered, "Adrian," hoping to draw her mind fully into this reality, but the marsh quickly faded to darkness. She focused again on the pain, but that, too, had vanished. Did this mean she was really dreaming, or was the marsh scene a dream? It seemed impossible to know for certain.

"Marcelle?" someone called. "Are you all right?"

She blinked her eyes open. Gregor stood in the corridor, a look of concern on his face. Her heart no longer raced. In fact, it no longer beat at all.

"Yes, I'm fine." She shook her head to clear the cobwebs. "Why?"

He pointed. "You drew my ... uh ... your sword."

"Oh." She raised her arm. Her fingers tightly clutched Gregor's sword. "Something startled me."

"And I as well. I thought I heard a growl, like a big cat."

"A growl? How strange."

Gregor leaned to the side as if trying to peer around her. "But it was nothing?"

"Right. ... Nothing." She slid the sword back to the scabbard. "Thank you for checking."

"Not a problem." He turned and walked back toward the door, patting his hip where his sword once was.

Marcelle followed. When she reached the vestibule, she crossed to the other side and entered a corridor that led to the palace's two courtrooms, one for the noble class—the so-called high court—and one for the peasants—the commons court. It seemed unusual for a meeting of royal officials to convene in the lower courtroom, but Orion had already proven himself an unusual governor. Maybe learning what he was up to would help her cause, that is, if this was really something more than a dream.

She passed by a stairway to the nobles' court and continued to a set of double doors that opened to a lobby. She paused at the entry and peeked inside. The familiar layout hadn't changed—hard benches lining the walls, another set of double doors to the left leading to the courtroom, and a vaulted ceiling with a rustic candelabra hanging low and providing flickering light. In contrast, the high courtroom lobby had energy channels in the walls, providing radiant light that bounced off a central crystal chandelier and spread an array of glittering rainbows throughout the room. It was beautiful, to be sure, but it was synthetic beauty. It was nail polish and silk stockings instead of courage and integrity.

Marcelle stepped into the lobby, touching the closest bench. If a peasant were charged with any sort of crime, he would sit at one of these until the magistrate called him in to face the charges, sometimes waiting all day. Even now it seemed that phantom peasants sat here and there, their hands wringing as they wondered what lay in store. A man might get a small fine for forgetting to tip his hat to a lady of high rank, or he might be shackled in the pillory for a day and a night, losing his wages for the duration. Of course, real criminals found themselves in the dungeon or dangling at the end of a rope, but too many fell victim to the inconsistent enforcement of fickle customs, a weapon for those in the noble class who bore grudges.

The courtroom doors were open, an odd sight, and the guard who usually stood there during trials was nowhere to be seen. The various judges enjoyed secrecy, allowing them the freedom to accept bribes in proportion with their mercy and exact penalties in keeping with their mood. A bad cup of morning brew or a lingering spat with a spouse could mean a doubled fine or extra time in the pillory, so the peasants prayed for blessings on the judges' heads while waiting to stand before them.

Using the open door as a shield, Marcelle skulked to the courtroom entry. As she drew close, a voice from inside became clear, a masculine voice forced into an unnaturally low register.

"So as your new governor, I have implemented these reforms for the good of all, to ensure fair treatment for all classes of society. Even my decision to gather in this courtroom has symbolic purpose. Trials here will be for nonviolent offenses, regardless of class, while charges regarding violent crimes and crimes against nature will be heard in the high court. Social infractions will no longer be prosecuted, except, of course, for spitting and profane words and gestures. These reforms should break down the divide between those of more substantial means and those of less fortunate circumstances."

Governor Orion took a breath. "Are there any questions?"

As he paused, Marcelle peeked inside. About ten rows of benches stood on either side of the courtroom with a carpeted aisle down the middle. Richly dressed men and women filled the front half, some fidgeting, obviously not accustomed to wooden seats that lacked cushions for their delicate posteriors. One woman in the second row squirmed mightily, tossing a tall purple feather on her hat back and forth.

A solitary man wearing a rust-colored tunic and trousers sat in the back, left row, his shoulders straight and his head erect. Bending low, Marcelle sneaked in and took a seat to the man's right.

He blinked at her, apparently taken aback by her appearance.

"I'm Marcelle Stafford," she whispered, unable to suppress a shiver, "the banker's daughter."

"Yes, I know." He took off his outer cloak—woolen and forest green—and laid it over her shoulders. "I am Philip."

She gave him an appreciative nod and, staying low, turned her attention to the front where Governor Orion paced on a rostrum, two steps up from floor level. Marcelle glanced around, hoping to spot her father. With only backs of heads visible and many of them sporting neatly brushed gray hair, he could be any one of twenty men in attendance.

Stopping at the center of the stage, Orion waved a hand. "Come, now. With all these changes, I am sure there are many questions. These reforms are without precedent, and it will take time to grow accustomed to a new set of norms. Feel free to express your views. This is a new day. No one will be persecuted for a civil statement of opinion, even an opposing point of view."

A man in the front row stood. When he turned to the side, his identity became clear—Issachar Stafford. "Governor Orion," he said in his most courtly tone, "the greatest concern I have, and I assume I speak for many others, is the release of dungeon prisoners. I understand your point that this new era of freedom of speech cannot allow for political persecution. That is all well and good, but we know that some of the former prisoners went far beyond speech when they protested Prescott's regime. I know of two in particular who resorted to arson, which, I am sure we all agree, is an uncivilized way of expressing one's views."

Marcelle smiled. Although father looked frail and worn, at least he was speaking with vigor and standing without teetering. Maybe he had successfully avoided the poison.

"So, I am wondering," he continued, "what you can do to assuage our fears that such menaces will not ignite their fires of rage again."

"Justice," Orion said without hesitation. "Uprisings have their birth in injustice. There is no other source. And our show of mercy toward those whose frustrations led them to violence should be enough to quell future expressions of rage. Yet, even though we will tolerate all forms of opposition in speech and print, any violence from this day forth will be dealt with swiftly and with a firm judicial hand."

As her father took his seat again, apparently pleased with the answer, Marcelle scanned the room. The smiles and nods of heads gave silent echo to Father's approval. Yet why would that be? Orion fed them nothing but words, well-spoken words, to be sure, but these were the same promises Governor Prescott made. He never prosecuted anyone for simply speaking out against the regime. He just found ways to charge them with other crimes. It seemed that a change in administration simply meant a shift from one liar to another, but few took notice. Those carrying a favored status cared little about the backsides of the oppressed as long as their own remained covered and cushioned.

The woman with the tall feather stood, her silky ivory gown accentuating a svelte figure. "These new norms," she said with perfect poise and enunciation, "are certainly borne of noble intent. Justice should be applied uniformly across the classes, and mere disrespect of distinguished personages should be handled with delicacy and utmost tolerance." She scanned the courtroom, her pointed nose seemingly probing for a reaction to her dramatic pause. "So, I wonder, dear Governor, if you will be employing similar reforms to the enforcement of laws against sorcery. The witches and Diviners have always risen from the peasant ranks, so if the classes are truly equal in value and nobility, does not common sense teach us that such sorcery should be discovered equally among the classes? If so, will you test every pubescent girl among the nobles as you have among the peasants?" As murmurs buzzed through the audience, she waited through another pause until the buzz subsided. "Or will you cease the practice altogether? With your experience and wisdom, I am certain you understand all too well the inherent risks associated with either option."

The lady sat again, now perfectly still, as if her speech had expelled whatever had been wiggling inside.

"Allow me time to give your question the deliberation it deserves." Orion began pacing again, his hands clasped behind him and his tall frame slightly bent.

During the new pause, Marcelle leaned toward Philip, whispering. "Were you the only one invited from the working class?"

He shook his head. "All were invited, but few could afford the time. Even fewer thought it worth the trouble. I was elected as a reporter of sorts while the others pitch in to take care of my horses."

"Do you operate a livery?"

"No, the military barn. Orion requested my transfer here. We are breaking in new horses."

Marcelle gave him an inquisitive look. Mesolantrum had been at peace with its neighbors for years. Why would they be training new horses? She scanned the courtroom again. No military uniforms adorned any shoulders. Although the last war had become merely a memory, the officers still maintained military discipline, which included the spit and polish of perfect dress-uniform assemblage, from reflective black boots to shiny brass buttons to shoulder pads that accentuated even the frames of those lacking in masculine muscle.

Orion stopped again at the middle of the rostrum. "Katherine has raised a question that exhibits her acute grasp of fairness as well as her valid concerns. If I were to expand my search for those who practice sorcery to include young ladies whose delicate constitutions could not fathom the reason for such an examination much less tolerate its rigor, I could do great damage for no good reason." A wry smile broke out on Orion's face. "It would be as if we were conducting a search for dust devils in Katherine's closets, for we all know how meticulously clean her household is."

A few chuckles passed across the audience. Katherine looked at the man next to her, a smile dressing her profile.

Marcelle nodded. Katherine was her manners instructor only a few years ago. Although she was a busybody who could display a hot temper at times, she didn't mind a joke told at her expense, at least most of the time.

When the laughter stopped, someone walked in from the entry and slid onto the bench across the aisle. Marcelle ventured a glance. The man in black and orange stared at her, his jaw still grinding.

Jerking her head toward the front, she began breathing in a slow, natural rhythm, hoping to mimic normal respiration. Obviously this man was suspicious, but as long as she had a sword at her side, no rookie guard was about to do anything she couldn't handle.

Orion, his expression now serious, continued. "I believe it is better to err on the side of freedom than on the side of security. I prefer to withhold trauma from the obviously innocent and trust in the quality of our citizens. We are a courageous people, so we can withstand the risk of allowing sorcery to rise among us. If it rears its ugly head, we are strong enough to sever it from the serpent's body. We have nothing to fear. Therefore, I have decided to cease all routine examinations. No one will be tested to see if she is a Diviner unless she publicly engages in sorcery."

As new murmurs spread across the room, Orion waved his arms, his palms down, as if batting the noise toward the floor. "There is no need to fear. I have created a new enforcement position and appointed the perfect man for the job." As his gaze reached the back of the room, his brow shot upward. "Ah! There he is. Leo, come forward and allow me to introduce you."

Marcelle lowered her head. This would not be a good time for Orion to see her.

As Leo slid toward the aisle, Marcelle watched his polished boots out of the corner of her eye, feeling his stare burn into her. When the sensation eased, she looked up. He strode toward the rostrum, his gait confident as he clutched the hilt of a curved dagger attached to his belt by a leather loop. Sharply serrated and gleaming in the light, it seemed odd that it wasn't in a sheath.

He leaped over the steps, vaulted up to the stage, and made a graceful turn toward the audience, his chewing no longer evident.

"Leo," Orion said, clasping his shoulder, "was one of three ministers serving the king's court in Tarkton. He was in charge of locating and executing Diviners and witches, and he had great success even without routine examinations. He is able to detect sorcery whenever he is in its presence, allowing him to investigate the suspicious rather than the innocent. This way the daughters of every class will be protected."

As polite applause broke out, Marcelle mumbled under her breath. "Then that makes him a Diviner, doesn't it?"

"Did you speak to me, Miss?" Philip whispered.

She shook her head. "Sorry. Just concerned, that's all."

"As you should be. I know this man. If I were you, I would leave. He has his eye on you."

"I noticed." She touched the hilt of her sword. "But I'm not one to run from trouble."

"I have heard tales of your prowess, but I have also seen him ply his trade." He leaned so close the warmth of his breath caressed her frigid cheek. "Please trust me. Leave while you have the chance."

When the applause settled, Leo stepped to the edge of the rostrum and spoke in an even tone. "I am here to do the Creator's will, to cleanse the land by uprooting any foul weed that threatens to spread its seeds on Mesolantrum's fertile soil." Leo locked gazes with Marcelle, his stoic expression unchanged. "For a while, the stench of burning witches will spoil the air as the purifying flames devour the devils, but a time will come when no hint of sorcery will darken the sky, for once the roots are burned, no shoots will be able to sprout."

As a new round of applause erupted, Philip whispered in earnest. "Go! I will create a distraction."

"Okay, okay." Marcelle slid to the edge of the bench. "Create your distraction."

"Stay low." He touched a sheathed knife at his hip. "You'll know when to leave."

As soon as Marcelle ducked, Philip stood on the bench and shouted. "I know who you are, Leo. The Tarks call you …" He cleared his throat. "Excuse me. The people of Tarkton call you Maelstrom, because you are a vortex that absorbs power. You find sorcerers by identifying those who are able to resist you with their dark arts."

Leo kept his body straight, one hand on his dagger's hilt. "You speak the truth, my good man, but why are you engaging in this noisy display?"

"Because …" Philip stepped over Marcelle and jumped down to the center aisle. "Because I want the people to witness your abilities. It seems to me that their applause is premature. Shouldn't they see what you do before they show their approval?"

Leo nodded genially. "A fair statement. What do you have in mind?"

"Demonstrate your skills on me, but I beg you to spare my life."

A smile spread across Leo's face, making the bulge in his cheek visible. "I will do as you ask. What sort of demonstration shall we arrange?"

"Try to stop me!" Philip drew the knife from its sheath and charged down the aisle, screaming a battle cry. Just as he leaped toward the stage, Leo raised a hand as if signaling for him to stop. Philip halted in midflight, bounced back, and fell to the carpet, writhing in pain. With every eye locked on Philip, Marcelle tiptoed out the door, then quickly spun and peered around it.

His hand still raised, Leo stepped down to the floor level. As the people gasped, Philip withered like a plum drying into a prune. Soon, he was little more than a skeleton with sagging skin.

Leo grasped Philip's wrist and hoisted him to his feet. The poor man wobbled in place, his eyes bugging out and his clothes sliding down his emaciated frame.

Holding Philip steady, Leo breathed on him, speaking into the flow. "I grant you mercy." Slowly, Philip's body filled out until he appeared as he had before, shaky, but restored.

Leo patted him on the back. "As you can see, this is a man of noble character. I am unable to use my ability on a wielder of dark arts."

Philip nodded. "You are right. I am a man of noble character. That's why I have to do this." With a lightning fast sweep of his arm, Philip stabbed Leo in the chest, then ran toward the door.

Holding a hand against the bleeding wound, Leo thrust out an arm as if throwing something. Philip tripped and fell headlong, sliding on the carpet until he stopped near the bench where he and Marcelle had sat. Again he withered, this time more quickly. While the audience looked on in stunned silence, his flesh crumbled to dust and streamed toward Leo in a swirling ribbon of sparkling light. When it struck his chest, the flow of blood stopped, and his frame swelled. Soon, all that remained of Philip was a pile of clothes with skeletal hands and feet protruding from the sleeves and trousers.

Leo jerked out the knife and glared at it. "I am thankful to the Creator that I could use his flesh to patch my own." He slung the knife to the carpet. "I trust that this demonstration has been sufficient to enhance your confidence in me."

While the crowd applauded, this time with nervous hands, Marcelle searched again for her father. He was nowhere in sight. She backed away in the direction she had come. This Maelstrom person was trouble, probably more than she could handle with just a sword.

When she reached the corridor, she turned and ran. If Maelstrom had his eye on her, he had to suspect her of sorcery, probably because of her appearance. But how long could she stay away from him while trying to gather an army, especially considering the odd absence of officers? How could she look for her father again without risking another meeting with Mr. Maelstrom?

She stopped at the rear entrance, just out of Gregor's view. Could *anyone* face Maelstrom? If he was so power hungry, why wasn't he king by now? And why would he be here in Mesolantrum instead of on the throne? He must have a weakness that kept him from assuming the throne, but what might it be? Who would know? One of the Tarks?

Turning in place, she surveyed her options. Maelstrom knew where she lived, so searching for Father there wasn't feasible. Going back toward the commons courtroom might be suicide. Running out of the palace wouldn't solve anything; all the answers were within its walls.

She faced away from the exit. Straight ahead lay a corridor leading to the palace's main offices, weapons cache, ballroom, and a stairway down to the archives.

She marched ahead. The archives were the best option. Old Professor Dunwoody knew just about everything about everyone in the kingdom. Maybe he could reveal Maelstrom's secrets.

As she strode through the corridor, she glanced at the framed paintings on each side, portraits of past governors of Mesolantrum. They started with Theodore Blake, the ruler of the region about four hundred years ago. Before that, the history books said that Mesolantrum was just a wilderness, so Blake was the first governor, a balding man with a thick mustache and piercing brown eyes.

Quickening her pace, she allowed the rest of the parade of portraits to fly by until she neared the end of the corridor where Orion's portrait hung across from Prescott's. Orion hadn't wasted any time in getting his proud mug preserved in oil on canvas.

After passing the massive ballroom on her left, she turned right on the shiny marble floor and crossed the front foyer, the location of the faux battle with Jason. Although it now seemed like weeks ago, the test of skills took place only ... three days earlier?

She shook her head. Traveling through a portal between worlds had skewed her sense of time, especially considering the fact that the length of a day on Starlight didn't quite match that of Major Four.

After passing a statue of Prescott's father, Marcelle entered a dark, narrow corridor. With every step, the surroundings dimmed, washing away the side doors leading to some offices no longer in use. Finally, the corridor ended at a barely visible wooden door. As she reached for the knob, a clatter of footsteps sounded behind her, then a deep voice.

"You check the weapons cache, and you search the ballroom. I will look in the business office."

A palace guard ran into the entry foyer and turned toward the ballroom, away from Marcelle. Maelstrom strode behind him and headed straight toward her, his arms pumping and his fists clenched.

She crouched low. If he was going to the business office, he would turn again before reaching her corridor, that is, if he didn't see her first.

He stopped at the entrance to the corridor and peered in. Blinking, he took a step and halted again, apparently waiting for his vision to adjust. A catlike purr rumbled with his words as he called out, "Is someone here?"

THREE

MARCELLE sat on the floor and pulled her knees up to her chest, closing her eyes and hiding her face between her arms. She couldn't afford to look. The light behind Maelstrom might reflect in her eyes.

Gripping the hilt of her sword, she listened for the sound of her heartbeat, but only silence reached her ears. Normally, her heart would be racing, and she would have to hold her breath. At a time like this, being semiphysical had its advantages. She could hide here indefinitely without making the slightest sound.

As she concentrated on staying perfectly quiet, a nagging thought returned. Maybe this was all a dream. The courtroom meeting seemed surreal, especially Philip's execution. In what reality could someone like Maelstrom exist? Of course, Cassabrie was powerful beyond all reason, but did Starlighters have such destructive abilities?

Again she concentrated on trying to wake up, but the sense of Maelstrom's looming presence grew. Was he drawing closer? If so, maybe he chose a slow approach, concerned that she carried a sword. After all, only a fool would chase a well-armed opponent into a dark room. If he really believed her to be a sorceress, he likely thought she could best him in her domain. Still, she couldn't afford a glance. Giving her position away could be fatal. She would have to rely on sensing his approach.

As she trained her ears on her surroundings, an image of Maelstrom came to mind, stalking toward her with his dagger drawn, now about fifteen paces away. He took a furtive step. Something squeaked. Boot leather? Or was her mind continuing to manifest the dream, making it come to life in all her senses?

She pushed her thoughts toward reality once more. Might Adrian still be carrying her unconscious body? Was he still in that marshy area?

The image of Maelstrom melted away, replaced by a crude log cabin in the midst of a dense forest. Drexel stood near the front door, surrounded by children. Her vision blurred and swayed, as if she were walking toward him in a drunken stupor.

When she arrived within reach, Drexel bowed, then looked away. "Marcelle appears to be quite ill."

Someone shouted, "Captain Drexel is here!"

Marcelle opened her eyes and peeked over her arm. Maelstrom loomed within three steps, his dagger in hand. He spun in place and marched toward the entry foyer. "Where is he?"

"Out here!" A short pause ensued. "At least he was here a moment ago."

Marcelle rose to her feet, opened the door to the archives stairwell, and slid inside. Laying her palm on the door, she pulled the knob, turning it to make sure it latched without a sound. Now in complete darkness, she felt for a locking bolt, but only smooth wood met her fingers.

She probed for a switch on the wall but found nothing. Since so few of the upper crust journeyed to the archives, no extane channels had been installed here. Anyone descending these stairs would know to bring a lantern.

With a hand touching each side of the narrow stairway, she tiptoed down the old steps, cringing at every squeak. The only time she ever visited here was during a school trip at the age of ten.

Professor Dunwoody, her teacher before he was transferred to the archives, hoped to explain the importance of historical records, but since he included other palace offices in the tour, they had stayed in the archives only a few minutes. Her lone memory was how dark and scary it seemed, even with a lantern.

When she reached the bottom of the stairs, something blocked her way. She found a knob, turned it, and pushed a much heavier door than the one above. It opened into a chamber less than half the size of the royal dining room, maybe twenty feet in length and width. A row of dim lanterns hanging from the low ceiling, separated from each other by about three paces, lit up four wall shelves on the left that stretched from the front to the back of the room. Books, scrolls, stacks of papers, small boxes, and several hourglasses of various sizes lay scattered on the shelves in haphazard array.

Oddly lettered labels identified the boxes—Sneezing Powder, Sleeping Potion, Smoke Balls, and Metal Polish, among others.

The lanterns' flickering lights cast wavering orange silhouettes on the right side of the chamber, casting a dim glow on haphazard piles of old books.

Marcelle stepped in and closed the door behind her. To the left, a key tied to a leather string dangled from a nail embedded in the jamb just above her head. She pulled it down and locked the door.

"What are you doing here?"

Marcelle pushed the key into her pocket and spun toward the voice. "Professor Dunwoody?"

"Of course." The dignified voice emanated from the darkness at the back of the chamber. A tall, gray-haired man strode into the light, blinking. "Whom did you expect to find here, a sparring opponent?" He scanned her body, pausing at her face. "Or perhaps a physician."

"I know I look kind of pale, Professor, but—"

"Kind of pale? Marcelle, I have seen more color in a corpse. In fact, I have seen more color in hailstones or in—"

"Just listen a minute. What do you know about a minister from Tarkton named Leo? His nickname is—"

"Maelstrom." Dunwoody nodded. "I am quite familiar with him."

"Well, he's here as Orion's enforcement officer, and he has power you wouldn't believe."

"That *I* wouldn't believe?" Professor Dunwoody said, pointing at himself. "Marcelle, do you remember the stories I told you when you were knee-high to a ... well, to an unusually tall person?"

"The dragon stories, of course. But no one believed ..." She took a step back and looked him over, noticing his clothes for the first time, disheveled and wrinkled, as if they hadn't been changed in weeks. "How long have you been down here?"

He straightened, as if reporting to a supervisor. "I was transferred to the archives twelve years ago, two years after I taught you in school."

"No, I mean, when was the last time you came up for air?"

He waved a hand. "There is no need. My wife died long ago, and a boy brings me food and water, trims the lanterns, freshens my wash basin, cleans my chamber pot, and brings me the morning journals as well as the latest gossip. I jog in place, and I have a solar lantern. I am well supplied."

"Then it's been weeks? Months?"

"Years. By now, I doubt that anyone up there would even recognize me." He picked up a hefty old book from a countertop under the nearest lantern and squinted at it. "What is this doing here?"

"Anyway," Marcelle continued, "what do you know about Maelstrom?"

Dunwoody lifted a finger. "I remember! He brought it to me as a gift from Lady Moulraine."

46

"He? You mean Maelstrom?"

"Of course not. Maelstrom wouldn't know a book from a broomstick." Dunwoody opened the book and began leafing through the pages. "I meant the boy who brings me supplies."

Marcelle tapped her foot. "Okay, forget your delivery boy for a minute. I just saw Maelstrom knock a man down from twenty paces away, absorb his body like a leech drawing blood, and pull a knife out of his own chest like it was nothing more than a splinter."

"He did all that, did he?" Dunwoody withdrew a pair of spectacles from his tunic pocket and put them on, blinking at the book. "This is all very interesting."

"Interesting? I'd call it mortifying."

"No, I mean this book." Keeping his stare on the page, he walked toward the back of the chamber, dodging two stools and three stacks of dusty newsletters. "Come with me. I'll show you what I mean."

She followed. "But I need to know about—"

"Maelstrom, I know." He picked up the last lantern in the row and continued toward the back. "You certainly have quite an obsession about him."

"Obsession?" She balled her hands into fists. "The only reason I keep mentioning him is because you keep changing the subject."

He stopped and turned, his face now clear in the lantern's light. "Ah! The sword maiden's infamous temper has shown its fire. I remember when you knocked Sandon across three rows of desks."

She crossed her arms over her chest. "He questioned my gender."

"When a girl always wears trousers, cuts her hair short, defeats her classmates in every sport, and possesses the curveless body of a ten-year-old, then don't you think punching an inquisitive boy in the nose is a bit of an overreaction?"

Marcelle sighed. "I grant your point."

"You do?" Dunwoody chuckled. "Well, that's a new development. You're not as stubborn as you used to be. Perhaps your illness has sapped your energy."

"Can we dispense with the Marcelle examination and get on with the Maelstrom news?"

"Of course. Exactly why I led you back here." He sat in an overstuffed armchair near the back wall and laid the book on his lap, balancing the lantern on the chair's arm. "This gift from Prescott's widow is both relevant and timely, and an earlier cursory examination proved it to be filled with corroborating evidence that confirms theories I have held for quite some time. It appears to be a journal of some kind dating back to …" He glanced at the door. "You did lock that, didn't you?"

She patted her pocket. "Yes. Why?"

"Do you remember when the governor's enforcement unit barged into our classroom and went on a wild rampage, tearing books from the shelves and throwing them around the room?"

"Yes. I was terrified."

"As was I." The lantern flames danced in his wide eyes. "They were looking for evidence that I was teaching a view of our origins that differs from the officially approved history."

"Was there any evidence?"

"Of course not. I fully believed the official version of history, ignorant fool that I was."

"What changed your mind?"

Dunwoody waved a hand at his surroundings. "Working here in the archives. I pieced together enough evidence to cast a great deal of doubt on the dogma of my peers and my predecessors, and I also unearthed other evidence that is startling, which I plan to show you soon." He opened the book to its first page. "Even with all that I have learned, there are many mysteries remaining, and this journal might be the key to unlocking those mysteries."

Marcelle shifted to a position behind the chair and looked over his shoulder. The page displayed a series of scrawled, illegible notes. "Pretty careless writing."

"Careless? Not likely. A handicapped scribe, I think."

"Okay. I can believe that." She leaned closer. The markings took on some familiar shapes, letters and words, but too many were illegible. "Can you read it?"

"As a teacher I had to read some of the sloppiest handwriting imaginable. I'm sure I could read this, as well, if I took the time." He flipped to a page near the back. "Take a look at this."

Marcelle scanned the pages. The handwriting was much clearer now, and some of the letters formed recognizable words—*genetics*, *procreation*, and *nutrition*—along with many simple articles and conjunctions. Yet most words still seemed too messy to read.

"This is a child's handwriting," Dunwoody said. "I have seen enough samples to recognize a young person's pen."

Marcelle leaned over the back of the chair and studied the page. "How old are the entries?"

He pointed at a series of marks set off by themselves near the top. "This newer one is about five hundred years old." He turned to the front of the book and pointed at a similar place on the first page. "This is much harder to read, but I believe it tells us that this was written about five years earlier."

"Could the handicapped writer have later dictated to a child?"

"An excellent assumption. My guess exactly. Once I tell you my theories, perhaps you will understand why."

Marcelle pulled back. "I'm sure I really want to hear your theories, but right now I have a bigger problem on my hands."

"Yes, yes, I know. Maelstrom." He heaved a sigh. "Leo, son of Prince Bernard and nephew of King Popperell, was the Counselor of Sheelan."

"Sheelan? I haven't heard of that province."

Dunwoody pointed at a map on the back wall to his right. "It's Mesolantrum's neighbor to the northwest. Its name changed to Bernardium due to Leo's desire to flatter his father." He wagged a finger at her. "You learned that in history. It seems that you were too busy playing with swords and punching inquisitive boys to remember your lessons."

Marcelle rolled her eyes. "Enough scolding. Let's get on with the story."

"Very well, but I will make it short. My boy is due here soon." He took off his spectacles and tapped them on his chin. "Leo became interested in some rather esoteric teachings, which he claimed gave him the power he has now. Since he can kill with a wave of his hand, who can argue? Anyone who is able to resist—"

"Is called a witch or a sorcerer. I know that much." Marcelle shifted to the front of the chair again. "So if you oppose him and aren't able to resist his power, you die at his hand. And if you oppose him and are able to resist, you burn at the stake."

Dunwoody pointed his spectacles at her. "That pretty much sums it up."

"Then if he's so power hungry, why isn't he king already? Why has he been transferred here?"

"The king himself is able to resist his power, but Leo has not yet dared accuse him. The king's guards are many and loyal. Instead, he plays the humble servant who wishes to rid the land of witchcraft. Orion, in his perplexing plan to hunt for witches in a new way, was foolish enough to call Leo here, or perhaps Leo requested the transfer. I am not privy to the deals made in secret places where scribes are not present to record the contractual protections and promises."

"You mean threats and lies."

"You are quite savvy for your age." He set his spectacles on his lap and folded his hands over them as he gazed at her with a serious aspect. "As I was saying, when Leo assumes the governorship, he will have the means to use our own soldiers to enforce a charge of sorcery against the king."

Marcelle nodded. "No wonder they've been bolstering the cavalry. Leo is getting ready."

"I expect to see conscription next. Many young men will be forced into military service, and older men will be called out of retirement. All of this will be done with another pretext, though I don't know what that might be."

"I know of a pretext. Maybe I can work this out for my cause."

Dunwoody's eyebrows lifted. "Do you need to raise an army?"

"A big one, and I need to do it quickly."

"May I ask the purpose?"

"Let's just say that it involves a certain gateway."

"The Underground Gateway?" Dunwoody put his glasses back on and stared at Marcelle. "By all means, tell me."

Marcelle rubbed her arms. The icy chills had subsided recently, but they seemed to be returning. "How much do you know about the Underground Gateway?"

"My dear girl, I have been the head of research for the organization for ten years."

She pointed at him. "You're the editor of the newsletter?"

"One and the same."

"Then you believe in the dragon planet."

"I don't merely believe. I *know* it exists." He slid his spectacles down near the tip of his nose. "Do you believe?"

Marcelle studied his sincere, probing eyes. Spilling all she knew would be easy but potentially dangerous. "First tell me how you know."

"Research." He tapped the first page of the book. "I said the writer of this part of the journal was handicapped, but that was a bit misleading. His only handicap was that he was a dragon who

51

had no opposable thumb, making the handling of one of our pens quite difficult."

Marcelle stared at the book. "So do you think this journal came from Dracon?"

"Not at all. I think the dragon wrote it here." Dunwoody touched the arm of his chair. "Of course I don't mean in this spot. A dragon couldn't squeeze down that stairwell, much less sit in this chair."

"I knew what you meant." Marcelle closed the book and touched the cover. Scratches marred the leather at every edge. "If this was a gift from Lady Moulraine, that means Prescott probably knew about the dragon planet all along."

"No need to state the obvious. His persecution of those who believed in Dracon was enough to convince me that he knew. Those who attack the adherents of a harmless story are the best witnesses for the story's veracity. My question is why would he hide the truth? What benefit did he gain?"

"Gas trading," Marcelle said.

"Extane?"

"Right, but it would take too long to explain, and I'm not sure of the details." She kept a finger on one of the cover's deeper scratches. "Why would dragons have been here five hundred years ago? And where did they come from? Where are they now?"

"As I mentioned earlier, I have theories, along with some enigmatic evidence. I never included them in the newsletter, however, for various reasons, including a lack of context that explains what I have found." He rose, leaving the book on the seat, and moved the lantern from the arm to the floor. Then, setting his hands on the back of the chair, he lifted his brow. "If you'll help me with this, I will show you a hidden—"

The doorknob rattled. Spinning, Marcelle whipped out her sword.

Three firm knocks followed. "Dawson, are you in there?" The solid door muffled the masculine voice, but the tones and inflections were familiar all the same.

Marcelle glanced at Dunwoody, whispering, "That sounds like my father."

"I believe you're right." Dunwoody cleared his throat and called across the room. "Yes, Issachar. What may I do for you?"

"The new Counselor is searching for my daughter, bearing an insane pretext that she is a sorceress of some kind. I was hoping you could shed some light on his past. He has already put a lot of pressure on me to reveal her whereabouts, though I have no idea where she is. She left on some fool mission to save Adrian Masters, and I haven't heard from her since."

"Interesting. What gives him the idea that you would know where she is?"

"He claims he saw a woman her age and size going into my room, and one other person said he thought he saw her in the residence area, but he wasn't sure." The knob rattled again. "Dawson, I am not accustomed to speaking to a door."

"One moment, please. I have to move some things around." Dunwoody leaned close to Marcelle and whispered. "For your father's sake, it would be best that he not know where you are."

"I agree." She slid the sword back into its scabbard. "Is there a place to hide?"

"Where I was about to take you. It's an escape tunnel." He extended his hand. "But first, give me the key."

She withdrew it from her pocket and laid it in his palm. "Now, if you would excuse the frailties of an old man, kindly pull the chair away from the wall. If it makes noise, all the better."

As he held the lantern high, providing a yellowish halo, Marcelle shoved the chair, letting it scrape loudly across the floor. When she had created enough space between the chair and the wall, he scooped up the book, crouched in the gap, and set the lantern on the floor. "Come. Your father's patience will likely wear thin."

She lowered herself to her knees. The light shone on a design in the paneling, painted with vibrant colors. Starting at the floor and rising to about thigh level, it appeared to be a sun, though yellowish white, unlike Solaris's more reddish hue. A red-haired girl stood at its center, her arms spread as if ready to make a sacred proclamation. Wearing a white dress and blue cloak, her green eyes stood out in sharp contrast to the surrounding colors.

Professor Dunwoody touched the girl's mouth. A door popped open, its hinges hidden on the left. "Take the light with you, and feel free to explore. When your father leaves, come out, and I will explain."

Leading with the lantern, she crawled into the low opening, the sword dragging at her side. As soon as her feet cleared the door, she pivoted on her knees and looked back.

Dunwoody pushed the book in with her. "If your father tarries here, at least you will have something to read." After the panel closed, the sound of his hurrying feet filtered in. Seconds later, Father's voice came through, agitated but controlled.

"I thought you would never open that door."

"I apologize. Since I live here, I have to attend to personal matters from time to time."

The door closed, and the click of the locking key followed.

"That's all well and good, but I think the Counselor has someone following me, so standing out there was rather risky. I think I eluded him, but I cannot be sure."

"Why does Leo think your daughter is involved with sorcery?"

"Some fool notion about the woman he saw. He said she was as pale as a corpse and was able to repel his spiritual probe, whatever that means."

"Maelstrom is relentless," Dunwoody said. "He will not soon turn from an obsession."

"Maelstrom? During our meeting, a man called him that name and attacked him with a knife. Leo killed him without even touching him. It was an extraordinary display of power that seems to have everyone licking his boots."

"Great power breeds fawning followers. It seems that only a few are wise enough to avoid the poison."

"I just want to keep Marcelle safe. She's my only child. Ever since her mother died, she's been …"

A pause ensued, then Dunwoody's voice returned. "Shall I fetch you a handkerchief?"

"No, no." Father's voice trembled. "Just give me a moment."

"That's fine. While you compose yourself, I will look for something that will provide more information about Maelstrom."

Marcelle pulled in her bottom lip. Daddy was crying. If only she could burst out of this place and tell him she was all right! But that wouldn't work. She wasn't all right. Her ghostly appearance would raise a hundred questions she couldn't answer. Just as Dunwoody said, it would be better to stay put and relieve her father's fears when the crisis was over.

Turning with the lantern, she scanned the area. It looked like one of the dungeon tunnels, long and narrow with a ceiling high enough for her to stand up, yet no cell doors anywhere. About five paces away, a trunk sat near the wall to the right.

She rose and set the lantern on the floor next to the trunk, giving light to its surface, a combination of wood and metal with two leather belts wrapped over the top and under the bottom. She ran a finger along one of the belt buckles, a metallic clasp that appeared to have no means of release.

She pressed on the sides of the buckle and pulled. The clasp popped open, responding to the pressure. She did the same to the other buckle and slid the belts off the top. The lid opened easily, revealing four eggshell halves resting on a cushioned bottom, the remains of two eggs, each the size of a large melon if the sections were to be joined. The jagged edges gave evidence that something had broken free from within, maybe a large bird of some kind.

Flush against the trunk's left inner wall, a keyhole was evident at the center just below a small knob. She pulled on the knob, bending a square door slightly, but it wouldn't give way.

A framed plaque lay against the trunk's back inner wall. She picked it up and read the message, written in gold ink by a careful hand.

The Abode of the Transported Humans
In the Year of Starlight - 2526
A Monument of Thankfulness
To Our Dragon Rescuers
Arxad and Magnar

Marcelle gasped. Arxad and Magnar! Dragon rescuers? What could this mean?

As she returned the plaque to its place, her knuckles bumped a small book that leaned against the right side of the trunk. She picked it up and let the ancient cover fall open over her palms. The first page read, "The Book of the Code—The Creator's Love and Wisdom in Words."

She closed the book and caressed its leather surface. Ever since Prescott banned the Code several years ago, only a few copies remained in the land. The Cathedral priest owned one, from which he preached his interpretations of its holy contents. Father said that the priest skipped the parts about freedom for the oppressed, that no man had the right to enslave another, and that those in authority were to be servants to those they watched over. The only other copy she knew about lay under glass at the palace museum, always turned to the page that commanded people to respect authority. A guard watched it day and night, lest anyone steal it and spread its supposedly dangerous contents.

Voices again emanated from the archives room. Marcelle returned the book to its place, closed the trunk, and stepped back to the access panel. Dunwoody's voice came through, more muffled than ever.

"Here is a journal from a magistrate in Tarkton who retired here in Mesolantrum. When he died, it came into my possession. It will tell you much more about Maelstrom than I could recite from memory."

"Thank you. I know this magistrate, a very levelheaded man. This should make for interesting reading." A lock clicked again, and the door at the exit stairway squeaked. "If you see Marcelle, please warn her about Maelstrom, and tell her I am looking for her."

"I will be sure to—"

A loud thud sounded, followed by the breaking of glass. "Take them both!" a man shouted. "The rest of you search this place. Turn it upside down if you have to. If Marcelle isn't here, report to me at the high courtroom."

As loud bumps and crashes pierced the wall, Marcelle slid out her sword. How many were out there? "The rest of you" likely meant at least three, and the ruckus sounded like a herd of cattle stampeding through the room. Could she battle past them and rescue her father? If she tried and lost, they would find the access panel, giving away the secrets that lay inside, including the book Lady Moulraine had sent. Even if she managed to escape, they would just chase her, leading to more trouble.

Her muscles tightening, she looked at the sword, eyeing her reflection in the blade. She really did look sick—an unearthed corpse who didn't know she was dead. If only she could attack!

Fighting had always been the quickest, easiest way to defeat the enemy. Brute force would rescue her father, wouldn't it? Yet, Adrian would say to use brains, to employ stealth, to exercise patience, no matter how bad things looked.

Marcelle shivered hard. The frigid claws of cold had embraced her again, worse than ever. She looked over her shoulder at the dark passage. Professor Dunwoody had said this was an escape tunnel, so it had to lead to an exit somewhere. Maybe finding it was the best option. Getting to the courtroom by stealth would provide many advantages.

She sheathed her sword and picked up the book. "Okay, Adrian," she whispered. "Let's hope you're right."

With the lantern lighting her way, she strode into the tunnel, passing a barrel of water with a dipper attached to a long, thin chain. A basin with sponges, a scrub brush, and a bar of soap sat nearby along with five large footlockers marked "Rations." A pile of woodchips overflowed from a smaller, unlabeled box. She picked up a chip and sniffed it. Manna bark.

After a dozen or so paces, the passage narrowed, and the ceiling lowered, forcing her to stoop. An acrid film formed on her tongue, a sure sign of extane gas. That meant the mining tunnels or a pipe-line lay close.

The lantern's wick sparked green and orange, another sign of extane. If the concentration increased, a flame could ignite an explosion. She set the lantern and the book on the floor and, after warming her hands near the flame, continued on. Maybe the glow would provide enough light, at least for a while.

After a few more steps, the tunnel ended at a pile of rocks, apparently the result of a collapse. Obviously no one had used this as an escape route for a long time.

She smacked her lips. The bitter film sharpened. If extane was able to pass through, this rubble couldn't be too thick. She grabbed a head-sized stone at waist level and set it down on the floor. A hole the size of two fists appeared, and dank air breezed through. The lantern sparked wildly, but when the hole drew back the air, the flame settled.

Marcelle peeked through the hole. Since she blocked the lantern's glow, darkness flooded her field of vision. The chamber on the other side seemed to breathe, sending air through the hole, then inhaling it again.

Sliding her arm into the opening, she stretched it through a narrow tunnel and felt for the end. Her fingers touched the lip of the hole into the other chamber. After withdrawing her arm, she pulled another stone away, widening the opening on her side. A large stone tumbled down from near the ceiling and struck her hand. The scrape raised a tiny cloud of dust that rose into a stream of air that flowed through the hole.

She squinted at the wound. No blood oozed from the slender cut, though particles of skin flaked away as dust. Smaller rocks cascaded down the side of the pile. The tunnel's roof cracked, sending sand and pebbles drizzling to the floor. She glanced toward the archives room. Had the guards heard the noise? Maybe their own commotion kept them from hearing hers.

Backing away slowly and quietly, Marcelle studied the ceiling. Large cracks radiated from the collapse point. It wouldn't take much to bring the whole thing down, and the noise would surely give her presence away.

She sat next to the lantern and book. Bumps and crashes still sounded from the archives chamber. Maybe waiting for them to go away was the only safe option.

She laid the book in her lap and opened it near the back where the handwriting was more legible. The careful strokes of a heavy pen told of living in a forest near a crystal spring, growing crops and cooking rabbits and fish over an open fire. A boy and girl, both seven years old, relied on their "big winged friend" who visited once in a while and provided supplies and instruction on survival. At times, they wrote as scribes, communicating their friend's wisdom.

After several pages, the details of their lives became tedious. The sentences blurred, and the letters blended into indecipherable shapes, but when the word *Starlighter* appeared, Marcelle jerked the book closer to her eyes. Their friend told them to watch for signs of a Starlighter among their descendants—a child with red hair and green eyes. If such a child appeared, they were to send a message to him in the usual manner. Then, a full page described the powers of a Starlighter.

A female possesses the ability to absorb tales and tell them with great ease and liveliness, and the characters in the tales come to life in ghostly images. Because of her, tales of courage and sacrifice are reborn and strengthen those who hear. A male is able to absorb power and substance from another creature. Although he can do this while looking at his target and with only one victim at a time, this ability can make him a powerful warrior against evil as he uses his gift to destroy oppressors and rescue the innocent.

With both genders, however, there is danger. Either one is capable of great harm if he or she rebels against the Creator. The female might turn to collecting the tales of dark sorceresses and learning their ways, thereby corrupting her and making her a powerful sorceress herself. A male can transform his energy-draining power into a means of usurping authority, thereby gaining a crown for himself, and if he draws power from the innocent, his heart will become dark indeed.

Therefore it is essential that you teach all your children the Code so that they will know and follow the Creator. Otherwise, a dark Starlighter will become a threat that no one in your world who lacks Starlighter genetics can withstand. Only dragon fire can stop such a fiend, but if he is able to avoid the flames and absorb a dragon's energy, he will be unstoppable.

Her mouth dropping open, Marcelle lowered the book to her lap. Maelstrom was a corrupted Starlighter! All the evidence fit— his hair, his eyes, his absorbing power as he looked at Philip. That meant the king probably had Starlighter genetics, protecting him from Maelstrom.

She looked at her hand. And Maelstrom probably couldn't absorb from her, because she was no more than a collection of dirt.

Something banged against the wall separating the tunnel from the archives room. The searchers were closing in.

Pulling her knees up to her chest, she rested her head and closed her eyes. *Think, Marcelle! You've gotten out of tighter jams than this.*

After a few seconds, darkness entered her thoughts, and the feeling of wetness, as if she were back in the underground chamber on Starlight where the bastra injected her with venom. That was certainly a tighter jam. Yet, this was different. Something rubbed her legs and thighs, as if washing them with a cloth. Little-girl voices entered her ears—soft, gentle, soothing, though no words formed from the whispers.

A tickling sensation rode up her legs, ending with pressure at her hips. Then, the whispers became words.

"Her trousers are still damp."

"Can't be helped. They're clean, though."

"I guess they'll dry soon."

"I hope she doesn't get a chill."

"We could put Frederick's cloak on her."

"Good idea."

A sudden sense of warmth covered her body from chest to toes.

"That should do it."

"Someone's coming."

Marcelle tried to open her eyes, but they wouldn't budge.

A man's voice filtered in. "You girls go outside for a moment. I need to get this wet tunic off."

"What will you put on?" one of the girls asked.

"I saw Frederick's cloak in the corner this morning. Where is it?"

"We put it on Marcelle. She looked cold."

"Ah! How very kind of you. But go on now. I need privacy."

"Have you seen Adrian?"

"I think he's still looking for Frederick."

"Should we take Marcelle with us?"

"Don't worry about her. She's asleep."

"When should we come back?"

"I will call you."

The voices silenced. In a sudden gust of wind, the warmth vanished.

"I'm sorry, Marcelle, but I have more need of this than you do."

She forced her eyes open. Drexel stood with his back turned, a shaft of light from an open door illuminating his bare skin. Multiple scars ran from his shoulder blades to his hips.

A thousand thoughts stormed through her mind—her mother's corpse under a white sheet, a coroner lifting her arm, a fingerless hand with a limp thumb. Then her father's words streamed in. *We found a considerable amount of skin under her nails, so we searched the soldiers for someone with a fresh wound. ... His wounds would have become scars, and who could discern scars earned through courage on the battlefield from scars incurred while committing a crime?*

Shifting her body as quietly as possible, Marcelle climbed to her feet. Her legs felt so weak! Every muscle ached, and her head throbbed. Yet she had to challenge this murderer, no matter what the cost.

As Drexel wrapped the cloak around his body, Marcelle spied a sword on the floor near his heels. Just as she picked it up, he spun and faced her. His eyes shot wide open, and he backed away. "Oh … Marcelle. I didn't realize that you were awake. My apologies for making a false assumption. I hope you were not offended."

A barrage of words caught in her throat. As she tried to force them through her lips, only a few managed to escape. "Scars … on … back. … How?"

"Oh, that?" Drexel laughed nervously. "A fall on the battlefield. I tripped and rolled down a hill."

Marcelle looked at Drexel's wet tunic, now lying inside out on the floor. Something protruded from the inner pocket. A finger? No. Two fingers. Both severed from their hand. And the pocket still held more hidden within.

Heat roaring through her cheeks, she shouted. "Liar!"

Drexel leaped for the wet tunic and snatched it up. Holding it in a ball close to his chest, he backed toward the door, trembling. "I can explain. I found your mother's murderer and took the fingers from him."

Marcelle forced the word out again. "Liar!" Then, drawing back the sword, she shouted, "Now die!"

Drexel dashed through the doorway and into the forest. Seconds later, he ran out of sight.

Dizziness flooded Marcelle's mind. Darkness veiled her vision. A falling sensation took control, pain jabbing her elbow and hip. Soon, cool water spilled over her face. She was back in the underground chamber leading to the river beneath the dragon world's barrier wall, crawling through one of the narrow holes while water funneled through. As before, she squeezed herself into the channel, making her body as small as possible. A scraping sound reached her ears, like metal on stone. Her sword was probably dragging against the sides.

Soon, the feeling of wetness evaporated. Pressure on her arms and legs returned. Now sitting, her arms were again wrapped around her knees, and her head rested on them.

She blinked her eyes open and shivered hard. She sat in total darkness. No. There was a light—a small, oval-shaped glow to her left.

She rose to her feet and walked to the light, a hole in the wall. She peered through it. Something vertically bisected the opening on the other side, slicing her view in half. Several paces beyond the opposite hole, a lantern sat on the floor, its flame sparking green and orange. A book lay nearby, along with a smaller object, too far away to discern.

She pushed her arm into the hole and extended her hand through a narrow passage, very much like the one she had explored while in Dunwoody's escape tunnel. She felt for the object dividing the view. Her fingers slid around the hilt of a sword. As she drew it through, a metal-on-metal snick made her stop. A scabbard?

She touched her belt with her other hand. The sword was gone. She groped past the hilt and came across the strap that fastened the scabbard to the belt. Grasping it, she pulled the entire assembly. The sword's crossguard scraped within at the top and bottom of the narrow passage, but after a few seconds of twisting and jerking, she pulled the sword and scabbard free.

With a firm snap, she fastened the belt in place. This was Gregor's sword and scabbard, not part of the body and clothing she had fashioned from the soil of Major Four. She felt for her mother's mirror in her tunic's inner pocket. It wasn't there. She patted her tunic from chest to waist, but no telltale lump met her fingers.

She looked through the hole again. The small object next to the book had to be the mirror. It was also not part of the ensemble she arrived with.

Blinking again, she backed away a step. Just moments ago, she sat next to that lantern with the mirror in her pocket. She had widened this hole in the wall, and now she stood on the other side wearing only what she materialized with when she arrived on Major Four.

She nodded. This really was a dream. It had to be. Somehow her real self was still in the world of Starlight, and once in a while she was able to awaken enough to do something there, something vital. Maybe this dream was a way to show her the truth, a crucial fact she needed to know.

Biting her lip, she clenched a fist. Drexel had to be her mother's murderer! Her fingers were in his tunic. He had scars, giving evidence that her mother had scratched his back while she battled for her life. He was a former soldier who had enough pull to keep from having his genetics tested. And he was also a conniver who would stoop to murder if he thought it would benefit him.

Yet, he had escaped. He was probably long gone. And it had seemed impossible to chase him. Since her real self had such a terrible headache, she must be badly hurt, explaining why she kept falling again and blacking out.

Could she go in search of him? It seemed that she could still connect with her real self whenever she concentrated on rising to consciousness. Was it safe to do so? Might she injure herself again? Should she rather just let the dream play out while her body healed?

She let her fingers relax. Waiting seemed to be the only reasonable option. In her condition, she could never catch that weasel. At least the dream was interesting, and she could march through it with reckless abandon, knowing no permanent damage could occur.

With the glow from the hole providing a little light, she looked around. A large pipeline dominated the passage, running parallel to the walls. She touched the pipe's metallic hull. This had to be an extane conduit. Maybe this would run to the section of wall where she exited the lower level of the dungeon and redirected the gas. If she could find the valve, locating the wall wouldn't be a problem.

She closed her eyes and drew a mental picture of the palace. Which way to the rear grounds? She swiveled toward the hole and traced her route back to the main floor, turning her body with each turn in her mind. When her mental image reached the palace's rear entry, she opened her eyes and pointed. That way!

FOUR

ADRIAN trudged toward the cabin with Frederick over his shoulder. He weaved through the trees, pausing and peering around trunks as he tried to stay out of sight. His legs quaked. Pain throttled his hand, sending spasms up his arm. Yet, he couldn't call for help. If Drexel heard him, he might grab one of the children and hold him or her hostage.

He checked the sword wedged between his belt and trousers. It was still there. Soon it would be put to good use—skewering a scoundrel.

When he drew close, he laid Frederick down in a patch of grass and slid out the sword. Then, gripping it in his left hand, he marched toward the door. Dispatching the likes of Drexel with a left-handed slice wouldn't be a problem.

He stopped at the edge of the open doorway and peeked in. A small window at the back added to the light from the door, both illuminating the eight children as they stood or sat around Marcelle. A table abutted the rear wall, and a handmade stool perched atop a large deerskin under the window, but Drexel was nowhere in sight. Tiptoeing in, he whispered, "Where's Drexel?"

Orlan stepped forward. "Long gone as far as we can tell." He touched the head of one of the girls. "Cassandra saw him running out of the cabin, and he never stopped running. When she came inside, Marcelle was lying here just like you see her now, with Drexel's sword in her hand. Either he moved her, or she moved herself."

Adrian knelt at Marcelle's side and scanned her face and body. Except for the rise and fall of her chest and movement under her eyelids, she lay motionless. Shellinda and Penelope shuffled close.

"Has she opened her eyes?" he asked, glancing at each girl. "Has she talked at all?"

"No," Penelope said. "Nothing."

Adrian touched Marcelle's thumb, still loosely gripping the hilt of a sword. "Drexel's scared to death of her. He wouldn't have given her his only way of protecting himself."

Orlan pointed at Adrian's hand. "What happened to you?"

"I got impaled in Frederick's pit." He showed them the stake's entry point, just below his palm. The shard of wood still protruded a few inches on both sides. "It looks worse than it is."

Seven of the children stared, wide eyed, while the girl with the feather hat gazed aimlessly. "We have medicine," one of the smaller girls said. She then ran out the door.

"And we'll need something for bandages." Adrian laid his sword down and rose to his feet. "Make a bed for Frederick. I'm going to bring him in."

"Bring him in?" one of the girls cried. "Is he hurt?"

"Yes, quite badly."

As Adrian walked out, Orlan joined him. "I'll help. You look like you're about to collapse."

By the time Adrian and Orlan carried Frederick inside, the children had prepared a thick bed of huge green leaves and straw. Adrian laid Frederick on his back, carefully aligning his leg. Since he had already shaved the point off the spike, his leg rested easily, though Frederick gasped with every move.

One of the small girls set a damp sponge in Adrian's palm. "Stops infraction."

"Infection," Cassandra said as she laid a wad of cloth strips next to Adrian.

The girl crossed her arms over her chest. "I say *infraction*."

Adrian smiled. "Either way works for me." He picked up one of the cloth strips. "Where did you get these?"

The little girl spoke up. "Frederick goes into the village sometimes and gets stuff."

"Is that so?" Adrian eyed the cloth, torn and ragged, but serviceable. "Do you have anything for stitching up wounds? A needle and thread?"

One of the smaller boys nodded. "Frederick got some the last time he went."

"Then please get them. I'm going to need them very soon." Gritting his teeth, Adrian eased the stake out of his hand, then swabbed both wounds with the sponge. He pressed a wadded strip of cloth over the entry and exit and lifted his hand. "Will one of you please wrap the bandage?"

Penelope grabbed two strips, doubled them, and carefully wound them around the heel and back of his hand.

"Tightly now," Adrian said. "We have to stop the bleeding. Maybe I can teach one of you how to stitch it later."

When she finished, he gave her the sponge. "Will you soak this again in the medicine and bring it back?"

With the children hovering around and running to and fro fetching water and whatever else he needed, Adrian removed the spike from Frederick's leg, stitched the wounds, and set the bone. He placed a shaved branch against each side of the leg and wrapped it tightly with cloth strips.

Soon, he was finished. The boys had already moved Marcelle to the bed, and she and Frederick rested quietly side by side.

"Now …" Adrian lifted his hand. Blood had soaked through the bandage on both sides. "You watched me stitch up Frederick. Who would like to stitch my wounds?"

"I'll do it," Orlan said. "It'll hurt, though."

Adrian began unwinding the bandage. "No worse than it already does."

While Orlan stitched Adrian's hand, the four smallest children introduced themselves and told their stories, though some of the details might have been skewed by their wide-eyed perspectives. Frederick rescued all four from the cattle camp, taking one at a time to the wilderness. He began with Tom, a six-year-old with a birthmark on his cheek, who claimed that Frederick swam upstream under the river's exit gate and helped him swim back out. Although Frederick held his breath, Tom breathed through a reed until they were out of the guardian dragon's sight.

Ariella, a black-haired, brown-eyed five-year-old, told a tale in which Frederick scooped her out of her hovel in the middle of the night and flew her over the wall. How he could have grown wings, she couldn't say, but she did remember getting a cut on her finger from a claw on one of the wings. Fortunately, as she put it, "I didn't get an infraction."

Regina, the blind girl with the feather hat, was eight years old and spoke with an endearing lisp. She remembered very little, just waking up in Frederick's cabin, warm and cozy, with the smell of stew cooking nearby. She had dreamed of running a great distance in the dark, but her legs weren't any sorer than usual. She had lost her eyesight a few weeks earlier. Whether the reason was malnourishment or disease, she didn't know, though both had ravaged her body. Even after Frederick had used all the herbal remedies he knew, parasites and fungi still stubbornly clung to her skin.

Zeb, a seven-year-old with bright hazel eyes, told the wildest tale. One evening, he was the last in the cattle camp to leave the feeding area. Being scrawny, he rarely won the skirmishes over the meager distributions, so he was grazing the pebbly soil in search of morsels. When the guardian dragon lashed him, Frederick jumped on the dragon's back and strangled it with its own whip until it fell unconscious. He then scooped up Zeb, climbed over the camp's thorn-covered wall, and hustled to the cabin refuge.

Since that evening, Frederick never brought more children, saying circumstances had made rescue attempts too dangerous. If he were to be captured, who would care for the children he had already saved? Besides, he thought he couldn't feed more than four.

Orlan and Cassandra told how Drexel helped them escape from the pheterone mine. When they added up all the details, it seemed clear that he orchestrated the deaths of the miners and the other children. If not for Orlan's skepticism, he, too, would probably have been killed. It seemed clear that Drexel desired to burden his journey with just one little girl, hoping to get sympathy for the plight of the Lost Ones and glory for himself.

When the last story ended, Adrian gazed at the children. Dressed in patched trousers and tunics, they stared back at him. Orlan and Cassandra, though firm and wiry, were thinner than the original four. Apparently Frederick had managed to care for his refugees quite well. Shellinda now wore a set of clothes that matched the others, though they appeared a bit rattier. Maybe they were castoffs that had been stored in case other refugees arrived.

Adrian shifted his gaze to Frederick and Marcelle. Both still lay unconscious on the bed of leaves and straw. It seemed that he would have to take Frederick's place. The original four could probably teach him their survival tactics. With his ability to hunt and trap, caring for them shouldn't be too hard.

And what of Drexel? What might he do? Although a trained soldier, he wouldn't know how to forage in a strange world. He could easily come back at night and steal what he wanted, including one of the girls, so they would have to post a guard. In any case, Drexel's obsession with returning home to achieve glory would be his driving force. If he couldn't soon find a way through the portal, he might become desperate and unpredictable.

The sound of beating wings rippled from one side of the cabin to the other. Adrian grabbed his sword and jumped up. "A dragon," he whispered.

Zeb ran to the door, his worn sandals slapping the uneven wood. "It's Arxad. He hasn't been here in a long time."

Adrian joined him and looked out. From about thirty paces away, Arxad approached on foot, his head and neck snaking around closely packed trees as he squeezed his body between the trunks.

Keeping his grip on his sword, Adrian glanced between Zeb and the dragon. Zeb appeared to be excited rather than frightened. Obviously Arxad's previous appearances here had not been menacing.

"What business do you have here?" Adrian called.

Arxad halted next to a leafy bush and extended his neck past the last tree before reaching the cabin, bringing his spiny head within fire-breathing distance. "I came to see if you arrived safely."

"What do you care? You seemed content to watch me die at the cooking stake."

"And you seemed content to die there." Arxad edged closer, his eyes fixed on Adrian. "I do not expect you to understand my actions, but I do expect you, an alien to our world whom I could have killed long ago, to listen to me without a threatening posture."

"Fair enough." Adrian laid his sword on the threshold and walked out. When he came within reach of Arxad, he stopped and crossed his arms over his chest. "I'm listening."

"Good. Perhaps now that the Starlighter is no longer within you, you will be able to heed wise counsel." Arxad's head eased slowly past Adrian and swayed from side to side as he scanned the doorway. "Where is your female companion? I saw you carry her into the forest."

"You saw us?" Adrian resisted the urge to look back at the cabin. Letting him know Marcelle's whereabouts might not be a good idea. "How long did it take for us to elude you?"

"Elude me?" As Arxad drew his head back, twin plumes of smoke shot from his nostrils. "If not for my efforts, the patrol dragons would have eventually caught you and your companions. I simply lost track of you because I was leading the patrol away from your trail."

"But why? Why do you care about what happens to us?"

Arxad's eyes drilled into Adrian's. "I care very little about what happens to you. I desire only justice and peace. If you perish in these pursuits, I will honor your efforts, but I will shed no tears. Many die on such paths."

Adrian broke away from the stare. "Then why did you mislead the patrol dragons?"

"To protect Frederick, not you. My concern was that they would have caught you as you neared this lodging, thereby exposing this refuge and ending Frederick's efforts."

"So you do have sympathy for the slaves. You want to protect the children."

"I seek long-term justice. If a few human children die during the short-term struggle, I cannot allow that consequence to skew a broader perspective."

"Very well. Then tell me plainly. Why are you protecting Frederick?"

Arxad shuffled back a step, his ears twitching. "Frederick holds a secret that I have yet to learn, so I need to protect him until I persuade him to give it to me. There is much more to be done in this wilderness area than simply rescuing slaves."

"Then kindly tell me what else must be done. If it's a noble cause, I will do all I can to help you."

"I find that to be quite unlikely. Your brother refused to help me, thereby purchasing my protection with his silence, so I assume you will join him in his refusal. It seems that distrust between our species has prevented cooperation that would result in mutual benefit, and no amount of persuasion is able to break the distrust barrier."

"What harm would it do to try me?" Adrian asked, spreading out his arms. "I am not my brother. Perhaps my perspective will be different."

Arxad's brow bent. He scanned the area as if searching for a spy, then he drew his head close and lowered his voice. "I apologize for my presumption. My own brother and I often differ, so it was foolish of me to assume that human brothers would necessarily be of the same opinion. Yet, if you learn what I have in mind, you might try to stop me."

Adrian displayed his empty hands. "How could I stop you? I'm not carrying a weapon."

"It is not your weapons I fear. It is your influence." Arxad peered past him again. "May I speak to Frederick?"

Adrian stepped back, blocking Arxad's line of sight. "He's resting, but I'll be glad to pass along a message for you."

Arxad gave him a skeptical stare. "Tell him that I am going to Darksphere with Magnar. He will understand the significance of this journey."

"To Darksphere?" Adrian bit his tongue. His tone had exposed his excitement. He had to settle down. Eagerness was the worst of negotiating tools. "Might you be able to take someone with you? One or two of the children, perhaps? A ride on your back might frighten them, but—"

"No!" Arxad shook his head as if casting away his own eruption. "I will not take anyone with me," he said, his voice now calm. "Magnar would strenuously object, and if he refused their company, I would have no choice but to leave my passengers stranded at the portal site, in which case, Magnar might choose to kill them."

Adrian glanced back at his sword. Could he get to the portal in time to try to stop them? Magnar going to Major Four had to be bad news. "What is the purpose of this journey?"

"You saw the black egg. Taushin the prince recently hatched, and he will soon take his prophetic place as ruler of this realm. Magnar and I hope to bring an army from your world to help us stop him. In return, we will free the slaves."

"Why do you need an army? If he hatched recently, isn't he vulnerable?"

"I cannot tarry long enough to explain the reasons. Ask Frederick. He will tell you. If you inform him that Taushin will try to capture a Starlighter, he will be able to put all the pieces together for you."

"How can he capture Cassabrie? She's just a spirit."

"Not Cassabrie. Koren. She is physical and is already very powerful."

Adrian nodded slowly. "Yes. Koren. You mentioned her once. You said she went with Jason to the Northlands."

"And now she is in danger. Perhaps Jason can protect her, and perhaps he cannot. Time will tell. In any case, there is also a third Starlighter in our world. I know nothing about her or what she might do, only that she exists. The white dragon told me as much."

"Is the white dragon the same species as you? He once told me that his definition of his own kind probably differs from mine."

Arxad wagged his head. "The white dragons are barely dragons at all. They have no ..." He looked to the side, his expression faraway.

Adrian waited for nearly a minute before speaking up. "They have no what?"

With a quick snap of his neck, Arxad's stare returned, his eyes fiery. "I have spoken too much about them already. You have more important issues to be concerned about."

Adrian stood his ground. He couldn't let this dragon use his threatening postures as a manipulating tool. Still, it seemed obvious that getting more information wasn't in the offing. "I do have more important issues. Have you heard anything from Jason? Is he all right?"

Smoke again rose from Arxad's snout, though whiter and thinner than before. "I have heard nothing since I gave him safe passage beyond the barrier wall."

"Thank you for doing that." Adrian watched Arxad's pupils. The fire slowly diminished. Apparently his anger was fabricated or at least easily extinguished. "What will Magnar do if my world refuses to send an army?"

"That I cannot predict. I will, however, try to keep Magnar in check." Arxad bowed his head in a submissive manner. "If you have any suggestions regarding how to persuade your people, I am ready to hear your counsel."

Adrian studied Arxad's position—a body, wing, and tail structure that could break a human's bones, attached to a curled neck and lowered head that begged for human advice. The contrast was striking, and Arxad's sudden changes in posture seemed orchestrated, as if he had planned every move in advance. Still, answering this request couldn't hurt. The counsel was obvious. "Take the children. Nothing will inflame human passions more than the sight of a suffering child."

Arxad shook his head. "That would inflame them to violence against us. They would slay us and invade without us."

"Well ..." Adrian stroked his chin. "I have to admit, you're probably right."

"If you have counsel that does not involve dragon deaths, please deliver it. Otherwise, I must be on my way."

"Just do whatever you can to show a compliant posture, like the head bow you just gave me. Also, allow very few to see you. If the people in power believe they control a secret that the citizens at large do not know, the knowledge will feed their egos. When they reveal the secret later, they will be able to crow that they conducted dangerous negotiations without spreading panic. Their desire to bask in self-importance will aid you greatly."

New strings of smoke twisted up from Arxad's nostrils. "I detect that you have much experience in this human frailty."

Laughing, Adrian nodded. "I guarded the backside of a pompous governor long enough to learn that his ego was bigger than his heart."

"Yes, I have had dealings with Governor Prescott. I will remember your advice and apply it as the need arises." Arxad began a slow turn of his body while keeping his eyes aimed at Adrian. "Tell Frederick that we need an army, but the Benefile are not the answer. Their emergence might well signal the destruction of your species ... and ours."

Arxad beat his wings, helping him scoot along the path. After dodging a few trees, he entered a small clearing, beat his wings again, and rose almost vertically into the air.

Adrian walked back to the cabin. Zeb stood at the door, holding the sword. "Are the Bloodless coming?" he asked.

"The Bloodless?" Adrian grasped the hilt and propped the blade against his shoulder. "What do you mean?"

Zeb pointed at the spot where Arxad had stood. "He called them the Benefile, but they have another name—the Bloodless. I heard him and Frederick talking about them before."

With his bandaged hand on the back of Zeb's head, Adrian led him to the bed where Frederick and Marcelle lay. "What can you tell me about the secret Arxad mentioned?"

"Not much. Arxad always came at night, and he and Frederick talked outside. I listened sometimes, but not every time. But that's how I learned they're called the Bloodless."

Adrian sat on the floor next to Marcelle. The smaller children gathered around and seated themselves in a circle, as if expecting a story. Adrian smiled. Apparently Frederick carried on the Masters family tradition of storytelling. "Okay, Zeb, just tell me what you know."

Sitting across from Adrian, Zeb gestured with his hands as he spoke. "Some dragons are trapped somewhere, and Frederick and Arxad talked about it."

"And those dragons are the Bloodless?"

Zeb nodded. "He and Arxad argued about whether or not they should be let out."

"Which side was Frederick on, and which side was Arxad on?"

"I'm not sure. They just argued. All I could figure out is that they're both worried about what the Bloodless might do."

Adrian slid his hand into Marcelle's and caressed her knuckles. "Very interesting."

"Maybe just because the Bloodless hate Magnar." Zeb shrugged. "Maybe not."

"Do you know where the Bloodless are?"

Zeb shook his head. "Frederick never mentioned it to Arxad while I was listening. We just know that he goes to a secret place once in a while. Maybe the Bloodless are there."

Regina, sitting to Adrian's right, raised her hand. "I know where he gothe."

Adrian looked her way. "You do?"

She nodded firmly, shaking the hat from her head. Her scalp, nearly bald except for short bristles of indistinguishable color, displayed a mottled pattern of scales and fungus.

"Where?"

"Not clothe. I have to thow you."

"Show me? How could you have seen it?"

"Thinth I'm blind, Frederick took me with him one time. He doethn't want anyone elth to thee it, but I can find it by thmell."

"Really?" Adrian smiled. This little girl was so pathetic, yet so beautiful. "What does it smell like?"

She shrugged. "I can't dethcribe it. But I know Frederick took me for a walk that way." She pointed toward the rear of the cabin. "And I tharted thmelling it after we pathed the thkunk tree."

"Skunk tree?"

She nodded again. "I can't thmell it from here, but the otherth can thow it to you."

"Well, then." Adrian rose to his feet and took Regina's hand. "If one of the others will be my eyes and Regina my nose, we'll find the skunk tree and Frederick's secret."

"I can show you the skunk tree," Zeb said, "but it's not real close, so we'll be gone for a few minutes. What will the others do if Drexel comes back?"

Adrian looked at Marcelle and Frederick lying motionless on their bed while Orlan stood next to them with a sword in hand. It seemed strange to see these warriors under the protection of a child they had come to this world to protect. "Go on," Orlan said. "I'm not afraid of that rodent."

"Perhaps not." Adrian patted Orlan's shoulder. "Maybe I can sneak out. If we leave the door open, Drexel will believe I'm in here, and he won't come close enough to see that I'm gone, especially if you talk and chatter as if everything is normal. My guess is that he's far away and won't show his face again."

After concocting a plan, Orlan wheeled the cart into the cabin. Adrian climbed inside with his sword and covered himself with the deerskin. Orlan, accompanied by Zeb and Regina, pushed the cart out the front door, around to the back, and deep into the forest until they were hidden in a thicket—ivy-covered bushes nestled under a low, arching limb from which thick, vertically hanging vines created a gapped curtain.

When Adrian climbed out, Zeb pointed at a narrow path that weaved through the trees and sloped gently downward. "That way," he whispered.

"Thank you." Adrian laid a hand on Orlan's shoulder. "I trust that your strength will endure. Have courage."

Orlan nodded and hurried back to the cabin.

Staying low and holding Regina's hand, Adrian skulked along with Zeb at his side. Regina kept her head high, her scalp bare, having forgotten to bring her hat. The path bore traces of recent foot travel—trampled leaves, broken twigs, and nearly invisible impressions. All three sniffed the air. At least two scents dominated, a moldy odor signaling their nearness to wet, organic debris and some kind of pungent musk, perhaps the skunk tree.

"You can see it from here," Zeb said, pointing.

About forty paces ahead, a massive tree stood to the right of the path, its hefty limbs hanging so low, they partially blocked the way. With white bark covering the tree from its trunk to its twigs, and leaves of blue and silver filling its branches, it didn't resemble any trees back on Major Four.

When they reached it, Adrian touched a limb crossing the path at waist level. Its bark felt smooth and cool, almost like marble. He inhaled deeply. Indeed, the odor resembled that of a skunk, though sweeter somehow, not as noxious. He rubbed one of the blue leaves between his fingers. It was tacky, leaving a thin residue on his skin. A silver leaf grew next to it, smoother and silkier. Both displayed fingerlike projections, four long and one short, very much like a human hand, though the silver ones ended at a point while the blue ones were rounded.

Adrian brushed the residue off on his trousers. "I've never seen a tree like this. Does it bear fruit?"

"None that I've seen," Zeb said. "But its colors change. The leaves switch from blue to silver and back again. It's hard to tell unless you mark a leaf. It takes about three days."

"Do the ends change as well? I mean from rounded to pointed and back again?"

Zeb nodded. "Pretty strange, isn't it?"

Adrian studied several leaves. It seemed that they all were mature in their colors and forms, not at a stage in between. "Strange is an understatement."

"Well, I got you to the tree," Zeb said as he ducked under the limb. "But I don't know where to go from here."

Adrian bent low and guided Regina to the other side of the limb. The path split into three—one straight ahead and the others veering off left and right. The path to the left, narrow and overgrown, was clearly the least traveled. "We'll start that way," he said, pointing to the left. "I'll let Regina guide me from here."

Zeb scratched his head. "What do you want me to do?"

"Go back to the cabin with the cart. Help Orlan any way you can."

Zeb plucked one of the blue leaves and pushed it behind his trousers waistband. "These are the smelly ones. I like to carry them around. It keeps the beasts away." He pulled another leaf from the tree and extended it to Adrian. "Want one?"

"No, thank you. It might confuse Regina's sense of smell."

"Okay. See you later." Zeb crawled under the limb and ran back toward the cabin.

When the sound of his footfalls died away, Adrian crouched next to Regina. "Are you ready?"

She nodded, smiling broadly. Even her crippled eyes seemed to glow with delight. He took her hand and strolled at her pace down the path. Regina hummed a tune, taking in a deep draught of air during each pause.

Adrian drew his sword and chopped a bramble from the path. Although the bandage protected his hand, the cut throbbed. "I've heard that tune somewhere. Did Frederick teach it to you?"

"Yeth. He called it Thon of Tholaruth."

"Oh, yes. Son of Solarus. My mother taught us that when we were little, but I don't think she has sung it in years." He swung their arms with her beat. "Do you know the words?"

"Thome of them."

"Sing as much as you can, and I'll see if I can fill in the gaps."

"Okay." With her eyes aimed at Solarus, she sang in a warble.

Tholaruth give me light today
And warm my little theedth
O help them thprout and grow tho tall
Give …

She paused. "I can't think of the word."

"Bounty," Adrian prodded.

"Oh yeth. Give bounty for our needth." She took in another draught. "That'th all I can remember."

"That's okay." Adrian lifted his nose higher. "Do you smell anything yet?"

"The tree behind uth. I think it'th thtill pretty far to the thecret plathe."

"Okay. Then I'll finish the song." He looked down at her. "If that's okay with you."

She grinned. "Oh yeth. Pleathe do!"

Adrian cleared his throat and sang in a quiet tenor.

I want to be a son of yours
And shine a light for hours
To warm cold hearts and help them see
Creator's love and power

And when they sprout and spread more seed
I'll warm their little shells
Then people everywhere will see
His light and love as well.

When he finished, he let out a sigh. Mother used to sing the simple rhymes quite often, but after Prescott banned the Code, allowing only the priest to read and interpret selected passages in Cathedral, she used her singing time to quote the portions of the Code she had memorized, often in singsong to enhance her children's ability to memorize the verses as well.

Regina stopped, her head swiveling as she sniffed. "I thmell it."

"Good girl!" Adrian inhaled. The skunk odor was gone, replaced by a faint hint of rotting flesh. As with the skunk odor, it carried a pleasant nuance, a flavor that promised something less fetid than a decaying carcass.

Regina pointed to their right. "It'th that way."

Adrian looked in that direction. They would have to depart from the path and plunge into dense brambles that would surely cut Regina's delicate skin.

He scanned the path ahead. If Frederick came this way, bringing Regina with him, traces of his veering away should still be evident. "Did he carry you from this point?"

"On hith thoulderth. It wath fun."

"Okay. We can do that." He hoisted her onto his shoulders and held her bare legs. "Are you all right way up there?"

She giggled. "It'th not that high!"

"Oh, no?" He marched away from the path, hacking at the brambles. "Pretend you're flying like a bird. I'll take you through the treetops."

"Okay!" She giggled again, flapping her arms. "I'm flying!"

"Don't forget to follow the smell and tell me which way to go!" Adrian plunged into the thicket, constantly glancing between the floor of the forest and his little bird above. As her hands brushed by leaves, vines, and twigs, she caressed each sensation with her probing fingers. At times, he had to duck low to keep her head from colliding with a limb, and with each sudden dip, she gasped, then giggled once again.

After a few minutes, she pulled on his shirt. "Go that way."

Adrian looked up. Her rigid arm and finger indicated a sharp left turn. The ground sloped downward in that direction, diving into a much darker part of the forest. The trees grew so dense, Solarus couldn't possibly warm any seeds in there. "Are you sure?"

"I hear the water. It'th at a thtream."

"You didn't mention water. Is the smell that way, too?"

"Both are."

"Okay. Let's go." Hacking at bushes again, Adrian strode down the slope. After several steps, he came upon a wall of massive trees that appeared to encircle a central point beyond his view. He squeezed between the closest two trees and emerged in a dark glade.

The forest floor lay perfectly flat, a round table of earth stretching about thirty paces across without a hint of leaf, root, or grass. Above, tree branches intertwined in a thick web, beginning just a foot or so over his head and rising out of sight, completely blocking the sky. Since the gaps between the trees provided the only source of light, the center of the glade lay in near total darkness. Except for the tinkling sound of running water, all was quiet.

"We're here," Regina said. "Do you thmell it?"

Adrian inhaled. The odor of rotting flesh hammered his nostrils. "I certainly do."

As he walked toward the center, his boots made squishing sounds in the damp soil. With every step, the ground grew wetter and wetter. Soon, his eyes adjusted. A spring welled up at the focal point, bubbling and gurgling as it flowed from below and spread out over the ground.

Adrian inched closer, sliding his feet to find the spring's edge. As if burping, the spring expelled loud gaseous bubbles, bringing with each burst an odorous draft.

When his toes found the border, he stopped and looked around. What secret lay here that Frederick kept from Arxad? And why would he bring Regina with him? Surely a flying dragon would be able to see this place. Maybe Arxad knew it was here but was unaware of all the mysteries within. The trees were packed so closely together, he could never enter the glade.

Adrian pushed his sword between his belt and waistband, then pulled Regina down and set her gently on her feet. Crouching, he spoke softly. "What did you and Frederick do when you came here?"

"Firtht, we drank thome of the water. Then, he put thome in my eyeth."

"He washed your eyes with this water?"

She nodded. "And my thkin. It feelth good. It tathte good, too."

"Interesting." Using his bare left hand, Adrian scooped up the cool water and drank it. Although somewhat fetid, it carried a sweet flavor, much like vanilla-laced cream and sugar. "Do you want some?"

She nodded vigorously. "Yeth, pleathe."

Adrian gazed at her. Although her face was now veiled in the dim light, it seemed that her eyes and skin shimmered, like the faint luster of dew on a moonlit night. What properties had this water transmitted?

"Wait just a moment." He stripped off his bandage and dipped his right hand into the water. The cool flow stung his wound, but after a few seconds, the pain eased. He raised his hand close to his eyes, but the darkness and the presence of stitches wouldn't allow a clear view of the cut. He closed and opened his hand, flexing the muscles. It didn't hurt at all. The water had healed the wound!

Adrian's mind flashed back to Regina's earlier revelation. She was the only one Frederick ever brought here. And why? The realization breezed through his lips in an excited whisper. "Frederick was trying to heal your eyes!"

FIVE

M Y eyeth?" Regina said. "He didn't tell me that."

"He probably didn't want to disappoint you if it didn't work." Adrian scooped up some water and held it to her lips. "Here."

She sipped, but most of it spilled to her tunic.

"Sorry. That was clumsy of me."

"It'th okay. I can get thome mythelf." She knelt and drank straight from the flow, slurping loudly. When she rose again, she smacked her lips. "That was so good!"

Adrian jerked his head toward her. "What did you say?"

"I thaid that wath tho good!"

"No you didn't. You said your esses correctly."

She blinked. "I did?"

"Here." He scooped another double handful. "Drink some more."

She slurped, but again it spilled. "It'th eathier my way." Still on her knees, she bent low and drank, this time taking her time to swallow big gulps. When she finished, she raised up and wiped her lips with her forearm. "Yummy!"

Adrian touched her cheek. "Say, 'See the slithering snake.'"

She grinned. "See the slithering snake." She slapped a hand over her mouth and breathed between her fingers. "I said it!"

"Yes, you did!" He wrapped his arms around her and pulled her close. "That's wonderful!"

She pushed away, her eyes again shimmering, yet wandering. "But you said I did it right before. Then I messed it up again."

"I know. It's strange." Adrian looked at the gap between the two trees where they had entered. "When you came with Frederick, did you drink much?"

She nodded. "More than this time. He brought a cup, and he never let me off his shoulders."

"So he dipped it for you and lifted the cup to your hands."

She nodded again.

"Interesting." Adrian imagined the process—Frederick stooping with Regina on his shoulders. He likely wanted to protect her from falling into the spring. And he had brought a cup, knowing he would use it for that very purpose. He had planned this healing attempt carefully. Yet, the water didn't work. Why? What was the difference between then and now? Only one possible difference came to mind. "Let's try washing your eyes and skin again. This time, I want you to do it yourself."

"Okay." She knelt and scooped handfuls of water, splashing her face and eyes. After rubbing it over every exposed part of her body, including her scalp, she blinked away the moisture. "I'm waiting," she said, a hopeful smile dressing her face.

Adrian passed a thumb across a blemish on her cheek. The black mark smeared. Using his sleeve, he cleared it and several other marks away, revealing healthy skin from her chin to the top of her head. His chest heaving, he barely held back a sob. "It ... it worked."

"It did?" As she rubbed her forearm, her brow shot upward. "It did!"

He looked into her eyes. The shimmer strengthened until a dim aura emanated. "Can you see anything?"

She blinked several times. "Not yet. Maybe it will come soon."

"Maybe." He kept his gaze locked on her oddly glowing orbs. At this point, it probably wouldn't do any good to tell her about the phenomenon. It might get her hopes up too high. "Just let me know when it comes."

She threw her arms around him, brushing her face against his. "Thank you."

He laughed. "I didn't heal you; the water did."

Pulling back, she pressed her palms against his cheeks. "But you brought me here, and you let me get wet."

"Let you get wet? What do you mean?"

She rose and splashed with her feet. "No one lets me do anything on my own. They're always scared I'll hurt myself."

"They're just trying to protect you."

She stomped, raising a bigger splash. "I'm blind, but I can do things!"

"Of course you can," he said, ending with a shushing sound. "And you brought me exactly where you said you could. I wouldn't have found it without you."

Closing her eyes, Regina crossed her arms and nodded firmly. "That's right!"

"So this is where the Bloodless are trapped." He scanned the area again. "But where?"

She pointed at the water. "Down there, maybe?"

"Underground?"

She nodded.

"You mean down in the spring?"

"There's a spring?"

"Sorry. I forgot. You can't see it." He formed a circle with his hands and let her feel the shape. "There's a hole in the ground where the water comes out, but I don't think a dragon can fit through it."

"Okay. What else is here?"

"I assume you felt the trees I squeezed through. We're in a clearing that's surrounded by a circle of big trees, and up above, the branches intertwine so thickly and tightly, they create a ..." He gazed at the branches, allowing his eyes to survey the intricate pattern. "A net, like a spider's web."

Regina clasped her hands together, intertwining her fingers. "Spiders catch things!"

"Yes, I was just thinking that." He rose to his full height and jumped, grabbing a branch. Hanging from it by one hand, he snatched out his sword and slashed the wood. The branch snapped, and he fell back to his feet.

"What did you do?"

"I cut off a piece of the net." He drew the wood close. The section was about a foot long and as wide as a broom handle, but nothing else was apparent. "It's too dark to study it carefully."

She reached out. "Let me!"

"Sure." He pushed it into her grasp and closed her fingers around it. "It feels like normal bark to me."

She ran her fingers all along the surface, then suddenly stopped. "What's this?"

"What's what?"

She groped until she caught hold of his wrist. She pulled his hand close and pressed his finger against a spot on the branch near the center. "Feel it?"

Adrian rubbed the spot. "A notch?"

"Uh-huh. Like it's been cut."

"I see what you mean." He slid it away from her and felt the gap. His own blade hadn't done this. His single slash had cut it at the end.

He looked up again, straining his eyes. Since there appeared to be no design in the snaking, twisting branches, it was impossible to tell if the web had suffered any earlier wounds. Even the branch he had cut away had already grown back. "If Frederick's been trying to break the trap, he hasn't had much success."

"Can you see any dragons up there?"

"I can't see anything but branches." Standing on tiptoes, he reached with his sword and poked through a gap. The point struck another branch. "I think there are multiple layers."

"No wonder the dragons can't get out."

"True. Arxad said they aren't the answer to the need for an army. That could mean that Frederick wants them out to help him rescue the slaves."

"So is Arxad afraid of the Bloodless?"

"That's a smart conclusion."

She grinned. "I told you I could do things."

"I never doubted you for a moment." He looked again at the web. "If they're trapped up in those branches, maybe Frederick was trying to help them by breaking a layer. But as fast as the branches grow back, it's no wonder he hasn't made a dent."

Regina pointed at the water. "The spring makes the trees grow. It makes the branches stronger."

"And heals them." Adrian rubbed her newly cleansed scalp, feeling the stiff bristles. "You really are a smart one!"

She crossed her arms again, this time saying nothing.

Adrian pushed a boot against the water's flow. "So, maybe the secret to getting them out is to plug the spring somehow."

"But …" Regina touched her finger to her chin. "But should you do that? If Arxad is scared of them, shouldn't we be scared of them, too?"

"Maybe these Bloodless are enemies of Arxad's kind. If Frederick was trying to set them free, maybe they would be our friends."

"And maybe not."

"So we need to learn more and proceed with caution." Adrian knelt and pushed his arm down into the spring. Several seconds of probing produced nothing but cold water and another smelly belch. "Well, I can't find a smaller hole down there, so if we decide to plug it, we'll have to get a boulder big enough to cover the top."

Regina spread out her hands. "Where would the water go then?"

"Good question. If it doesn't have another outlet, it could burst out somewhere else. It might be better to divert it."

She pointed upward. "Shouldn't you make sure the dragons are there?"

"Well, I just assumed Frederick already checked."

She shrugged. "Maybe they got out since he checked."

Again gazing at her, he shook his head. "The more I listen to you, the dumber I feel."

She felt for his back and patted it. "It's okay. At least you're not blind."

Adrian caressed her cheek, shadowed and barely visible. On Major Four, with her lesions, hairless head, and dead eyes, she would have been considered ugly, useless, fit only for simple farm labor, never for a position of nobility. Even with newly cleansed skin, most males would never give her a second look, considering a sightless female an unsuitable wife or bearer of children.

So who were the blind ones? Easy. The fools unable to see inner beauty, the hidden treasures that lay beyond the eyes. And now, veiled by shadows, this precious girl's splendor shone as bright as Solarus.

His throat tightened, pitching his voice higher. "I think you've helped me to see better than ever."

"Good." She patted his back again. "Maybe that'll help you find the dragons."

As he rose, he looked once again at the web above. "I'm going to try to climb up there. Maybe I'll find more space than meets the eye from here."

"Can I come, too?" She raised her arm and flexed her bicep. "I'm strong. I can climb."

Adrian opened his mouth to say no, but quickly shook the word away. "Sure. Let's see if we can scale the trunk and go up where the branches are bigger."

Regina clapped her hands. "Fun!"

Taking her hand, he led her back to their entry gap and searched the trunks, now much easier to see in the light between the trees. Every limb protruded toward the center, branching off quickly and in dozens of directions. The closest limb hung low enough for her to reach with a boost.

He laid down his sword and spoke in a cheerful tone. "I'm going to lift you up, so reach your hands as high as you can."

She stretched her arms over her head. "Like this?"

"Perfect." Grabbing her just below her hips, he heaved her upward until her hands wrapped around one of the smaller branches. "Got it?"

"Got it."

"Now hang on while I move my hands. You'll need to swing up to the big limb that's in front of the branch you're holding."

"I'm ready."

Adrian shifted his grip to her feet and boosted her higher. She pulled free from his hands, swung her legs up, and straddled the limb with her face toward the center of the glade, bumping her head on a branch above in the process.

"Ouch!" She rubbed her scalp.

"Are you all right?"

She nodded. "You didn't warn me."

"I'm sorry. I forgot again."

"That's okay. I just have to keep reminding you."

Adrian picked up his sword and, holding the end of the blade, extended the hilt. "I'm lifting my sword. Grab the hilt."

Regina's brow shot upward. "Your sword?" She reached out. When her fingers touched the hilt, they curled around it slowly. "Wow!"

"Okay. Hang on tight. I'm coming up."

She gripped her supporting limb with her free hand. "I'm ready."

Adrian leaped, grabbed the same branch Regina had used, and swung himself up to the limb. He also faced the glade's center, Regina sitting behind him. When their bodies stopped shaking with the bouncing bough, he studied the inner workings of the web. As expected, the branches created multiple layers of concentric circles with the center directly over the spring. The limb they sat upon was the source of this tree's contribution to the lowest layer, and fewer branches sprouted than farther out into the web. With more space here, if they climbed close to the trunk, it would be a lot easier to ascend into the upper levels.

He twisted his body toward her and took the sword. "Are you ready for more climbing?"

Her grin returned, wider than ever. "I'm ready!"

"Up above, there are thick limbs and thinner branches. We'll use the limbs to stand on and the branches for grabbing hold and climbing."

"I understand."

"Good. Now reach up and grab the branch you bumped your head on, and try to stand."

She complied, standing steadily as their limb bounced again.

"Now climb to the limb on the next level and reach for another branch. Use the branches as handholds and the limbs as steps. Keep doing that until I say to stop."

"I'll race you!" She scrambled up, as agile as a monkey.

Adrian followed, making sure she had gained control of a higher level before he heaved his body to the limb below her. With each level, he peered toward the center, checking for any sign of life within. Finally, after the sixth level, something white appeared. "Stop!"

Regina skittered down to his limb. "What do you see?"

"Something white. Follow me, and be careful." Keeping his head low and the sword in hand, he crawled toward the center over the network of branches. Although they bent under his weight, cracking at times, they held firm enough. The sound of Regina's quick, shallow breaths stayed close behind.

Near the area above the spring, a white shape protruded from the upper level, as if a huge ball had been wedged there from above. When he reached it, he halted, laid his sword down, and touched the shape's cool surface. His fingertips ran across tiny lines—shallow gaps that divided it into sections that felt like scales, though not nearly as pronounced as those of the dragons of the Southlands. The dragon he had ridden in the Northlands, however, had skin very much like this.

"I think it's a dragon," he whispered.

She scooted up to his side, her hand falling through a gap once before finding solid support. "Is he alive?"

His hand still on the protruding shape, a slight buzz tickled his skin. "I think so."

"And you said it's white?"

"Yes. I saw a white dragon in the Northlands. Up there they call him a king."

"So is this one of the Bloodless?"

"I suppose so. That means the king of the Northlands is of this dragon's species, not Arxad's."

"If the Bloodless dragons have a king, why doesn't he help them?"

"That's a good question. Not only that, the white dragon and Arxad seemed to be friendly with each other, so it's odd that Arxad would be frightened of the ones here."

She pushed on a branch beneath her hand. "These are strong. How are you going to get him out?"

"I'm thinking about that." Adrian touched the point where the body met the upper level's matrix of branches. The woody spears pierced the dragon's flesh, skewering it, but no blood flowed from the wounds. "Bloodless," he whispered. "No wonder they haven't bled to death."

"Are they hurt?"

"Very much so. This isn't going to be easy."

"Are you going to take the water away?"

"First we have to figure out who they are and how dangerous they might be. If they're awake enough to answer, I have some questions for them."

Regina shuddered. "I don't. If they're dragons, I don't want to talk to them."

"That's fine. I'll do the talking." Adrian patted the dragon's scales and shouted. "Hello! Can you hear me?"

The dragon's body shifted, and a low rumble emanated. "Who is there?"

"I am Adrian Masters. I have come from Darksphere to rescue the human slaves."

"A human?" The dragon's tone seemed annoyed. "We have no business with humans."

"You do now." Adrian pushed on the dragon's scales. "I don't think you can do much about it."

"You mock my captivity." The dragon groaned, mixing in a shallow growl. "If you wish to speak on friendly terms, I advise that you dispense with posturing and speak plainly."

"Very well." Adrian grabbed a branch above his head and steadied himself. "My brother thinks you might be able to help us."

"Your brother? What is his name?"

"Frederick. Frederick Masters."

"I do not recall the Masters part of his name, but I remember Frederick. He tried to set us free, but he failed. He has not been here in quite some time."

"What did he do to try to free you?"

"He is your brother. Why are you asking me?"

"I'm afraid he is incapacitated and unable to communicate."

A new purr vibrated the branches. "Interesting."

"Well, can you tell me?"

"I assume you saw the spring."

Adrian looked down, but darkness at the glade's center prevented a view of the upwelling water. "I did. I already guessed that it heals the trees."

"It flows from an underground river. Someone blocked that river and redirected the flow to the surface."

"Who did that?"

"The same beast who trapped us here. Our king."

Regina gasped. Adrian raised a shushing finger to his lips. Letting this dragon know what they knew might be a mistake. "Why would your king do that?"

"To keep us from bringing retribution. The very soul of this world was violated, so it was our duty to punish the evildoers."

Adrian regripped the branch. Keeping his body steady on this shifting foundation wasn't easy. "How was it violated, and who are the evildoers?"

"Since you are Frederick's brother, you are not one of the guilty. I see no need to explain."

"Has your king sided with the evildoers?"

The dragon grunted derisively. "Aleph does what he must, and what only he can do. That is all I will say."

"If you won't tell me more, I won't be able to decide whether or not to help you."

"Frederick was unable to help us. Are you wiser than he?"

"Not wiser, but I think I have journeyed in this land to a wider extent than he has. Maybe I have learned more than he was able to learn."

"A fair statement." The dragon shifted, shaking the network of branches. "It hurts to move, but staying motionless eventually brings a greater ache."

Adrian clutched the branch with one hand and Regina's arm with the other until their ground and ceiling settled.

After a low groan, the white dragon continued. "Members of both the human race and the dragon race have committed grievous violations against our world. The humans have been appropriately punished, and all those at fault are now dead. Among the dragons, however, some who committed atrocities are still living. When we attempted to exact punishment, we were defeated, but only because our own king prevented us from doing what we were born to do. We are the enforcers of this world, and all who violate its soul must die."

"Why would your king prevent justice from being served?"

"This is a question you would have to ask him. Although Alaph is not one to speak without provocation, he will respond with honesty to questions. He is unable to lie."

Adrian searched for the dragon's head. It lay somewhere to his left, veiled by darkness. "Well, if he were here, I would be glad to ask him. But he's not."

"So you think." The dragon groaned again, this time with a mournful tone. "He is close, much closer than you realize."

Adrian nodded. Now they were getting somewhere. Detecting a lie in this beast would determine whether or not it was trustworthy. "So, where is your king?"

"In the Northlands."

"The Northlands? But you said he was close. I've been to the Northlands, and it isn't close at all."

"Nor is your world close to this one, yet, if you took Frederick's path, you crossed from one to the other in the blink of an eye."

Adrian nodded. This dragon had indeed spoken to Frederick. "So there's a portal nearby?"

"Of a sort. It is quite different from the one you passed through."

"Where is it?"

"Climb. You will find it. It is an arduous climb, but it is a much quicker route to the Northlands than any other. That is, if the portal allows you to pass. Not all are able."

Adrian looked up, but it was much too dark to see through the gaps in the network of branches. At least this dragon hadn't lied about the king's location, but could he be lying about a portal in the trees? There was only one sure way to find out. "If I were to climb, how many more of your kind might I see?"

"There are three of us. Perhaps you will see them. Perhaps not. I do suspect, however, that the higher you climb, the slower the branches will be to heal, so if you can free the highest of us, she might be able to help you with the rest."

"She? I take it that you are male. What gender is the third?"

"The third is also female, my mate, the king's sister. The highest one is my sister, the king's mate."

Adrian set a hand over Regina's mouth, stifling another gasp. "The king entrapped his mate and his sister?" he asked. "How could he be so cruel?"

"Again, that is a question to ask him. We might consider it to be cruel, but apparently he does not, for he thinks himself to be gentle and just."

Adrian glanced back at the trunk. "Did Frederick attempt the climb?"

"He did not. He was concerned about taking care of some children in his charge and thought it best not to risk being unable to return."

Adrian looked at Regina. Her mournful expression said it all. They had to learn the truth and find out if the dragons should be freed. Everything this dragon had said rang true. Maybe a human could climb up to the Northlands and learn more. Since Frederick would recover eventually, someone would take care of the children.

He laid a hand on the dragon again. "Very well. I will try the climb. If what I learn tells me that you should be set free, I will do what I can to help you."

"May the Creator guide you." The dragon shifted again and groaned once more. "Our agony is unrelenting."

Making enough noise for Regina to follow, Adrian crawled toward the trunk, his sword again in hand. He glanced back at her every few seconds. Feeling carefully for each support, she kept up beautifully. At one point, her hand stopped at a gap. Her fingers felt the edges of the hole, and, avoiding it deftly, she continued on.

A tear welled in Adrian's eye. Her every move painted a portrait of courage. What must it be like to glory in the splendor of sight only to lose it because of the brutal cruelty of horrible beasts? They scourged her back, forced her to carry her weight in stones from dawn to dusk every day of her life, and fed her just enough to allow for survival but not enough to soothe the gnawing hole that scourged her from the inside and never let her forget the meaning of suffering. They robbed her of the gift of vision, and now she was being called upon to help a member of a similar species.

When they arrived at the trunk, he pushed the point of the blade into the branch, making the sword stand upright, and turned to face Regina. As they both straddled the limb, he took her hand. She pulled his hand close and wrapped it with both of hers. They were cold and trembling.

"Are you going to climb farther up now?" she asked.

"Yes." He lowered his voice to a whisper. "Wait here for me, but if I don't come back, can you find your way home?"

She nodded, also whispering. "I counted our steps, and I know the smells, but I'm not worried about me."

"Good. You're a brave girl."

"I know." Her brow knitted with two deep creases. "But I am worried about Marcelle. I can't bring her here. She's too heavy."

"Why would you bring her—" Adrian cut off his own words. What a fool! How could he miss the obvious? The spring could probably heal Marcelle, and it hadn't even crossed his mind! "You're making me feel stupid again."

"Think of it this way. You're getting smarter all the time." Grinning again, she touched her chin with a finger. "I should go with you to make sure you keep getting smarter."

"There's no need for that." He gazed into her eyes. Even in the brighter light, they shimmered. Why had the water healed the rest of her body but not her visual gateway to the world? "I'll just go up a little way. If I see anything dangerous at all or it gets too far, I'll come right back, and we'll go get Marcelle. Otherwise, I'll keep climbing. Sound good?"

She nodded. "Sounds good."

"Hang on. I'm getting up." As she braced herself, he reached for the limb above and pulled himself up, plucking the sword from its perch in one motion. He pushed the blade behind his belt and began climbing. From level to level, the gaps in between seemed to be about the same, though the limbs grew progressively smaller. Below, Regina became harder to see, her form shrinking and veiled as the distance expanded and the branches obstructed his view.

At each level, he looked toward the center. Vague white shapes appeared, maybe various parts of the lowest dragon or his first view of the second one. With long necks and tails, who could tell where one dragon began and another ended?

When he passed what seemed to be the third dragon, he stopped and looked up. The distance to the next limb was about ten feet instead of the usual four to five. A layer of fog floated just above his head, thin and swirling, as if stirred by a breeze.

He licked his finger and raised it. Not a breath of air cooled his skin. What could be stirring the fog? And why would it be there at all? It was so thin, seeing through it wasn't a problem, so it couldn't be hiding anything.

He pushed his hand through the layer. The fog rushed toward the contact point and wrapped around his wrist. Resisting the urge to jerk back, Adrian stood on tiptoes to get a better look.

The mist ran up to his fingertips and swirled around them, as if trying to dress them in a white glove. A tingling sensation trickled down his skin and spread toward his elbow. The mist trickled down with it, enveloping his forearm.

Adrian pulled his arm down and backed toward the trunk, but the mist stretched out from the layer, as if reaching and trying to hang on. It crawled along his body until the tingles and white raiment covered him from head to toe.

A ribbon of mist connected his hand to the layer above. The tingles radiated toward the connection, as if drawing him. As the pull intensified, his feet lifted from the branch, and his body drifted upward.

Adrian thrashed, slowing the ascent, but he couldn't pull free. He drew his sword and slashed at the fog. The blade passed harmlessly through, doing nothing but adding to the swirl. "Let me go!" he shouted, but the words sounded foolish even in his own ears.

"What's wrong, Adrian?"

From below, Regina climbed toward him, her bright eyes pulsing.

"Stay back! Something grabbed me, and I can't get loose."

She scrambled up to his level and groped until her hand swiped across his foot. She wrapped her arms around his legs and pulled with all her weight. "I'll get you loose," she called.

"No, Regina! Let go! I can't let you get hurt!"

"But you need me!" She rocked her body, lifting off the branch and making them both swing. "You can't be smart without me."

Unable to kick, Adrian put the sword away and kept his lower body as still as possible. If she fell now, she might tumble all the way to the ground.

"I'm hanging on, Adrian! Is it helping?"

He bent over, grabbed her wrist, and hauled her into his arms. Holding her tightly, he kissed her cheek and whispered into her ear. "Thank you for helping me."

They continued rising slowly with the fog, both penetrating the swirling layer. After nearly a minute, they stopped in midair, now within reach of the limb above.

Adrian kept his lips close to her ear. "I'm going to boost you to the next level. Just reach out and grab whatever you can."

"Okay."

Grasping just below her hips, Adrian hoisted her to the branch. When she latched on to it, he pushed her higher until she was able to climb up and straddle it. The mist surrounded her, as if it adhered to her body, following her every move.

Adrian looked at his hands. He, too, wore the misty clothing. Streams of white ran across his skin in both directions, like an external circulatory system.

He stretched to grab the branch, but it stayed just inches above his fingers. With no foundation from which to jump, it might as well have been a mile.

She reached down and grabbed his wrist. "I'll pull you." Grunting, she heaved until his hand came in contact with the branch. He latched on and hoisted himself the rest of the way.

Now facing Regina, he took a deep breath. She smiled so broadly, her face seemed ready to crack.

"What is it?" he asked.

She covered her mouth, masking a giggle. "I have a secret."

"A secret? What?"

"Hold up some fingers and ask me to guess how many."

"Okay." He held up three fingers. "How many?"

"Three!"

"Good guess."

She bounced in place, making the branch sway. "Again!"

He closed his hand, then held up three fingers. "Now how many?"

Her brow furrowed. "You didn't change the number."

"Regina?" Adrian bent low and looked into her eyes. "You can see?"

Her smile growing even wider, she nodded. "That's my secret!"

"That's wonderful!" He grabbed her and held her close. "The water did heal you after all!"

"Maybe it had to soak in."

"I suppose so." He looked up. The next level was well within reach. "Are you ready to keep climbing?"

"Ready! This will be even more fun now."

She pushed to her feet and scrambled up to the branch above. Adrian followed, staying close behind her, just in case.

As they climbed through level after level, the trunk began to bend to one side, forcing them to ascend at an angle. Soon, another trunk came into view, angling toward theirs. The individual branches became thinner, though they grew in number. The two climbers squeezed through smaller gaps, pushing the spindly branches aside as if they were real spider webs.

Finally, at the point where the two trunks merged, Adrian poked his head through a hole. In a much larger gap between levels, a bed stood within reach on the matrix of branches, the back of the headboard facing him so that the bed's occupant stayed out of view. Bracing himself on what appeared to be the floor of this new level, he squeezed through the opening and crawled into the room.

When Regina followed, he grabbed her arms and lifted her through, her smaller body fitting much more easily. He stood and eyed the tree. With the twin trunks merging into a single trunk just below the floor, and with two branchless limbs overhead, it seemed that the tree resembled an extraordinarily tall man with woody arms and legs. One of the arms extended over the bed, its five-fingered hand open with its palm facing up.

Adrian raised and lowered his feet. With the thin branches intertwining underneath, they looked more like roots than branches, and they seemed too fragile to hold up his weight without bending.

A gasping, wheezing sound came from somewhere nearby. Adrian walked gingerly around to the side of the bed. As his eyes adjusted to the dim lighting, he clutched the bed's rail and felt the sheet for an occupant. No one was there.

Regina joined him and held his hand. The mist swirled around their melded fingers. "I see other beds," she said.

Now able to focus clearly, Adrian looked around. They stood at a bedside in a rectangular room with beds lining the nearer wall to the right and the farther wall to the left. This empty bed seemed to be the middle of five on their side. Light in the room emanated from two lanterns on each wall. Their flames, barely visible, seemed insufficient for such a large chamber.

A glimmer appeared from behind the first bed in their row. A radiant girl, perhaps a teenager, stood on the opposite side, leaning over a heaving lump covered by a sheet. "Breathe, Edison!" she called with a plaintive cry. "Please keep trying!"

"Edison? My father?" Adrian ran toward the bed, the thin branches easily supporting his weight. He stopped at the side across from the girl, clutched the rail, and reached for the occupant's head. Adrian's mist-covered hand glowed, illuminating the face of Edison Masters.

SIX

EDISON sucked in a gurgling, halting breath, then exhaled with a nasally whistle. His eyes stayed clenched shut, as if pain throttled every second of respiration.

"Father!" Adrian called. "It's me—your son."

He offered no response, just another round of excruciating gasps for breath.

Adrian looked at the girl across the bed. Like himself and Regina, glowing mist coated her body. "What's wrong with my father?"

When she looked at him, her face twisted in anguish. "Adrian, I'm afraid he has taken a turn for the worse. When you left, he was resting comfortably in a normal bed, but when he worsened, we moved him to the healing trees."

"Healing trees?" Adrian looked at the tree behind his father's bed, a duplicate of the one he had climbed. It, too, extended an arm over the bed. "How do they heal? Why isn't it working?" He paused, squinting. "And how do you know my name?"

"I am Deference. We met when you came here before."

"But you were invisible then. Now you're—" Irritated, he waved a hand. "Never mind. Just tell me about the healing trees."

Deference pointed at the extended arm. "We need to place a stardrop in this tree's hand. Only that will heal your father."

"A stardrop? How can I get a stardrop?"

"By scooping out a piece of Exodus in the star chamber."

His father wheezed again, this time unable to breathe for several seconds. Finally, air broke through.

Adrian exhaled with him. How long could he survive? "Where is this star chamber?"

Deference pointed across the room. "Through those doors and down the hall. When you reach the foyer, turn left through the opening in the wall."

Adrian looked in that direction. An open double doorway led to a wide corridor. A young woman stood there, facing him. With shining green eyes, flowing red hair, and a white dress and blue cloak draped over a thin body, her identity was unmistakable. "Cassabrie?" he whispered.

Cassabrie walked toward the bed, her bare feet light on the branches. When she arrived, she stood nearly toe to toe with him and tilted her head up, looking him in the eye. "Will you trust me to give you counsel?"

Adrian locked gazes with her. As always, even in her emaciated state, her beauty was mesmerizing. Yet, since she no longer resided within, blocking her hypnotic effect seemed much easier. "I will listen."

"First, allow me to ask, how is Marcelle faring?"

"Still unconscious. She woke up to help me in a fight, and she seemed to recognize me, but she slipped back again."

Cassabrie looked away. "Her ability to see through her physical eyes is sharpening. That's a good sign."

"We can talk about Marcelle later. What can I do about my father?"

"Nothing." She refocused on him. "You will not be able to get a stardrop, not in your current state."

"My current state? What do you mean?"

She fanned out her cloak. "As you will remember, whenever I am in your presence here on Starlight, I am invisible. The same is true with Deference. Now you and your young traveling companion are in the same state, invisible to the living souls here in the Northlands, though we are visible to each other."

Adrian glanced from Regina to Deference to Cassabrie. All three wore shrouds of mist. "But I'm not a spirit. I didn't die."

"When you climbed through the portal, you transformed. When you go back, you will revert to your normal state, though that wouldn't work for Deference or me, since our bodies are elsewhere."

Adrian nodded briskly. "Okay. That's a good enough explanation for now. Just help me figure out how to get the stardrop. If I can't do it, who can?"

"Your brother Jason is here, and he is attempting that feat as we speak. Since he must scoop out some of the star's radiance and carry the hot material a great distance, his success is not at all assured, so I suggest praying for him. There is nothing else you can do."

A white dragon flew through the doorway and settled close to the bed, barely bending the floor at all. Adrian resisted the urge to back away. This was the king, the dragon who had saved his father's life earlier, the one the other white dragon called Alaph.

Regina thrust a hand into Adrian's and held it tightly, trembling but saying nothing.

After studying Adrian and Regina for a few seconds, Alaph blew a stream of icy vapor. "Your presence is unexpected, especially your lack of physical state and your mode of entry." Adrian bowed his head. "I didn't know the path would lead me here. If I am intruding, I apologize, but I have to find a way to help my father."

"The best way to help your father is to go back the way you came and continue your quest to free your people. There is nothing you can do for him here. Your brother will have to be your surrogate. You may watch his efforts, if you dare, but you will not be able to help or even speak to him. You will be invisible in his perspective and unable to move anything here, save for the tree branches."

"You said *dare.*" Adrian glanced at Regina. "Is there any danger?"

Alaph drew his head back, bending his neck into an S shape. "There is danger, but only to you and the girl, not to Deference or Cassabrie."

"Why? What danger?"

"I assume you saw others of my species as you climbed the trees."

Adrian nodded. "I saw three. I was going to ask you about them."

Alaph stared at him, his head bobbing as his eyes scanned Adrian from head to toe. After nearly a minute, Adrian backed away. "Well?" he asked.

Alaph's brow arched up. "Well what?"

"Aren't you going to tell me about the other three white dragons?"

"If you ask, I will tell. You merely said that you were going to ask."

Adrian let out a huff, then enunciated carefully. "Who are the other three dragons, and why are they imprisoned in the trees?"

Alaph's head floated a few inches from Adrian's face as he spoke with a tone of mystery. "The four of us are the Benefile. We are prophets of Starlight who are able to influence humans. The longer you stay in your present state, the more susceptible you are to the influence. My subjects have been here in my palace for a long time, so they are fully submitted to me and to the precepts of the Creator. They began their submission by choice and are now captivated, slaves by their own free will, if you can accept that paradox. The other three members of my race conspired to guide humans away from the Creator, thinking they themselves could be worshiped in the Creator's place."

Drawing back again, Alaph altered to a normal tone. "There is much more to tell, but this is not the time. For now, you must decide whether you will stay and watch your brother's efforts or leave before the influence grows beyond your limits or the limits of the girl who accompanies you."

Adrian looked Alaph in the eye. The influence didn't appear to be strong, but experience with Cassabrie's indwelling proved that discerning his mental competence was almost impossible. Still, he had to see what would happen to Father. He could withstand an entrapped dragon's wiles, and he could protect Regina as well. She would follow him no matter what.

Taking Regina's hand, Adrian gave Alaph a firm nod. "I will stay."

Alaph let out a sigh. "As you wish."

Cassabrie whirled around, making her cloak swish in a wide circle. "I think I hear Jason. I'd better meet him at the door." She ran across the floor, her bare feet not even touching the branches.

"Stand wherever you wish," Alaph said, "but do not speak. You will confuse him and potentially hinder your father's recovery."

Hand in hand, Adrian and Regina walked closer to the doorway, stopping at the halfway point. As Cassabrie looked out expectantly, her cloak flowed as if blown by the wind. Soon, Jason appeared well down the hallway, running with all his might while holding something in his fist.

Cassabrie reached out her hands. "I'll take it the rest of the way!"

"I've got it!" Jason ran past her, but when his foot landed on the branches, it punched through, sending his leg into the floor up to his thigh. Adrian took a hard step, but Regina pulled him back. "You can't help," she whispered.

Jason grabbed a vine and tried to climb out, but he stiffened. With his teeth clenched and his eyes tightly shut, he seemed unable to move.

Cassabrie ran to him, her hand open. "Give it to me, Jason! Hurry! I will save your father."

"I'll take it to him!" Jason reached with a bloody hand. "Help me out!"

"Don't be a fool!" Cassabrie shouted. "Give it to me!"

Deference cried out from the bed. "He's not breathing! I can't clear the airway!"

"Okay! Okay!" Jason presented a shining sphere between his thumb and finger and placed it on Cassabrie's palm. "Hurry!"

While she ran to the bed, Jason struggled to climb out of the hole. Adrian flexed his muscles, mentally trying to help. Somehow Jason had injured his hands. Both bled profusely as he pulled on the branches, but he soon managed to stand.

Now stepping more carefully, Jason hurried to his father, while Adrian and Regina followed. Cassabrie stood on the mattress, staring at the tree's extended hand. The shining sphere lay on its palm. It shrank in a splash of sparks that penetrated the hand's bark, making it glow from top to bottom and radiate down the tree's arm to a knot that looked like an elbow. Soon the sparks drizzled over Father's head and covered his forehead and cheeks, erupting in an array of colors before transforming to white snow-like flakes.

Father gasped, and his body heaved. Then, he took in a long, deep draw of air before settling into a rhythmic pattern, breathing without a rattle.

Cassabrie climbed down from the bed, leaned over Father, and collected the glowing flakes. "Show me your wounds," she said as she turned toward Jason.

Jason held out his hands. Cassabrie spread the particles over the lacerations and pressed his palms together. White smoke and glittering radiance leaked between his hands and spilled over his skin.

When the smoke cleared, Cassabrie released him. "Let's see how they look."

Spreading out his fingers, Jason smiled. "Thank you. They feel perfect."

Adrian leaned over Jason's shoulder to get a better look. Dried blood covered his brother's palms and fingers, but the wounds were gone.

Jason stepped to the bed. Adrian edged back, holding his breath. Oh, to embrace him and shout out congratulations! He had brought the stardrop and healed Father! But the king had forbidden it. Just looking on proudly would have to do.

"How is he?" Jason asked.

"Let's see if he'll wake up." Deference gently stroked Father's forehead. "Mr. Masters. Edison Masters. It's time to wake up."

Father took in a deep draw of air again, this time through his nose. "I detect a familiar scent. Dreams of my son have leaked into the air."

"Father," Jason said. "Open your eyes."

Father's eyes opened. "Jason? Son, is that really you?"

"Yes." Jason's voice cracked. "Yes, I'm here."

Father sat up and scanned the room. "We're in the dragon world. Not at home. This is the same castle, the white dragon's castle, where the dragon brought me after I fell into the river. All the legends were true, and I wasn't dreaming."

"They're all true," Jason said.

Adrian glanced at the white dragon. His stare seemed to draw him closer. "Go now," Alaph whispered. "Your father is well, and there is no more for you to see."

While Jason and their father continued to chat, Adrian guided Regina to the tree behind the bed. Although this wasn't the same tree they had ascended, maybe it would be a good idea to risk taking a new path. Maybe they could meet and talk to a different white dragon.

He lowered himself through the gap feetfirst, then helped Regina climb to the next limb down. Once both had settled in a face-to-face straddling position, Adrian whispered, "If what the king said is true, those white dragons might try to tell us to do something we shouldn't do, so don't listen to them."

Regina covered her ears. "I won't listen."

"Good girl." Adrian climbed down the limbs, watching Regina with every step, until they reached the level above the misty portal. He stooped on the sturdy limb and held Regina at his side.

"It's a long way to the next one," she said.

"I can jump and catch you when you jump."

She looked at him, her eyes filled with doubt. "How good are you at catching?"

Half closing his eyes, he touched his chest. "I will have you know that I am the most expertest of catchers. Once Jason fell out of a tree, and I caught him. Even though he was young, he was bigger than you, and I'm bigger now than I was then. Besides, the mist might grab us and slow our fall."

"Okay," she said, stretching out the word. "I guess I can do it."

Adrian sat on the limb, letting his legs dangle. After gauging the distance, he slid off and dropped. He burst through the mist and landed with a thump on the limb, bending his knees to absorb the impact. The limb cracked and shifted. Adrian flailed his arms to keep his balance, then toppled forward.

After dropping about four feet, he thrust out his hands just in time to keep from smacking face-first into the next level's limb, but even with the cushion, his cheek slammed against the hard wood, and his legs plunged through the branches. Dazed and aching, he hung on, his body dangling below the woody matrix.

"Are you all right?" Regina called.

Adrian swung his body up to the limb and lay prostrate on it. "I think so."

"I guess you're a good catcher but not so good at jumping."

His head throbbing, Adrian laughed. "I suppose you're right."

Regina leaned over from two levels up, her face obscured by the mist. The limb in between had separated from the trunk, but its intertwined branches held it in place.

He climbed to his feet, reached up, and pulled the broken limb. It sank with his weight, the branches cracking and breaking. It wouldn't support him, much less the added pressure of a girl jumping from above, and if she tried to jump two levels, she might crash into the broken limb in between.

Adrian glanced at his hand. The glow was no longer there. Obviously the portal didn't catch and hold people who traveled downward.

"You appear to need some help," someone said. "You have exhausted your options for retrieving your female companion."

Adrian turned toward the voice. A white dragon stared at him, its head bobbing at the end of a long neck stretching down from the level above. Branches impaled its chest, but very little else was visible in the dim light.

"Well, it does seem that way." His head still pounding, Adrian glanced at his sword. So far there seemed to be no need to draw it. "I could climb to the ground, come up another tree, and meet her in the healing room."

"An interesting idea." The dragon seemed to purr like a cat, its voice feminine and appealing. "That means you will trust me to watch over her in your absence or else trust that she will be safe alone in the palace. It is good that you have so much faith. I commend you."

Adrian stared into the dragon's blue eyes. Her words were perfectly reasonable, but listening to her for very long could be trouble. Her hypnotic allure was already evident. "I think I'll take my chances with the palace."

"Very well, but allow me to give you an option. I think I can stretch far enough to allow the girl to climb onto my neck and ride safely down while you watch at all times. That would eliminate danger for both of you."

"Only if you're not dangerous," Adrian said.

The dragon tilted her head. "Me? How could I be dangerous? I trust that you can see my dilemma. I cannot move anything but my neck and head. What benefit would I gain from harming you or this child?"

"A full belly came to mind."

The dragon's eyes widened. "Eat the child! How preposterous! Even if I were to conjure such a hideous plan, she would not even make it to my stomach. Branches from these trees penetrate every portion of my digestive system. Trying to pass food would bring torture beyond belief."

"I'll ride the dragon," Regina called. "I'm not afraid. She seems real nice."

The dragon's lips stretched out into what appeared to be a friendly smile. "There. You see? You need not fear anything, including fear."

Adrian kept his face expressionless. "It's not a good idea to trust a dragon who is trapped because she tried to usurp the Creator."

"Ah! You have spoken to Alaph!" Her smile evaporated, replaced by a pitiful frown. "It seems that when you were in the healing rooms, you allowed his influence to overpower you. He has a formidable mind, to be sure. Such is the way of the portal mist. When it covers you, you are easily manipulated."

"That's what I've heard, so I'm trying to keep from being manipulated."

"Perhaps you have already been manipulated." The dragon's eyes moved, scanning him. "You are not covered by the mist now. Your mind is free from Alaph's control, so you are able to make decisions on your own, if you so choose."

Adrian crossed his arms. "He told me that my time while in that state would make me vulnerable even after I left."

"Quite true. You are vulnerable. Yet not nearly as vulnerable now as you were while you were in Alaph's abode. So it stands to reason that you would believe his story, because he had a strong influence over you, much stronger than any influence I could have now. The fact is, he has given you a version of the past that is incomplete. If you will allow me to fill in the gaps, you will hear for yourself that he has manipulated you."

Adrian shifted his weight from foot to foot. It seemed that no position felt comfortable. "As you might be manipulating me now."

"I concede that possibility." The dragon drew her head a few inches closer, obviously straining at the effort. "Your logical faculties are sharp, and your thinking is clear, so may I suggest that I rescue the girl? That will alleviate a stressful situation and take the pressure off your mind. If you then decide not to hear my story, I will bid you a peaceful farewell."

"It's okay," Regina called. "I think she's a good dragon."

Adrian glanced between dragon and girl. Since mist fully enveloped Regina, she was still being influenced. Her assurances didn't mean anything. But what choice did he have? Every other option seemed dashed, but the inability to think of an alternative plan could be because of muddled thinking. Yet, wasn't simply considering that his thinking might be muddled a sign that it was clear?

He laid a hand on his throbbing head. It seemed impossible to know. And he had to think fast. Marcelle and Frederick were still unconscious with only children guarding them. He couldn't waste so much time.

Heaving a long sigh, he nodded. "Go ahead. Bring her down here."

Without a hint of emotion, the dragon nodded in return, then elevated her head, passing through the layer of mist. When she neared Regina's level, her head stopped short of her position—about five feet away and three feet lower. "This is the limit of my ability to stretch," the dragon said. "You will have to walk onto the branches until you are directly over me and find a hole you can push through to get to my neck."

"Okay." Regina crawled away from the trunk and onto the woody mat of intertwining branches. When she reached the point above the dragon's neck, she pushed her legs through a gap, but her trousers snagged. Tugging at the catch, she cried out, "I can't get it loose." Then, with a loud snap, she fell through. Her leg struck the dragon's neck, but she toppled to the side, screaming.

With a quick swipe, the dragon snatched her pant leg with its teeth and held on. Regina dangled under the dragon's chin, her arms flailing. She gasped, though her screaming had stopped.

Adrian grabbed the broken limb above, hoisted himself up, and walked on the branches, sinking as the broken foundation slowly gave way. Holding out his arms in a cradle, he settled under Regina as the dragon lowered her toward him.

When Regina passed through the layer of mist, the portal stripped her glowing raiment away. She gasped once more, blinking rapidly, but again said nothing.

Finally, the dragon set her gently in Adrian's arms and drew back. "I trust she is well. I apologize for tearing her clothes, but it could not be helped."

Regina threw her arms around Adrian's neck and buried her face in his tunic. "I'm blind again!" she cried, her voice muffled. "Adrian, I don't want to be blind!"

While the branches sank, Adrian stroked her arm. "It must be the portal. You're blind here but not there."

She pulled away and gazed aimlessly with teary eyes. They glimmered more brightly than ever. "Then take me up again! I want to stay there!"

"But I have to get back to the others, and I can't leave you up there alone." Still cradling her, he edged toward the trunk until he reached a sturdier part of the sinking limb. He hopped down to the lower level, dodging the branches as they snapped upward.

When they had settled on the firmer limb, Regina pressed her face against his tunic again and wept.

The dragon stretched closer. "It seems that you have a dilemma. You must choose between heeding the girl's tear-filled entreaty and protecting others. What will you do?"

"I have to get back to the others. I can always return for Regina's sake later."

"I see. Delaying gratification for the sake of protecting others is wise indeed. Yet, may I delay you one more moment with some information that should aid your cause?"

Adrian nodded. "I will take a moment."

"If you set me and the others free, I will show you how to restore her sight. With my help, she would not need to return to Alaph's palace to heal her eyes. Going back through this portal would strip her physical presence, and she would be no more than a phantasm. She would see, of course, but she would have no substance, and to keep from going blind again, she would have to stay in the Northlands forever. Would it not be better to strive for eyesight that includes freedom of body and movement?"

Adrian hugged Regina more tightly. "If you're so concerned about her, why don't you just tell me how to restore her sight?"

"Because I am the one who has to do it, and I cannot perform this feat from here and in a perforated condition. I must be set free so I can bathe in the healing waters. Only then will I be strong enough to heal her."

Regina drew back and pulled on Adrian's tunic. "Let's help her get out. She's a nice dragon. And then I'll be able to see."

Adrian set her down on the limb and looked again at the dragon. "How do you propose that I set you free?"

"The spring wells up because of a blockage in an underground river. If you can remove the river's obstacle, the spring will stop feeding the trees, and you will be able to break the branches. When we are free, you can restore the spring so the trees can continue to provide healing for those in need in Alaph's castle."

Adrian looked toward the forest floor, imagining the underground river with a boulder blocking its path. The task seemed simple in concept, but it could take hours to accomplish. "I don't have time for that right now, but I will consider your proposal when I am sure of the safety of everyone in my care."

"As you should." The dragon drew her head back. "Safe travels, Adrian. I hope to see you again soon. I cannot hear what occurs on ground level, so if you wish to speak to me, please climb up here again."

Wiping tears from her eyes, Regina turned toward her. "What's your name?"

The dragon closed her eyes and gave a stately bow with her neck and head. "You may call me Beth. I am Alaph's mate."

Regina blinked rapidly. "His mate? Why won't he rescue his own mate?"

Beth let out a long sigh. "I think you will have to ask him that yourself, for I can think of no valid reasons. He and I were united as one, battling the evil dragons of the Southlands who hoped to rule the entire world, but it seems that his own desire to rule overwhelmed his duty toward me. And now, as you see, he is free while I am locked in eternal torment."

"Poor Beth!" Regina tugged on Adrian's sleeve. "We have to help her."

"Let's go check on the others first." He added a whisper in her ear. "If Frederick agrees, we'll do whatever we can to help her."

SEVEN

MARCELLE groped her way through the dark tunnel, one hand brushing the wall to her left and one touching the pipeline to her right. If memory served, the wall's surface should alter from rock to brick, signaling the passageway to the dungeon. Since that passage's floor was a few feet higher than that of the gas line, she would have to probe at shoulder level or above.

After a few minutes, her fingers ran along a slight dip. She turned and felt the surface. Yes, these were bricks, stacked instead of mortared together. She pushed a brick forward until it dropped into the tunnel beyond the wall. The hole loosened the stack, allowing her to push other bricks more easily until the gap grew big enough to climb through.

She vaulted up to the dungeon's floor and crouched. With darkness still shrouding her vision, she drew a mental map of the surroundings. About fifty paces ahead, a stairway ascended to the left, leading to the upper level, and from there, another left turn would lead to a second stairway that climbed to the exit.

She began sliding the bricks back in place. Keeping her comings and goings hidden might prove to be a benefit. As she worked, her previous experience at this spot came to mind. Elyssa, a prisoner on this level, helped her find this secret passage to the pipeline. What had happened to her? Drexel had promised to help her escape, and Gregor had said that all dungeon prisoners had been released. Still, Gregor likely spoke hearsay. It wouldn't hurt to verify the claim.

When Marcelle finished with the bricks, she rose and ran her hand along the left wall. Her fingers brushed metal bars—a window, Elyssa's cell. She stopped, grabbed the bars, and set her mouth between them. "Elyssa?" she called. "Are you in there?"

No one answered.

She raised her voice. "Elyssa! If you're in there, say something!"

Only her echoing words replied.

Sighing, Marcelle released the bars and marched on. The upwelling cold returned, raising frigid chills across her skin. She shivered hard, mentally forcing the cold waves back to her body's core. That helped, though trickles of cold continued to seep through to her extremities.

After negotiating the stairs to the upper level, she turned left into the corridor and slowed her pace, listening and brushing her fingers along the right-hand wall as she counted the barred windows. The crazy old man claiming to be Tibalt Blackstone occupied a cell here. Maybe he could shed some light on what happened to Elyssa.

When she reached his cell, she stopped and peered in. Scratching noises sounded from within, just a faint rustle. "Tibalt? Is that you?"

Marcelle set her ear between the window's bars and pulled on the door. Locked. The rustling continued, perhaps a little louder, but no one answered.

Drawing back a step, she imagined the inside of the cell. Might Tibalt be gagged? Asleep? Drugged? Or might a rat be in there, scrounging for a meal? There seemed to be no way to find out, but since Elyssa was gone, maybe what Gregor heard was true after all, and only rats now roamed the dungeon.

She continued toward the entrance. When she found the stairway, she lowered her head and, holding one hand up, climbed slowly. Soon, her fingers touched the trapdoor at the top.

She pushed on the door, but it wouldn't budge. Feeling with her fingers, she came across the latch. A spring held it in place, too tight to move. Why was it locked? With no prisoners, it didn't make any sense.

She drew out Gregor's sword, inserted the tip between the spring's coils, and twisted with all her might. A grinding sound rattled in the chamber, then a high-pitched ping.

Keeping the blade in place, she sat on a lower step and shoved the trapdoor with her foot. It popped open like a book cover and thudded on the ground outside. Light poured in, revealing the latch mechanism protruding from a wood frame around the opening. A metal plate within the mechanism faced downward, a keyhole in the center of the plate.

She heaved a sigh, rose to a crouch, and peered out. If anyone noticed the door flinging open, all the stealth in the world wouldn't keep her from being seen. Still, she had to be careful, just in case.

The rear of the palace lay in view, the hangman's noose and the burning stake visible in between. Gregor stood at the door, leaning against a column, the same pose as before. With his eyes aimed at the porch's ceiling, he seemed to be daydreaming, apparently too lost in his thoughts to hear the trapdoor. Maybe she could slip out without him noticing.

Keeping her body in a tight crouch, she rolled out onto the lawn. Gregor didn't move a muscle, and it seemed that no one else was around. Moving quickly, she stood and closed the trapdoor, letting it drop softly in place. When the air blew out around the sides, it refastened itself with a muffled click. As she lowered herself to her belly, she eyed the latch. It had locked on its own.

Crawling with her elbows, she slithered to the gallows platform and hid behind it. A breeze stirred the rope, making the noose sway. Of course, this rope was just for show. Being out in the elements day and night made it unfit to bear much weight, but it looked ominous all the same.

The sound of the platform's trapdoor springing open knifed into her ears, then the grunt of the noose's victim. Gasps from the crowd followed, as well as a few weeping laments. Yet, the platform door had not moved. The display rope still swung without a neck in its noose, and the courtyard lay empty of gawking witnesses.

As ghostly shrieks of pain erupted, Marcelle laid her hands over her ears. Surely the blood spilled in this place of torture and death cried out for justice, but why was she hearing the calls? Dreams often included strange, unexplained sounds, but why now? Was she supposed to feel guilty about the injustices perpetrated here? Shouldn't the Creator listen to these cries and satisfy the hunger for freedom in this land?

Gregor opened the palace's rear door. Orion and Maelstrom walked out side by side, Maelstrom carrying a coil of rope. Apparently talking to each other, they walked straight toward the gallows.

Marcelle opened an access panel at the side of the gallows, squeezed through, and crawled under the platform. She knelt below the trapdoor, listening to the sounds of approaching footsteps.

The two men marched up the stairs to the top of the platform and stopped at the noose. Maelstrom's calm, even voice filtered down. "I brought this rope from Tarkton. I used it for all our hangings. It has special properties that make it useful for capturing a sorceress."

"Special properties?" Orion asked.

"Feel the fibers."

After a moment's pause, Orion continued. "Sharp. Like broken glass."

"Sharp, indeed, but not glass. I call this my truth-detecting rope. The shards are from a crystal that causes traitors to confess and tell us who their conspirators are. Before we open the trapdoor, we tighten the noose, and the shards cut into the traitor's throat. Then we offer clemency to his condemned wife and children if he will simply reveal the conspirators. Perhaps it is only pain and fear that squeeze the confession out of him, but I believe the crystal is part of the persuasion. I can see it shimmer as they speak, which helps me know that the traitor is telling the truth. When it turns black, he is lying."

"A truly helpful tool, I would say. What do you do after the confession?"

"We hang him, of course. The rope makes it a bloody business, but even that is a deterrent. We hear loud complaints about the gory practice from the witnesses, but ever since we started using it, the crowds have grown."

"Such is the thirst for the macabre."

Maelstrom laughed. "It seems that the loudest among us are the most fluent in hypocrisy."

"Gregor!" Orion called. "Come and install this rope."

"Now the witches' stake," Maelstrom said. "I would like to inspect it."

More footsteps signaled their descent from the platform. Marcelle crawled to the access hole and looked toward the stake. Maelstrom caressed the top as if he were petting a cat. A sword hung at his hip instead of a dagger, and his cheek still bulged. Whatever he was chewing, he never spat the juices, so it probably wasn't tobacco.

"This old piece of wood needs a coat of protectant," he said, his voice barely audible now. "It has not felt the flames in a long time."

Orion nodded. "Too long, but I am no hypocrite. I refuse to condemn a witch or a Diviner without proof. If, however, you're right about Marcelle, I will gladly light the wood myself."

"And I would never refuse you the pleasure." Still rubbing the stake, Maelstrom seemed to be speaking to the wood. "I look forward, my dear, to watching you embrace your lover with arms of exquisite torture. Your caress will make the witch writhe in blissful agony. The crowds will gasp in mock dismay, but they will never take their eyes off you and your partner as you simmer together in mortal ecstasy."

Heavy footsteps pounded up the gallows stairs, then a voice sounded directly above Marcelle. "Governor," Gregor said, "you have fifteen minutes until the court convenes."

Orion turned. "Very good. Perhaps the gallows will receive a certain archives keeper soon."

"And a banker," Maelstrom added.

Marcelle dug her fingers into the ground. They intended to hang Father and Professor Dunwoody. She felt for her sword. It was still there. With this crazy dream acting in such unpredictable ways, she couldn't be sure of anything. Since there could be no permanent consequences in a dream, maybe jumping out and whacking their heads off would be the best option. Still, what might she learn in the deep recesses of her mind if she let the dream play out? She had already invented a new torture device in Maelstrom's hanging rope, copying the Relfections Crystal's ability to detect truth and falsehood. This could be an interesting adventure, and no harm could come no matter what she chose.

After waiting for Orion and Maelstrom to return to the palace, Marcelle crawled out from under the platform and rose to her feet. Gregor stood on a box, tying the rope to the beam that hung over the trapdoor.

"Excuse me, Gregor, may I ask you a question?"

He teetered on the box, nearly losing his balance. "Marcelle!" he hissed. "What are you doing here?"

Smiling, she offered a mock bow. "I need to rescue my father and Dunwoody. Where are they right now?"

"In the holding chamber next to the upper courtroom." Glancing at the palace, he hopped down to the ground, keeping his body between Marcelle and the palace door. "You'd better get out of here. Orion wants to spill your blood."

"Well, he won't get blood." She grinned. "I don't have any."

"Seeing how pale you are, I can believe that." He grabbed her shoulders, then jerked back. "You're as cold as ice!"

"I know. It's all part of the dream, I suppose."

"The dream? What are you talking about?"

She spread out her arms. "This is all my dream. It can't be real. I'm ice cold and white as a sheet. I passed through a small hole in a pile of rocks. I have no heartbeat."

"No heartbeat?"

She extended a hand. "Here. Feel for a pulse."

He backed away a step, his brow deeply bent. "I think your illness is affecting your mind. I'm awake, so you cannot be dreaming."

"It's no surprise that a figment of my imagination would say that." Marcelle walked past him. "The adventure should be exhilarating. At least I can't get hurt this way."

Gregor pulled her back and drew her close. "Listen to me," he whispered, his eyes focused on hers. "Put that thought out of your mind immediately. I don't know what devilry has infected you, but if you don't come to your senses, your recklessness will be the death of you and your father. If you march into the courtroom to defend your father while looking like this, Orion and Maelstrom will kill you both, you as a witch and your father as a heretic who supports witches. And old Dunwoody will be on trial as well, though I have no idea what they're charging him with."

"Interesting." Marcelle looked at Gregor's sincere face. Maybe his counsel was part of the dream adventure. Saving her father by stealth could be more exciting than a direct assault, and the mental effort could stimulate her physical brain and promote healing. "Will you help me?"

"To save your good father, I would give my life." Gregor winked. "For you, however, I would merely sacrifice an arm and a leg. We have to be wary about entanglements with witches, you know."

Marcelle clasped his arm. "Very well, then. Do you have the keys to the holding cell?"

"I have a key that works in every cell in the palace."

She held out her hand. "Then give it to me. I'll need access to the prisoners."

"Let's think for a minute." He pushed her hand down. "Maelstrom brought a personal military force from Tarkton, and two of them guard the door. I can employ a distraction to allow you to slip inside, but you wouldn't have time to flee with your father and Dunwoody. They're too slow, and you won't be able to fight your way out. I'm sure you can best one of the guards, but I'm not so sure about both at the same time."

"I see you got another sword," she said, touching the hilt at his belt. "The two of us could handle them. Remember, you said you'd give your life for my father."

"Indeed, but I prefer an alternative to death."

"If you have a plan, then tell me."

Gregor glanced between Marcelle and the palace, still shielding her with his wide body. "I think they arrested your father and Dunwoody to lure you out of hiding. They know you won't stand idly by while they're being executed."

"That's true, but I can't just let it happen."

"I know you can't, but we can use their zeal against them."

"How?"

"Get the two guards to chase you, and I'll get the prisoners out."

Marcelle stroked her chin. That could work. And maybe she could disable at least one of the guards in the process. If she were to be captured, that would matter little. Facing Orion and Maelstrom in the courtroom while her father was safely hidden could be entertaining. "I like the idea. How shall we proceed?"

Gregor took off his cloak and wrapped it around Marcelle, pulling it closed over her face. "You are now my ill mother who fears spreading a contagion. That will keep people from getting too close. When we get near the courtroom, we will go to the holding cell, but stay far enough away from the cell so the guards can't see you. Then, when I speak to them, come closer and drop the cloak. While you run, I will do the rest."

Marcelle pulled the cloak tight and peeked through a tiny slit. The covering did little to ward off the chill. "Let's go."

Gregor led her through the corridor leading to the lower courtroom, then up the stairs. At this level's spacious anteroom, the upper court's doors lay directly ahead, perhaps fifty paces away. The hall to the holding cell lay forty paces ahead and to the right. A dozen or more nobles milled about, apparently waiting for the proper time to be seated inside.

Marcelle stooped and added a slight limp to her gait, hoping to mimic the hobbling pattern of a diseased old woman. Along the way, several people glanced at her. A few stared. When Marcelle neared the double doorway to the courtroom, Gregor pointed to a hallway to the right and whispered, "You stay here while I go to the cell. When you hear me cough, show yourself in that hall."

She nodded. Trying to speak loudly enough to penetrate the cloak might give her away.

Gregor strode quickly to the hall and disappeared around the corner. Marcelle shuffled that way, continuing her old-woman gait as she kept her sword from dragging on the floor.

One of the courtroom doors opened, and Counselor Orion walked out with Maelstrom at his side. "You may now enter," Orion called. "We will join you in a moment."

After everyone filed in, Orion glanced at Marcelle, then bent close to Maelstrom. "When you read the charges," Orion said, "make sure you use a fiery tone and blistering insults. If she is listening from a hiding place, we want to enrage her, to stir her passions and force her hand as early as possible. The longer we wait, the more likely that people will become impatient."

Maelstrom's cheek still bulged, though not as far. "What if she fails to show?"

"Then she will surely come to the hanging. She won't let her father die without a fight."

"Agreed." Maelstrom returned to the courtroom while Orion headed for the stairway.

Marcelle sidestepped but tripped over the too-long cloak and toppled to the floor. Still holding the cloak together, she rolled to her back and peeked through the slit. Orion dashed toward her and dropped to a knee, touching her covered arm with a tender hand. "Are you hurt?"

She cleared her throat and attempted an old lady's voice. "Only my dignity, dear Governor."

"Then allow me to help you up." He grasped her wrist and hoisted her to her feet. "Why are you covered like this?"

From the corridor, Gregor coughed.

Marcelle glanced that way. She had to get rid of Orion, and fast. "Ah! Good question!" She coughed, hoping to mimic Gregor's sounds. "My beloved son said I was too ill to come at all, but how could I miss this trial? It should be quite a spectacle. He told me I should protect others from my very contagious disease, so I am trying to do so."

Orion brushed his hands on his trousers and backed away. "Who is your son?"

Gregor coughed again, louder this time.

"Why, just the finest guard in your service. Gregor." She cackled, ending with another series of coughs. "Of course, a mother would think that, right? Even one who is certain to die of a plague."

"Yes, I'm sure."

Gregor coughed once more, adding gasps and gurgling breaths.

Orion leaned back and looked down the hall. "It seems that your son has contracted your illness."

"That well could be." Marcelle leaned with him and added a wheeze to her respiration. "I kissed my dear son this morning before we learned how sick I had become."

"Guards!" Orion called. "All of you report to the infirmary at once!"

Gregor emerged from the hallway, the other two guards trailing—Tarks, by all appearances. Their orange uniforms with black trim matched Leo's. As they approached, Orion backed away several more steps, pointing at Marcelle. "Apparently Gregor has contracted his mother's illness. Take her with you and submit to quarantine."

One of the two guards glanced back at the hallway. "Who will watch the holding cell?"

"They will be unguarded only five minutes. I will send Leo for them when they are summoned to trial."

While the two Tarks marched toward the stairs, Gregor laid an arm around Marcelle's shoulders. "I will take her, Governor. I think her cloak probably protected you from her illness."

"I certainly hope so. The trial starts in mere moments. I have no time for quarantine." Orion hurried toward the stairs.

Gregor passed a key into Marcelle's hand. "You'll have to do it yourself. Make haste. I'll go to the infirmary and explain your absence."

"Godspeed, Gregor." Pulling up the cloak to keep the hem from dragging and again pinching the hood closed in front, she strode to the corridor. About twenty paces down the hall, a sign on the metal door to the right read THE ACCUSED. She inserted the key, turned the bolt, and flung open the door. Her father and Professor Dunwoody sat on a cushioned bench against the opposite wall. "Father!" she called in a loud whisper. "Professor! Come with me!"

"Marcelle?" Her father shot to his feet. "Is that you?"

She made a shushing sound. "Hurry! We don't have much time!"

Her father took three steps to reach the door, his gait shaky. "If I leave, they will think I am guilty."

"If you don't, they'll hang you. They've already decided you're guilty."

He spread out his hands. "There is nowhere to run, nowhere to hide."

Professor Dunwoody joined them. "Actually, there is a place to hide in the archives, and there are provisions."

"Perfect," Marcelle said, sliding the key into her pocket. "Let's get your necks out of a noose."

Her father shook his head. "Rebelling against the authorities is not the best way to—"

"Those authorities tried to poison you!" She released the cloak, allowing the hood to fall to her shoulders. "If you don't hurry, you're going to end up looking like this!"

Her father's mouth dropped open. "Marcelle! What happened to you?"

"I'll explain later." Marcelle shook the cloak the rest of the way off and drew her sword. "Let's just get going."

They skulked down the hall toward the courtroom, Marcelle leading the way. When they reached the end, she slowed and tiptoed into the anteroom between the stairs and the courtroom entry, scanning the area for Orion. With the doors closed and the people seated in anticipation of the trial, the anteroom lay empty. A chandelier hung over the center of the floor, but with abundant skylights in the ceiling, the extane-burning bulbs sat dark in their sockets.

Marcelle stopped and listened. The sound of rapid clopping drew close. Spreading her arms, she blocked her father and Dunwoody and forced them back to the hallway.

Orion ascended the stairs, his head low and his eyes focused on the floor. When he reached the courtroom, he opened the door and rushed inside.

As soon as the door clapped shut, Marcelle pointed at the stairs with her sword. "Professor, take my father to the archives. I'll join you there as soon as I can."

"Why aren't you coming with us?" her father asked.

"I'm coming. I'll trail you to make sure no one's following."

Just as the two men started for the stairway, the courtroom door swung open. Maelstrom strode out and turned toward the hall. When he spied Marcelle, he whipped his sword from a hip scabbard. As radiance from the skylights above shimmered on the polished blade, Maelstrom smiled. "Orion told me about the diseased woman he encountered, but he was too kindhearted to guess the truth."

The two escapees paused, but Marcelle waved them on. "Go!"

"Halt!" Maelstrom shouted, raising a hand.

Her father stopped in midstep. Professor Dunwoody pulled on his arm, but he seemed unable to move.

Marcelle flung herself at Maelstrom, her sword swinging. He parried her blow with a powerful shove, sending her into a wild spin. She slammed into the courtroom doors with a loud thud.

After bouncing off and regaining her balance, she stalked toward Maelstrom again. With his attention diverted from her father, his hold on him collapsed, and the two escapees hurried down the stairs.

She lunged and crossed swords with Maelstrom, firing imaginary darts with her eyes. Since he stood at least eight inches taller and weighed a hundred pounds more, bending her knees and pushing with her legs was the only way to keep from collapsing under the pressure. He glared back at her, his pupils pulsing like throbbing black pearls and his cheek still bulging as he gnawed on the ever-present wad within.

Marcelle jumped back, making the blades zing as they parted. Now standing just out of his reach, she gave him another hot stare, her sword lifted and her feet set for battle. "Let's see how good you are without that energy-sapping power of yours."

He lifted his own sword. "I will be glad to demonstrate."

As they sidestepped around a central point, creating a makeshift tourney ring, the courtroom doors opened. Several men and women peered out, and a buzz grew. Soon, a bustling line of finely dressed men and women gathered around the impromptu match, making a semicircular line.

Orion burst through the crowd. "What is the meaning of this?"

"I am exposing the sorceress," Maelstrom said, keeping his eyes on Marcelle. "Everyone can see her appearance now, and they will soon see the color of her blood … if she has any."

Orion's face reddened. "I will not have a summary execution here!"

"Don't worry," Marcelle said. "I'm not going to kill him. I'm just going to cut off his hands so he can't use his …" She looked around, extending her pause to bend every ear toward her. "His *sorcery* against anyone else."

A few gasps rose from the onlookers, but with a glare from Maelstrom, they quickly silenced. "Her bravado stands on mere words, Governor. I should like to silence her here and now, but since you wish to see her burn, I await your instructions on how to seize her without doing harm."

"Marcelle," Orion said, altering to a gentle tone, "if you will submit to a trial, I pledge that you will get a fair one. There are reliable tests that prove whether or not a person is a witch or a Diviner, so if you are not one of those evil breeds, you have no reason to fear. I am sure everyone is anxious to hear why you appear the way you do. If it is mere sickness, we will get a doctor to—"

"Spare me the hot air, Orion, and open your eyes. The only sorcerer here is Leo. Everyone's just too blind to see it ... or too bewitched by him." She glanced around. Not a single person seemed affected by her words. They just stared wide eyed.

"Leo," Orion said calmly, "bring her father here. I'm sure you can persuade Marcelle to acquiesce."

Maelstrom nodded toward the stairway. "He escaped with the other prisoner."

"Likely to the archives. My guard there will soon bring them back."

Marcelle tightened her grip on her sword. Her father and Dunwoody weren't young enough to flee from a hidden guard. Only one chance remained. Fight!

She leaped at Maelstrom and slapped his sword from his grip, slicing part of a finger off with it. Then, reversing her swing, she slashed again, but he ducked out of the way and dove for his sword. He grabbed it and jumped to his feet.

With blood dripping from his index finger's stub, he charged and swiped at her waist. She leaped over the blade and turned a flip in the air before landing on her feet.

She faced him again, her sword ready. How strange it felt to leap in this body. Without real muscles, weakness ought to have disabled her, but her lack of substance made her light and nimble. Her mind had conjured a complex dream, indeed.

Just as Maelstrom charged, a desperate cry rang out. "Marcelle!"

She threw herself on the floor and tripped Maelstrom, sending him flying. Then, springing back to her feet, she turned toward the voice. Her father stood at the top of the stairs, a guard's spear at his back. Orion walked to his side, his arms crossed and his face painting the portrait of a weary but patient observer.

Marcelle stared at them. What had become of Dunwoody? Had he escaped?

"Are you quite finished?" Orion asked.

"Perhaps." Marcelle looked at Maelstrom. His mouth twisting in rage, he staggered alongside a trail of blood. When he reached his fingertip, he picked it up. "Wicked witch attacked while I was distracted." He set the bleeding digit against the stump, holding it there as he continued. "Fighting with my left hand is a great disadvantage."

"Typical excuses from a whining loser," Marcelle growled, "but I wouldn't expect any better from the likes of you."

When he let go of the finger, it stayed in place as if surgically stitched. Shifting his sword to his right hand, he gestured for her to approach. "Come to me now. A fair match is all I ask. Unless you fear to fight without trickery."

"Stop!" Orion barked. "This display is becoming tiresome."

Both combatants lowered their swords. "I'm not going to subject myself to your tests," Marcelle said.

"We'll see about that." Orion nodded at Maelstrom. "Drain her father's energy, but not too quickly. He is old and frail."

His frown reflecting the anger of a humiliated man, Maelstrom raised an arm and pointed at Marcelle's father with the same finger she had severed.

As if pierced by an arrow, her father clutched his stomach. His eyes shot wide open, and he gasped, his face growing pale as it warped in pain. He whispered, "Marcelle, I ..." He dropped to his knees, unable to say anything more.

"Stop!" Marcelle's cry came out in a whisper, lacking any breath.

Orion raised a hand. "Leo. Cease immediately."

"As you wish." Maelstrom lowered his arm.

"Drop your sword," Orion said, "and Leo will restore your father."

Marcelle rested the tip of her sword on the floor. "What will you do with him?"

"If you are asking for a bargain, I am willing to spare your father all prosecution if you will surrender." Orion nodded toward the crowd. "You see the witnesses to my promise."

Marcelle scanned every face, from the gawking onlookers, to Maelstrom, to Orion, to her father. How startling that her dream had created such detail! So many people, so many varied expressions. Since it was a dream, she could fight on. If Maelstrom killed her father, it wouldn't matter. He would be fine in real life. No harm would be done. Yet, even in a dream, how could she deny love? How could she abandon her father to the ravages of this monster? A violation of conscience might wound her soul and slow her recovery.

"Will you give me a moment to speak?" she asked.

"Take all the time you wish. Just remember that your father is in pain."

She looked at her father again. Giving her a weak smile, he nodded but said nothing. She smiled back at him. He had given his okay.

Turning in a slow circle, she searched for the words that might shake Maelstrom's hypnotic hold over these people. "As you have noticed, my friends, my appearance is not what you're accustomed to seeing. I have been on a journey of unspeakable terror that has drained my vitality. I have been to Dracon." She paused for dramatic effect, but only dry stares met her own. A few people even chuckled in a derisive way.

Anger flaring, she bent her brow. "You are such cowards! Yes, I said cowards! As long as you can keep your satin dresses, your velvet capes, and your pungent perfumes, you'll let tyrants hold sway. You don't care about the peasants who gather the crumbs that fall from your tables. You don't hear the cries of the children when they go to bed hungry. You ignore evidence of Dracon, that the Lost Ones still toil under the whips of dragon masters, their emaciated frames bleeding from their lashes. In fact, you persecute those who search for the truth. You punish those who disturb the status quo. Using your own whips, you inflict lashes on those who dare to imply that you have ignored the plight of the pitiful. And why is that? Because you know that you have treated the peasants here with beastly contempt. You are the dragons of this world."

"Marcelle," a man called out. "How can you say that? You know my family. We give to the charities. We make clothes for the orphans."

She nodded at the man, Charlton, the head of Orion's board of overseers. "Yes," she said with a sarcastic sneer, "I'm sure we're all aware of your good deeds. You trumpet them every chance you get, and the applause of your peers is your reward. But as long as you keep dragging members of the Underground Gateway into prison, you'll get no applause from me. Your wings and scales are all too evident. You don't want the slaves here to be free. You want them fed and clothed so they can plow your farms to make sure your dinner plates are heaping and spilling over the sides. You want them to pluck your poultry so your cushions can hold up under your fat backsides. You want slaves to continue bending under the whip both here on Major Four and there on Dracon, because if a heroic warrior returns from Dracon with a band of freed captives, the cry of liberty will resound throughout the land. And that cry will echo from mountain to mountain and valley to valley until every ear in every rundown shack hears it and catches the contagion. Yes, freedom is a contagion. It is a wildfire that burns the tares of hopelessness. It is rain that sweeps across the land and cools parched thirsts. It is a hammer that passes from hand to hand and breaks the chains and manacles of slavish strife, enabling those set free to flex their muscles and rise up against their oppressors. And their oppressor is you." She pointed at Charlton and let her finger shift from face to face. "And you. And you and you and you."

Narrowing her eyes, she threw a hot stare at Orion and growled. "You don't want the slaves to return, because you fear freedom." She threw her sword on the floor and stepped away from it. "I have said all I need to say. Release my father, and I will go with you."

Maelstrom took a hard step toward her, but Orion raised a hand, halting him. Many in the crowd grumbled, some whispering vague threats. The words *burning stake* rose above the murmurs more than once. Charlton and a few others said nothing, their lips straight and their brows knitted. It seemed impossible to tell if they were scowling or contemplating.

Orion picked up Marcelle's sword and caressed its shiny surface. "Your eloquence and passion are sharper than your blade. I'm sure we're all moved." He nodded at Maelstrom. "Restore his energy."

Maelstrom stepped up to Marcelle's father and laid a hand on his head. Within seconds, color returned to his pallid face. When Maelstrom stepped back, her father rose to his feet but said nothing, though his tight lips told of burning anger.

"Issachar," Orion said as he gestured for the guard to lower his spear, "you are free to go, but you must stay within the confines of the palace until I say otherwise. I want to make sure your daughter keeps her promise."

He nodded but again said nothing. With no more than a glance at Marcelle, he turned and walked down the stairs, his gait stronger than ever.

Orion waved the sword at the courtroom doors. "Now let us reconvene. We have a trial to conduct."

As Marcelle walked toward the courtroom, she kept her head down, avoiding the stares of those filing back inside. The tiles passed under her feet, clean and shining, without a trace of blood from Maelstrom's wound.

She looked back and scanned the floor. Indeed, no bloodstains appeared anywhere. Like dew evaporating in the heat, they had vanished.

EIGHT

MARCELLE stood at the center of the courtroom inside an encircling, waist-high guardrail. About eight feet away, the floor for the spectators sloped upward like an amphitheater with stairs between sets of chairs that fanned out to each side, every seat filled by one of the soft-skinned set. Ladies fanned their rouged faces while men mopped their foreheads with lace-trimmed handkerchiefs. As usual, hats with wide brims and garish plumes covered every priggish female, making the crowd look like a peacock's feathered nest.

After scanning the walls, Marcelle nodded. Every window had been closed. The inquisitors hoped for a grilling, and she was to be the main course. A shadow passed across one of the windows, fleeting and obscure, too big for a bird, yet too small for a man. A child, perhaps?

Ahead, Orion sat behind a high desk perched on a stage, glaring at her while Maelstrom paced the floor just beyond the guardrail. With no bulge in his cheek, he looked less like a gritty soldier and more like one of the nobles, none of whom would be caught chewing anything while outside the dining hall. He seemed paler than usual. Perhaps the battle and loss of blood had had more of an effect than he had shown earlier.

In one hand, he clutched a glass rod with a sharpened point. The other he used to grasp the rail from time to time as he walked around Marcelle like a cat stalking its prey. "To begin this investigation," he said with an air of gentlemanly dignity, "I ask you to vow to cooperate and answer all my questions without fail."

Marcelle glowered at him. "I make no such vow. You wouldn't request it unless you have a sinister reason."

He laughed softly. "Not sinister at all. The purpose is simply to determine whether or not you have decided to be cooperative. With the vow in place, we will pursue a polite form of questioning. If, on the other hand, you maintain your hostile posture, we will have to resort to methods appropriate for questioning an antagonistic defendant."

"I see." Marcelle scanned the audience. Many nodded, whispering to each other. Very few, if any, saw through the charade. To them, it made perfect sense. Just promise to be civilized or you will be treated like a savage. Of course anyone should acquiesce to answering questions. What could be the harm in that?

Marcelle pressed her lips together. The ignorant simpletons were unable to plumb the depths of Maelstrom's malice. If she made the vow, he would ask a question that would prove her to be a sorceress no matter which way she answered, and not answering would be breaking a vow, which only a sorceress would do. And, of course, refusing the vow gave him an excuse to employ torture. His longing gaze seemed to hope for the refusal, a look that bound her in chains and clapped a manacle around her neck.

Maelstrom gripped the rail and leaned within an arm's length. "And your answer?"

"I vow to answer every civilized question with a civilized answer."

A murmur arose and quickly settled. Maelstrom glanced at Orion, who gave him a nod.

"Very well." Maelstrom held up the glass rod. "This is a truth crystal. I know you have no experience with such things in Mesolantrum, but this crystal is why we have had so much success with ridding Tarkton of sorcery. It detects whether or not someone is telling the truth. If a lie is told, it turns black. With truth, it shimmers with clear light. And it takes on various shades of gray if the speaker's words are ambiguous or false without the speaker realizing it." He extended it toward Marcelle. "Hold it in your right hand."

She folded her hands behind her. "I will not."

"Ah!" he called out, spreading out his arms toward the onlookers. "Perhaps the investigation is already complete! Who but a liar refuses to have her lies detected? She fears that her heart will be exposed."

"I have no fear that my heart will be exposed. I fear that this device is not what you say it is."

Orion spoke up. "A test is in order, Leo. As you said, we are not familiar with this lie-detecting rod. It is natural for our citizens to be suspicious of something so wondrous."

Maelstrom bowed. "I apologize. I jumped to a faulty conclusion." Turning slowly in place, he held the rod out for all to see. "May I have a volunteer who wishes to cleanse the scourge of superstition and further the cause of science in Mesolantrum?"

A man in the front row stood. Dressed in long sleeves and draping a jacket over his arm, he raised a hand. "I'll be glad to, if it will help us get this over with. It's as hot as an oven in here."

"Yes, 'tis true," Maelstrom said. "Yet, there is a reason for the lack of ventilation, which will come to light soon." He handed the rod to the man. "Now tell me your name."

"Stanton."

The rod glowed with a bright aura.

"Excellent!" Maelstrom said with a genial laugh. "You know your name!"

Chuckles spread across the crowd. It seemed that Maelstrom was winning them over.

"Now tell a lie." Maelstrom quickly raised a finger. "But don't worry. 'Tis not a sin, because you are not intending to deceive anyone."

While Stanton looked up at the ceiling, apparently conjuring a clever lie, Marcelle instinctively touched her hip where her sword should have been. Maelstrom's smooth-talking tongue should have been cut from his throat long ago. Now he was catering to the cathedral pew sitters. Probably half the audience never missed a service, genuflecting in front of statues three times a week in order to keep from slipping on the stairway to heaven. For most of them, an eloquent two-minute prayer made up for two hours of backstabbing gossip, though they never bothered to take the dagger out of their victim's back.

Stanton shrugged. "Here's the most obvious one I could come up with. It's comfortably cool in this courtroom."

The rod instantly turned black in his hand.

Stanton pointed at the rod, grinning. "Look, Margaret. I suppose you'll want to buy one of these."

While the crowd laughed, Maelstrom took the rod and walked it to Marcelle. "Are you satisfied that it works as I have suggested?"

She again moved her hands behind her back. "I noticed it never glowed or turned black in your hand."

The laughter ceased. A grumbled "Stubborn wench" drifted from somewhere near the middle of the crowd.

Marcelle let her eyes dart around. Another shadow passed across the window, larger and slower this time. It could easily have been a man. What might he be up to?

She snatched the rod from his hand. "Get on with your charade. Everyone else here is fooled by your manipulation, but I'm not. You're so humiliated that you can't control me like these stupid sheep, you're determined to see me burn."

More scolding murmurs erupted, but, with a wave of his hand, Maelstrom quieted them. Turning back to Marcelle, he glared at her. She returned the stare. She had rattled everyone, and the aghast expressions of her former friends were truly entertaining. If not for this being a dream, she would never be able to face them again.

"Tell us," Maelstrom continued, "why are you so terribly pale?"

She kept her stare locked. "I have no blood pumping through me. I have no heartbeat at all."

The audience laughed, but when Maelstrom grabbed her wrist and lifted the rod, they all quieted. It glowed with a brilliant light. "You see!" he shouted. "She tells the truth! What need is there of further questioning?"

Silence filled the room. Every eye locked on Marcelle, blistering stares that could have skewered her if they had sharpened points.

"Leo," Orion said. "Since we all know that a bloodless person who has no heartbeat is incapable of speech or motor activity, is it at all possible that the rod is malfunctioning?"

"Not in my experience, Governor."

"I see." Orion looked up at a window. "Regardless of how obscure the chance might be, I am going to grant the possibility and ask that we move directly to the final proof that we discussed earlier. If that evidence provides the conclusion you seek, then we can assume that this test is valid as well."

Maelstrom bowed. "I wholeheartedly agree." After taking the rod from Marcelle, he produced a small round ball of dark resin from his pocket and showed it to Stanton. "Do you know what this is, my good man?"

Stanton took it and gave it a long sniff. "It smells like lava gum."

"Correct. What do you know about lava gum?"

"Highly spicy and flavorful. We use it in stews. Just a bare shaving can spice up an entire pot."

Maelstrom nodded toward the ball. "What would happen if you chewed on it?"

"As everyone knows," Stanton said, "the first thing you would do would be to sweat. Although it doesn't burn the tongue, it induces profuse perspiration."

"Since you have shown such courage already, would you care to demonstrate?"

"Glad to." Stanton dried his brow and cheeks with a handkerchief, then peeled off a tiny sliver of lava gum with a thumbnail and put it into his mouth. As he chewed, sweat beaded on his forehead, then streamed down his cheeks and nose, a far more profuse flow than he or anyone else in the courtroom had suffered.

He spat the sliver into his handkerchief and mopped his face. "That's lava gum all right."

"Exactly. Now notice, although it is uncomfortably warm in here, and even the most delicate among us has at least dressed herself with a shimmering glow, Marcelle has not shed a single drop."

Again a buzz spread around the courtroom. This time Maelstrom did nothing to quell it. He took the gum from Stanton and presented it to Marcelle. "Put a sliver into your mouth. It will not take long to see what you really are."

Marcelle took it, popped the entire ball into her mouth, and began chewing. It produced no flavor in either taste or smell. In other dreams, situations like this were unpredictable. Maybe she would sweat in spite of having minimal bodily fluids. Maybe she would sprout wings and fly. Who could tell?

While she continued chewing, everyone looked on in silence. Although she had very little saliva for dissolving the ball, it began to dwindle. When it shrank to the size of a pea, she spat it out in her palm and let it drop to the floor.

Maelstrom withdrew a handkerchief from his pocket, reached over the guardrail, and mopped her face and forehead. He walked back to Stanton and presented the handkerchief. "Would you please check this for moisture?"

"Glad to." Stanton took it and wadded it in his hands, then held it up by two corners. "It's completely dry."

"Then there is no perspiration at all."

"None that I can detect."

Maelstrom grabbed the handkerchief and waved it like a flag as he strolled back to Marcelle. "By her own confession, she has admitted that no blood flows in her veins, that her heart is a stone within her breast. And now we have demonstrated that she has no perspiration in her pores. In fact ..." He grabbed her wrist again. "Would my most helpful examiner please come and touch Marcelle's hand and tell us what you feel?"

Stanton rose and strode across the gap, his graying head held high. When he wrapped his hands around Marcelle's, he jumped back, letting go. "She's ... she's as cold as Miller's Spring!"

The audience erupted in chaotic chatter. Maelstrom shouted above it, waving the glass rod as his voice rose to a crescendo. "Only a sorceress could have no fluids of life. Only a sorceress could move and speak without a beating heart. Only a sorceress could be frigid to the touch while the rest of us roast in this oven." Spinning back toward her, he jabbed a finger at her face. "Marcelle is a sorceress!"

Orion pounded his desk with a flat stone. "Silence!"

The crowd grew quiet. With a hint of a smile growing on his face, Orion began with a tsking sound. "Leo, my own wife's feet are frigid to the touch, even on summer nights. She tries to warm them on my feet every night."

Laughter skittered about. When it died away, Orion continued. "And just because Marcelle doesn't sweat when chewing lava gum, that proves only that she has a high tolerance for the spice. And we are all unfamiliar with your truth-detecting rod, so how can we rely on it in this life-or-death trial? We cannot return to the ignorant, superstitious ways of the past and burn every female who exhibits unusual qualities. That would be barbaric. I promised Marcelle a fair trial, and I intend to keep that promise."

His smile growing, he rose to his feet and placed his hands on the desk. "If you are unable to provide more evidence than these superficial tests have uncovered, I will have to decide in favor of—"

"Wait!" Leo's voice echoed throughout the chamber. "I have one more test."

Marcelle eyed him warily. Something in his tone gave away a deception, as if every word had been staged, even Orion's near dismissal of the case. The climax of the drama had come. She would have to be ready to react.

With another quick spin, Maelstrom lunged at her with the rod and drove its point into her chest, shoving it several inches in. The crowd gasped. Marcelle staggered back a step, but Maelstrom held on to the blunt end of the rod. Then, he jerked it out and displayed it for everyone to see. With dramatic flair, he yelled each word in a punctuated rhythm. "I ... rest ... my ... case!"

Marcelle clutched her tunic, feeling the hole and her skin underneath, dry and already sealed. Although pain ripped through her body, there was no blood. His blow caused no permanent damage, but it proved to be the fatal stroke. Maelstrom had won. He and Orion had concocted a brilliant plan. There was no denying it. Yet, the verdict mattered little. Since the dream had lasted so long, it had to end soon.

As ladies cried and men shouted oaths, Orion pounded his rock on the desk again and again. "Silence! There is no reason to fear! We know how to dispose of a sorceress. When she burns at the stake, all will be set to order."

A crash sounded at the window. Several smoking balls flew through a hole, one after the other. As smoke filled the room, sneezing broke out until nearly everyone in the crowd bent over in sneezing fits.

Maelstrom lunged at Marcelle. She jerked away, leaped over the guardrail, and plunged into the smoke, climbing the stairs between the seats. This had to be Professor Dunwoody's doing, but where could he be? What escape had he planned?

When she found the window and the hole, she looked out. Dunwoody stood in a hedge with a sword in hand. "Hurry to the archives," he whispered. "The guard is no longer there, but it's the first place they'll look, so we'll have to duck into the escape tunnel immediately." He extended the sword's hilt through the hole. "Don't kill too many people."

She grabbed the sword and tried to hurry to the exit, but the swarm of coughing and sneezing people funneling down the stairs blocked her way. The smoke began to clear, revealing Maelstrom knocking men and women out of the way as he stormed toward her with a sword in hand.

Marcelle dashed back to the window, smashed the pane with her boot, and leaped out. With a spin, she slashed at Maelstrom just as he burst through the hole, grazing his thigh and drawing a trickle of blood. Roaring, he swung his blade at her. The edge cut deep into her waist, tearing her tunic. Again no blood spewed, but this time there was no pain.

She leaped and kicked him in the face with both feet, sending him staggering backwards. She then spun and ran around the palace, sprinted up the steps, and burst through the unguarded rear door, retracing her previous path to the archives. When she arrived at the bottom of the stairs, she found Dunwoody standing at the open door, holding a lantern. "Get in quickly! We must hurry!"

As soon as she entered, he slapped the door shut and locked it. Taking her by the arm, he pulled her past the ransacked room to the back and opened the panel behind the chair. After she crawled through, she turned and knelt. When Dunwoody appeared, she took the lantern and helped him crawl inside.

He pulled the panel closed and ran his finger along the edges. "It appears to have sealed properly. We should be safe now."

"Have you seen my father?"

He nodded. "He is well. I advised him to stay out of sight until the chaos settles. I guessed that you would need funds for the army you're trying to raise, so I asked him to transfer a large sum to a secret account." He handed her a scrap of paper. "Here is the account number. Memorize it quickly, and I will destroy it."

"Good. Excellent." She read the number—142103—then pushed the scrap back into Dunwoody's hand. "Do you know where Father is?"

A loud thud sounded, then a crash. Angry voices burst into the archives room. "Search everywhere! Don't worry about what you might destroy. Just find her. If she's not here, post three guards. Make sure they're expert swordsmen."

Dunwoody raised a finger to his lips, his eyes wide in the glow of the lantern.

Marcelle studied his expression. Not being a warrior, he likely had never faced such danger. Yet, a look of excitement grew on his face. The old teacher seemed to be having the time of his life.

She turned toward the tunnel. The lantern she had left behind still glowed, and the book and mirror lay next to it unharmed. Apparently no one had discovered this refuge between her visits.

After a few minutes, the noise ceased. Dunwoody kept the finger in place, still waiting. This was not the time to risk making a single sound. A misplaced step or an inadvertent grunt might give them away. They had to wait for the dust to settle and for the guards to grow less wary.

Marcelle shifted to her bottom and pulled her knees up close. Normally in situations like this, she would be taking slow, even breaths to quiet her thumping heart, but without a heart or a need to breathe, staying perfectly silent was easy.

She closed her eyes. Maybe this would be a good time to try to wake up again. Now that her father and Professor Dunwoody were safe, her real mind might be satisfied, and healing wouldn't be hampered. This imagined adventure was over. It was time to go on with the real adventure, rescuing slaves on Starlight.

As she concentrated, the blackness of inner thought slowly faded. Light filtered in, then color and contrast. She lay on her back on a bed of leaves and straw. This was the same room where she had confronted Drexel, but now several children sat on the floor. The closest one, a wiry boy of about twelve, carried a sword, though far from expertly.

With three other children huddled near his feet, the boy's eyes darted from one side of the room to the other, often pausing at an open door at the far end. Light poured through, along with a breeze that kicked up dust and swirled it in a tiny cyclone.

Blinking, she lifted a hand and looked at it, though the effort felt like lifting a boulder. Was she awake now? Was this real life? It seemed real. Yet something was missing, something crucial— the embrace of mind and body. A wall still divided thought and response. It seemed as if she were telling a young dog what to do. The dog wanted to obey, but it didn't understand her commands. She would have to retrain her body, become reattached to it.

To her right, a bearded man lay on the same bed. She gasped mentally, but her body didn't respond in kind. She just stared at the familiar face, similar to Adrian's. Could it be? Yes! Frederick!

She tried to speak, but her lips barely moved. Only a breath of a whisper emerged, a feeble, trembling, "Frederick?"

The boy jumped toward her and dropped to his knees. "Marcelle! You talked!"

She forced a weak smile. "Who ... are you?"

"Orlan, but that's not important. Adrian's gone, and I think somebody's outside who wants to hurt us. An axe is missing."

Pressing her tongue against the roof of her mouth, she forced out, "Drexel?"

"That's what I think, but I haven't seen anyone."

"He is ..." Again she had to push out her words. "Evil."

"I know." He touched her hand. "Do you feel like you can fight?"

She lifted her arm again and flexed her bicep. It seemed more flaccid than usual, but probably strong enough for the likes of Drexel. "I think so."

"I was hoping you'd say that." He pushed the sword against her palm. "Adrian told me about you. I'd feel a lot better if you took this."

She wrapped her fingers around the hilt. It felt good and right. "What ..." She swallowed through her parched throat. "What ails Frederick?"

"He fell into a deer trap. He bumped his head, and a spike broke his leg. Adrian thinks Drexel pushed him, maybe even whacked him on the head."

"He ... he knows I am here. ... He's a coward. ... We are safe."

"Maybe we are, but Zeb was supposed to come back after leading Adrian to the skunk tree. He should've gotten here a while ago. The cart he took with him is in sight out back, but no Zeb. I know Drexel pretty well. I'm sure he'd hurt Zeb."

"He would." Marcelle climbed to her knees and looked at Frederick. "Has he moved? Spoken?"

"A little. I thought he was about to wake up a few minutes ago. He's close."

"Water? Cold water?"

"We've been trying that, but not for a while." Orlan took four strides to reach the opposite side of the room. He retrieved a bucket, sloshing a bit of water as he hurried back. After setting it down, he dipped his hand in and sprinkled it on Frederick's forehead.

"No." Marcelle touched the bucket's rim. "All ... at once."

"But won't that startle—"

She firmed her tone. "Do it."

"If you say so." Orlan picked up the bucket and dumped it over Frederick's face. He jerked up and shook his head hard, slinging water from his hair. "What? Who?"

Marcelle laid a hand on his shoulder. "Frederick. Calm ... yourself."

He stared at her, then at Orlan, then all around the room. As the seconds passed, his shocked expression twisted into anger. With a low growl, he muttered, "Drexel!"

Orlan nodded vigorously. "Adrian said Drexel must have pushed you into the deer trap."

"Adrian?" Frederick's brow shot up. "My brother?"

"Yes, he rescued you from the trap."

Frederick blinked at Marcelle. "You're ... Marcelle?"

"I ... I think so." She laid a hand on her face. Even the simplest actions seemed as if she were manipulating her body with marionette strings. The separation wouldn't go away. "I am not ... myself. So dizzy. So ... dis ... dis ..."

"Disoriented?"

She nodded.

"Fill me in." Frederick's words shot out in quick succession. "What's going on? Why are you here? Where's Adrian?"

"Orlan. Tell him. I have to ... lie down." She lowered her body to the bed. Although the leaves and straw were now cold and wet,

155

it didn't matter. With her head spinning, she would soon collapse if she didn't rest.

Orlan related his experiences with Drexel, then shifted to what he knew of Adrian's story, including his recent excursion with Regina and Zeb. Marcelle tried to add details about her journey with Adrian, but when blackness dimmed her vision, she had to settle for answering Frederick's questions, which were many and rapid-fire.

Finally, he nodded at the huddled children. "Tom, fetch the shovel. That will be my crutch. Ariel, you and Orlan get the cart and collect the animal traps. We're all going to leave. Marcelle and I need to visit a place that should aid our healing, and we need to find Zeb. We'll set some traps along the way."

"What about Adrian and Regina?" Tom asked. "They won't know where we went."

Frederick mussed Tom's hair. "Trust Regina. She knows the signals."

Marcelle reached for Frederick's hand and compressed it in her own. "Not sure … I can walk … so dizzy."

He returned the clasp. "Don't worry. We'll haul you in the cart if we have to."

Spreading his arms, Frederick gestured for the children to draw close. When they gathered around, Tom and Ariel each looping an arm around one of his, he whispered, "We've had a lot of scary days and nights here, haven't we?"

Tom and Ariel nodded. Orlan and the other children just looked on, their faces tense.

"Well, let's do the same thing we always do when it gets scary."

Tom firmed his jaw and made a fist. "Fight the darkness!"

Ariel waved an arm as if tossing a gift. "Spread the light!"

"Exactly!" He wrapped his arms around them and pulled them close. "Sing the songs I taught you, and maybe Drexel will hear us and try to follow." Grinning, he looked at each child in turn. "Let's see if we can catch a skunk!"

Marcelle pushed against the floor, but her arm gave way. She flopped back to the damp bed. Darkness flooded her vision. As her mind swam through a spell of dizziness, she closed her eyes. Garbled voices pecked at her ears, like crows squawking, competing to be heard.

Finally, one broke through in a soft whisper. "Marcelle? Are you all right?"

She forced her eyes open. Professor Dunwoody stared at her, his expression worried. She swiveled her head. Frederick and the children were gone. "Where are they?" She blinked. It seemed so easy now to move and speak. The marionette strings had been severed.

He kept his whisper low. "Where are who?"

"Never mind." She blinked rapidly. "I'm fine."

"Were you dreaming?"

She smiled. "I wasn't then, but I am dreaming now."

"You think so?" He touched her cheek with his hand. "Your illness is devastating your body in many ways, probably affecting your mind as well, perhaps taking you to the brink of insanity."

"I guess I should expect someone in my dream to think I'm insane." She looked at the panel. "Shouldn't we stay quiet?"

"Whispers are fine." He nodded toward the access panel. "The men left and closed the door to the stairway. They are likely guarding the room from the outside."

"So what do we do now?"

"First, I want you to explain the special powers you have."

She blinked again. "Powers? What are you talking about?"

"While you slept, I saw images around you—a boy with a sword, a man with a beard, other children. They were like glowing fog, semitransparent and ethereal."

Marcelle pointed at herself. "Professor, are you sure *I'm* the one who's insane?"

"What I saw is not insanity, I assure you." Dunwoody picked up the lantern and slowly rose to his feet. Hunching over to keep his head from bumping against the ceiling, he hobbled farther into the tunnel. "Come with me. We have much to talk about."

✳ NINE ✳

MARCELLE and Dunwoody stopped at the trunk that bore the eggshells. He reached in, picked one up, and cradled it in his palm. "This might come as a shock to you, but I believe our ancestors arrived here in these eggs, a male and female from Dracon."

"Humans from eggs?" Ignoring a new chill, Marcelle touched the shell's jagged edge. "How is that possible?"

"I assume it was the only method the dragons knew for safe transport of embryos. My guess is that something terrible happened that made Dracon unfit for human habitation, so in order to save the species, the dragons put harvested embryos in these eggs and brought them here."

"You mean Arxad and Magnar."

"Yes." He touched the side of the trunk. "I take it you read the plaque."

She nodded. "And I know them personally."

"Ah! You will have to relate your exploits. If dragons are cruelly enslaving humans on their planet as we have long believed, it's good to know that there are two dragons we can count on for help."

Marcelle huffed. "Magnar? Impossible. He's the cruelest among them. Arxad isn't much better. I haven't figured him out yet, but he was going to allow both Adrian and me to die at a cooking stake, so I'm counting him on the enemies list."

"Very interesting." Dunwoody laid the shell back in its place. "My hope is that the journal Lady Moulraine sent will shed more light on these mysteries."

"Right. It's over here." She hustled to the lantern and picked up the book. "I read some of it."

"You left it on the ground?" Dunwoody shuffled over and set his lantern next to Marcelle's. "Couldn't you have at least put it in the trunk? If someone had tipped the lantern over, it might have burned."

Marcelle rolled her eyes. "As if this tunnel were a thoroughfare."

"An animal, then. Or bugs. They might do damage to such an old tome."

Marcelle sighed. It was better to let him rant. Explaining her exit from the tunnel seemed impossible anyway. "You're right, Professor. I apologize."

"You do?" His brow arched. "Have those words ever escaped your lips before?"

"Cut the comedy. We have work to do."

"As you wish." He took the journal and sat facing the lanterns. "Join me. Let's see if these entries verify my theories."

Marcelle retrieved her mother's mirror from the floor and slid it into her pocket, then sat at his side and watched as he leafed through the early pages. "I read a section near the end about Starlighters," she said. "I think Leo is one."

"Is that so?" He turned to a page that displayed a crude drawing of a dragon sitting on its haunches, simple outlines, as if sketched by a child. "Tell me more."

"It said a male Starlighter can absorb energy, but he can do it only with one person at a time, and he has to be looking at the person. Not only that, he can be destroyed by dragon fire."

"Not other fire?" Dunwoody asked.

"It didn't say."

"How strange. I fail to see why dragon fire differs from other flames. Fire is fire."

She shrugged. "I'm just telling you what I read."

"Fair enough." He dipped his head toward the book and turned a page.

Marcelle leaned over. As she tried to read, the scribbled text blurred.

"Ah! Look at this!" Dunwoody pointed at a messy line of text near the top of the third page. "Arxad traveled here with the eggs, and each had an embryo with a specially prepared genetic arrangement, but he doesn't say what that arrangement is."

She blinked at the handwriting, or rather claw-writing, spotting the malformed *genetic*, but little else.

"Let's see if I can find a clue …" He ran his finger down the page. "Ah!" His brow lifted for a moment before settling into a knitted scowl.

"What is it?"

"I thought perhaps the dragons were trying to spawn humans of great strength and durability so they could come back and harvest them for slavery."

"Through genetic manipulation?"

"Exactly." He thumped his finger on the page. "This proves me wrong."

Marcelle tried again to read the text, but *disease* was the only legible word. "Something about a disease?"

"Precisely! The purpose of the genetic manipulation was to ensure that the two hatchlings were free of a disease that had spread on Dracon. Arxad brought them here to rescue the species from annihilation." He laid his palm on the page and looked at Marcelle. "The plaque honoring the dragons isn't propaganda. It's the truth. If not for Arxad and Magnar, neither you nor I would exist!"

Marcelle shook her head. "If you could have seen what I saw on Dracon, you wouldn't want to honor them."

"Very well. Tell me."

She rose to her feet and gazed at Dunwoody. He returned her stare, an expectant look on his face. He was a ready audience, a soul hoping to absorb truth, and it seemed that his willing aspect pulled at her, like a sponge drawing water. An urge rose within her, a longing to deliver what he begged to learn.

Then, mimicking a valve releasing pressure, she spread out her arms and voiced the words flowing from within. "I see children who are barely more than skeletons, either half-naked or completely naked, with oozing welts on their backs, burn marks on their faces, and fungus and lesions rotting their skin. They carry pails filled with heavy stones, their feet bloody as they march along a stream where rafts float, rafts that could carry their loads, but the dragons force them to do useless labor, trying to weed out the weak."

Lowering her head, she narrowed her eyes. "All the while, a dragon bearing a whip watches over them like a hungry hawk. If any child should falter or fall, the dragon pounces on her like a mad dog, ripping her flesh with a brutal whip. The other children look on, emotionless, their empathy torn from their hearts by the repetition of such cruelty day after day after day."

She rubbed her fingers together as if sprinkling something onto the ground. "And as Solarus lowers herself to the horizon, a dragon drops an inadequate supply of stale bread and a bricklike wafer of fish. Like starving rats, the children swarm for the food, clawing, shoving, biting, just to get enough morsels to ease the gnawing hunger so they can survive through the night in their glorified anthill of a home."

She hugged herself, shivering. "There the sick lie naked and starving because bigger children steal their clothes, and the few with more sensitive hearts can only share a crumb or two and clean up the vomit and feces of the invalid waifs, what little their starved bellies can produce."

Finally, she took a deep breath. The pressure began to ease, but more words remained. Before she could rest, they had to come out. Dunwoody sat wide eyed, tears flowing. Her story was definitely working as designed.

With a flourish, she pointed a shaking finger at the trunk. "And for one hundred years, our heroes, Magnar and Arxad, have allowed this to go on, knowing that children's backs are being flayed, their dead bodies tossed away like garbage, and their memories wiped off the face of the planet." She kicked the book closed and whispered through clenched teeth. "They weren't trying to preserve a species. They weren't protecting poor, suffering waifs. They just needed healthy slaves!"

Dunwoody stared, tears dripping from his chin. "Remarkable," he murmured. "Simply remarkable."

"What's remarkable?" Marcelle turned in a circle. "What are you staring at?"

"Nothing now." He climbed to his feet, the book in hand. "How long have you been able to do that?"

"Do what? Tell a story?"

He nodded. "We can start there."

"I've told stories from a young age. Not so much lately, though. I've had more important things to focus on."

"I dare say you haven't. This ability is crucial. If you can repeat what you have done here, you will be able to call up a formidable army without even hinting at conscription." He balled his hand into a fist. "Yes, with your ability, you can summon a legion and smash those foul beasts. The passion you ignite will foment a blaze that will be terrible to behold."

Marcelle grabbed his sleeve. "Will you just get to the point? What have I done here? How can I call up an army?"

Dunwoody stroked his chin and gave her a skeptical stare. "You really don't know, do you?"

She hissed out her reply. "Know what?"

"Marcelle …" He clasped her shoulder. "While you told the story, every detail came to life around you, like misty images, ghosts really. I saw the pitiful children. I saw the evil dragon. I saw the anthill, as you called it, though I think a burial mound is a more accurate word to describe it. In any case, if you could tell this story again in front of a group of sympathetic men, the sight of these poor children would set their hearts on fire. You wouldn't be able to stop them from taking up arms and marching to Dracon."

Laughing under her breath, Marcelle backed away. "Wait a minute. This is all getting out of hand."

"What do you mean? Is there a flaw in my thinking?"

"No, it's just that in all the excitement, I forgot what was going on. I can't call up ghosts while I tell a story. Only a Starlighter can do that."

"A Starlighter? I thought you said they absorb energy."

She nodded. "The males do, but females tell stories that come to life, and the people who listen become hypnotized. Cassabrie can do it, but explaining who she is would take too long. The point is that this is all just a dream. I must have been hoping to be able to do something like that, so I'm dreaming about being a Starlighter."

Dunwoody waved a hand. "Marcelle, I felt the hypnosis about which you speak, and I had to fight it to stay alert. I assure you, you are not dreaming. Your sickness is—"

"Of course I'm dreaming." She touched her cheek. "I'm as pale as snow and just as cold. I don't have a heartbeat. I don't sweat or bleed. If I'm not dreaming, then how do you explain all that?"

"I see your point." He crossed his arms over the book. "I will have to come up with solid proof that you aren't dreaming, won't I?"

"I don't see how that's possible. Anything can happen in a dream."

"True. This will be a difficult task." Dunwoody scanned the room, his eyes narrowing. "Ah! Maybe that will suffice!" He pointed at the trunk. "How do you explain learning something about the dragons that you couldn't possibly imagine? Did you think humans could hatch from eggs? That dragons could preserve genetically altered humans that were protected from disease?"

She stared at the trunk. Could she have imagined such a wild tale?

"And look at this." He opened the book to a page near the back. "I saw this when I glanced at it earlier. It didn't register then, but it makes perfect sense now."

Marcelle looked on while Dunwoody read out loud. "The children are old enough to learn about the genetic code so that they can work to prevent any disease-susceptible recessive genes from manifesting. After they fully understand the genome, I will suggest that mating be allowed between males and females who cannot produce children who might contract the disease. Of course, such a policy would demand strict control of mating practices, which they never followed while on Starlight, but in a new society, perhaps it will be perceived as normal."

"But that never happened," Marcelle said. "As controlling as the government is, no one is told whom to marry."

"Which pulls another stone out of your silly dream theory. You wouldn't have come up with this idea on your own. You have never heard of government-arranged marriages." He pointed farther down the page. "Now allow me to read this."

She looked on again as he continued. "I trust that Magnar will never read this journal, so I will express my feelings for the sake of any humans who might care about the motivations of a dragon.

Since I will be leaving soon, only visiting from time to time in order to check on your progress, I will not have an opportunity to express my thoughts. Although Magnar acquiesced to this plan reluctantly, I pursued it with vigor. He hoped for a world without humans, so he is pleased that the outcome of this plan keeps your kind away from Starlight. Since humans enslaved us and treated us so brutally, I cannot find guilt in his pleasure at the thought of a world without your species.

"Yet, I believe in new beginnings. I have read your holy book, the Code, so I know that your people worship the same Creator I do, and I know that if you follow that book, you will never return to cruelty. You will never be slave masters again. You will learn what I have learned, that the way you would have others treat you is the way you should treat them, whether human or dragon. That is the way of the Creator. So I provided you, my surrogate children, with the Code and warned you to keep it safe at all costs, and, above all, to remember the deity who inspired the words. If you fail to honor the source of the words, you will eventually fail to honor the words themselves, and calamity will result.

"So I now must leave you. I have grown to love you beyond any affection I believed possible. If someday I meet your descendants, I hope I will be able to help them in any way I can without, of course, revealing my role in their survival. For, as the Code says, it is most blessed to give to those who are blind to their benefactors, for kindness that is never repaid is the sweetest to the soul."

Dunwoody slowly closed the book and rubbed the back cover with his palm. "Tell me, Marcelle, is it possible that your dragon-despising mind could have imagined such a heartfelt exhibition of affection for humans? Did I just read something that, even in a dream, your heart could not possibly envisage?"

"I ..." She bit her lip. Of course anything could happen in a dream, even the most bizarre ideas, but this one was almost too difficult to believe. If not for the more objective evidence of her bodily functions, or lack thereof, this journal entry would be conclusive. "I don't know what to say. For the sake of argument, I suppose I can pretend this isn't a dream."

"I will accept that." He tucked the book under his arm. "So now we have to get you in front of a large group of potential soldiers."

"How should we do that?"

"Why, surrender to Maelstrom, of course."

"What? Are you crazy? He'll tie me to that stake and ..." She let her voice trail away. Even as the words spilled out, the image of the execution came to mind—hundreds of people gathering at the stake to witness her burning.

Lowering her head, she whispered, "I see what you mean."

"So it's settled." Dunwoody rubbed his hands together. "And I thought using my smoke balls and sneezing powder to get you out of the courtroom was exciting. This will be an adventure to top them all."

"An adventure? What do you mean?"

"I am assuming, of course, that the people will be so aroused by your story that they will halt the execution by sheer force of public outcry, but I will have to come up with an escape plan, just in case."

"Just in case." Marcelle shook her head, laughing under her breath. "This is my life we're talking about. If the crowd doesn't come around, and I get cooked, there won't be anyone left to summon an army. I'm willing to die to free the slaves, but I'm not willing to die for a crazy scheme."

Dunwoody shrugged. "It's up to you. If this is a dream, you don't have anything to worry about. If it's not, then you'll have to summon an army some other way, but your appearance will make that task improbable, if not impossible. And if you show your face in public, Maelstrom will hear about it. Either way, you will likely end up facing the fire."

Marcelle laid her palms on her cheeks. He was right. With Maelstrom on the rampage against sorcery, everyone would think her a witch at first glance, especially after news of the trial spreads. Most would be glad to turn in a sorceress for whatever favors Maelstrom might offer.

"Okay," she said, nodding. "If we can come up with a good escape plan, I'll do it."

*　　　*　　　*　　　*　　　*　　　*

After leading Regina back from the healing spring, a quiet journey because of her weariness, Adrian stopped within sight of the cabin, and hid with her behind a hefty tree. "Something's wrong," he whispered.

She blinked, her gaze again aimless. "What?"

"I'm not sure." He peered at the cabin's small rear window. No sounds came from within. "Do you normally nap in the afternoon?"

"Sometimes, but never all of us at once. Someone is always on guard."

"That's what I guessed. It's too quiet."

"I know. You told everyone to make noise while we were gone."

"That's why I'm concerned." He set her hands against the trunk. "Stay hidden. I'm going to have a look."

She ducked behind the tree. "Okay."

Drawing his sword, Adrian bent over and skulked to the rear of the cabin. He stood on tiptoes and peeked inside. The bed the children had made for Frederick and Marcelle still lay near one side, but neither they nor the children were anywhere in sight.

After hurrying back to Regina and leading her to the cabin's front door, they entered and looked around. Except for two potatoes under the table against the wall, every scrap of food had been taken. Only the deerskin and the bedding remained on the floor. "It looks like everyone packed up and left. Everything is gone."

"Everything?" Feeling her way along the wall, Regina walked to the back of the cabin. She reached under the table and felt the potatoes. "There are two potatoes."

"I saw them. I guess they missed those."

Regina shook her head. "It's a signal. Frederick told us if we ever came back from working in the garden or anything else, and everyone was gone, to check for the potatoes. One means to run into the woods and hide. Two means to stay until they come back. It shouldn't take more than a few hours. Three means to wait one day. If no one comes back, then something awful happened, so go to the mines and try to join a family. The other food isn't missing. It's just hidden. I know where to find it."

"I assume Frederick invented the system," Adrian said. "It sounds like something he'd come up with."

"He did." She brought the potatoes to Adrian. "Can you read any markings on them? Frederick said he would try to leave a message on them if he could."

He picked one up and examined it. Someone had scratched letters in the peel that spelled out HEAL MARCELLE. He grabbed the second and read the words TRAP DREXEL. Nodding, he stooped next to Regina. "It seems," he whispered, "that my brother has recovered enough to go to the healing trees with Marcelle, and he hopes to set a trap for Drexel."

"Oh, good!" she said, clapping her hands. "I hope the water works for them."

"I hope so, too." He rose and looked out the window. Nothing stirred in the quiet forest. "Do you know what kind of trap Frederick might use?"

She nodded. "A rope trap. If Drexel steps in it, the rope will jerk him up by his foot." As if watching the sight in her mind, she rolled her eyes upward and laughed. "And he'll hang there like a rotten fruit!"

"I can see it now," Adrian said, laying a hand on her shoulder. "Frederick will give each of the children a thorny branch, and they'll take turns whacking Drexel until he understands what it feels like to be a slave."

"Right! That'll teach him!" She took in a breath to say something else, but it died on her lips. Then, her head drooped.

"Regina?" Adrian lifted her chin with a finger. "Is something wrong?"

"Um …" A tear sparkled in her eye. "Never mind."

Adrian studied her forlorn expression. This girl was so deep, so introspective. "Okay. So I suppose we'll just stay here until Frederick comes back."

Wiping the tear away, she sniffed. "I don't think we have a choice."

He caressed her cheek. "Are you tired?"

She nodded.

With a hand at her back, he guided her to the bed. For some reason, the straw was damp in one spot, as if someone had bathed there. He swept fresher straw into place and helped her lie down. After covering her with the deerskin, he slid his hand into hers. "Frederick must have taken a different path to the spring. That's why we didn't see him on our way back."

She touched her chin with a finger. "To hide the traps, probably. They would be too easy to see the way we went."

"So now," he said, gently pushing her eyelids closed, "you can dream about Frederick and Marcelle washing in the spring. When they're finished, maybe they'll play with the children and splash around."

Smiling, she nodded again. "I can see it already."

"Me, too. They're laughing and singing, and they're getting soaked."

"I wish I could be there with them." She pulled Adrian's hand up to her chest and held it there. "Why did the water heal my tongue and skin this time but not last time?"

As her thumb kneaded the back of his hand, he watched its rhythmic motion. "Well, I'm not sure, but from what you told me, I think you have to apply it yourself."

"Oh …" Her reply was like a stretched-out hum.

"Still, I can't figure out why it didn't heal your eyes. That's why I asked you to wash them yourself."

"It's really strange. I feel like I can see some things in my mind instead of through my eyes, sort of like memories, but I could see with my eyes for a while."

"Yes, I know, but we were on the other side of the portal, and we were invisible to everyone else. Would you trade your ability to be seen for an ability to see?"

"I'm not sure." Her lips pursed, the thumb-to-hand massage continuing. "Why do you have to wash yourself?"

"I don't know how it works. Only the Creator knows."

She opened her eyes and turned her head to the side. "I think I know."

"Okay. Let's hear it."

"When I do something bad, I'm the only one who can say I'm sorry. No one can do it for me."

"That's true." Adrian watched Regina's wandering eyes. There was so much going on in her mind. Again, it would be best to draw her out, let her make her own conclusions. "What does saying you're sorry have to do with the healing water?"

"Well …" Her grip on his hand tightened. "Isn't saying you're sorry like healing a wound?"

"Definitely. The words *I'm sorry* are just about the most healing words someone can say."

"Okay." She turned her face toward him, though her eyes didn't quite line up with his. "I'm sorry."

"You're sorry?" He cocked his head. "For what?"

"For saying what I did … about Drexel." Her lips quivering, she turned away again. "I don't want anyone to know what it feels like to be a slave."

"You didn't say that. I did. I guess I'm the one who should be sorry."

"But I agreed with you." She shook her head. "You don't know what it's like to be a slave. I do."

"I see." He pressed his lips together. She was right, of course, but there was no need for such a burden to fall on her shoulders. "Well, Drexel didn't hear you, so he wasn't offended."

"But *you* heard me." She clenched her eyes closed. As her body shook gently, tears seeped through. "Now I know why my eyes weren't healed."

"Oh, Regina!" His own tears welling, Adrian passed his hand across her bristly hair, the only visible sign of her cruel captivity. She had been liberated, rescued, redeemed. And now blindness remained as a constant reminder of the toil and misery.

He took a deep breath, hoping his voice wouldn't crack. "There's a saying in the Code. Afflictions are stripes for the valiant, those the Creator chooses for a great purpose. He catches their tears in a crucible and grinds their bones within. With each cry of pain that rises, the Creator weeps, adding his own tears. Then, when the mixture is prepared, he pours it out, and there stands a warrior, hardened on the outside and tender on the inside, for he has endured bitter trials, and he never forgets the tears, either his own or the Creator's."

She blinked, saying nothing, yet her expression probed for more.

"That means you're one of the valiant ones. Your blindness, even your slavery, might be the grinding of your bones that has prepared you to be the Creator's warrior. And your sorrow over what you said proves that you haven't forgotten the tears. You are tender inside, exactly the kind of warrior the Creator needs."

She sniffed again. "You think so?"

"I know so." He caught a tear with a fingertip and brushed it from her cheek. "You're an inspiration to me."

Her lips trembled into a smile. "I am?"

"You are. It seems that every moment I'm with you, I learn something about love and endurance. If I were to be put in the crucible you endured, could I have withstood the pain? Would I still love the Creator after my bones were crushed? It's hard to know."

"I hope you never have to, but if you do, I'll try to help you." She pulled his hand up to her mouth and kissed his knuckles, letting her lips linger. "So never leave me, okay?"

"Never?" Adrian wiped his own tear away. "I'll tell you this, to stay with you, I will fight all the beasts of the wild and plunge the darkest of depths. The only thing that will be able to separate us is death." He poked her ribs. "Or if you get married to some lucky young man."

She giggled and pushed his finger away. When she settled, she faced his direction again. "I've heard about getting married. It must be wonderful."

"My parents think so. I hope to take you home and introduce you to my mother. She always wanted a girl. Maybe you could live with us, and you could learn what being married is all about."

"And I would be your sister?" Her mouth dropped open. "Wow!"

"It would be a great honor to be your brother."

After a moment's pause, she took his hand again. "Do you want to get married?"

"I do. ... Someday."

"You should marry Marcelle. She's about your age, right?"

"She is. We're the same age. We were best friends as children."

Her brow arched up. "But not anymore?"

"Let's just say that we drifted apart for a while, but we're close friends again now."

"So you *will* marry her?"

Adrian laughed. "I haven't even asked her. I'm not sure if she'd say yes."

"Well, I think there's only one way to find out."

"And what if she says no?"

"Then you won't get married, and it would be the same if you didn't ask her at all." She let out a yawn and smacked her lips. "It's like something Frederick said to Orlan yesterday. You'll never hit a target unless you shoot at it."

"That's true, Regina. I'll be thinking about it." He pressed her palm down on her chest and patted her hand. "Now go to sleep. There's nothing to fear."

Sighing, she pulled the deerskin up and closed her eyes. "Not as long as my big brother's around."

Adrian's throat tightened, reducing his voice to a bare whisper. "That's right."

Soon, her breathing settled to a steady rhythm, a sign of approaching sleep. As if dreaming, she spoke with her eyes closed, more of a murmured thought than lucid speech. "Adrian? What's a crucible?" Then, her breaths became even once again as she drifted off into true sleep.

Adrian gazed at her pursed lips, the source of so many profound words and now a probing question. What was a crucible?

He looked at the open door, the path to the world outside. Starlight. A world of cruelty. A land of broken bodies and broken hearts, where little girls who should be dancing and singing find only backbreaking marches and cries of agony. Starlight. A crucible. Yet, was it the Creator's crucible?

Letting his mind wander, Adrian drifted back to Major Four, to Mesolantrum, to the Enforcement Zone behind the governor's palace. Images of punishment flashed one after the other—his friends suffering in the pillory for believing in the dragon world; political prisoners living out their days in the dungeon because of their convictions; and finally, the widow Halstead burning at the stake for having vision that saw beyond what the blind fools in the palace could see.

Adrian sighed. Major Four. A crucible. Perhaps as much of an affront to the Creator as any other.

He rose to his feet, strolled to the door, and surveyed the dense forest. Beyond the trees, dozens of children like Regina still toiled in their slavish crucibles, some maimed, some crippled, all barely hanging on to life, a tiny flame within providing a spark of hope that maybe tomorrow their rescue would come. … Maybe tomorrow.

Looking up, Adrian whispered. "Don't let them suffer another night. Let today be their tomorrow. I am your warrior, gladly pressed into service to stay here and protect this little angel, yet my arms ache to charge out and destroy her oppressors, to set her brothers and sisters free. I ask you to take my sword and cut loose their bonds, even if I cannot be there to swing the blade. Use the tracking skills you have given me to lead them to safety, to lead them here. To lead them home." Adding a sigh, he pushed the door open wider. "I will be waiting."

✳ TEN ✳

MARCELLE paced in a circle around an iron ring embedded in the stone floor of the courtroom's holding cell. Chains attached to the ring led to more chains fastened to manacles encircling her ankles and wrists, providing enough slack to wander three steps in any direction. A lantern sitting on a wall mount to the right of the door cast her shadow on the opposite wall. The dark, undulating copy of herself mimicked her pensive stride.

After making at least a hundred orbits while mulling over Dunwoody's escape plan, she sat heavily on the bench at the back of the cell. Dawn would arrive in only a few hours. Life or death rested on Dunwoody's fragile promises. He would try to locate Gregor, assuming he escaped from the Tark guards at the infirmary, and they would conceal her sword in the kindling and wear earplugs to avoid her hypnotic effect. Then, if her storytelling failed to persuade the crowd, he would rescue her at the last moment with help from unnamed members from the Underground Gateway. And as if that promise wasn't brittle enough, his assurances that the storytelling would again conjure pitiful images that would enflame the crowd now seemed thinner than the eggshells back in the trunk.

She shook her head. It wouldn't work. It couldn't work. Her best chance now rested on the idea that this was all the dream of an injured sword maiden who couldn't stay awake longer than a few minutes. If only she would rouse herself and end this nightmare!

She stood and glared at the ceiling. Shaking a fist, she shouted, "Wake up, Marcelle!" but only the rattling of her chains replied.

Sitting on the bench again, she closed her eyes and concentrated. That always seemed to be the best way to get in contact with her real self. Still, the fleeting images of facing Drexel and talking to Frederick might be the dream, while this cell and these chains were the true reality, a nightmarish gauntlet of unfathomable horrors. But how could that be? A bloodless body of dust and dirt couldn't be real.

"Do you need help, Marcelle?"

She opened her eyes. Cassabrie stood inches in front of her. Wearing her now-familiar blue cloak and white dress, she crouched and wrapped Marcelle in a tight embrace. "I'm so sorry I left you here for so long. I had much to do on Starlight, but now I have come to give you guidance."

Marcelle pushed her back. Cassabrie smiled, her hands on her knees as she stooped, each hand missing a ring finger. "How did you find me?" Marcelle asked.

"It wasn't difficult. The entire village is gossiping about your imprisonment here. I heard that the dungeon is empty, so I searched the palace. When I saw the guard outside the door, I assumed you might be here, and I was right."

"How did you get past the guard?"

"Oh!" Cassabrie looked back. "He was asleep."

"Asleep?"

Laughing softly, Cassabrie faced her again, her hood shading her sparkling green eyes. "I'm surprised you didn't know. He snores quite loudly. I think he'll get in trouble if—"

"Forget the snoring! How did you open the door?"

Cassabrie looked back again. "I didn't open it. I passed underneath it."

"Underneath?" Marcelle looked at the gap under the door, a space less than an inch high. "Okay, that settles it. This really is a dream. No one could fit through a—"

"No one except me ..." Smiling, she pointed at Marcelle. "And you."

"Me?"

Cassabrie sat next to her and rubbed her back. "Oh, Marcelle, the shock from the Reflections Crystal has surely purged your brain of the memories you need to understand your state. You are not dreaming. Don't you remember what I told you when we arrived in this world? The crystal drew your spirit out of your body, so you're a spirit who has created your body from the materials of this world, and if you return to the Northlands, you will again be a spirit unless you reunite with your physical body."

"I remember, but that could also be part of a dream." Marcelle laid a hand over her chest. "No one can exist without a heartbeat, without vital fluids. I can feel moisture in my mouth and eyes, but I don't have blood or sweat."

"Then try to go further back in your mind. Do you remember when you and Adrian first saw me? I was in this state, cold and pale. The soldiers thought me dead because I lacked a beating heart. Then my body dissolved into the dust that formed me. Later, I reconstituted into the same state I was before, again without color or circulation." Cassabrie got down on her knees, took Marcelle's enchained hands, and looked into her eyes. "You were awake then. You weren't dreaming, just as you aren't now."

As Marcelle returned her stare, the memories began flowing. This cadaverous girl with two missing fingers indeed did crumble and reconstitute before her eyes. That wasn't a dream. Yet, couldn't a real event reoccur in a dream? Of course. But the fact that a bloodless girl without a heartbeat actually once existed in reality worked to destroy the best evidence that this was all a dream. "Okay, you've shot me down. I'll have to think about it. But tell me why you've come."

"I told you that I would leave the portal open, but that proved to be impossible. Magnar has come to this world, and—"

"Magnar?" Marcelle tapped the bench with a finger. "Magnar is here on Major Four?"

As Cassabrie nodded, her hood slid down, revealing her bright red hair. "If he learns of that portal and passes through it, our troubles will multiply, so I closed it. When you return there with an army, if it isn't open, be patient until it is. One way or another, I will make sure it opens as soon as possible."

"So you expect me to risk my life gathering an army, march them through the forest while they're all grumbling about why they're following a dead woman to a dragon planet they don't really believe in, and then when we get there, you want me to wait until you decide to show up?"

Cassabrie smiled. "Yes. That's exactly right. I'm glad your faculties are returning."

"What do you expect me to do? Entertain them with that dissolving-to-dust trick you do?"

"Oh, Marcelle," Cassabrie said as she laughed, "you're so funny!"

"Funny?" Marcelle glared at her. "I'm serious. You have no idea what it's like for a woman who tries to lead military men. It's difficult enough when I'm one of the best swordplayers in the land, but getting hardened soldiers to believe me when everyone thinks I'm some kind of witch? Impossible!"

"Then you'll have to come up with some other form of persuasion. Perhaps the governor—"

"The governor's the reason I'm here!" Marcelle shot to her feet, dodged Cassabrie, and began pacing in a circle again. "You see, I turned myself in to the governor because I thought it would give me a chance to speak to a lot of people at once. A teacher of mine said that when I told a story about the cattle children, they came to life around me, like moving ghosts."

"How strange!" Cassabrie sat on the bench and stared at Marcelle. "That is a Starlighter's gift, and you are not a Starlighter."

Marcelle stopped pacing. "How do you know? If I'm doing what a Starlighter does, what else could it mean?"

"I admit that I am perplexed. Your hair is somewhat red, and your eyes have a greenish hue, which means you might have Starlighter genetics. But since you were not born in my world, I don't think you can be a true Starlighter, though I don't understand how you could conjure the manifestations, especially since we aren't on Starlight now."

"Adrian told me you were able to create images here. You showed Frederick rescuing one of the cattle children."

Cassabrie pulled her hood back over her head. "I had never exercised my gift here before, so I was unsure of what I could show him. I looked into the matter later and learned that I can show what occurred on Starlight wherever I am, as well as what I can remember from my own mind or what I am able to pull from the minds of those around me."

Staring at her shadow, Marcelle watched herself nod. "What I brought to life was from my own mind. I told a story about what I had seen."

"Interesting. Clearly you possess a gift of some sort, but a greater proof will be if you can display a tale you have not seen, perhaps something from Starlight's past. It could be that you have this ability only when you're in this form. Perhaps energy from the Reflections Crystal endowed you. It absorbed quite a bit of my energy at one time."

"That experience I'll never forget." Marcelle set a hand on her hip. Memories of the burning pain she had suffered roared back. She had disguised herself as a Promoted slave in order to rescue Adrian from that crystal, and it took some time for him to get the will to fight. Cassabrie had lived within him for quite a while, and he seemed to change during that time, apparently hypnotized by her charms.

She drilled a stare into Cassabrie. "Why did you go inside Adrian? What were you doing to his mind?"

Cassabrie blinked rapidly. "My purpose was not my own. I was compelled by a higher authority."

"That's a dodge. You didn't answer my question."

"I didn't answer in the way you hoped, but it wasn't a dodge, as you call it. I was letting you know that my purpose was guided by another, so the *why* is not something I can fully answer."

"Well, if you want me to trust you, you'd better tell me what you know."

Cassabrie stared for a moment, her green eyes soft, yet piercing. "Should I purchase your trust with information that is private between two parties?"

Keeping her eyes on Cassabrie, Marcelle turned and sat to her right. "Two parties? You and Adrian?"

"Yes, of course. I dwelt inside him. We had many private conversations." As their gazes locked again, Cassabrie's expression took on a melancholy air. "As Arxad's agent in communicating with your governor about a pheterone transfer, I visited this world frequently, and I took the liberty at times to explore, so I learned a great deal about the people here. I had seen Adrian before, but I had no idea that he would be the one to facilitate the gas tank transfer until I arrived to get it. When Alaph, the king in the Northlands, learned that you and Adrian were coming to Starlight, he told me that he wanted the two of you to be separated and that I should be Adrian's guide for his journey to the Southlands."

"You mean that our separation was orchestrated?" Marcelle pointed at Cassabrie. "By you?"

Cassabrie nodded. "I wasn't told why, but I think I figured it out. Each of you learned something on your own, something crucial that you could not have learned together. I assume that you had quite a harrowing experience getting past the barrier wall."

"I did." Marcelle forced a skeptical tone. "Go on."

"Alaph wanted me to guide Adrian, not so much in direction, because the Southlands region is easy to find, but more so in purpose and clarity of mind."

"Clarity of mind? Your presence made him lose clarity."

"Only when I intentionally created a fog. That was part of my goal, to provide him with the experience of giving control to a powerful presence so that he would be ready for a greater test."

"What greater test?"

Cassabrie shrugged. "I don't know."

"But you nearly got him killed."

"I know. I tested him to his very limits. I challenged his mind with wooings of love and testings of the quality of his heart."

"But why? Adrian is a good, honest man. He doesn't need testing."

"We all need testing, Marcelle, not only to learn what we are lacking, but also to learn who we are, to be reminded of what has been buried within, treasures that need to come to the surface. When I finally left Adrian, it seemed to me that he resurrected exactly what he needed to complete his journey."

"And what is that?"

Cassabrie's brow knitted. "You don't know?"

Resisting a scowl, Marcelle kept her tone calm. "If I did, I wouldn't have asked."

"I suppose not." Cassabrie looked away. "I thought a real woman would have seen it clearly."

"A real woman?" Marcelle gritted her teeth. "What are you implying? Just because I prefer trousers over—"

"Oh, Marcelle! I wasn't questioning your femininity. I was referring to your physical presence. You were in a real body during Adrian's ordeal." Cassabrie gave her a disarming smile. "You're a real woman, to be sure. I just thought that since you were physical and able to call on natural womanly instincts, you would empathize with Adrian's plight and understand his dilemma and his final choice. It's fair to assume, however, that your own torture has crippled your faculties."

"Crippled my faculties," Marcelle whispered, as if echoing. What could Cassabrie have meant by womanly instincts? Did she think there might be a romantic relationship of some kind? "Adrian and I are on a mission to rescue slaves, not to get involved with each other. This is war, not love."

Cassabrie let out a tsking sound. "If not for love, Adrian would have stayed at home. If not for love, he wouldn't be shedding his blood to rescue slaves." She drew so close, their noses nearly touched. "If not for love, he wouldn't be carrying your soulless body through Starlight, whispering encouragement to you, praying for you, and ignoring the mess and smell when your body, unable to control its functions—"

"That's enough," Marcelle said, waving a hand. "I get the picture."

"Is that so?" Cassabrie looked into her eyes. "I'm not sure you do."

"What am I missing?"

"You're missing the reasons behind your trials. The only way for you to raise an army was to come here in this form, and the only way to preserve your body was to make sure that a certain warrior so loved you that he would never forsake you, even if you became a voiceless vegetable without hope of recovery. He would keep you safe from harm."

Marcelle let her voice drop below a whisper. "I see."

"And I taught him a lesson about where great faith and brutal practicality meet. I wanted him to consider where he would draw the line between a faithful risk and suicidal foolishness. You see, our faith to do the impossible grows as the value we assign to the impossible task grows. At first, he told me you were a fellow warrior, so his risk to protect you ought to be in keeping with the value of a fellow warrior. I did not contradict him, but this expression of worth let me know how much work I had to do. He was suppressing his true view of you, so I had to show him what he really wanted you to be."

"And what was that?"

"I am amazed that you don't know." Cassabrie spread out her fingers, displaying the gap. "Your lack of knowledge is far more crippling than a missing ring finger."

"Just give it to me straight. What does Adrian want me to be?"

Cassabrie caressed Marcelle's hand. "More than a warrior. A spiritual companion. A deep-abiding friend. Someone he couldn't live without. I bonded with him and showed him what it's like to be spiritually united with a powerful ... tender ... needy woman."

"Needy?" Marcelle instinctively reached for her sword, but it wasn't there. "I have trained for—"

"Oh, stop it, Marcelle! You can't be your own hero forever. When are you going to put down your armor? When are you going to realize that your heart needs a friend? When are you going to shed that façade?" Cassabrie's eyes blazed like a copper fire. "Adrian needs a woman, not another man!"

"A woman can be a woman without dresses and perfume. Just because I can fight with a sword doesn't mean—"

"I'm not talking about swords or dresses or perfume! You can wear a gunnysack and skunk oil for all I care. A woman isn't a costume you wear on the outside; it's what you are on the inside. And Adrian needed to feel the love of a woman before he could see you as something other than a fellow warrior."

Marcelle gave her a skeptical stare. "So you showed him. You melded with him and made him love you."

Cassabrie nodded firmly. "In fact, at the point of decision, I wooed him so thoroughly and with such tantalizing power that I invited him to die at the cooking stake and be with me forever in spiritual ecstasy."

"You did?" Marcelle painted a mental image of Cassabrie and Adrian dancing, their bodies pressed close together as they swayed in the midst of a calm breeze that gently brushed their hair and clothes. Their faces reflected perfect serenity, far from the dangers of mortal battles and slavish strife. "And what if he had chosen to die?"

"I don't discuss hypotheticals, Marcelle. He didn't choose me; he chose you. That's all that matters."

"That's all that matters," Marcelle repeated with a doubtful tone. "Are you trying to tell me that you had no desires for yourself? That you didn't want Adrian to be your eternal love?"

Cassabrie crossed her arms over her chest. "I see no reason to discuss my desires. They're irrelevant."

"You want me to trust you, don't you?" Marcelle spiced a vibrant whisper with a low growl. "You undressed my soul. I don't see why you shouldn't undress yours."

Cassabrie and Marcelle stared at each other for a long moment. Finally, Cassabrie lowered her hood again, allowing her red tresses to spill over her cloak's shoulders. "I had an older brother, well, half brother really, who was a lot like Adrian, brave and noble and loving. Trace was eight years older than I, and he treated me like one of your princesses here on Darksphere, so kind and thoughtful. With every tender touch, I felt loved and cherished, a wonderful rush of emotions that told me I was something more than a stone mover." Cassabrie closed her eyes and seasoned her words with a gentle hum. "Some of the older women told tales of romance, being loved by a heroic man, something we never saw in real life. But when I was twelve, Trace attempted an uprising. He killed a dragon with a homemade sword and tried to herd a bunch of us to the wilderness. For the first time in my life, I saw true heroism, and the image made my heart leap."

Marcelle looked at the center of the cell. A semitransparent man who looked much like Adrian spread out his arms, frantically guiding women and children into a line.

"But he couldn't get any of the other men to help, so he had to defend the women and children by himself. A dragon blasted him with fire and killed two of the women and three children."

A ghostly dragon flew across the room and blew a blast of fire that slammed into Trace and splashed over some in the line, setting them ablaze. Then, as quickly as the scene appeared, it vanished.

Cassabrie opened her eyes. "Maybe if more men had joined us, ready to fight, we could have escaped, but they said the best way to protect us was to acquiesce, to just do what the dragons tell us. They even accused Trace of hating the women and children, saying he would be the cause of our deaths."

"That's so wrong," Marcelle said. "Trace was the real man. He fought for their freedom."

Cassabrie nodded. "And that brings me to my point. The fire crippled Trace, and the dragons chained him to the Basilica, providing him just enough sustenance to keep him alive. Unable to speak a word, he became a public display, a blackened shell of a man, a visual warning against rebellion. After many years, he died of old age, a relief, really, for his suffering was abominable. Anyway, ever since Trace's valiant attempts, I dreamed of finding a man like him, a man with a backbone, a man of courage who could lead me with a muscular arm while massaging my heart with a compassionate hand. And in Adrian I found him. So when I went inside Adrian, I poured my love into him, showing him the passion and purity of a woman's unbridled affections, an empowering infusion he had never experienced before. You see, men are willing to fight for what they believe in, but when they face brutal persecution, their resolve might wilt if not for this inner sense of purpose."

"The love of a woman."

"Yes. A man will fight to the death for what he believes in, but he will suffer for all eternity for his woman. He will even endure the shame of failure. You see, when he falls, his woman picks him up, dusts him off, and whispers words of intimacy in his ear that only he will understand, and these words become fuel for his fire. Then, reignited by love, he charges into battle once again, confident that his sacrifices have meaning to someone he loves, someone who loves him." Cassabrie nodded slowly. "Yes, it is easier to die for a cause than it is to live in daily sacrifice, and it is a woman who helps a man understand the difference."

Marcelle sat mesmerized. This Starlighter's gift for words truly did pierce hearts.

"So," Cassabrie continued, "when I had fully infused that love into Adrian, I challenged him to decide between me and you. While he suffered, my heart was ripping in two. I so wanted him to be mine, but that was not my mission. I came to give him power and purpose, and I had fulfilled my quest, so I pulled back to give him a moment of clarity, to allow him to see what you were doing for him. When he fully understood, he hesitated not one second."

Cassabrie took Marcelle's hand. "He loves you, Marcelle. Now that he has experienced what I have shown him, he wants you to be the one to infuse him with this power that only a woman can give, the purpose that will cause him to sacrifice whatever he must to accomplish an impossible task. For your sake, he will do whatever love tells him."

Marcelle stared at their joined hands. "And you could have kept him. You wanted him, but you gave him up."

Her chin quivering, Cassabrie nodded. "But now that he's yours, you have to, as you said, undress your soul for him. Keep your sword. Keep your trousers. But lower your shield. Let him see your heart, the heart of a woman who will be at his side to the ends of the earth. For such a woman, he will slay every dragon in every world."

Marcelle looked into her eyes again. "What shield? I'm straight-forward. I tell everyone exactly what I think. I don't hide anything from anyone."

"Straightforward, yes. Your sharp tongue fends off fools, but it also repels those who wish to draw close. You have wrapped your wounded heart in armor, and in that sleeve it will never be harmed again. Within that cowl, you still shiver in the shadow of your mother's murderer. To this day, he still stalks your nightmares, and as long as you cower in fear of another attack, as long as you push everyone away to protect the open wound, you will never heal; you will never conquer the villain who did this deed. He will continue to stab you again and again until you decide to muster courage and stand up against him, and not just him, but also any intruder who threatens your security."

Marcelle tried to slide her hand away, but Cassabrie held firm. Their gazes locked again. Cassabrie's eyes sparkled, not from tears, but from an eerie light shining within. Her words were powerful, indeed, persuasive, mind-changing. But was it because of truth or rather because of her Starlighter gifts? How could anyone know for certain?

"How did you learn all this?" Marcelle asked. "You live on a world without examples of what you're talking about. Even Trace was with you for too few years to give you all this wisdom. Who taught you?"

Cassabrie averted her eyes. "I have had many long conversations with the white dragon, the king of the Northlands. He has great wisdom."

"How could a dragon understand a human heart?"

"His kind has many emotional similarities with our kind, and he has a mate, so he understands what love can do, how love can affect the heart."

"You said *has* a mate. When I was there, I didn't hear about any queen."

"They are currently estranged, but I will say no more about that. Their heartbreak is not our concern."

"I see."

Marcelle imagined Adrian as he struggled to free himself from the Reflections Crystal. He had cried out, "Cassabrie, I beg you. Let me go! Don't let me die a coward. Let me fight at Marcelle's side!" Then, like a stream of light, Cassabrie emerged from his body. The moment Adrian made his decision, she set him free. Every word of her story was true.

"I need to get back to him," Marcelle said. "He needs me to help him. Right now I'm just a limp body who can't give him a sword or a heart."

Cassabrie nodded once more, her eyes again fiery. "Yes, you must get back to him, but do so with as many soldiers as you can muster. Then you and he can lead them in battle together. Yet, how will you find each other? Starlight is smaller than this world, but it is still too vast for a pair of humans to randomly meet."

"Adrian will find a way. He is the best tracker in Mesolantrum. He notices everything—smells, sounds, and tastes. He can tell a man's weight just by the angle of the grass he trod."

"Is that so?" Cassabrie let out a low hum. "Then perhaps there is no concern."

"Okay, that's settled," Marcelle said, firming her jaw. "So back to the portal issue. Whatever you have to do to be there to open it when we arrive, just do it. If this isn't a dream after all, I'm taking a huge risk going to the stake."

"Indeed you are. If you don't escape the body you created from the soil of this planet, your spirit will not be able to survive the flames. You will be sent straight to the Creator, and your physical body on Starlight will also perish."

"So there's still a real connection between my body and my spirit?"

"Oh, yes. My own body still exists on Starlight. I can sense it, feel it. Sometimes I can even see through my body's physical eyes, though only brief glimpses. I hope someday to reunite with it, but it's impossible right now."

"I *thought* it was real." Marcelle sighed. "So it's risky, but it's not as if I have any choice anymore."

"You still have a choice." Cassabrie rose and pointed at the door. "You can leave the way I came in. In fact, we can leave together. We can crumble to dust, slide underneath, and reconstitute right in front of the guard." She laughed. "I have to admit, being able to surprise people and take advantage of their shock can be quite amusing. In fact, I experienced a recent standoff with Counselor Leo. The look on his face when I dissolved was worth the risk of the encounter. His face became as pale as yours and mine."

Marcelle set her hands on her hips, rattling her chains. "You certainly are an interesting character."

"Since you are the same …" Cassabrie curtsied. "I will take that as a compliment."

"I suppose it was … in a way. I prefer people who are honest and straightforward."

"Then will you go with me?" She walked to the door and knelt. "It's not hard. All you have to do—"

Someone banged on the door. "Quiet in there!"

Covering her mouth with her hand, Cassabrie skulked back to Marcelle. "I'll lead him away," she whispered. "That will give you a chance to escape."

Marcelle kept her voice down. "But you haven't told me how to do it yet."

"Urgency. A need to escape. You have to feel it deep within."

"But I don't want you to risk your life for me."

"Don't worry. I've done this many times." Cassabrie hurried back to the door, raised her hands high, and crumbled to the floor in a pile of dust. The sudden fall raised a breeze that swept her remains under the door and out of sight. Several tiny pebbles rolled out with her in the trailing vacuum.

Marcelle stepped as close as her chains would allow, listening.

A gasp sounded, then a shout. "What the blazes?"

Cassabrie's voice followed. "You can't hold me in there. I can escape any cell."

"We'll see about that."

The clatter of pounding footsteps erupted, then quickly faded.

Marcelle took a step toward the door, but the chains kept her in place. She stamped her foot. Now what? Cassabrie left without explaining how to dissolve. She mentioned feeling urgency, but what did that mean?

Looking at a chained wrist, she imagined her arm crumbling to dust and leaking out of the manacle. Cassabrie said it wasn't hard, but anything can be hard to someone who has never done it before.

She sat on the floor. So this wasn't a dream. Now all the pieces were falling into place. When she traveled from Dunwoody's escape tunnel through that hole in the pile of rocks, she must have dissolved on her own, and just as the pebbles were swept up in Cassabrie's flow, her sword went partway along with her transport to the pipeline. At the time, she had been trying to wake up, trying to get in touch with her sleeping self. Was that the key to dissolving? To put herself in a state somewhere in between Major Four and Starlight? Maybe attempting the connection would make her dissolve, but if that were true, why hadn't Professor Dunwoody mentioned a dissolving event when she made a connection while he was present?

Whatever the case, she seemed to have no control over the situation, and leaving now didn't fit into the plans. Staying here and facing the stake remained the best option for raising an army. If the Starlighter gifts were real, she would have to tell a tale that would make every warrior weep.

She sat on the bench and pounded it with a fist. She could do it. She had to do it. The slaves needed help.

The door rattled, then banged open. The guard stormed in with a sword gripped in a tight fist. He snatched one of her chains, jerking her wrist. "You're still here," he grumbled. "Good."

Marcelle glared at his bearded face and watery eyes. "What did you think? That I could fit under the door?"

He slapped her with the back of his hand. "That'll teach you to be smart with me!"

She refused to flinch. "Did hitting a woman in chains make you feel more like a man?"

"I hit a sorceress, not a woman. I'd like to slit your throat, but Orion would have my head."

She growled under her breath. "Not if I were trying to escape. Give me a sword, and I'll give you a chance to be a hero."

"The only other sword around here is a display blade on the wall in the courtroom."

"That'll do." She nodded at his hilt. "Even if I had a sword as unaccustomed to expert handling as yours, I could shave your beard and trim your nose hairs before you could draw yours from its scabbard."

He slapped her again, this time more savagely, and again she kept her glare unmoved. "It's a good thing you have to wear a gag when they tie you to the stake. No one would want to hear your witchy talk."

"A gag?" She blinked at him. "Since when do they gag a condemned prisoner?"

The guard laughed. "Counselor Leo's orders. He doesn't want you casting spells at anyone, least of all him, I suspect."

Marcelle let her shoulders slump. Not being able to talk would ruin everything.

"I think you need a little more darkness," the guard said. "I hear witches are thrown into the abyss, so you'd better get used to it." He grabbed the lantern from its bracket and shuffled to the door, muttering, "Fool nightmares. I have to stop drinking that cheap ale."

Just before he exited, Marcelle rubbed her smitten cheek and looked at her finger. A thin layer of dust coated the tip. Crumbling and escaping through the crack seemed to be her only chance. If she waited until they tied her to the stake, it might be too late.

When the door closed, shutting out the light, she lay on the bench and looked up into the darkness. Might Cassabrie return? Obviously she would notice that an inexperienced pseudo-Starlighter hadn't followed. Maybe she guessed that speaking to the crowd was the best option after all, or maybe she got sidetracked and couldn't return. Regardless of what she was doing now, her strident counsel had been piercing.

Marcelle sighed. How should she apply it? If she could connect with her body again, maybe she could let Adrian know that she was all right and tell him what was going on here on Major Four. If death really awaited with no chance of raising an army, at least maybe she could say good-bye. And maybe the process really could help her dissolve into dust and give her a way of escape at the execution stake.

Closing her eyes, she slid a hand inside her tunic and caressed the manna mirror's smooth wood. When she was little, sometimes Mother let her take it to bed. It always brought peace and calm, allowing her mind to settle and think pleasant thoughts.

Where might Adrian be now? Was it nighttime on Starlight? Even if so, it still could be daytime there, depending on where the dragons' village happened to be in the planet's rotational cycle. In any case, if she could connect again, she would soon find out.

After letting her mind drift for a few minutes, she opened her eyes. She sat in shallow water with her legs straight out. As little hands propped her up, two girls scooped water and poured it over her legs. One girl dipped a cloth and washed her face, while yet another girl with a cloth reached under her tunic and swabbed her abdomen and chest.

Marcelle blinked at her familiar face. Shellinda? Yes, Shellinda was here, the girl who escaped from the cattle camp.

Her legs and arms numb, Marcelle sat still and watched. A boy to her left held a lantern near Frederick, who sat in the water washing his leg. "Keep it up, girls," Frederick called. "My bone's healed, and every wound is closing up. It has to work for Marcelle soon."

Gathering her strength, Marcelle forced out, "Frederick."

"Marcelle?" He leaped to his feet and splashed over to her. "The water's finally working! Praise the Creator!"

Shellinda withdrew her cloth and patted down Marcelle's wet tunic. "I knew she'd be okay!"

Shaking her head, Marcelle took in a deep breath and spoke again. "My spirit … is in … pri … prison."

"Your spirit?" Frederick took the facecloth and mopped her brow. "Just relax. Shellinda told me what you went through. It will probably take you a while to recover."

"No!" She dodged the cloth. "I am … on Major … Four."

Frederick spread out an arm. "This is Starlight, or Dracon as we called it. But we'll get you back to Major Four as soon as we can."

"I … I am … not here."

Frederick squinted. "Not here?"

"My … my spirit … is in … Meso … Meso …"

"Mesolantrum." He smiled as if talking to a child. "I wish we were there, and we'll get there eventually, but not until we free the slaves."

"Have to … stop Leo."

"Who is Leo?"

Marcelle slowed her respiration and concentrated. Explaining who Leo was would take too much effort, and trying to convince Frederick that she was really in a prison cell in Mesolantrum wasn't going to work, but maybe another strategy would.

"Where … is Adrian?"

"I'm not sure. According to the children, he was coming here with Regina and then going back to my cabin. He and I must have missed each other. Since we've been here for hours working on you and my leg, he should have arrived at the cabin long ago. I left him a message, so everything should be fine."

Again she struggled to speak. "I have … a message … for Adrian."

"What message is that?"

"Tell him … I love him."

Frederick drew his head back. "Really? That's a new development. I thought you two were rivals … well, friendly rivals, but not … um … involved."

"Tell him," she repeated.

"Okay. I will."

"And tell him ... I will ... bring soldiers."

Frederick smiled, again using the kind of smile adults give to daydreaming children. "Well, I hope you do. We could certainly use that."

"Cassabrie ... will help."

"Cassabrie? Who is Cassabrie?"

She shook her head. It would take too long to explain the situation with the opening of the portal. "How do I ... find the cabin?"

"No need to explain, Marcelle. You should rest."

She forced a shout. "Tell me!"

"Okay," he said, lifting a hand. "If it will calm you down."

As he paused to rewet the cloth, Marcelle listened to the peaceful sounds. In the background of flowing water, the children whispered excitedly. Something above crackled, making her look up. A network of intertwined branches constructed a ceiling. An animal, maybe a squirrel, was probably skittering around up there.

Frederick partially wrung out the cloth. "Do you know where the river flows into the barrier wall?"

She nodded.

"Then I'll explain the easiest way to find the cabin from there." He dabbed her forehead and cheeks as he talked. "If you follow the river southward and upstream, it splits into two smaller streams. One goes east toward the mining mesas, and the other continues generally south and into the wilderness, running parallel to the western part of the barrier wall. Eventually, you will go past the end of the wall. At that point, the western side of the stream is a horrific swamp, creating a natural barrier to keep slaves from venturing westward, so a wise traveler will stay on the eastern bank. Actually, either side is hazardous because of snakes and poisonous vines, but a good sword will hack those obstacles out of the way."

As Frederick paused again to wet the cloth, the crackling sound repeated. This time, Marcelle kept her head still as she tried to find the source. With the boy's lantern providing the only light, the entire ceiling looked like a mottled pattern of shifting shadows. One shadow stayed constant. The size of a large cat, it appeared to be crouching, ready to pounce, but with so many people around, it was likely not a danger.

"The stream will divide once more," Frederick continued, again dabbing her face. "From that point, follow the left-hand fork until you see a moss-covered log that bridges the stream. Turn left away from the log and walk until you reach an embankment where you'll have to climb the vines to get to the top. There, you will see a narrow path that runs through the woods to the southeast and leads directly to the cabin. This path is also a haunt for various beasts, but ... " He reprised the condescending smile. "I doubt they will be a concern for armed soldiers."

Marcelle dodged the cloth again and glared at him. "I will ... bring them. ... You will see."

"I know you would if you could." He grasped her wrist. "Let's see if you can stand."

He hoisted her to her feet, then slowly released her. She wobbled, her legs shaking. After a few seconds, everything turned black. A falling sensation followed along with excited chatter. The only words she could pick up were Frederick's.

"It's okay. I can carry her back now. My leg's fine." Then all fell silent.

Marcelle blinked open her eyes. Darkness still shrouded her vision, but now the wetness was gone. She was again lying on the bench in the prison cell.

She rose to a sitting position, making her chains clink. At least now she knew the way to the cabin. That's where Adrian probably was, and since Frederick left him a message, he wouldn't be worried.

Heaving a sigh, she lay back down. Morning would come soon, as would her execution. It would be best to try to sleep, but with no real body, was sleep necessary? Probably not. This shell of dirt she wore didn't seem tired. Maybe it would be better to come up with an idea to persuade Orion to remove the gag order. If he acquiesced, then she would have to be ready for her speech.

What words might set hearts on fire? What would get potential soldiers to shed their skirts and become men? Shame? Ridiculing cowards? Making them fear doing otherwise?

She shook her head. Fear motivates to action only until a greater fear arises. Shame fades from red to white in the face of danger. The fiery breath of a dragon burns away all memories of ridicule. Negative energy never lasts.

As she lay quietly, the image of Adrian appeared, again struggling against his chains at the crystalline stake. Another image followed, Adrian in battle in the forest on Major Four, using a pair of swords while combating Darien and his lackey simultaneously. What empowered him to fight with such passion? What transformed him into a raging bull?

Cassabrie said that love drives Adrian; love is the fuel for his fire. But how does a woman get a man to find the fountain of fire within? Could mere words kindle the flame? Or must he see the danger for himself? Yet, if she showed the people images of brutalized children, fear of her so-called sorcery might douse the flame.

She blew out another sigh. Whatever lay ahead, she had to be ready for the performance of her life.

ELEVEN

ADRIAN paced the floor in darkness, keeping his footfalls quiet for Regina, who slept peacefully on the bed of leaves. He strolled to the open door for the twentieth time and looked out, listening. Birdcalls filled the air with nighttime twitters, and a wolf howled in the distance, but no human sounds found their way to the cabin. Traveling with so many children, Frederick couldn't possibly keep them quiet.

Stepping out, he looked up at the sky. Trisarian shone brightly, painting the surrounding clouds yellow. What time might it be? Close to midnight? It didn't seem reasonable that Frederick would be gone so long, not with all those young children in tow. And with Drexel lurking out there like a crafty dragon, who could tell what trouble might be afoot? Even with Frederick's trapping skills, Drexel wasn't likely to be snared. He was too wary, never trusting anyone.

He walked back to Regina and stooped next to her, barely able to see her sleeping form in the darkness. Wearing her feather hat again, she seemed as content as could be. It was a shame to wake her up, but there wasn't much choice.

Just as he reached for her shoulder, she shot up, knocking her hat off. "Drexel!" she shouted.

He pulled her into his arms, wrapping her up tightly. "Don't worry. It's me, Adrian. Drexel's not here. He's not anywhere close. I would have heard him."

She heaved shallow breaths, her heart beating so rapidly, it pounded against his chest. "Not here," she said, her voice pulsing with her breaths. "At the healing trees. With Frederick and Marcelle. But Frederick doesn't know he's there."

"Don't worry. It was just a bad dream."

"Are you sure?" Her breathing slowed. "It seemed so real."

"Of course I'm sure. You don't even know what Drexel looks like, or even Frederick or Marcelle or the other children."

"I suppose you're right. I could've made them up in my mind." She nestled into Adrian's arms, her head resting against his chest. "Marcelle was really pretty in my dream, though. And strong, too. She has muscles like a man's."

"That's right. Did you get to feel her muscles while she was sleeping here?"

"Maybe. I don't remember." She reached up and touched him under his nose. "Drexel had this strange mustache. It had curls on the ends, like a—"

"Curls on the ends?" Adrian stiffened. "How could you know that?"

"You mean he does?"

"Tell me Marcelle's hair color."

"I don't know. It was too dark."

Adrian tried to imagine the scene Regina had conjured in her mind. What element could prove that it was more than a dream? "Did anyone say anything? Frederick? Marcelle?"

"They both did. Frederick talked a lot, but Marcelle didn't say much. She was still sick. She mentioned you and someone else with a strange name."

"A strange name? Do you remember it?"

"I think so." She paused a moment. "Cass ... Cassa something."

"Cassabrie?"

"That's it. You said it."

"We have to go." Adrian rose, setting Regina on her feet. "It's obvious you saw something real. No one else would know that name, not even Frederick."

Regina felt for her hat and put it on. "Who is Cassabrie?"

He took her hand and walked her toward the door. "She's a Starlighter, someone who can tell tales she hasn't seen."

"Like I just did?"

"Maybe." When they exited, he checked the sword at his hip and looked at the sky again. "I'm beginning to think you might be one, but Cassabrie can also make the tales come to life around her, like ghosts showing what happened. I didn't see any while you were dreaming."

"Could it have been too dark to see them?"

"That's reasonable." He led her around the cabin and toward the skunk tree. In the darkness, the trail was impossible to see. He would have to travel by memory. "From what I hear, Starlighters have red hair and green eyes. I noticed your green eyes, but I can't tell what color your hair is."

"I know." She pushed a hand under her hat and rubbed her scalp. "It's too short. I hope it grows back soon. But before it all fell out, it wasn't red."

"Okay, that might disprove the Starlighter theory."

"It was bright orange."

Laughing, Adrian stopped and touched her nose. "Regina, you are so funny sometimes."

"I am? Is that good?"

"It's excellent." He picked her up in a cradle and carried her, accelerating to a quick march. "We have to go faster."

"Do you want to know what Drexel was doing?"

Adrian gazed at her excited eyes, barely visible in the veiled moonlight. "Sure. Tell me everything."

Regina pointed upward. "He was in those tree branches, the ones above the spring, and as soon as Frederick and Marcelle left with the others, he climbed higher and higher until he met one of the white dragons."

Adrian stopped. "And then what?"

"That's all. The dream ended."

Adrian imagined Drexel talking to the lowest of the three white dragons. Whether the dragon was good or evil, surely he would tell Drexel how to unblock the river and stop the spring's upwelling. If Drexel thought the dragon could benefit him, he would comply. "If your dream is true, that means Frederick and the others are on their way back to the cabin. Maybe we'll meet them on the way."

"Maybe. Should we wait for them?"

"I think I should see what Drexel's up to. Like I said before, I want to talk to Frederick about those dragons before anyone tries to set them free." Adrian focused on the path. With Trisarian now peeking through the clouds, the narrow lane between the low-hanging branches of hardwoods and needle-laden conifers was clearer than before. Only the breeze stirred the foliage, no sign of returning cabin dwellers, either by sight, sound, or smell. How long would it take them to return? Would they even come this way? Their physical condition might influence the answers to both questions. "Did the healing waters help them?"

Regina nodded. "A lot for Frederick. He was walking like nothing happened. Marcelle talked some, but she didn't walk. She just sat in the water until Frederick helped her up."

"We'd better get going. Maybe we can—" A strange odor filtered in. Besides the distant skunk tree, something else tinged the air, something alive, wet, and foul. He lowered his voice to a whisper. "Do you smell that?"

"The skunk tree?"

"No. It's more like—" A rustling sound cut him off. He stooped behind a bush and set Regina on her feet at his side. Letting out a low shush, he withdrew his sword. A human figure broke through the tree line and emerged onto the path. Holding a thick branch with a sharpened point, he looked both ways, apparently listening carefully. No taller than Orlan, he appeared to be about twelve years old. As the boy turned their way, a feature on his face became clear. He had only one eye.

The boy turned toward the trees and waved an arm. "It's clear. Come on."

A smaller boy pushed past a pine bough, followed by a little girl. Then, as if someone had broken a dam of juvenile humanity, child after child walked onto the path until dozens filled the forest lane. The boy with the branch, now in the middle of a sea of children, began touching heads, apparently counting.

"What do you see?" Regina whispered.

"Children. Lots of them." Adrian tucked his sword away and, taking Regina's hand, straightened to his full height. "Hail, friend!"

The boy's head jerked up. "Who's there?"

"Adrian Masters." As a whispered buzz rose from the children, Adrian slowly closed the gap. "Who are you?"

"The name's Wallace." He lowered his branch. "I came here to find Frederick Masters. Are you related to him?"

"Yes!" Keeping a hold on Regina's hand, Adrian waded into the crowd. With heights ranging from his thighs to just above his waist, the children appeared to be from four to eight years old. Displaying protruding ribs and gaunt faces, they had to be half-starved.

As he passed, some touched his hips and hands with fawning fingers, while a few whispered hopeful questions.

"Is this the refuge?"

"Did we make it?"

"Who is that kid with the hat?"

When Adrian reached Wallace, he extended his hand. "I'm glad to meet you."

Wallace took his hand and shook it vigorously. "Not as glad as I am to meet you."

"How do you know my brother?"

"If you mean Frederick," Wallace said, "I've never met him. I do know your brother Jason, though."

"Jason?" Adrian's heart pounded. "Where did you last see him?"

"At one of the pheterone mines. It's a long story, but since he killed a dragon, they took him away. Elyssa and I found Arxad who told us Jason is on his way to the Northlands with Koren."

"Yes, I learned that from Arxad as well. I was hoping to get more recent news."

Wallace shrugged. "That's the last I heard."

Adrian scanned the children again. "Where is Elyssa?"

"She went to find Jason. She and I set up a camp not too far from here, but someone came by and took one of the girls while I was asleep. Her screams woke me up, and one of the other girls told us that a man carried her away. We've been looking for her ever since."

"Drexel!" Adrian hissed through his teeth. "He keeps stooping lower."

"I wonder if he was the murderer," Wallace mumbled.

"What do you mean?"

Wallace leaned close and whispered. "I don't want to scare any of the younger kids, but one of our older boys was scouting our path, and he followed a scent, something that smelled like a skunk. Anyway, he found a boy whose throat was slit. He wasn't one of the cattle children. Too well fed. The blood was still warm, so he hadn't been dead for very long. That's one reason we're staying together and on the move."

Adrian stared straight ahead. They had found Zeb. Drexel had likely killed him and hidden the body, but the leaves from the skunk tree led the scout to where he lay. Why would Drexel kill him? Did Zeb try to rescue the kidnapped girl? They might never know.

Fighting back a surge of pity, Adrian shook his head. "Poor Zeb."

"Zeb? Was that his name?"

Adrian nodded. His throat cramped. He couldn't say a word.

"So," Wallace continued, "I'm worried about what happened to Sarah."

"The girl Drexel took?"

"Right." Wallace nodded toward Regina. "When I first saw this boy, I thought he might be Sarah. Sarah has flyaway hair, but then I saw he's just wearing a feather hat, so I knew he wasn't her."

Regina stomped her foot. "I'm a girl!"

"Oh!" Wallace laughed nervously. "Sorry."

Adrian swallowed, loosening his throat. "It's all right, Regina. He didn't mean anything by it."

"If you say so." She gave Wallace an icy glare. "Just don't forget I'm a girl."

Smiling, Wallace lifted a hand of surrender. "I promise."

Adrian looked into the section of the forest from which Wallace had emerged, an area of closely packed trees and brambles. "Why did you go through there? Did you find a trail?"

"I smelled that skunk odor, so I decided to follow it. I thought it might lead to the killer. I guessed that the killer and the kidnapper might be the same person."

"You're a good tracker." Adrian scanned the children. With heads down and mouths quiet, they appeared to be exhausted. "Come with me. We have shelter."

"For forty children?" Wallace asked.

"It will be a tight squeeze. We might have to sleep in shifts."

"Who will look for Sarah?"

207

"I will." Adrian nodded at Wallace's branch. "Are you good with that?"

Wallace looked at the point. "Not really. We're not allowed to have weapons. But I can ram it through someone if I have to."

"Good enough. Since Drexel has a girl, I don't think he'll go back to the cabin. I'll leave you to guard the others while I look for Drexel and Sarah. I have a good idea where they might be."

"The trees," Regina whispered. "And I'm coming with you."

Adrian clasped her shoulder. "You need to stay with Wallace. I can go a lot faster without you."

"But I can help." Her wandering eyes pleaded. "I know things you don't know."

"Like what?"

"Like where Drexel is right now." She bounced on her toes, her tone growing impatient. "You have to trust me!"

"How could you know where Drexel is?"

"Remember how I saw him in my dream? How I knew what he looks like?"

Adrian nodded. "I remember."

"It's the same now when I'm awake." Regina grasped his hand. "Let me come. Since it's dark, I can find him better than you can."

Adrian gazed into her eyes, sparkling with life in the moonlight. Without a doubt, she had proven her ability to see Drexel. Maybe she could help. "Okay. I'll take you. Let's see if we can get these kids some food and a place to sleep, and we'll go."

✳   ✳   ✳   ✳   ✳   ✳

Sitting on the bench, Marcelle stared at the cell door, not quite as dark now that more light seeped in through the gap at the bottom. Morning had arrived and with it the rays of dawn, likely coming through the skylights in the courtroom's antechamber. With the execution scheduled for one hour after sunrise, someone would soon come to escort her to the stake.

Something clicked at the door. The lock turned with a low squeak, and the door opened, revealing Orion carrying a lantern. After glancing over his shoulder, he walked in, careful to keep the door ajar, and set the lantern on the wall bracket. He stooped next to the ring on the floor and lifted one of the chains. "This is unfit adornment for someone of your stature, Marcelle. The Stafford name deserves better than this."

She crossed her arms. "Did you come to have me burned at the stake, or are you going to mock me to death?"

Chuckling, he dropped the chain and straightened. "I came to ask you a favor."

"A favor?" Marcelle squinted at him. "You're going to kill me. Why should I do you a favor?"

"The guard told me about seeing someone at your door last night, a red-haired girl wearing a blue cloak. What do you know about her?"

Marcelle leaned to see around him. The guard didn't seem to be at his post. "Why do you want to know?"

"You are aware that we hope to rid the land of witches, Diviners, and other practitioners of sorcery, so we would like to find her." He took a step closer, his voice now taking on a slight tremor. "You see, she appeared to have slid under the door from your cell, so it's fair to assume that she is a sorceress of some kind and that you saw her while she was here."

Marcelle scanned his face and posture, both exposing a hint of anxiety. Might feeding him some tidbits help her situation? It probably wouldn't hurt to see what he had in mind. "What do you think she was? Some sort of phantom?"

"I'm not sure. I had an experience with a creature of similar description many years ago, so I want to know if she is the same person I met." He glanced at the door. "So did you see her? Do you know who she is?"

Staying seated, Marcelle loosened her arms and leaned back against the wall. "Since you're going to kill me, why should I say anything?"

"I see your point." He clasped his hands and pressed his thumbs together. "You want to exchange information for clemency."

"Are you willing to make such an exchange?"

"It depends on how valuable the information is."

She pulled at a protruding thread on the bench's cushion, feigning detachment. She couldn't appear to be too eager. "If I give you the information, I will have nothing left to bargain with."

"I cannot argue with your point. Do you have a solution?"

She looked at him, raising her brow. "How about a simpler trade? No matter what my information is, allow me to stand at the stake without a gag."

"A gag?" Orion nodded slowly. "Oh, yes, I remember Leo's request. He seemed quite insistent. I didn't see any harm in granting it."

"Of course," Marcelle said, copying his nod. "But there is also no harm in granting my request. Allow me to speak freely while at the stake. Just ten minutes. That's all I ask."

Orion gave her a skeptical stare. "Your request appears to be benign, but its lack of real value to you makes me suspicious. What are you hiding from me?"

"Hiding? What could a condemned prisoner who is shackled to a stake hide?" Marcelle altered to a condescending tone. "What are you afraid of, Orion? Is it Maelstrom? Surely you have enough authority as governor to rescind this order and repel the counselor's obsessions, don't you?"

Orion's face hardened. "Patronizing me will not help your cause. I'm just trying to discern why the freedom to speak is so important to you."

She returned her focus to the cushion, picking at the purple thread until it unraveled enough to make a tiny hole. "I assume you are unwilling to tell me why the female phantom is so important to you."

"You're right. I am unwilling."

She glanced at him furtively. "Then we're on level ground, and I assume it would be patronizing to ask why you fear the words of a woman who is tied to a stake."

"Yes, it would be patronizing." After maintaining his stare for a few moments, Orion let out a sigh. "Very well. I grant your request. There will be no gag, and your arms will be free. You will have ten minutes to speak from the stake before you burn."

She continued pulling on the thread, making the hole big enough to fit her fingertip. "And how will I know you will keep your promise?"

"I don't suppose my word as a gentleman will suffice."

Marcelle shook her head. "Not a chance."

"Do you have a suggestion?"

"A witness to our agreement." She released the thread and looked up at him. "Someone we both know who has unquestioned integrity."

"Given that parameter, I think you should name the person. You might not trust my estimation of integrity."

"That's true. I don't." Marcelle bit her lip. He would have to be someone in the military, someone she might be able to persuade to mount an invading force into Dracon. "Captain Reed?"

Orion nodded. "Reed is a good man. I will summon him at once."

"And I want him to lead me to the stake. I don't want Counselor Leo to lay a hand on me."

A scowl etched Orion's face. "How many more demands are you planning to add?"

"I'm not sure yet, but the sooner Captain Reed arrives, the less time I'll have to think about it."

His face slackening, Orion laughed softly. "Marcelle, if nothing else, you are certainly a persuasive woman."

"Then allow me one more word of persuasion."

"And that is?"

"You've seen the power Maelstrom—"

"I wish you wouldn't call him that. He is not—"

"He is dangerous!" Marcelle shot to her feet. "And I will call him whatever I please. Think about it. With his power, why is he here? As important as the Counselor position is, it was a step down for him."

Orion gave a light shrug. "He obviously has an obsession with rooting out sorcery and—"

"Oh, stop it! He didn't come here out of the goodness of his heart. His only obsession is with gaining power. Witch hunting is just his pretext, his mask." She jabbed a finger toward Orion's nose. "And when he finally removes that mask, you'll learn that you can't control him. Then he will take your place and command our military forces. Mesolantrum can muster a fine army, and if he uses his magical influence, he can forge alliances that will overwhelm Tarkton. Maelstrom will soon be king, and you will be a trampled pawn."

Orion's expression didn't flinch. "An intriguing theory, but you have forgotten one factor."

She set her fists on her hips. "And that is?"

"I am no fool. You might not approve of my ideals or methods, but you would do well to honor my intellect. I would not have brought Leo here if not for the safeguards I have put in place."

"Safeguards?" She cocked her head. Normally Orion wouldn't provide any further information, but maybe her Starlighter gifts, even if weaker than Cassabrie's, could draw out his secrets.

Focusing on his eyes, she altered to an alluring tone. "What do you mean by safeguards?"

"Let's just say that the military commanders would not dare make a move without my approval. I have leverage that our new counselor cannot remove."

Marcelle batted her eyes, feigning surprise. "You wouldn't stoop to threats, would you?"

"Not threats. Certainty. It seems that a few families have reported missing children, and it would be a shame if they were never found."

Biting her tongue, she kept her expression calm. This monster had to be stopped, but blistering him verbally now would dam the stream of information. "Missing children," she said with a hum. "Do you have any idea where they are?"

Orion laughed again. "Your anger makes your attempts to probe my mind all too transparent, Marcelle, but I will tell you that the children are well cared for. My purpose is to protect the king, and as long as Leo stays in check, the king will enjoy a prosperous reign for many years, and as long as the military leaders maintain appropriate discipline and honor the line of command, everyone will be safe."

"Safe," she murmured as she crossed her arms in front. "Just summon Captain Reed, and let's get on with this."

"Very well. He is part of the security detail for your execution, so it shouldn't take long. Still, I am not sure whether or not I will grant your desire to be led to the stake by him. I have to throw Maelstrom some kind of bone in this affair." Orion walked out and closed the door behind him, dimming the cell again, though the lantern remained on the wall mount, providing a weak, flickering light. A moment later, the lock clicked.

Marcelle sat heavily on the bench. The scoundrel! Threatening children to keep himself in power! And with the military leaders under his thumb, what good would it do to try to muster an army? They would be too paralyzed by fear to join her.

She grasped a chain and threaded it between her fingers, letting the links drop to the floor one by one as the minutes passed. The lantern's glow flickered on her hands. In the wavering light, her fingers appeared to be burning, writhing in the dancing fire. Soon, if her plan failed, she would be in a real fire, a spirit trapped inside a burning shell.

She looked at the door. When would Captain Reed arrive? Might his children be among those Orion held captive? If so, maybe he would be sympathetic to her cause and willing to listen to a plan.

But what plan? To rescue the slaves from Dracon? To rescue a sword maiden from the stake? Or to rescue children from an evil tyrant here on Major Four?

Marcelle dropped the chain and sighed. The slaves on Starlight would have to wait. Her own rescue was now secondary. The children of Major Four had to come first.

＊　　　＊　　　＊　　　＊　　　＊　　　＊

Adrian stood at the outside edge of the healing trees, the light of dawn sending his shadow between two trunks. Holding Regina's hand, he tapped his sword high on the bark. "You saw Drexel up there?"

She nodded. "But only in my dream. He's not there now."

"Do you know where he is?"

Staring straight ahead, she spoke in a hush. "It is too dim to see what's around him, but he's wet. I can tell that. A girl is with him, Sarah I suppose."

"Are they at the spring?"

A muffled cry sounded from within the glade.

"That answers my question. Come on." Holding Regina's hand, he squeezed between the trunks and into the darker interior. As they skulked closer, the bubbling stream masked their splashes, though the water seemed shallower than before.

Soon, Drexel's voice rose above the din. "Try once more, and then we can stop. I promise."

A girl's voice followed, punctuated by sniffles. "But you promised last time."

"I know. But you almost have it. Just nudge it a little bit more. If you stop the water, I'll let you go back to the others."

Bending low, Adrian drew within a few steps, now close enough to see Sarah standing at the opposite edge of the spring's opening. Drexel stooped next to her, holding an axe in one hand and her ragged braid in the other. Wearing nothing but dripping short trousers, she sobbed through her words. "Okay. ... I'll try once more. ... Just don't cut me again."

Touching Regina's lips to signal for quiet, Adrian advanced a foot. If he could get within five paces, he could charge and knock Drexel down before he had a chance to react.

Just as Adrian took another step, Drexel's eyes flared. He grabbed Sarah around the waist from behind and held the axe's blade next to her throat. "Don't come any closer," he shouted, his voice quaking, "or I'll slit her throat!"

Adrian stood upright, his fist tight around the hilt of his sword. "Are you playing the coward's role again? Hiding behind a starving little girl?"

"You give me no choice, Adrian. I am merely trying to survive."

Regina tugged on Adrian's belt from behind and whispered, "Keep him talking." Adrian reached to grab her, but her hand slipped from his grasp. With barely a sound, she blended into the darkness.

"Survival as a cowardly dog is worse than death."

"Stop the preaching! You've been reading too many hero story-books!" Drexel's breaths came fast and heavy as his words squeezed through his straining throat. "Only fools never learn that survival is the most basic instinct. They think dying as a martyr is honorable, but their dead ears cannot hear the eulogy from the grave."

Adrian scanned the area. What was Regina planning? It seemed clear that Drexel was unaware of her presence. Maybe she could create a distraction that would allow a rescue, but she needed their voices to keep track of where they were. Appealing to Drexel's desire to pontificate might work. "I see your point, but won't the martyr's descendants be blessed? You have to admit that's a benefit to heroism."

"A temporary benefit." Taking in a deep breath, Drexel rose slowly, the axe blade still at Sarah's throat. Bare-chested and wet, she shivered in place. "Heroic acts warp into fanciful myths that no one really believes. We all assume that the hero was motivated by the desire for fame, which even you seem to confess."

"I was simply asking a question. I am motivated by love, and I hope to avoid fame."

"Then I will grant your wish. Just throw your sword next to me and leave. No harm will come to you or this girl, which is what you and I both desire. Since it would be madness for me to relate this unsavory event, no one will ever know what happened here."

Adrian again scanned the glade. Of course Drexel would never let the girl live. Otherwise, she would eventually tell the tale.

Walking on tiptoes, Regina approached Drexel from behind. Adrian forced himself not to focus on her. If she were to be successful with a distraction, he had to create one of his own. He laid his sword across his palms. "Where shall I throw it?"

Drexel nodded at the space to his left. "There will be fine."

Regina drew within three steps, a hand reaching toward Drexel's head.

"Are you ready?" Adrian asked.

Both Drexel and Regina nodded, Regina now only a step behind him.

Moving slowly, Adrian regripped the hilt. "Here it comes." With an underhanded motion, he tossed the sword to Drexel's left, aiming for a point out of reach. When it splashed at the perfect spot, Drexel reached for it, momentarily loosening his hold on Sarah.

Regina grabbed his hair and jerked him back. The axe flew from his grip and sailed into the darkness. Adrian charged. Drexel lunged for the sword and scooped it into his grasp. Regina grabbed Sarah and tried to push her away, but they both plunged into the spring, Sarah first and Regina dropping after her.

Adrian skidded to a stop at the edge of the spring's opening. Gasping for breath, Drexel stood a few steps beyond the opposite side. Water dripped from his hair and mustache as he pointed the blade at Adrian. "I am not the swordsman you are, but I'll wager I can defeat any unarmed opponent."

Adrian glanced at the spring. Water streamed around his feet more slowly than before, and noxious gasses rose with every bursting bubble. He dropped to his knees and thrust an arm deep into the hole, but there was no sign of the girls.

Drexel leaped forward, swinging the sword. Adrian ducked under the blade, rolled to his back, and thrust out his legs. His feet planted in Drexel's stomach, sending him flying backwards. Still clutching the sword, he landed on his bottom and slid out of sight.

Adrian rocked to his feet and jumped into the spring. For a moment, his hips wedged at the sides of the opening, then like a slurping drain, the water pulled him down through a vertical tunnel until he splashed into a rushing current. His feet struck ground first, then his hands plunged up to his wrists in the sandy bottom of a shallow stream. His momentum sent him into a horizontal roll that deposited him at the water's edge.

Sitting up, he extended an arm. "Regina? Are you here?" His voice echoed in the cavern.

"I'm here. Sarah's here, too. She moved a stone that was blocking the river."

Reaching again, Adrian grasped a hand. "Is this Regina or Sarah?"

"Regina. Sarah's right here."

She guided Adrian's hand to a wet, trembling wrist. He pulled both girls close and wrapped them up in his arms. "Is either of you hurt?"

"Not me," Regina said. "Just wet."

"I'm wet and cold." Sarah shivered in his embrace, her bare back hot to the touch.

Adrian rubbed her back briskly. She seemed to be feverish and suffering from chills. "So you swam down here and dislodged a stone?"

"A big one. I kept pulling and pulling, but I always ran out of air before I could get it loose, so I had to swim back up. Drexel kept making me go again until I got the rock out of the river's way. He wanted the water to stop coming up the hole."

"Where is the rock? I could push it back in place so we could swim up with the spring."

"That way."

"Are you pointing?"

"Yes." Sarah grasped his wrist and pushed it in the downstream direction. "You can almost reach it."

"Let's get you to a safe place." After guiding the girls onto the bank, Adrian rose, lifting a hand as he straightened. When his fingers touched the ceiling, he halted his rise and stayed bent over at the waist. He took in a breath. The air was fetid, the same smell the spring's belches carried to the surface.

He walked through the calf-deep water. After only two paces, his legs bumped against something hard. Feeling with his hands, he painted a mental image. The hard object was the stone—round and about a foot and a half high. The water rushed around it on both sides and exited the chamber through a hole in a wall that was slightly smaller than the rock. It seemed that Sarah had taken advantage of the fact that the water, which had filled this cavern at the time, had buoyed the stone's weight, so she was able to pull it away from the hole just enough to allow the current to sneak around the edges.

He touched the outer borders of the wall's exit hole, perhaps just big enough to crawl through. The edges were somewhat soft, probably the result of years of being assaulted by a never-ending barrage of water.

Using both hands he pushed the rock into place, sealing the hole. Water splashed against the blockade and began to rise. He lunged back and stooped with the girls, wrapping each in an arm. "Get ready to hold your breath. We'll ride the water up to—"

A loud crunch sounded along with the splatter of debris striking water. As the splashing eased, the water level receded. Sighing, Adrian set the girls down again, crawled to the hole, and felt around. The rock still sat in the middle of the stream where he had left it, but the hole was now much larger, probably big enough to walk through. Apparently the new surge of water had broken the edges of the hole away.

"Well, we won't be swimming to the top with the current." Adrian looked up and again created a picture in his mind, this time an image of what might be happening on ground level. Drexel succeeded in stopping the spring's upwelling, and now he had the sword and probably an axe as well. What would he do? Use the blades to get the Bloodless out of the trees? Go to the cabin and kidnap another child? Maybe both.

"Can we climb?" Regina asked. "I'm a good climber."

"I'm not sure." Adrian rose and, reaching up with both hands, ran his fingers along the ceiling until he found the tunnel leading to the surface. Its smooth sides and narrow width made the prospects of climbing low, especially while carrying a girl. Even if he could get to the top alone, without a rope, there would be no way to pull them out.

Sighing again, he shook his head, though they likely couldn't see it in the dark. "There's no way."

"So what do we do?"

"I'm thinking." He stared into the blackness. The only other choice seemed to be to follow the river, but in which direction? With both girls so cold and wet, making the wrong decision could cost them their lives.

Listening to the water, he drew a map in his mind. Upstream appeared to head toward the rivulet where the boys found Frederick's sword. Maybe that stream plunged underground somewhere nearby. After finding the entry point and digging out, it would be easy to get back to the cabin. Yet, downstream might come out somewhere beyond the barrier wall, and he could take the girls to the Northlands where they would be out of danger for good.

He shook his head. Too cold. They would freeze before he could get there. Still, it might be worth seeing where it came out. Maybe all the refugee children could escape that way. And since rivers tended to get wider as they progressed, there might be plenty of room to walk between here and wherever the river finally surfaced. Not only that, he could allow Sarah to bathe in the healing river all along the way. The longer she applied the water, the better her chances of being healed would be.

Crouching, he scooped up a handful of water and drank it. The river would, indeed, provide a cool, healing flow, but choosing to follow it in either direction would allow Drexel to have his way with the healing trees. If he released the white dragons, who could tell what evils they might unleash on the world? The result might bring about the deaths of many more little girls than Regina and Sarah. He could try to climb by himself, promising to return. The girls would be safe here for a little while, but with Drexel standing up there with a sword ready to whack off any head that popped up from the ground, returning to the surface might be impossible.

Adrian drew in a deep breath. Taking care of the girls in his care was the best choice. He would have to trust others to watch over everyone else. Frederick was still out there somewhere, and maybe Marcelle found healing in the spring after all. And didn't the Creator care for the children of Starlight more than did any of the rescuers from Major Four?

"Are you still thinking?" Regina asked. "You've been awfully quiet."

"I'm finished ... for now."

"I can help you think, you know. I told you I could help you."

"You were right. You did a great job distracting Drexel, but I was worried when you two fell in the hole."

"Oh, we didn't fall. I pushed Sarah and jumped in after her so we could move the stone and hide down there. I knew you'd fight better if you weren't worried about him hurting one of us."

"That was good thinking," Adrian said, laughing. "I wish I had known ahead of time. I was worried anyway."

Regina sighed. "I'm sorry. I was hoping you'd figure it out."

"I probably should have. I need to learn to trust you completely." He took a hand of each girl. "Let's see if we can find a way out of here."

TWELVE

WITH the rays of dawn shining through the palace's rear doorway, Marcelle looked around the brightening lobby. Captain Reed stood at attention to her left, Maelstrom to her right, each holding one of her chains. Out in the Enforcement Zone, a crowd had already gathered, watching the executioner as he arranged bundles of wood at the burning stake's base. Orion paced near the perimeter, pointing at the wood as if giving instructions.

"You are lucky," Maelstrom said. "The governor is showing you far more mercy than I would."

Marcelle stared straight ahead, not wanting to look the Starlighter in the eye. "You mean besides countermanding the gag order?"

He nodded. "I would use slow-burning green wood to make you suffer for a long time, but Orion is placing manna bark around the stake. It burns quickly and provides a sedating effect. You will likely feel very little pain."

"But if I'm sedated ..." Marcelle let the thought die. No use tipping her hand to Maelstrom about her plan to whip potential soldiers into a passionate frenzy. Since Orion had agreed to allow her ten minutes to speak before the execution commenced, the sedation issue might not matter since the wood wouldn't yet be on fire. Still, doubt remained. Orion had already shown signs of negating their bargain. Only moments ago he had refused her request to be led only by Captain Reed, which allowed her to reciprocate by holding back information about Cassabrie, at least for now. She had promised to reveal everything while at the stake, which was enough for him to rescind the gag order. At least his desire to hear about Cassabrie would force him to allow her speech to finish.

She turned to Captain Reed, a broad-shouldered man with a slim waist and a graying beard, and looked at his hands, both clutching the chain so tightly, his knuckles had turned white. A wedding band adorned his left ring finger, and two red squares and one blue square had been stitched onto his uniform's cuff, a sign to anyone who might find his body on the battlefield that he had two daughters and a son to care for at home. Every region in the kingdom used the same system, though sometimes the colors differed.

Shifting her gaze to his face, she studied his expression—solemn, anxious. Orion likely held one or more of these children captive.

"What are their names?" she whispered.

He responded in a low voice. "Whose names?"

"Your son and two daughters." She nodded at his sleeve.

"Oh, yes." As he traced the outline of one of the squares, his jaw quivered slightly. "I prefer not to discuss them at this time."

She studied his finger. The tip continued tracing the red square closest to his wrist, not deviating to the other patches. She leaned closer and spoke in the barest of whispers. "I can help you get her back."

Captain Reed gave her a quizzical stare, but just as he pursed his lips to reply, Maelstrom barked, "The signal is given. Let's send this witch to the hell she deserves." He marched ahead, pulling on the chain and jerking Marcelle along.

She looked back. Captain Reed, still holding one of her chains, kept pace, blinking at her. She signaled with her head to come closer. As he neared, she whispered, "Stay close after he ties me to the stake."

"Silence!" Maelstrom bellowed, jerking the chain again. "You will have your opportunity to say your last words in a moment."

Marcelle followed Maelstrom out the rear exit, now unguarded. Where was Gregor? Had he escaped the Tark guards? If so, might he and Father and Dunwoody be carrying out the plan? With Orion inspecting the pyre so carefully, they might not have had a chance to hide the sword in the wood.

As she marched, silence descended on the crowd. The throng separated, creating a path to the stake. Every soul peered at her in wonder, eyes wide and mouths agape. Some gave her tremulous smiles, while others scowled. No one displayed a neutral aspect. It seemed that they were either for her or against her.

Forcing a smile, she met each gaze. Maybe a dose of friendliness would give her detractors something to ponder.

Among the sea of humanity, Father, Dunwoody, and Gregor were nowhere to be found. Unfamiliar faces dotted the masses. Several at the front wore orange-and-black uniforms, similar to Maelstrom's. His personal soldiers from Tarkton were making their presence known. Orion had to be pretty confident in his position to allow such an obvious show of strength from his potential usurper.

Ahead, the stake loomed at the center of the stacked wood, like a bare tree trunk protruding from the midst of its fallen branches. A space of about a square foot had been cleared in front of the stake as well as a foot-wide path leading to it from one side.

Orion stood at the edge of the pyre near the path. Carrying a burning torch, his expression was the only stoic one among the witnesses. Maelstrom stopped at the path, pulled a key from his pocket, and unlocked Marcelle's manacles. As the chains dropped to the ground, she glared at her captors. While Orion remained expressionless, a smug grin formed on Maelstrom's face. He untied a rope from around his waist, unwinding multiple loops before letting an arm-length section dangle from his hand. "I have tested this and found the crystals to be fireproof."

Turning, Marcelle looked at the gallows. The hangman's noose was no longer there. She shifted back and studied the rope. Particles embedded within the fibers sparkled in the rising sun.

She swallowed. The truth-detecting rope. The crystals would cut into her skin and turn black if she uttered a lie. But what did that matter? She planned to tell everyone the truth about everything.

"Proceed," Orion said, waving the torch. "Let her speak her mind and then let us be done with her."

Captain Reed let go of her chain. Marcelle looked back at him, giving him a questioning stare. Why wasn't he following? With his hands folded behind his back and his head down, he gave no hint as to what he was thinking.

Maelstrom guided her along the path, a hand on her shoulder as he prodded her from behind. As they neared the end, the height of the wood rose to chest level. When they reached the cleared space in front of the stake, she stepped up to the prisoner's block and stood calmly, forcing a stoic expression.

After circling behind her, Maelstrom looped the rope around the stake, then around her throat and chest. As he fastened it behind her, he growled a whisper into her ear. "You have no gag, witch, but this rope will make you regret every word you speak, and it will reveal any lies you try to utter. I have a suspicion about what you really are, so I will be back to collect the crystals when the embers cool." With a final tug, he tightened the knot and walked backwards down the path, pulling wood from each side to fill in the gap.

Orion withdrew a sandglass from an inner pocket and displayed it in his fingers. "My cook uses this for timing eggs. The sand lasts for five minutes, but it will be sufficient for your ten-minute reprieve. I will merely let the sands run through twice."

Marcelle glanced at Captain Reed. He made no effort to come closer. She swallowed, but even that motion tightened the rope, causing it to cut into her throat. Although little more than dust, her body again registered pain. "You have been unfaithful, Governor. You promised no gag and time to speak, but you have allowed Counselor Leo to stifle my speech far more effectively than if a gag were in place."

Obviously trying to hide a smile, Orion shook his head. "I will move the rope from your throat as soon as you tell me about the girl with the hood."

Marcelle frowned. Between the cutting rope and the burning torch, he held all the leverage. Could she reveal more about Cassabrie? What might he do with the information? Maybe telling the most benign facts would be enough. "She is a wandering spirit, a girl who died long ago, and she has the ability to tell amazing tales that mesmerize her hearers. It takes great strength to withstand her prowess, so a wise man takes heed and stays away from her."

Orion set the flame closer to the wood. "Do you believe her to be a sorceress?"

As the torch crackled and popped, Marcelle glanced at Maelstrom. He had backed away at least three steps. "I am not qualified to judge, Governor. Since you believe me to be a sorceress, what validity would my evaluation have?"

"A fair statement." Orion nodded at Maelstrom. "I think we will learn nothing more from her. Move the rope from her throat."

"Governor," Maelstrom said, "we have already given this sorceress more liberties than she deserves. You have kept your word, and now she demands—"

"Allow me!" Captain Reed said, raising a hand. "I will obey your will."

Orion scowled at Maelstrom. "Very well. A condemned prisoner is allowed such a simple request, and a captain in the army who is loyal will soon find new decorations on his chest."

His fists clenched, Maelstrom bowed and backed away several more steps. Then, standing at attention again, he fixed his stare on Orion. "The Governor is wise to reward his most loyal supporters. He knows that some powerful men in his service might be able to usurp him at any moment, in spite of his ever-present bodyguards, so giving honor is judicious."

Marcelle scanned the onlookers standing near Orion. Two muscular young men dressed in Mesolantrum attire clutched the hilts of their swords and stepped to the front of the crowd, apparently Orion's bodyguards.

Captain Reed climbed the pile of wood, dropped to ground level, and stood behind her. "Speak quickly," he whispered as he loosened the rope around her throat. "I cannot dawdle here for very long."

Trying not to move her lips, she whispered in reply. "Help me muster an army. Our first task will be to rescue your daughter and any others who have been kidnapped. Then we will march on Dracon."

He shifted the loop down to her waist. "Dracon is a myth."

"No. I have been there myself. I will prove it in a moment."

"How will you keep the children from harm?"

"By capturing Orion."

He retied the knot. "Are you serious?"

"Look at the rope. Are the crystals glowing?"

"They are."

"That means I'm telling the truth. I'll prove that as well. When I get the men fired up, we will be able to build the army secretly. In the meantime, I'll work on a plan to capture Orion before we go to Dracon."

"But how will you escape the fire?"

"A plan is in the works, but if I fail—"

"Marcelle!" Orion waved the torch. "If you have something to say, kindly share it with the others, as you promised. With everyone waiting to hear from you, it is impolite to carry on a private conversation with Captain Reed."

"I was simply explaining to him how I was planning to escape this execution." She looked down at the rope around her waist. The crystals within turned dark.

"I believe you," Captain Reed whispered. "But I can do nothing to help you until my daughter is freed." He jumped up to the pile, walked carefully down to the edge, and stood at the side, his arms crossed over his chest.

"The black crystals in the rope prove your lie." Orion laughed. "I hope you don't plan to waste your ten minutes by speaking falsehoods."

She fixed her stare on him. "I plan to reveal to these people the truths that have been hidden for one hundred years."

"Very well." Orion turned to the crowd. "But let it be known that the rope detects only what she believes to be a lie. It is possible for her to utter an untruth, believing it to be true. In such a case, the rope's crystals will not turn black. As a sorceress who has sold her soul to evil, she likely has been deceived about many things. We will have to take great care in discerning fact from fiction."

Marcelle pushed against the encircling ropes, trying to catch a deep breath. "You are one to talk. Letting Counselor Leo come here proves that you have the discernment of a tumbleweed in a tornado."

"Is that so?" Orion turned the sandglass over and set it on the ground. "And is my discernment any worse than yours? I promised you ten minutes to speak before your execution." He pushed the torch under the edge of the wood. "That's about how long it will take for the fire to reach you."

"What?" Marcelle fought the ropes again, but the shards cut through her clothes, pricking her skin. "You tricked me!"

"I did no such thing. I am merely keeping my promise exactly according to my words." He nudged the sandglass with his shoe. "I suggest that you begin."

Turning her head back and forth, Marcelle scanned the crowd again. Where were Dunwoody and Gregor? As the flames crawled slowly toward her, she looked down into the wood. No sign of the sword. Maybe Orion's eagle eyes kept them from depositing it there.

"Has the loquacious lady suddenly become speechless?" Grinning, Orion spread out an arm. "Come now! We are all waiting for the promised oratory. Surely you won't waste your final request to die without a gag."

She tried to spit at him, but nothing came out. "Someday you'll choke on your own tongue, you vile serpent!"

"Marcelle!" someone called from the crowd. "Speak! You're running out of time!"

She looked for the source. A gray-haired man ducked out of sight. Could he have been Dunwoody?

Turning her head to avoid the smoke, she took in a deep breath. Although she didn't need to breathe, she had to inhale in order to speak. Would the manna's sedative affect her? Only time would tell.

She focused on Orion again and called out, "Governor Orion, you asked me to reveal the truth about the female your guard witnessed outside my cell, but since you are so ignorant, you need to know a bit more history. She comes from a planet called Starlight, the same planet we call Dracon, and she has traveled here through a portal between our worlds."

As a wave of murmurs raced across the crowd and the flames marched closer, Marcelle continued. "Now I know this sounds strange to all of you, and since you can see glowing crystals in the rope, you likely already think me mad. Yet, even a madwoman is unable to display what she has never seen. If I were to show you a leaf, you would know that I have been near a tree. If I were to show you a feather, you would know that I have been in contact with a bird. But if I were to show you a scale, would you believe that it came from a dragon?" She shook her head. "Not likely, for scales cover a number of animals. What about a claw? No. An eagle has similar claws. A long, sharp tooth? No again. The mountain bears have teeth every bit as long and sharp as those from a dragon. But if I were to show you an entire dragon, would you believe?"

A slight wave of dizziness made her head swim. She had to fight the sedative! Closing her eyes, she spread out her arms, her palms pointing skyward. "I stood in the midst of deprivation. Children marched in a staggered line. Bleeding from whip marks on their backs, they dragged pails laden with stones. For some, dirt and bloodstains served as their only clothing, while others covered their loins with filthy rags. With ribs protruding from emaciated bodies, they scratched and clawed for bread crumbs thrown from the sky.

"After the bigger children scooped up the lion's share, trampling the little ones in the process, the bony hands and sunken eyes of the defeated waifs scoured the barren ground for the tiniest morsels, hoping to silence the growling in their stomachs, praying that the gut-gnawing beast within would cease its savagery and allow them a few hours of sleep within their dirt hovels, just enough to give their aching muscles time to rest and recover from their back-breaking labor, just enough peaceful slumber to prepare them for yet another day of blood loss, stinging sweat, and tearless weeping."

Marcelle folded in her arms and peered through a slit in her eyelids. A parade of cattle children walked between her and the crowd, exactly as she had described. Although their bodies and pails were semitransparent, all the gory details were easy to see—the slashes on their backs, the dirty bare skin, and the protruding ribs. A stream flowed at the feet of the onlookers, so real and sparkling, some backed away to avoid the water.

Leaving her eyes partially open, she took in as little breath as possible and continued. "And all the while, these pitiful creatures labored and suffered under the watchful eye of ..." After a dramatic pause, she flung out her arms. "A dragon!"

A drone flashed into the scene, its whip cracking over the children's backs. Gasps erupted from the crowd. A few ran, while most shuffled a few more steps away.

Marcelle snatched a quick glance at Maelstrom, Orion, and Captain Reed. With wide eyes and slack jaws, all three appeared to be mesmerized. If only Captain Reed had kept his wits about him, he might have been able to help with the escape.

Scanning the crowd once again, she searched for anyone who might have resisted the hypnosis. At the left side, a gray-haired man appeared again, skulking low in the midst of the swaying heads and pushing toward the front. Near the center, a dark-haired man did the same, and to the right, a third man with only a few wisps of gray approached.

The man in the center popped out of the crowd. Marcelle recognized him immediately. Gregor!

With a sword in hand, he rushed toward her, his back bent low. "Keep talking!" he hissed. "They might wake up!"

"Don't breathe the smoke," Marcelle said. "It's already affecting me."

Gregor pointed at his ear. "I can't hear you. Just keep talking." As he circled to the rear of the pyre, avoiding the now-towering flames that drew near from the front, Marcelle winced at the growing heat but managed to shout over the crackling fire. "This dragon you see is merely a drone. Though evil and cruel, he is but a shadow of the greater dragons, yet his whip still slices the backs of these poor children, drawing blood they can ill afford to lose."

The other two men emerged from the crowd, Professor Dunwoody to the left and Father to the right. Carrying a black burlap bag, Dunwoody sneaked up to Maelstrom from behind. Father rolled a barrel toward the wood, a dagger in hand.

"A more ferocious dragon stalked the skies," she continued, "ready to plunge to the ground and scorch anyone who offered resistance, whether one of the children or an adult rescuer."

Gregor began slicing the rope with the sword, grunting. "The crystals are making it hard to cut."

Marcelle studied the faces in the crowd. On many of the men, the vacant expressions had altered to scowls of anger, while tears flowed from the eyes of men and women alike. They were almost ready. Maybe it was time for a final entreaty before Gregor finished breaking her bonds. Then Captain Reed could muster the army while she fled with her rescuers. And maybe telling Orion more about Cassabrie would be the best way to punch through to the people's hearts.

As flames crawled within a foot or so, her dizziness heightened. Heat blistered her skin. If Gregor and Father didn't hurry, the end would come soon.

She took in another breath and shouted, "And among the slaves, there were many potential rescuers. One was Cassabrie, a young woman with a special gift, the ability to tell tales from the past and conjure lifelike phantoms who acted out those tales. She has visited this world, hoping to gain favor and help in her efforts to set her people free. While here, she appeared as a pale, corpselike girl who can crumble into dust and then rematerialize from the same dust, but during her life on Dracon, she was a vibrant, healthy teenager who dared to try to rescue the unfortunate children."

Dunwoody crept closer to Maelstrom's back, the bag uplifted. Father plunged the dagger into the barrel. Water poured out over the wood at the right side of the pyre, but it didn't appear to be nearly enough to douse the inferno.

"Only a couple of threads to go," Gregor said, his voice labored. "Keep talking."

The flames marched to within inches of her waist, their tongues beginning to lick at her belt. She drew her stomach in, but how long could she stay out of its reach? "The dragons captured Cassabrie and tied her to a stake much like this one, but the heat to cook her body came from a crystalline ball mounted behind her." Cassabrie appeared between Marcelle and the crowd, replacing the dragon and children. Bound by chains, she writhed in the Reflections Crystal's radiance. "She suffered for thirteen days, no saliva to moisten her tongue, no sweat to cool her roasting skin, no tears to signal her despair as her spirit departed from her body. Then, as now, she longed for another chance to liberate her fellow slaves, but the rulers of that land maintained their power because they had grown addicted to the benefits of slave labor, so they chose to execute the one who yearned to set the children free."

Dunwoody threw the bag over Maelstrom's head and jerked him to the ground.

"No!" Gregor hissed. "She's not loose!"

While Dunwoody wrestled with Maelstrom, Marcelle glanced all around. Fire and smoke veiled her view, and heat pummeled her face and hands, making her skin feel as if it were melting. Cassabrie faded away. The onlookers blinked rapidly, their hypnosis fading. Orion shook his head as if casting off a fog. Father slung water over the flames with a dipper, but he looked like a boy trying to empty the sea with a spoon.

Marcelle craned her neck again. What was Gregor doing back there? Was he succumbing to the sedative? To the smoke? Soon the flames would engulf him as well. As heat blasted her face, she called, "Gregor! Save yourself!"

"I got it!" After a final slice, he slung the rope into the flames and grabbed Marcelle around the waist. "We'll have to leap through. Brace yourself."

Maelstrom threw Dunwoody off, ripped the bag from his head, and thrust out a hand at Gregor. "You will stay where you are!"

Gregor froze in place, Marcelle locked in his arm. She wriggled, but he was too strong. She couldn't pry herself loose. Father scrambled up the wet side, a dripping piece of wood in his hand. He beat it against the flames as he advanced.

Heat from the fire ripped into Marcelle. Something trickled down her cheek. Was it sweat? How could that be? She brushed a finger across her skin to mop the moisture, but the tip dug into her cheek, pulling away a chunk of damp, pale dust. The particles drizzled to her feet along with the fingertip. Her other fingers crumbled, then her hand. Wet dust rained in front of her eyes.

Her father burst through the flames. With his clothes on fire, he jerked Gregor's arm away and pulled Marcelle into an embrace. "Hang on. I'll get you out of here."

As she stared at his desperate face, the raining dust thickened until it veiled her vision. She fell away from his grasp, feeling only a plunging sensation. Every sight, every sound, every other feeling vanished. Then, nothingness.

THIRTEEN

MARCELLE looked around. She lay on a bed of leaves and straw. A flickering light somewhere sent a shaft of wavering radiance over her, dimly illuminating the room. Small, half-naked bodies lay across the floor, one on each of her sides, pressing her arms in, while others sprawled in haphazard array, some intertwining limbs or even lying partially on top of one another. Steady breathing proved that they were alive, probably sleeping.

Finding the lantern sitting on a table to her left, she studied a man who sat in its glow, his back against the wall—Frederick. He held a boy nestled in his left arm and a girl curled in his right. His eyes were closed and his head hung low. He, too, appeared to be asleep.

In front and to her right, a young male stood at an open door. Bearing a sword and leaning against the jamb, he seemed to be guarding the entry, but with his own head bobbing, he was obviously ready to join the others in slumber.

She scanned the rest of the dim room. This was the same cabin she had been in before when she faced Drexel and scared him away. Where was Adrian? Could he be patrolling somewhere outside?

Sliding her fingers across her trousers, she felt the material— wetter than merely damp. She sniffed the air. Although the odor of sweaty bodies hovered close, no hint of urine infiltrated the scent. For some reason, she had been bathed with her clothes on.

She closed her eyes and pondered the data. The children sleeping in close quarters meant newly escaped slaves had come to Frederick's wilderness refuge, maybe dozens. Apparently major developments had occurred in the world of Starlight. Yet, since they still needed protection in this cabin, they weren't free yet. The dragons must still be trying to capture them.

She turned her head toward Frederick and tried to speak, but her voice barely managed a whisper. "Frederick?"

He didn't flinch.

Summoning all her strength, she pushed out a groan. Frederick's head bobbed for a moment, but his eyes stayed closed.

A whisper brushed her ear. "Are you all right?"

Marcelle turned her head toward the sound. The lantern light shone on a familiar face. Calling for another breath, she whispered in reply. "Shellinda?"

Smiling broadly, she nodded. "Frederick said to sleep close to you in case you need anything." She rose to her knees and looked Marcelle over. "So … do you need anything?"

Marcelle lifted a hand and pointed at Frederick. "Him."

"I'll be right back." Shellinda shot up and tiptoed around the sleeping bodies. When she reached Frederick, she touched his shoulder and whispered into his ear. His eyes flashed open, and, after setting the children to the side, he sprang toward Marcelle.

He stepped over her and knelt at the spot Shellinda had occupied. "What is it?" he asked, his voice spiking with concern.

She curled a finger, gesturing for him to lean close. When he complied, she whispered, "Captain Reed."

"Yes, I know Captain Reed. What about him?"

"He will lead the army."

Frederick straightened, twisting his lips as if trying to hide a condescending smile. "Oh. Right. The invading army you're sending."

With a surge of strength, she grabbed his tunic and jerked him closer. "Don't … be … difficult!"

"Okay! Okay!" Frederick slid his hand into hers and gently loosened her grip on his tunic. Keeping their hands clasped, he stroked her knuckles with his thumb. "If you want me to believe you, you have to give me some proof. I mean, you have to admit that what you're telling me is pretty far-fetched."

Closing her eyes, Marcelle exhaled. He was right. Why should he believe this crazy story? She summoned another breath and whispered, "I have no proof."

She forced her eyelids up. Frederick gazed at her, his beard still disguising the face she once knew so well. Still, his eyes were unmistakable, so much like Adrian's, yet more analytical, more brutally logical. He would be far less likely to succumb to a Starlighter's charms.

Frederick gave her a nod. "Let's say, for the sake of your sanity, that you really are in touch with our world, with Major Four. What do you want me to do?"

"I am … spirit there. … Must unite with … my body." She patted her chest with her free hand. "This body."

"Should I take you somewhere? The healing spring didn't seem to help."

"Northlands. … Portal."

"Yes, I know about that portal, but it's a long way off, and I have more than forty kids to take care of. Drexel has already kidnapped one and killed another."

"Where … is Adrian?"

"I haven't seen him. From what I can gather from the kids, he went back to the spring searching for Drexel and the missing girl.

Just guessing, but it's been long enough for him to search quite a bit, so I'm hoping he'll come back soon."

Her arm trembling, she reached up and grabbed his bicep. His muscles felt toned and hard. "Will he take me ... to the portal?"

"Like I said, I haven't seen him. I was unconscious when he hauled me out of my hunting pit, and when I woke up, he was gone. So I can't be sure, but knowing Adrian, he'll do whatever you ask. You know how chivalrous he is."

"Yes." Marcelle let her hand fall to the floor. "I know." She closed her eyes. It had taken so much effort to move and talk. But she had to make sure Adrian got the message. She had to get her spirit and body reunited. The moment her spirit stepped back into Starlight, she would vanish again. Who would lead the troops south then? They would think it was a trick, that a sorceress had led them to an icy wilderness in order to trap them. And warning them in advance about her disappearing act probably wouldn't work. Even if they believed her, they wouldn't want to be led into a land of dragons by someone who would vanish before the battle began. They would cry "sorceress!" and have an excuse to stay home.

Her heart thumped. A sorceress. That's right! She had just been burned at the stake! Had the shock made her forget? Since she still could connect with her body, didn't that mean her spirit survived the flames? If so, how? And what happened to Father, Dunwoody, and Gregor? The only way to find out would be to try to disconnect from Starlight and return to Major Four. But could she? Had the fire damaged her fabricated body too much?

With a final effort, she opened her eyes and whispered again, "Tell Adrian ... to do ... whatever love tells him."

As if sinking into the floor, she dropped away from Frederick. His face and the surrounding room looked like a fuzzy ball flying into the darkness. Seconds later, the ball disappeared. Then, from the opposite direction, a new light drew closer. Shaped like a rectangle, grayish white and undulating, it looked like a smoky curtain floating down from the sky.

The curtain draped her body, warm and wet, as if someone had dipped a blanket in hot, sooty water and spread it over her. It felt heavy, suffocating. She tried to push against it, but her arm wouldn't move. Yet, it did move … slowly. She turned, trying to swing her arm around. As the curtain swung with her, it felt lighter, as if fanning out. She spun faster. The curtain lifted higher. Finally, it slung away.

She slowed her rotation. Dizzy, she tried to blink. Light filtered through her partially open lids. A pile of scorched wood lay around, wet and smoking. The gallows stood to her right, and the pillory to her left. Straight ahead lay the governor's palace, a high-noon sun gleaming off its central dome.

Marcelle looked around. No one was in sight. Somehow she had survived the execution and reconstituted herself from her own ashes. The wet wood might mean that Father had managed to douse the fire after all.

"Psst!"

She turned toward the sound. Someone waved from the crawl-space under the gallows. While glancing in every direction, she skulked that way. When she arrived, she stooped low and looked into the open access panel. Dunwoody peeked out, his eyes wide. "Get under here before somebody sees you!"

As soon as she scooted in, he handed her a bulky black cloak. "Put this on. It should be big enough to hide your shape."

Marcelle ran the material through her fingers, searching for a sleeve. "What is it for?"

"You are short enough to pass as a young teenager."

"I know. I've done it before." She slid her arms through the sleeves and raised the hood. "What's the occasion?"

"You are now an orphan named Ophelia."

"An orphan?" She lifted an arm, making the baggy sleeve ride down to her elbow. "That explains the mourning cloak."

"I chose this deception with the cloak in mind. It will keep your identity hidden." He patted the cloak's side near her waist. "Your mirror is in the pocket. I found it in the ashes. It appeared to be unharmed."

"Oh!" She pushed her hand inside and felt the familiar shape. "Thank you."

"You're welcome." He touched the edge of her hood. "Do you know the rules regarding female orphans?"

She nodded. "They are to cover their faces in public, and no man is allowed to touch them, but I can't remember why."

"No man except for a prospective father. He alone may lower your hood to see your face. It is a tradition, of sorts. A girl without a father is vulnerable to the lusts of predatory men, so if she shows her face, such vile men might be tempted to take advantage of her vulnerability. So, as the logic goes, a true gentleman refrains from touching an orphan girl, lest others think him depraved." He touched a scabbard on the ground next to him. "And this sword will help you in case you run into one of the depraved sorts."

Smiling, Marcelle pinched the hood closed in front of her face. "You have chosen well."

"Actually, your father conceived the plan." He pushed a folded parchment into her hand. "This order will secure a guide for you at the front entrance."

"I assume Drexel is no longer on duty there."

He shook his head. "No one has seen him in quite some time. How did you know?"

"It would take too long to explain." She looked at the order. "What does it say? Give me a summary."

"Your parents died yesterday, so you are in mourning. You are supposed to report to the orphan administrator. I have arranged for you to be transferred temporarily to the care of Captain Reed."

"Perfect. Where did he go after the execution?"

"Home. Well, to the tunnel. After you dissolved, I escaped while Orion's men were still somewhat hypnotized. Some guards came looking for me in the archives, so I listened in on their conversation. I gathered only snippets, but it seems that Orion made up a grandiose story about how a certain kind of sorceress crumbles when subjected to heat. Supposedly, this type of witch is also able to conjure phantoms and hypnotize those who watch them. With you destroyed, he declared a holiday for all officers."

Marcelle rolled her fingers into a fist. "So he succeeded in ruining my credibility. Our plan did no good at all. The men will be too cowardly to join us."

"Not so fast. Try to suppress your disdain for masculine responsibility for a moment. My gender might surprise you if you don't watch out."

"I judge what I see." She shot him an icy glare. "The men went home. They didn't listen."

Dunwoody touched his chest. "I'm here, aren't I?"

"Right," she said with a nod. "What's your point?"

Laughing softly, he shook his head. "Think, girl! Think! Why should I be here right now?"

"I don't know. As far as you could tell, the flames burned me to a heap of ashes. You had no reason at all to be here."

"That's exactly my point! If I was the irresponsible fool you paint men to be, I would have shrugged my shoulders and gone on as a collector of dusty documents, squirreled away in my cozy little hole with my feet propped up while perusing an old tome that no other eyes have seen." He raised a finger. "But, no! I am a man!

I have faith! I believed in you!" He grabbed her bicep and compressed it. "I believed in the strength of a woman, and not just any woman. I believed in a woman who doubted my gender's faithfulness. I believed in—"

"Cut the crowing, Professor!" She jerked her arm away. "Just tell me why you're here!"

"Well ..." Still on his knees, he clasped his hands and pressed his thumbs together. "Actually, I was back in my cozy little hole with my feet propped up while perusing an old tome that no other eyes have seen."

"Oh, so your self-aggrandizing speech was just—"

"Wait a minute!" he said, lifting a hand. "Let me finish. There was a method to my masculine moorings."

She nodded, resisting the urge to roll her eyes. Dunwoody had worked a long time on this presentation. She might as well let him entertain himself. "Go ahead."

"Well," he said, gesturing with his hands, "I was curious about Leo's lie-detecting rope. I returned here wearing the orphan's cloak and found a section of the rope still attached to the gallows, so I pocketed a sample of it and took it with me to the archives. Suspecting that the crystals in the rope are somehow related to Dracon, I hoped to find something in the dragon's journal. So, there I was, sitting in my tunnel and reading the tome, just as I said. Then, on page one-fifty-five, I saw it. Arxad described a large, spherical crystal that is capable of absorbing a spirit. He wrote much about its properties, including the curious idea that dragon fire might be able to destroy it. As I indicated concerning the male Starlighter, it seems strange that an intelligent beast such as Arxad would believe that one fire's destructive qualities exceed another's.

"And there is more." Lowering his voice to a rasping whisper, he pulled a piece of burnt rope from his pocket and shook it in front of her face. "Arxad's large crystal also divines between truth and lies in the very same way these small ones do."

"That's all well and good, Professor, but you still haven't explained why you came here."

"Must I spell it out for you?" He pointed toward the burning stake. "The place where you stood is littered with these shards. Leo has already come twice to collect them, but the embers were still too hot. It was a strange sight. Although he carried fireplace tongs, he seemed quite hesitant to get close to the embers, as if terrified by the heat. Yet, I was able to retrieve your mirror. It was blazing hot near the stake, to be sure, but it was tolerable. Anyway, while I was reading, the thought struck me that the crystals might have absorbed your spirit as your shell crumbled around you, thereby protecting you from the flames. You see, Arxad wrote that intense heat initiates a spirit's migration into the crystal, so I hoped that you would escape and reconstitute yourself when the environment cooled. Perhaps Leo wants to gather your remains, but his flawed timing worked to our benefit. I assume he will be back again, so we cannot linger here."

"Professor, you're brilliant!" She threw her arms around him. "And masculine!"

He returned the embrace. "Yes, 'tis true. I risked a lot coming here."

She pulled back. "Why didn't you collect the crystals when you picked up my mirror?"

He showed her the section of rope again. "I grabbed this while I could, but I saw that Leo was on his way, so I hurried to this hiding place. The other crystals were still fiery hot, and there was no way to collect them all in time, so I hoped you might be in one of these. I was wrong, to be sure, but it all worked out."

"What would you have done if Maelstrom's timing was better? I mean, what if he collected the crystals before they cooled enough for me to escape?"

"I don't know." He winked. "Gone back to reading dusty tomes, I suppose."

She gave him a shove. "I don't believe that for a minute."

"Suit yourself." He touched her cloak's sleeve. "No time to chatter. We need to get this new plan started."

"You're right." She pushed the adoption order into an outer pocket and fastened the cloak in front with a silver sash. "Where is my father?"

"In the upper court's holding cell. Considering Leo's thinly veiled threats, I think Orion is worried about a forced takeover of his office. He will want all government money secured only for himself, so holding your father serves his purposes."

"That makes sense." She began smoothing out the sleeves. "Is Gregor with my father?"

Drooping his head, Dunwoody replied in a whisper. "Gregor died in the flames."

She stopped in midstroke. "Oh. ... I'm sorry."

"Yes, he was a good man, a good friend, actually. He often brought me letters sent to prisoners in the dungeon. They didn't have anywhere to keep the letters after reading them, so Gregor told them the archives would welcome the historical records." Dunwoody sighed and shook his head. "What a shame ... what a crying shame."

Marcelle took his hand. "Then we will fight back. We will get my father out of prison, strike Orion in the heart, and end this reign of tyranny."

"I agree. But how? You still have slaves on Dracon to rescue."

She peeked out from under the gallows and looked at the pile of smoking wood. Somehow she had to return to Dracon with an army, find Adrian, reunite with her body, and march against the cruel dragons. "Yes ... I know. But the men—"

"Trust me. The men will come if they have a leader. When you meet Captain Reed as his newly adopted daughter, you just have to convince him of the truth."

"He believes me, but his heart is chained." She picked up the sword. "His daughter is Orion's prisoner. I have to find her and the other commanders' children."

Dunwoody stroked his chin. "There aren't many places he could keep them. The dungeon would be the obvious place, but he emptied every cell."

"I know. I was there not long ago. It was as quiet as a ..." She looked up at him, blinking. "A rat."

"No, my dear, the idiom is 'as quiet as a—'"

"I know the idiom!" she hissed. "I heard something down there. I thought it was a rat, but maybe it wasn't. I called, and no one answered, but maybe they were asleep."

"Or gagged. It seems that Leo is fond of that device. He prefers his prisoners to be silent."

"But he doesn't know about them. Orion captured them to keep Maelstrom—" She snapped her fingers. "Orion emptied the dungeon so they could leave it unguarded, and no one would think there are prisoners within an unguarded dungeon. He did it to fool Maelstrom."

Dunwoody tapped the side of his head with a finger. "Excellent thinking. You learned what I taught you after all."

She batted the comment away. "So Captain Reed and I will rescue his daughter and the others, and we'll have the leader we need."

"Then while you are amassing an attack force, I will take care of your father's situation. We will go into hiding until you return."

She tilted her head. "How will you get him out?"

"With a parting gift from Gregor." Dunwoody lifted a metal ring filled with keys. "And I have a potion that will make even the most diligent guard snooze for hours, and he need only sniff it to succumb."

"That's great, Professor, just great. I'll leave it to you, then." Marcelle crawled out and stood, shaking her arms and legs to straighten her oversized cloak. "How are you going to get to the palace?"

Still under the gallows, Dunwoody peeked out. "I will wait until dark. Your father's trial isn't until tomorrow."

She attached the scabbard to her belt. The baggy cloak hid it beautifully. "When the battles are over, should I look for you in your escape tunnel?"

"Yes. I have already stored enough food and water there to last for quite some time. If we run out, Gregor's keys will allow for nighttime kitchen raids. We will be fine."

She extended a hand. "I'll need the dungeon key."

"You might need more than that." He detached a long brown key with a notched square end and gave her the ring. "I will take the palace's master key. You take the rest."

She pushed the ring into her tunic's pocket. "Do me one favor. I need a letter of marque to invade Dracon. Can you make a copy of one from the archives?"

"Of course, but you would need the governor's signature before you could use it to gather soldiers and provisions."

She pressed a thumb against her chest. "Leave that to me. Just have it ready as soon as possible."

"Very well. I will put it in the tunnel tonight. Look for it there."

"Thank you, my friend." Marcelle pulled the hood over her eyes. "Pray for me."

Walking with her head bowed, she hurried around the palace and approached the guard at the front gate. With a peach-fuzz mustache and sandy hair tied in a ponytail, he looked familiar, one of the young men who had recently graduated from her training class. What was his name? Evan? Yes, it was Evan.

As she drew near, Evan stood at attention. "What may I do for you, Miss?"

Marcelle kept her head low and forced the same young-girl voice she used when impersonating Penelope. "I have an order here, sir." She pulled the page from her pocket and extended it, her hand shaking. "I hope you can help me."

Evan took the note, unfolded it, and began reading. "Ah! As I suspected, you're an orphan." He gave her a convincing look of sympathy. "I am terribly sorry to hear about your loss."

"Thank you, sir," Marcelle said, feigning a shattered voice. "You are kind."

"I will escort you to the lobby and summon one of the maids to take you to the society office." After ushering her through the gate, he closed and locked it. "Come with me."

As she followed him on a gently winding path across the pristine lawn, she looked back and gathered in the sights and sounds of the village. Beyond the guard fence, people walked along the cobblestone streets, going about their business, some pushing carts filled with produce or books or household wares, others carrying hoes, shovels, or other farming implements. One man gnawed on a loaf during his noontime break. Children ran in circles around mothers as they strolled to market. Some smiled, some laughed, a few even sang. Most had likely witnessed her execution earlier that day, and now they went about their business as if nothing had happened.

She turned again and focused on Evan's ponytail as it bounced while he marched. It seemed that no one cared that Marcelle, daughter of Issachar the banker, had died. No one wept for her. No one wore a mourner's cloak. What did her life mean to the townsfolk? If she could pass away in a violent death at the hands of a cruel tyrant while no one cared, what difference did it make whether she lived at all?

After they ascended the stairs to the main entry, Evan opened the door, again standing at attention. She stopped in front of him and, closing the hood around her face, looked up into his eyes—gray and sincere under dark eyebrows. "Excuse me, sir. I was wondering if you could tell me something."

"Just ask, Miss. I will do my best."

She ran her finger along the jamb. Unlike much of the palace, this door and its surrounding framework had no marble, only wood and glass. "Did you see the execution this morning?"

"I did. I went on duty shortly afterward."

"Did you know the woman?"

Evan nodded. "She was my training teacher for a year, a stellar swordplayer, one of the finest in the land."

"Then I suppose you're saddened by her death."

He shrugged. "I hadn't thought about it. She was a bossy sort, hotheaded and temperamental. She sliced me up with her tongue more than a few times, if you know what I mean."

Marcelle blinked. How could she argue with his assessment? She often had been hotheaded in class. Sometimes student laziness brought out the worst in her. "Yes, I think I know what you mean."

"I feel bad for her father, though. He is a fine gentleman who has been ill of late. I fear that her passing will be a burden too heavy for his weakened state."

"I understand." She kept her focus on his eyes. This might be a good time to get details she had forgotten to ask Dunwoody about. "When Marcelle's father rushed in to try to save her, I could no longer bear to watch. Could you tell me what happened?"

"It was extraordinary. I didn't know the old fellow had it in him." Evan began pumping his arms and legs. "He ran up the wood and through the fire, just like it was nothing. As soon as he jumped down to the stake, a wall of flames erupted around him and Marcelle. Then she exploded and disappeared." He snapped his fingers. "Gone in an instant."

"Then what did her father do?"

"Did you see the water barrel?"

She nodded.

"Well, he ran back and threw dipper after dipper on the fire. It was a tragic sight, really, a poor, grieving father working so hard for a lost cause. He cried so bitterly, nearly everyone cried with him, and since Marcelle was already dead, Orion did nothing to stop him. In fact, he called for two guards to help, and they kept pouring water until they doused the flames."

She lowered her head. "I know how her father felt."

"I'm sure you do."

"Did Counselor Leo help put out the flames?" She looked up at him again. "Or was it too smoky for you to see?"

Evan shook his head. "He seemed quite angry and left. I haven't seen him since. It's too bad, though. The governor made quite a moving speech about a father's love for his daughter and—" He looked back at the main gate. "Someone's waiting for entry."

"Oh. Well, I can find my way." She looked through a palace window and pointed at a maid dusting a statue. "I'll just ask her."

"Fine." Evan lifted her hand and made ready to kiss it, but she pulled away.

"I am an orphan!"

"Oh!" Evan's face flushed. "I forgot. I'm terribly sorry."

"I won't tell anyone if you won't!"

She hurried inside and pressed her back against the nearest wall. That was close. With the cloak covering her hand, maybe he hadn't noticed her frigid skin, but his lips would have.

After the maid guided her to the society office, and after the clerk—a fat, bearded man with an overly cheery disposition—

summoned Captain Reed, Marcelle sat on a cushioned bench in the corridor where she was told to wait for the captain to arrive.

With early afternoon business taking place, this part of the palace had come alive with passersby—couriers hustling to and fro with message tubes; members of the nobility set walking with heads held high, skin perfumed, and dresses and waistcoats pressed; and guards of various branches marching from station to station.

Marcelle studied the guards' body language. With eyes wide and constantly glancing about, they seemed to be on alert, as if searching for something. But what?

Finally, Captain Reed hustled down the corridor. Although he wore a soldier's uniform, no sword scabbard slapped his thigh as he hurried. Only a sheathed dagger dressed his hip. Marcelle stayed seated, playing her part. An orphan such as herself probably wouldn't immediately recognize the captain.

He sat next to her and laid his hands on her shoulders. She drew back, but he held firm. "I am your prospective father."

"Okay." She settled in her seat and summoned her little-girl voice. "I suppose it's all right, then."

He touched the top of her hood. "May I?"

She slid away. "I don't think I'm ready for that yet."

"Very well. I will honor your grief." He smiled, though his lips trembled. "Come. My sister will have a comfortable bed and a fine meal prepared by the time we get home."

"That sounds good. I'm terribly hungry." As they rose together, Marcelle turned and faced him. "Captain, thank you for taking me in."

"You're quite welcome." His smile strengthened. It was lovely—genuine and fatherly. "They tell me your name is Ophelia."

She nodded and curtsied, clutching the hood in front of her face. The charade was working perfectly. It was time to pierce his heart. "What should I call you?"

His lips trembled again. "If you would grant me the honor of calling me Father, I would count it a great blessing." He quickly waved a hand. "But I understand if you decline. The pain of your father's recent death is likely a horrible burden to bear."

She dipped her knee again. "I respectfully decline, Captain. Perhaps my heart will respond to your charity, and I will change my mind, but for now *Father* belongs only to one man."

"Of course. Of course." He laid a hand on her back. "Come, Ophelia. I will take you home and—"

"Wait!" Marcelle stopped. "Will I have any brothers or sisters?"

A tear trickled down his cheek. "Yes. One brother and one sister. I am bereaved of a wife and another daughter."

"I'm sorry. Death of family members is the greatest of tragedies."

"Actually, my daughter is missing, which has proved to be an even greater torture, and my wife died three years ago of consumption. I now live with my sister." His chin quivering, he seemed ready to say more, but he just pressed his lips together and nodded.

"What a shame!" She pushed her hand into the cloak pocket and felt for the dungeon key ring. This might be the perfect time to get Captain Reed on her side forever. "I think I have a gift for you."

"There is no need—"

"Oh, but there is." She marched away toward the stairs. "Follow me."

FOURTEEN

O PHELIA!" Captain Reed called. "Where are you going?" Marcelle didn't look back. He would follow, and he wouldn't try to stop her. A father grieving over a daughter wasn't about to upset a new one.

Holding the sword against her thigh, she scrambled down the stairs to the bottom level and hustled toward the rear exit. As she drew near, the guard at the door gave her a quizzical look.

"It's okay," Captain Reed said, now only a few paces back. "She's with me."

The guard opened the door and let Marcelle breeze past. Feeling Captain Reed closing in, she picked up her pace and headed straight for the dungeon. As she passed the burning stake, the odor of charred wood drifted by, raising the memory of her talk with Frederick. Soon he would believe her. Getting the army together was all that mattered now.

When she arrived at the dungeon entrance, she fished out the ring and pushed the largest key into the lock in the trapdoor embedded in the ground.

"What are you doing?" Captain Reed asked as he caught up. "And where did you get that key?"

"From a friend." She turned the lock, heaved open the door, releasing a loud squeak, and stepped down to the first stair. "I have something to show you."

His brow bent, he joined her on the stair. "It's dark and dank in there. It's no place for a girl."

"Exactly why we're here." As she continued down the stairs, she pulled the door, forcing Reed down with her. When the door dropped flush with the ground above, plunging them into darkness, the latch fastened, and she pushed the key ring back into her pocket.

"Now that we're down here, Ophelia, I hope you will explain yourself."

"I will." She brushed her fingers against the wall. "We'll have to find our way in the dark."

A spark appeared, then a flame crawled over the top of a torch. Captain Reed held the end, his face now illuminated by the rippling glow. "There is always a torch attached to the wall along with flint stones. I was assigned to patrol duty here in my younger days. I thought I would never have to come back."

"Let's hope this is the last visit for both of us." Marcelle took the torch and soft-stepped down the stairs.

"Don't go down there!" Reed's heavier footsteps clopped from behind. "There are rats and other vermin."

"I know, and maybe something else." She halted at the bottom of the stairs and lifted the torch, flooding the dungeon's antechamber with flickering orange light.

He hustled down the rest of the way. "Come, Ophelia, this is no place for—"

"Captain Reed," Marcelle said, reverting to her own voice, "haven't you yet figured out that I'm not who you think I am?"

He squinted at her. "You haven't exactly acted like an orphan."

She shook her head hard, making her hood drop to her shoulders.

Captain Reed gasped. "Marcelle! But how did you survive the—"

"Never mind. Just trust me." She waved the flame slowly from side to side, illuminating three corridors that led into darkness, one straight ahead and two angling to the sides. As smoke from the torch rose to the wood-beam ceiling and crawled back down the stone-and-mortar walls, she listened. The sounds she had heard during her previous visit here could very well have been rats, so the young prisoners might be anywhere. "Hello?" she called.

As her voice echoed in triplicate, she listened again. A scraping sound reached her ears, then the distinctive clinking of chains from the center corridor.

She waved the torch. "Let's go!"

When she reached the first set of doors, she pushed the torch between the window's bars, but the small space wouldn't allow a peek past the flame. "Hello!" she shouted. "Is anyone in here?"

More clinking sounded farther down the corridor along with louder shuffling.

"Give me the keys!" Captain Reed said, reaching out a trembling hand. "Hurry!"

She withdrew the ring and dropped it into his palm. He rushed to the next cell, jammed a key into the lock, and flung the door open. Marcelle caught up and extended the torch into the cell. Nothing. Just empty manacles and chains hanging from the back wall.

He leaped to the door across the hall and did the same. Marcelle's torch again found nothing.

After checking the next set of doors, a loud, rhythmic series of clinks sounded, then a matching series copied the cadence. A third joined in, then a fourth.

Captain Reed ran to the door closest to the sounds and unlocked it. This time, he opened it slowly while Marcelle eased the torch inside. A girl about twelve years old sat against the back wall with her arms raised, her wrists shackled by manacles attached by chains. With one arm, she was beating the chain against the wall, her mouth gagged and her ankles bound.

When the girl saw the flame, she stopped and squinted, then screamed into the gag as she pulled desperately against the chains.

"It's Ilana, the General's daughter!" Pulling his dagger from its sheath, Captain Reed rushed inside. He sliced away the gag and sawed through the rope binding her ankles. "Don't worry, honey! I'll get you out of here!"

"Oh, thank you!" she cried, tears flowing. "Thank you!"

As he tried to unlock the manacles, Marcelle walked in, providing more light. "Do you know how many others are here?" she asked.

Ilana shook her head. "I hear them, but I never see them."

Reed unfastened her left manacle and shifted to the other one. "Are you hungry? Thirsty?"

"Both. He gives me food and water once a day."

"He?" Marcelle asked.

"Sometimes two other men come," she said as Reed pulled the other manacle away from her wrist, "but the one I see most often is a man wearing a hood. It's always too dark to tell much about him, only that he's sort of tall."

Marcelle nodded. "Orion."

"Savage!" Captain Reed slapped the manacle against the wall. "He's the devil in disguise."

Marcelle grasped Ilana's hand and helped her rise. "Come with us, sweetheart. We have to find the others." With every stiff-legged step, Ilana winced, and when they emerged into the corridor, she leaned against a wall and breathed a sigh.

Captain Reed opened the next door. A male toddler sat in a similar pose, arms raised and shackled. He appeared to be asleep or unconscious.

While Reed worked on his bonds, Marcelle pulled out his gag, a pair of dirty socks that had been jammed deep inside. He coughed, then sucked in a deep breath, but his eyes stayed closed.

"The poor kid could barely breathe." She wadded the socks into a tight ball. "And Orion said they were well cared for."

"I don't know this boy, but I'm sure the general does." Captain Reed scooped him into his arms. "He might just be dehydrated."

Marcelle sniffed the air. "He was sitting in his own filth."

"I can see that." The captain looked at his soiled uniform. " This is the finest medal I have ever earned."

With Marcelle leading the way, the torch in hand, he carried the boy to the hall and set him on the floor. "He should be okay here while we find the others."

"Most likely." Marcelle tuned her ears. Although a slight shuffling still sounded here and there, the rattling chains had quieted. Maybe the prisoners had grown weary of signaling.

Ilana staggered closer. "I'll watch Alexander. He's Colonel Jarvis's son. I sometimes babysit for him."

"Excellent." Captain Reed showed the key ring to Marcelle. It trembled in his grip, rattling the keys. "Which cell next?"

She cupped a hand around the side of her mouth and shouted. "Shake your chains again so we can find you!"

The clinking of chains returned, this time coming from the cell across the hall.

"Shine the light on the lock," Captain Reed said.

She set the flame close to the door. As Reed's hand drew near with a key, his shaking arm made him miss the hole. With his second attempt, he inserted the key and disengaged the lock.

Marcelle yanked the door open and marched in with the torch. A dark-haired girl of about ten sat in the same position as the others, her expression forlorn as she tried to spit out the gag.

When Captain Reed walked in, her hazel eyes lit up. In spite of the gag, her muffled shout was clear. "Daddy!"

"Hazel!" He lunged to her, jerked a wadded rag from her mouth, and wrapped her in his arms.

Hazel sobbed. "Oh, Daddy! You came! You finally came!"

"Yes, honey." He drew back and wiped tears from Hazel's cheeks with his thumb. "And I'm going to get you out of here."

Forcing air through her tightening throat, Marcelle spoke softly. "Captain, if you'll give me the keys, I'll see if there are any others."

He tossed the ring to her. She snatched it out of the air, slid the door key off, and tossed it back. "If I don't return soon, come looking for me."

"I will." Smiling broadly, Reed worked on Hazel's manacles. "But if you can escape from that fire, I'm sure you can escape from anything."

Marcelle opened the remaining doors and found another boy and another girl, both about eight years old. After removing their gags and whispering assurances to them, she returned for the key to the manacles and set them both free. For the next several minutes, she checked every cell in the other two corridors but found no more prisoners.

When everyone had gathered in the central corridor, Marcelle stood in the middle of the cramped circle, the torch held high. "We can't very well parade them out the main entrance."

Captain Reed, again carrying Alexander, nodded toward the far end of the hall. "There are two staircases leading to lower levels. The one to the left ends at a maze. If we can find our way through the twisting passages, we would come out at the dungeon's rear gate, but that's always locked. I didn't see the key to it on that ring, and we don't have the tools to break through. The staircase on the right leads to more cells, but it's a dead end. Maybe we can hide the children in the maze and come back—"

"No," Marcelle said. "I know a way out using the staircase to the right." She lowered the torch. "We'll carry the torch as far as we can, but we'll eventually have to go in the dark."

"Why so?"

"Extane. The tunnel down there is full of it."

Reed nodded. "If you know the way, I'm sure we can follow."

"Everyone join hands." When the children had made a hand-to-hand chain, Marcelle nodded at Ilana. "Now hold my belt in the back."

Ilana slid her hand behind Marcelle's belt. "I'm ready."

A squeak sounded at the main entrance. At the end of the hall, light poured in from the trapdoor, illuminating the bottom of the staircase.

"Where's the torch?" a man asked.

"No clue. Maybe Orion forgot to put it away. Don't worry. I have glow sticks."

"Someone's coming," Reed whispered.

"Two someones. I'd better douse the light." Marcelle tamped out the torch and threw it into a cell. She reached for her sword but drew her hand back. A battle with two armed men might be dangerous. Since Captain Reed had only a dagger, and since vulnerable children surrounded them, a quick escape was the better option.

Walking swiftly with Reed at the tail of the line, she led the chain to the far end of the hall, down the staircase to the right, and then to the right again, retracing her steps toward the extane pipeline.

Voices echoed in the corridor above—two men, neither one alarmed or agitated, at least not yet. When they found the unlocked and empty cells, that would change.

She picked up the pace. As expected, a bitter extane film coated her lips and tongue. The air was saturated with it.

At the end of the passage, she began pushing the loose bricks out, hoping their muffled thuds in the tunnel wouldn't reach past her own ears.

A shout sounded from above. "They're gone!"

Marcelle whispered, "Help me! We have to hurry."

As several hands joined hers, the voices above continued.

"They couldn't have left through the main entrance. It's locked."

"Check the maze. I'll look on the lower level."

"*You* check the maze. The last time I went down there, I got lost."

"Then wait here while I check below. Then one of us can go around to the back gate. If it's locked, they must still be in the maze."

"Whoever got them loose has the keys. They could have gone out either way."

"If you want to report the escape to Orion without making a search, then be my guest."

"Get going, then! I'll wait here."

A hand touched Marcelle's shoulder. "It's big enough," Reed said. "Go through. I'll guide the children to you."

Loud clops sounded from the stairs. Marcelle crawled through the hole and began helping the children climb down to the pipeline tunnel's ground level, a drop of about three feet. The hands she held grew in size from child to child until Reed's muscular hand clasped her own. As soon as he settled on the ground, he jerked away but stayed quiet.

"I know," Marcelle said. "My hands are like ice."

He seemed to ignore the comment. "I'll collect the bricks while you patch it."

As he handed her brick after brick, she felt for a spot for each to fit and slid it quietly into place. They might do a sloppy job, but this was no time for perfection.

Through the hole, a tiny red light appeared, the guard's glow stick drawing closer. Every few steps, he stopped and shone the stick to each side, apparently checking the cell doors.

When Marcelle slid the last brick in place, the glow stayed visible through cracks in the poorly mended wall. Making a quiet shushing noise, she herded the children against the wall and pushed them low.

She returned to one of the cracks, her cheek pressed against Reed's as they peered through. The approaching glow stopped at the final set of cell doors. A red halo surrounded the guard, an older, unfamiliar man. He pushed the glow stick between the bars of the cell window to the left and checked the latch, then did the same to the cell on the right.

Finally, the glow drew closer, the guard's eyes directly behind it. Marcelle peeled away and pressed her back against the wall. Reed did the same.

The glow penetrated the cracks, sending a multitude of narrow red shafts of light into the tunnel, illuminating the pipeline. At the lower fringes of the scarlet halo, the children sat perfectly still. The slightest move would give away their presence.

A grunt filtered through, then the guard's voice. "Crummy wall. No wonder there's so much extane in here."

The red shafts vanished, leaving them in darkness. Marcelle pressed her ear against the crack. The guard's footfalls retreated into the distance.

"Join hands again," she whispered.

Fingers pushed behind Marcelle's belt. "We're ready," Ilana said.

Marcelle led them up the pipeline back to Dunwoody's escape tunnel. A narrow ray of light poured through the hole leading to the tunnel, providing enough illumination to make a head count.

After touching each head, Marcelle whispered, "It looks like everyone's here."

Captain Reed smiled. "Excellent, but where is here?"

"I'll explain soon. First we have to dig through this rubble."

Captain Reed transferred Alexander to Ilana's arms. "Let's get to work."

"The ceiling on the other side is fragile," Marcelle said. "We'll have to be careful."

After about fifteen minutes, they had created a hole big enough to get everyone through. Once Captain Reed and the children had settled around the lantern, Marcelle scooped water from the barrel and passed the ladle around, beginning with Alexander, who stayed awake and alert after his drink.

Finally, Marcelle sat down in the ring and put on an exaggerated smile. "This is an old tunnel that almost no one knows about." She nodded toward the entrance panel. "That leads to Professor Dunwoody's archives room. He's supposed to be coming in here tonight, and I hope he brings my father with him."

"Very well." Sitting with Alexander in his lap, Captain Reed pulled Hazel closer. "I will do anything in my power to help you gather an army, but even after we inform the other officers about their children, it won't be a simple task. The officers will be behind you, but without the governor's signature on an invasion order, we won't be able to get the rations and equipment we need unless, of course, you can pay for them in advance."

"I have access to funds," Marcelle said, "but I don't know how long it will take to get them, so I can't be sure we can pay in advance. Professor Dunwoody is going to draw up a letter of marque for me tonight. If I can get Orion's signature on a blank parchment now, maybe Dunwoody can use that for the letter."

"Now that would be quite a trick. Do you have a plan?"

"Follow him until he's alone and kidnap him."

"Kidnap him?" Laughing under his breath, Reed shook his head. "My dear Marcelle, whatever illness has made you pale has also drained blood from your brain."

"If you mean his bodyguard, he will be no match for—"

"Not a bodyguard." Reed lifted a pair of fingers. "He has two most of the time, one who stays close and one who usually stays out of sight. He has become quite anxious about assassins."

"When does he have only one?"

"When he leaves the palace, but then he has archers, usually six. They are quite adept at skewering someone from a distance. Some of the older ones were taught by Professor Dunwoody himself."

Marcelle gave him a skeptical look. "Dunwoody was an archer?"

"The best in his time, but I'm sure he hasn't picked up a bow in a while. No place to shoot an arrow in the archives."

Marcelle raised her own pair of fingers. "Then it will take two warriors to capture Orion, but one of us has to stay here with the children."

"I agree. It seems that we will have to wait for Dunwoody to return." Captain Reed set Alexander in Ilana's lap, rose to his feet, and nodded at the water barrel. "Do we have enough to wash them?"

"Probably, and we have sponges and soap, too." Marcelle joined him. "I hope they don't mind a bath that's not so private."

Ilana laughed. "After what we've been through, I don't think anyone will mind."

"Good, but first we'll break into the rations Dunwoody keeps here. When everyone's good and fed, we'll get cleaned up." Marcelle passed around the box of manna woodchips. While Captain Reed and the children chewed the bark to calm the effects of breathing extane, she opened one of the rations footlockers and handed out small paper bags filled with nuts and dried fruit.

When she gave a bag to the captain, he pushed a manna chip into her palm and folded her fingers over it. "Don't underestimate the extane. I heard about a man whose heart ripped in half from beating too hard."

"Thank you." Marcelle popped the chip into her mouth and chewed. There seemed to be no reason to explain the lack of need for it.

Captain Reed picked up a rations bag and extended it to her. "Aren't you going to eat?"

"I'm not hungry." After stealthily spitting out her manna chip, she stripped off her cloak and sword belt and began gathering the bathing supplies.

"You will be later." The captain pushed the bag into her cloak's pocket, now on the floor near the lantern. "Every warrior needs to eat."

She nodded. "Thank you again. I will be sure to eat when my body needs it."

After the children had finished their rations, Captain Reed helped the boys clean up while Marcelle helped the girls, the boys facing one way and the girls facing the other. They washed their clothes, rung them out, and put them on again, though they were still quite damp.

After lighting two more lanterns, they gathered around the flickering lights, close enough to feel the warmth. During the next hour, Marcelle told Captain Reed her story, including all the details she could remember from her adventures with Adrian on Starlight, though she left out the part about being separated from her body.

Captain Reed stretched his arms. "I assume you must have caught an exotic illness on Dracon ... or Starlight, I suppose."

She nodded. "Exotic is an appropriate term."

A tapping noise sounded from the panel. Marcelle leaped up and grabbed the sword and a lantern. She hustled to the entry, poised to strike the intruder.

When the panel popped open, Dunwoody poked his head through and crawled in.

Marcelle drew back and helped him up. "You're early ... I think." She leaned over and glanced into the archives room, but without windows, there was no way to tell the time of day.

Dunwoody pushed the panel closed with his foot. "Yes," he whispered, pulling her away from the panel. "How did you get here with the children?"

As they walked toward the others, she nodded at the pile of rubble, the gaping hole evident. "There's a way to get here from the dungeon without going out into the open."

"Excellent." Dunwoody patted her on the back. "Well done."

Marcelle picked up the cloak and sword belt and put them on. "So why did you come out of hiding?"

Dunwoody glanced at Captain Reed. "I see the captain is now our ally."

Marcelle pushed her hood back. "Absolutely."

"Very well." He turned toward the archives. "I heard some important news that was worth risking my capture, so I returned here to gather some things from my office. The guards were gone, I assume, because of your execution, so the risk lessened greatly. I heard a bit of splashing and giggling, and I guessed the cause right away. Since the door was closed and no one else was around, I went about my business. I am glad of the children's rescue, but they must be quieter."

Marcelle touched the top of Alexander's head. "I'm sure we can persuade them."

"Good. This refuge is only as safe as the refugees make it."

"So, what's the news?"

Dunwoody's brow arched up. "Randall, the son of the former governor, has brought two dragons from Starlight."

"Here?" Marcelle raised a pair of fingers. "*Two* dragons are here on Major Four?"

He nodded. "It is quite amazing what one hears while hiding under the gallows. Randall met some members of the Underground Gateway there and told them. I stayed hidden, just in case some of them couldn't be trusted."

"But why would Randall bring dragons? They're dangerous." She bit her lip. Would it be better to hide her knowledge that Magnar was here? He was probably the most dangerous of all. Why would Randall be so bold to bring *him* here? "Do you know their names?"

"Only that one is their king and one is a priest."

"Magnar and Arxad," she said with a sigh.

Captain Reed joined their huddle. "Your tone worries me, Marcelle."

"Magnar's the worry. Arxad might keep Magnar from going on a rampage, but I'm not sure we can trust Arxad, either."

"Well," Dunwoody continued, "it seems that Randall will send a message to Orion asking him to meet for a parley of sorts, but Randall was unclear about the dragons' demands, something about getting help to solve a crisis on their world."

Marcelle grasped the hilt of her sword. "Do you know where they'll be meeting?"

"At the rear entrance to the dungeon," Dunwoody said.

Captain Reed looked at the gap leading to the gas pipeline. "Randall must be hiding them in the dungeon. That entrance leads to a cave with a maze of passages. Based on Marcelle's descriptions of the dragons' size, it sounds like they could fit."

"Probably." She drew a mental picture of the dungeon's rear gate and the surrounding area. "Lots of woods there, right?"

Reed nodded. "There's a path leading to it from the palace, but it's not well traveled."

She grabbed his sleeve. "This might be my only chance."

"To do what?"

"To kidnap Orion, of course."

Reed laughed. "Are you serious? He'll have every archer at his disposal in those woods. Randall might be hoping for a neutral parley, but Orion will make sure the numbers are in his favor."

"But Orion probably doesn't know about the dragons. Randall would be a fool to send that as part of the message."

"True. So he'll have only six archers and one bodyguard." Reed stroked his chin. "You need to get a message to Randall. Find out what the dragons want. Maybe they'll help us get Orion's signature."

"On the letter of marque?" Dunwoody asked.

"Exactly." Marcelle began pacing a short path. "We could go to the dungeon, but if Randall's not there, we shouldn't trust those dragons with delivering a message."

"Pen and ink," Dunwoody said. "I can provide those along with parchment. Leave Randall a written message at the dungeon gate."

"That sounds good." Marcelle took Dunwoody's hand. "Will you stay with the children while Captain Reed and I go?"

"What of your father? If you are delayed, I won't be able to leave to set him free."

"Good point." Marcelle looked at Captain Reed. With two important goals to accomplish, either he or she would have to get the message to Randall alone. "I should go. Randall was a student of mine. He'll trust me."

Reed nodded. "Although I relish the thought of going on this secret mission, I will gladly stay with my daughter and the other children."

"Come," Dunwoody whispered as he walked toward the panel. "I will get three parchment pages, one for your message to Randall, one for the letter of marque, and an extra one just in case you make an error. When you were in my class, you often had to discard sheets because of ink spills."

"Professor. I was ten."

"Yes, of course." He stopped at the panel. "In any case, if you can get his signature at the bottom of a page, return it to me, and I will draw up the letter."

He opened the panel, poked his head back out, and motioned for Marcelle to follow. When they emerged in the archives room, she stood up and looked around. With papers and books scattered everywhere, the place was a mess. "I hope you can find a letter of marque to copy," she whispered.

"I hope I can find a pen and ink." Dunwoody rummaged through a box on the floor, then another. After kicking through several piles, he lifted a finger. "Aha!"

"A pen? Ink?"

"Both." He leaned over and picked up a quill pen and an inkwell. "It's an old-fashioned variety, but it should work." He drew the inkwell close to his ear and shook it. "I'm afraid there isn't much left."

"I'll make the note short."

Dunwoody retrieved three blank parchment pages from the floor. "You might as well use my table. I'll watch the door." He waded through the mess until he reached the door leading to the stairs. With his cheek pressed against it, he nodded. "All is clear so far."

Marcelle sat on a stack of boxes, spread a parchment page out on Dunwoody's worktable, and dipped the quill's tip into the well. Hovering the pen over the paper, she imagined Randall reading the note. Somehow, he needed to figure out who wrote it without the benefit of a signature at the end. If she had to leave it somewhere and someone else found it, signing it would give too much away.

Smiling, she nodded. A feminine flair would help.

She wrote carefully, recalling her best penmanship from her school days. Dunwoody was right about one thing; she had often scrapped entire sheets because of the smallest of errors.

Randall, I am working on gathering the troops we need for war on Starlight. Because of recent events that would exhaust my dwindling ink if I were to tell them, I was able to assemble a contingent of believers, but I will need more proof, or at least more leverage, if I hope to gather enough soldiers to do battle against the dragons. I will contact you in person soon so we can combine our efforts. Until then, I wish you well.

She paused. Would this be sufficient? Maybe just one more clue.

After dipping the quill again and finding very little ink remaining, she signed the bottom with the letter *M*.

"Finished." She folded the note and pushed it into her cloak's pocket. "But I'm out of ink. I'll need something for Orion's signature."

Dunwoody scanned his desk. "Aha!" He snatched an object that lay next to a haphazard pile of journals and displayed it in his palm: a stubby black cylinder no longer than a thumb. "It's a charcoal pencil. If one is careful, it will suffice for a signature."

"Won't it rub off easily?"

"It might smudge, but that won't matter. Such implements are common for battlefield signatures. Commanders rarely pack pen and ink."

She and Dunwoody ducked back through the access panel and returned to the hideaway. Once inside, the three adults huddled near the hole to the pipeline tunnel.

"I suppose this is the safest route," Marcelle said. "The pipeline will eventually lead to the surface somewhere, but it might take me a while to get to the dungeon's back gate."

Reed gestured with his hands, as if drawing a path. "Not if you go through the dungeon's maze. You could leave your message just inside the back gate where no one but Randall could find it."

"If Randall is housing the dragons in there," Marcelle said, "that might be suicide. I would have to pass right by them."

Dunwoody raised a finger. "Not if you use your speaking gifts. You could hypnotize them with your oratory. Then you could learn their purpose in coming."

"As if they'd tell me," she said with a huff. "Magnar is not one to reveal any secrets, and I haven't tested my gifts on dragons. If acting like a Starlighter angers them, a failed attempt might be my last attempt."

Captain Reed nodded at the sword bulging under Marcelle's cloak. "If you'll let me borrow that, I will deliver the message."

She shook her head. "The dragons don't know you. They might burn you to a heap of ashes before you had a chance to explain." Sighing, she pushed her cloak back and gripped the sword's hilt. "I have to go."

"Then we'd better get you some glow sticks. Otherwise you'll never make it through the maze." Reed raised his brow at Dunwoody. "Do you have any?"

He nodded. "Several. I will fetch them, but you should eat and drink before you go. There is plenty of food and water in the rations cache."

"Not as much as you think," Captain Reed said, laughing. "These children were famished."

"That's fine, as long as you're all fed."

Reed glanced at Marcelle. "Not all. Perhaps you can persuade Marcelle to eat. I couldn't."

Dunwoody waved a hand. "She is a warrior. No need to treat her like a child."

"Thank you," Marcelle said, bowing her head as she sneaked a grin at Reed. "I'm glad someone doesn't look at me as if I were an orphan girl."

"I'll be right back with the glow sticks." Dunwoody hurried to the panel and crawled into the archives room.

Captain Reed grasped Marcelle's wrist. "Listen!" Sighing, he loosened his grip and softened his tone. "Marcelle, I know you're a warrior and not an orphan, but I also know you're not well, and you're about to face dragons alone. Your reputation with a sword is unquestioned, but no one, man or woman, should go into battle against such fire-breathers while sick."

"Don't worry about me, Captain." She slid her hand back and grasped his in a thumb lock. "Just think about how you're going to use that letter to get your soldiers ready, and I'll let you know what the dragons are up to."

"Very well." He withdrew the key ring from a pocket and set it in her hand. "Godspeed to you, warrior."

FIFTEEN

ADRIAN walked hand in hand with Regina, carrying Sarah with his other arm, her head against his shoulder. In the darkness of the underground river channel, his mind drifted back to their recent journey—a long hike downstream to the river's exit point on the surface where the water spilled out at a rocky slope at least five arrow shots north of the barrier wall, then another hike back upstream past where the spring once upwelled.

The girls were now exhausted, but they had to go on. Traveling to the Northlands from the river's exit was out of the question. They weren't dressed warmly enough, and Frederick's cabin was much closer.

Although tired, Regina marched on through the darkness, chatting at times about visions she could see in her mind's eye. "It's strange," she said. "I think I see the place where we were a little while ago, the place where the river comes out from underground."

"Is that so?" Adrian high stepped over a boulder in the middle of the stream and guided her around it. The river's bank had long ago disappeared, and they now walked through ankle-deep water in the tube-like tunnel. The ceiling had been getting progressively lower as an occasional reach of a hand proved. The fetid odor had strengthened for a while, then diminished later, but without light, they never found a source for the smell. "Do you see anything unusual?"

"Just firelight on the great barrier wall. I've never seen the outside of it before."

Adrian pictured the barrier wall, covered with the flickering lights of lanterns and torches. Although Solarus had risen high in the sky, the undulating flames were still easy to see, but the complete darkness now made those moments seem like a dream. "What does it look like?"

Regina's voice took on a dramatic tone. "Like a dragon's eyes when he's angry, when he's about to crack his whip. You can always tell. Most of the time a dragon's eyes are dull orange, sort of like the clay around our mound at the camp, but when he gets mad, they burst into bright orange or even red flames. You can see the whip snapping in his eyes before he even draws the real whip back. It cracks again and again, just like a lantern's flame when a breeze bends its yellow back and then snaps it to attention. The flame is trying to do its job even though the wind isn't happy with its labors." She sighed. "Anyway, that's what the firelight looked like on the wall."

"That's exactly what it looked like." Adrian took in a deep breath. Regina was sounding more like Cassabrie all the time. Her Starlighter gifts were becoming more and more evident. "After we gather everyone at the cabin and get them ready for cold weather, maybe you and I will go back to the healing waters and try to heal your eyes again before we go to the Northlands."

Regina clapped her hands. "Yay!"

Soon, the stream and its tunnel sloped upward, and the space between ground and ceiling shrank. Adrian set Sarah down and crawled until he could go no farther. Water poured in from a small opening between two boulders in the ceiling. He pushed one with his hand, but it wouldn't budge.

Setting his head against the tunnel's dead end, he pushed the ground above with both hands and shoulders. Straining with all his might as water poured over his body, he lifted a boulder and shoved it to the side. Now standing with his head in fresh air, he rolled the other boulder out of the way, widening the opening.

After helping Regina and Sarah out, he scanned the area, aided by sunshine peering through the treetops. If this was the same stream where he had found Frederick's sword, it wouldn't take long to find the path back to the cabin.

He hoisted the girls into his arms. "Just relax. We'll be there soon." He marched upstream until he found the disturbed banks where he had crawled in and out earlier. Turning onto the path, he broke into a fast march.

When he closed in on the cabin, he slowed to a stop about a hundred paces away, set the girls down, and inserted his pinky fingers into his mouth to create a narrow blowhole. With quick spurts, he whistled a long, warbling note.

"I heard something," Regina whispered.

"I made the noise." Adrian wiped his wet fingers on his tunic. "It's a birdcall."

"I've never heard a call like that before."

"I'm not surprised. This particular bird lives on my world. If my brother hears it, he'll recognize it."

After a few seconds, a man emerged from the cabin's door and walked their way. Adrian swallowed. His gait was unmistakable. It was Frederick, at long last.

"Come on." He took the girls by the hand and hustled as quickly as their little legs would go.

Frederick burst into a sprint. "Adrian!"

Adrian let go of the girls and ran to meet him. The brothers embraced, patting each other on the back. "It's about time you showed up," Frederick said, keeping his voice low. "What have you been doing out there? Collecting flowers?"

"In a manner of speaking." As they drew apart, their hands and wrists still locked, Adrian grinned. "You're looking a lot better than when I saw you last."

Frederick's brow bent, but his smile stayed put. "It'll take more than a fiend like Drexel to keep a son of Edison Masters down."

Adrian glanced past him. "How is Marcelle doing?"

"Not too good, I'm afraid. She has moments of wakefulness, and she talked some." Frederick gestured toward the cabin. "She's inside. You can see for yourself."

Adrian pointed at Frederick's leg. "You're walking okay now. Were you faking earlier?"

"I wasn't faking it. You went to the spring, didn't you? Its water heals—"

Adrian punched Frederick's arm. "Still taking everything literally. You haven't changed a bit."

Laughing, the two embraced again. After a few seconds, Frederick tapped Adrian on the back. "Is that Sarah?"

Adrian turned. Regina and Sarah stood hand in hand, facing them. Still bare-chested, Sarah shivered, but her smile was as warm as sunshine. "Yes," he said. "We'd better get them inside."

When they entered the cabin, Frederick wrapped the two girls in a deerskin and guided them toward the back of the room, high stepping over and around the other children. As Adrian followed, he scanned the snoozing forms, illuminated by lanterns burning at each corner and daylight streaming in from the open door. Although most were half-naked, they slept without any covering. The closeness of the bodies kept them warm. A few sat up, awake and wide-eyed, watching as the newcomers passed by.

"Nap time," Frederick explained. "They had quite a harrowing night, so they didn't get much sleep."

When they neared the back of the room, Marcelle came into view, sleeping on her back. Adrian stopped a few paces away and stared. With her clean, brushed hair spread out over a bed of broad leaves, her hands folded primly over her tunic, and her eyes closed placidly without a hint of pain, she appeared to be the portrait of a storybook goddess.

Shellinda rose from the spot next to Marcelle and stood in front of Adrian with her hands folded behind her. "You can have my space."

"Thank you." He laid a hand on her cheek. "And thank you for watching her for me."

As she rocked from heel to toe, a gap-toothed smile spread across her face. "You're welcome."

Adrian crouched next to Marcelle and watched her chest rise and fall in a steady rhythm. Every now and then, an arm or leg twitched, and a shallow line creased her brow.

Frederick joined him, also crouching. "It's like watching someone who is witnessing a great adventure. Is she battling a dragon? Chasing a scoundrel? You can try to interpret what's going on, but you can never be sure you're right."

"I remember watching Jason dreaming," Adrian whispered. "He would sometimes punch his pillow and call it all sorts of names."

"Dreaming?" Pursing his lips, Frederick shook his head. "I'm not so sure Marcelle is dreaming. She told me she's on Major Four trying to raise an army. This is just her body. According to her, her spirit is on a journey."

Adrian set a hand on Frederick's forehead. "No fever."

Smiling, Frederick pushed his hand away and settled to the floor. "Relax. I'll tell you what she said."

Adrian sat fully and crossed his legs. "And I have a lot to tell you, but we can't take too long. When you hear what I think Drexel's up to, you'll understand."

After Shellinda brought bread and water to Adrian, Regina, and Sarah, Frederick settled back against a wall. "I learned about a portal leading to Starlight by following one of Prescott's confidants to a forest glade near a gas pipeline. It's west of the village about—"

"No need," Adrian said. "I know where it is. I used the same portal."

"Good. Well, I entered Starlight in a place called the Northlands, which is—"

"Yep. Been there. You don't have to describe it."

Frederick laughed. "Maybe you should tell my story for me."

For the next hour, the two brothers exchanged tales. Most of Frederick's included his rescue efforts at the cattle camp, filling in the gaps the children couldn't have known. Of course he ached to lead every child out of that horrific place, but taking care of four while making clandestine forays into the village without giving away the location of their refuge was already difficult and dangerous. His only hope to rescue the others lay in secretly building a larger nest of sorts until he could bring more refugees, while at the same time working to undermine the dragons by making swords and spears and giving them to the slaves, telling them to hide the weapons until a time when he would call for an uprising. So for now, it seemed that his dilemma still lay before him—let the cattle children suffer and possibly die in the camp or else bring them here where they might starve anyway. Their presence would certainly prevent him from arming the slaves, which would ruin his long-term rescue plans.

Frederick went on to relate his conversation with Marcelle and her wild tale. The evidence that she really was a spirit roaming their home planet seemed sketchy, not completely convincing. Yet Cassabrie was able to spin up a body on Major Four. Maybe Marcelle could do the same and recruit soldiers to participate in an invasion. If anyone could do it, Marcelle could.

While Adrian told his story, Shellinda snuggled up to Marcelle and fell asleep. Regina found her way into Adrian's lap and rested her head in the crook of his arm. Soon she, too, dozed, her mouth ajar and her hands loosely clinging to one of his. Wallace joined them as well, sitting quietly with a sword across his lap.

After explaining his theory regarding Drexel and the healing trees, Adrian let out a long sigh. "So when I talked to Arxad, he seemed nervous. He said to tell you that they need an army, but the Benefile are not the answer, something about their emergence signaling the destruction of his species and ours."

"Arxad knows that the Benefile are in those trees, but he isn't able to enter the glade because he's too big, so he doesn't know that they're skewered like rabbits on spits, and he also doesn't know that it's impossible to get them out. When you try to cut the branches, they grow back in seconds."

"I noticed," Adrian said, nodding, "but Arxad seemed to think you're keeping a secret about them. He's been protecting you so he can learn the secret."

Frederick chuckled. "That old fire-breather is spewing hot air. He refuses to admit that he has a soft spot for the children. He's protecting me for their sakes."

"So there isn't any secret?"

"Only that I can't get the Benefile out." Frederick shrugged. "I didn't see any reason to tell him. I just led him to believe that I would try to let them out if I thought they would be beneficial for us, which is true."

"Does Arxad know where they are?"

"He knows about the trees, but he can't get inside the glade." Frederick drew lines in the air. "The barrier wall ends on the west not far to the north of the trees. If you were to extend the wall southward, the glade would sit just outside of the boundary. An impassable marsh sits a little farther to the west, so it's just as good as a wall. I think the dragons didn't want to work on the wall so close to the trees because of fear of the Benefile."

"So the marsh was an excuse to stop the project?"

"That's my guess."

Adrian rolled his hand into a fist. "We have to stop Drexel. If he succeeds in cutting through the trees, that will ruin my plans."

Frederick arched one eyebrow. "Oh? Why is that?"

"I was thinking I should take Marcelle to the Northlands and put her in one of the healing beds so she could be healed by a tree."

"And a stardrop," Frederick added.

"Right, but even if Drexel can't hurt the trees, if her spirit is on Major Four, what good would taking her to the Northlands do? The problem wouldn't be with her body at all. If she's not dreaming, she's just an empty shell that has occasional visits from its soul." Adrian pressed a finger against the floor. "Maybe I should stay here and see what Drexel's up to. Trying to set the Benefile free would take a while, but if he eventually succeeds, who can tell what they'll do? You might need all the help you can get."

Frederick stared at Marcelle for a long moment before answering. "The idea that her spirit is in another world is just a theory, and a shaky one at that. Even if it's true, she'll come back to Starlight through the Northlands portal. One way or the other, you need to be there. You'll either get her healed or get her spirit reunited with her body. I can handle things here. We don't know if Drexel can release the Benefile or not, and even if he can, there's no solid proof that they'll be a problem." He turned to Adrian. "Go to the Northlands. Marcelle's life depends on it."

Adrian nodded. "You're right. Nothing else makes much sense. I just wish there was a way to protect the trees."

"Leave that to me. I'll have to pay the glade another visit. I hate leaving these kids alone, but there might not be any other way."

"Okay," Adrian said, "that settles it. I'll go to the Northlands."

"It's a long journey. You should take someone with you, a boy who can handle your sword. With all the beasts out there, two warriors are better than one, especially if you're trying to keep Marcelle safe."

Wallace raised a hand. "Take me. I can handle a sword."

Frederick smiled. "We have a volunteer."

"Good." Adrian scanned the room. "I'll need a girl as well, someone who can see to Marcelle's needs."

"Of course. Do you have one in mind?"

"Shellinda and Penelope have served that purpose well, but I don't need both."

Frederick nodded at Shellinda, still snuggling close to Marcelle. "It might be hard to separate those two."

Regina squeezed Adrian's hand. "Don't forget me," she murmured, her eyes still closed. "You can't separate me from you either."

"I'd love to take you, Regina, but you're—"

"Blind?" A pout formed. "I can see some things you can't. You wouldn't have found Sarah without me."

"I can't argue with that, but I still can't figure out how you did it."

She opened her eyes, revealing glazed green irises. "I don't know either. It's been like this ever since I washed in the spring, but sometimes it's all confusing. Things happen in my mind, and then it jumps back and happens again, almost like someone's telling me a story over and over. And sometimes I see things that aren't where I am, like right now I can see the spring and the trees again. Drexel is there with a sword, and he's climbing in the branches, hacking at them."

"Visions," Frederick said. "One of the village elders, a gentleman named Lattimer, told me about a phenomenon like this."

"What did he say?" Adrian asked.

"Quite a bit." Frederick nudged Adrian's leg with his foot. "You mentioned Cassabrie, but you didn't give much detail."

Adrian averted his gaze. Telling him about her indwelling presence would take too much time. "I wanted to keep my story brief. There's a lot more to say about her."

"As I suspected. Lattimer said she was, or is, a Starlighter."

"Right. Cassabrie has the ability to tell tales, and they come to life around her. She receives them from the air and expresses what she sees in her mind."

Frederick nodded at Regina. "Perhaps you have a Starlighter in your lap."

As Adrian gazed at Regina, his thoughts drifted back to his first meeting with Cassabrie, the cold, emaciated waif who had spun into existence as Arxad's emissary. When she later entered his body, she proved herself to be much more than a naïve child. She was an agenda-driven woman who inflamed him with passion. She had a purpose and a plan, and nothing would stand in her way. Now Regina insisted on accompanying him to the Northlands. Were all Starlighters cut from a similar cloth? Arxad had mentioned Koren, another Starlighter, who now traveled with Jason. Maybe Jason had also experienced the power and passion of her presence.

Adrian passed a hand across Regina's scalp, feeling the short bristles. Although young and inexperienced, this green-eyed redhead could very well be the third Starlighter. "I will take you," he said. "You and Shellinda and Wallace."

"I have extra clothes for the journey," Frederick added, "but I gave a lot of my homemade weapons to the villagers, so I can't spare another. You'll have just one sword."

Adrian nodded. "We'll have to manage."

"Oh, one more thing. During her murmurings, Marcelle was lucid enough to ask me to give you some messages."

"Really?" Adrian lifted an eyebrow. "What did she say?"

Frederick raised a finger with each phrase. "She said she would bring soldiers, that Cassabrie would help, and for you to do whatever love tells you."

"Hmmm. Those last two are rather cryptic."

"I thought so, but one other message was quite clear. You know how straightforward Marcelle can be."

"That's an understatement." Adrian raised his hands in mock defense. "I'm ready. Hit me with it."

Frederick lowered his voice, his expression turning serious. "She said to tell you that she loves you."

Lowering his hands, Adrian blinked. "She said that? Are you sure?"

"No doubt about it. She was emphatic."

"Emphatic," Adrian whispered as he looked away. "She loves me."

"Anyway, you'll also need my cart. It will be a tight fit, even for Marcelle, but we'll put plenty of straw under her to make her comfortable."

"That'll help, but ..." He looked again at Marcelle, still lying motionless on her back. "I think I'll carry her as much as I can."

"Why? I know she's small, but her muscles are like rocks. I've carried her, so I know. She's heavier than she looks."

"True, but I want to keep her close. We have a lot to talk about."

*　　　*　　　*　　　*　　　*　　　*

Marcelle looked down the staircase leading to the dungeon's maze. All was quiet. With the dungeon now empty of prisoners, there was no need for guards to roam the halls. The odor of sweat and filth still permeated the upper-level corridor, but the sense of heaviness had lifted. This was no longer a place of cruel oppression.

Holding a yellow glow stick out in front, she descended. After only a dozen steps, a bitter extane film coated her tongue, more biting than in the corridor leading to the pipeline. When she reached the bottom, a wall blocked the path. Condensation dripped down its black surface, drawing wavy lines around tiny crags.

A dark passage led to the left and to the right. The dungeon exit lay somewhere to the right, but in a maze, maybe the opposite way would be the better choice. Still, whoever constructed the maze likely knew that an explorer might guess that.

She shook her head. Trying to overthink this situation didn't make sense. She turned to the right, extended her glow stick, and padded slowly into the darkness.

Something skittered across her feet. She jumped back and lowered the stick close to the floor. A rat scurried away, hugging the right-hand wall.

Staying low, Marcelle followed. The rat probably knew the maze better than anyone, and it wouldn't run to a dead end when pursued.

The black ball of fur raced through several turns. Marcelle battled to maintain her bearings intact, always keeping the direction to the dungeon's rear exit in mind. After a sharp turn toward the exit, the rat stopped, stood on its hind legs, and stared ahead, its nose and whiskers twitching. Letting out a shrill squeak, it dashed between Marcelle's legs and scampered away.

She tucked the glow stick into her pocket and stared into the darkness, waiting for her eyes to adjust. Without a heartbeat or need to breathe, she became like silence itself. Air brushed by her cheeks, first from the front, then from the back, as if the dungeon maze took breaths in her stead. A slight rumble rode with the respiration, like the droning snores of sleeping old men. The dragons were there ... somewhere, most likely close to the exit so they could monitor the gate. Even if they were asleep, sneaking past them might be impossible. Of course, finding out why they were here was important, but so was staying alive.

Marcelle pictured the two dragons as they lay somewhere up ahead, their long necks and tails snaking across the floor. Maybe getting Arxad and Magnar to converse with each other would be the best way to learn their secrets. But how? If only she could be like Cassabrie, able to dissolve and become a disembodied spirit at will. Speaking to the dragons while invisible might prompt them to divulge their secrets.

She withdrew the glow stick, cupped it in a hand, and gazed at her fingers. Somehow she had dissolved twice now, once when she passed through the hole in the escape tunnel's rubble and once when she crumbled in the heat of the execution flames. Is that what Cassabrie meant about urgency? The two events certainly had aspects in common—a need to escape, a deep sense of necessity.

Marcelle closed her eyes. Could she conjure such a need? Or was it something that just had to happen on its own? When Cassabrie crumbled in the grasp of Darien's soldiers, she was in desperate trouble. If even she needed a real impetus, maybe that was the only way. Still, she didn't seem desperate at all when she left the holding cell.

With her other hand, Marcelle withdrew the note to Randall, the key to the next step in the slaves' liberation. She had to plant it where he would find it or else they might never escape. This was real urgency. Maybe being helpless would trigger the necessary passion.

Moving slowly, she unhooked her scabbard and laid it on the ground, then pulled her hood up and drew it over her brow. Holding her glow stick out, she ran toward the rumbling sounds. The yellow aura revealed the floor and walls at each side as she rushed past. After she turned with a bend in the tunnel, a light came into view, a rectangle with crisscrossing bars—the dungeon's exit.

From an alcove to the left, a dragon's head extended across her path, bobbing at the end of a long neck, but it was too dark to tell if it was Arxad or Magnar. She ducked underneath and kept running.

"Stop!" the dragon shouted.

Near the exit gate, Marcelle found a small stone and, shielding her actions with her body, set the note underneath.

"Good. You stopped." The dragon's voice carried a hint of relief. "Who are you, and what are you doing here?"

She edged backwards, not wanting the dragon to get a good look at her face. The voice sounded like Arxad's. She disguised her own voice, deepening it. "Perhaps I should ask you the same questions. It is not becoming of alien creatures to interrogate the aboriginals."

Arxad snorted. "Aboriginals. If only you knew."

"You might be surprised at what I know," Marcelle said. "The *hatching* of your plot is no longer a secret."

Another dragon voice joined in. "We cannot allow this woman to leave. She will reveal our whereabouts."

"What do you suggest?" Arxad asked with an annoyed tone. "Roasting her?"

"Only if she tries to escape. She must remain here until Randall returns. He will know if she poses a threat to our security."

Marcelle nodded. That was the cue. Steeling herself, she spun and sprinted back.

"Halt!" Magnar shouted.

She ducked under the two dragons' heads and ran on. The crackle of an inferno roared toward her from behind. She tripped and fell headlong. When her hands smacked against the ground, they broke and crumbled along with her arms, and when her chest landed, she slid forward, light and free, as if gliding along ice.

A ball of fire flew over her head and farther into the tunnel. The surrounding gas exploded, lighting up the walls until the flames dispersed. Marcelle rolled over and looked back. Sunlight from the exit gate gave a background for the two dragon heads.

"What happened?" Arxad asked.

"She disintegrated." Smoke rose from Magnar's nostrils. "Could the pheterone in this refuge have made my flames that hot?"

"I certainly feel an increased potency, but the exploding pheterone killed her. We are fortunate that it did not collapse the entire chamber."

"Perhaps, but the increased potency is an excellent development."

"Excellent?" Arxad again took on an annoyed tone. "You just murdered a human."

"Murdered? Humans are not sacred. Save that term for dragonkind."

"This is an old debate. The point is if we kill any inhabitants, whether sacred or not, the others will not be likely to do what we ask."

Marcelle pushed against the ground and rose to her feet easily, as if floating. She was probably invisible to them now, a perfect situation. Maybe the dragons really would talk about their purpose. Listening in could be crucial.

"Did you see something?" Magnar asked.

Arxad's head bobbed. "A glimmer of light."

Marcelle froze. Just as with Deference in the Northlands, movement brought visibility.

"Probably the human's embers," Magnar said.

"She was carrying a glowing stick for light. Perhaps we saw that."

"Perhaps." Magnar faced Arxad. "No one need learn about this death. The woman was likely a prisoner in the dungeon who sought a way of escape. Even if the humans learn about her fate, they will care little about her loss."

Arxad nodded. "Yet I am intrigued by her statement."

"What statement?"

Arxad enunciated carefully. "The hatching of your plot is no longer a secret."

"That is not stunning," Magnar said. "Perhaps Randall has succeeded in raising an army, and the humans here already know."

"That is not the plot to which she referred. She emphasized hatching with reference to aboriginals. The first humans here hatched from eggs."

"Nonsense," Magnar said. "Randall knows nothing about that. She could not have learned that from him."

"Then why the emphasis?"

"Taushin hatched from an egg. It is his hatching and ascension to the throne that has provoked our need for an army. It seems that Randall has told everyone the events leading up to our request."

Arxad snorted. "Our demand, you mean. Refusing to take no for an answer is not exactly a request."

"Another old debate. Since the fate of their own race is at stake, I have no qualms about forcing the issue if necessary."

"Your pretense at appealing to the greater good might fool them, my brother, but I have known you for too long. You care only for your continued rule."

Magnar growled. "Beware that you keep your insulting skepticism private. The humans must not know that we are at odds. We have a common goal with them, and whatever happens after we stop Taushin is not my concern. As long as Exodus is airborne and spreading pheterone, they can all leave Starlight. I hope to never see another human again."

"I understand."

The two dragons shuffled back into the alcove and disappeared from view.

Marcelle floated to the point where she had fallen. Near the glow stick, her mourning cloak lay spread out on the floor. She lifted it slowly, revealing dust in a humanlike shape, barely visible in the dimness. The key ring, mirror, charcoal pencil, and parchment pages still weighed down the cloak's pocket, and the sword lay underneath.

As she moved, she scanned her glowing body. Except for the cloak, she wore the same clothes she had on earlier, though now without color. Everything radiated white from top to bottom.

The cloak dropped from her grasp and fell to the side of the pile. Yet, she hadn't let go. It seemed to just slip away. Maybe that's how it was as a spirit. She could touch and carry physical objects, but only for a short time. Deference seemed to have the same limited ability.

She stepped onto the pile of dust. Now what? She had gathered a body from dust three times now—when first arriving, in the pipeline tunnel, and after the execution. Again, what were the common factors? In the two recent cases, she had been in mental contact with her body on Starlight. Was that true also with the initial generation here, when she first created her body? The details seemed fuzzy.

Yet, what did it matter? If it worked twice, maybe it would work a third time.

She stretched out over her dust and closed her eyes. Again, as if trying to awaken from a dream, she concentrated on rising from slumber. It seemed easier than before, maybe from practice, or maybe from no longer being confined to a body.

After a few seconds, it seemed that gravity pulled down on her in a bouncing rhythm. A voice came through, soft and gentle, but a background noise garbled the words. A foul odor rode the moist air, a rotting carcass perhaps.

She opened her eyes. Adrian's profile filled her vision, his face partially veiled by shadows. He carried her in his arms, cradled like a baby. A boy walked in front, wielding a sword and holding the hand of a child, perhaps a girl, who swung a lantern at her side. Behind them, another girl pushed a one-wheeled cart. Their footsteps splashed through shallow water, masking Adrian's whispers, but as Marcelle concentrated on his lips, the words grew clear.

"So even though you had good reason to lack trust in Cassabrie, I think she had a reason behind what appeared to be a selfish plot. Her presence within me and the circumstances it created taught me a great deal about myself ... and about you."

As he paused, marching onward toward the moving light, she gazed at Adrian's profile. A tear tracked down his cheek and into beard stubble, but with his arms occupied, he couldn't brush it away. And those arms! His muscles, so strong and steady, carried his burden effortlessly. How long had he been walking? How long had he been pouring out his soul?

Maybe this was what Cassabrie was talking about. The sword maiden's shield was down. She was vulnerable, open, in a state that allowed Adrian to speak what was on his mind.

Heaving a sigh, he continued. "Back when I forfeited our match, I made a big mistake. Not the forfeiting part. If I had it to do over again, I still would have done that. My mistake was in not talking to you first. I made a show out of it, and I realize now that I was trying to put my family's chivalry on display. You see, my father's reputation was ruined by a liar, and people don't give him the honor he deserves. I guess I wanted to show them the kind of man his teachings fostered, someone who practiced chivalry even at his own expense. I mean, a lot of people thought I was just afraid to fight you. You know, if I won, then so what? I defeated a woman. And if I lost, then the humiliation would have been a burden of shame I would carry to my grave. So, to some, forfeiting looked like a coward's way out.

"But that wasn't true at all. I wasn't afraid of fighting you. I didn't fear clashing swords or the letting of blood. Win or lose, I would still be Adrian Masters. I would still have my honor, in spite of the catcalls and snickering that might go on behind my back. That much I learned from my father's trials. Even with the venomous gossip that dogged him day and night, he never changed. He was always Edison Masters. He was always a father who tucked his little boys into bed each night, who taught them how to fight, how to defend, how to grow strong in body, mind, and spirit. And most of all, he taught us how to treat a lady.

"If you could see how he loves my mother, you would understand. He cherishes her. He would die for her without hesitation. Yet, what he does best of all, he *lives* for her. Every word he speaks to her is kind, never delivered in anger, never spoken to cut or wound."

Adrian laughed. "I think if he ever spoke an unkind word to her, I would be the first to punch him in the nose and shout, 'Who are you, and what have you done with my father?'"

After a short pause, his smile died away. "So what I'm trying to say is this—the reason I couldn't fight you isn't because I feared putting a nick in your sword or a scratch on your skin. My greatest fear was being your adversary. I didn't consciously realize this until Cassabrie's presence made it clear. When she was inside me while I was chained to the Reflections Crystal, and you were out there battling a dragon and Zena and everyone else, Cassabrie laid the choice out in front of me. Did I want to go with her to peace and safety, an eternity of bliss, immersed in her hypnotic charms? Or did I want to go to battle with you, to suffer and maybe die in the white-hot fires of evil?

"That's when I realized the truth. My greatest desire is to be at your side. We are warriors, and I want to be a warrior with you, not against you, and I couldn't bear to do anything as your adversary, whether it was in the heat of a real battle or in the showmanship of a tournament. I want our hearts to beat together. I want our muscles to flex together. I want our swords to swing as one, two blades in harmony, not in conflict.

"You see, battling you in the ring would have been a symbol, an illustration of conflict, and I wanted to avoid any shadow of that with every fiber of my being. So I make no apology for my decision to forfeit, but I hope you will accept my apology for neglecting the most important factor."

After adding another sigh, his voice began to crack. "I should have told you. I should have respected you enough to let you know why I was going to forfeit. I couldn't have told you everything, because I didn't know all of it myself, but I could have at least told you that I didn't want to cross swords with someone …" He licked his lips and took a deep breath. "With someone I love so much."

He nodded. "Yes, I knew that much then. And I think I feared the truth. My father taught me how to love a woman of peace, a woman of gentle ways. I had no idea how to love a woman of war, a woman who would choose sweeping a battlefield with a sword over sweeping a floor with a broom."

As he laughed again, Marcelle squelched her own laugh … and her own tears.

Another pause ensued, allowing the gentle splashes at his feet to again hold sway. Adrian's tear rolled to his chin and fell to the back of her hand. When it trickled around her finger and to her palm, she closed her fist and held it tightly.

"So the point is this, Marcelle, and I hope deep in your mind somewhere you can hear what I'm saying." For a moment, the splashes returned as the only sound. Then, Adrian's voice resounded, stronger and filled with passion. "Will you forgive me for not respecting you enough to tell you all that was in my heart? And if we get through all of this alive, will you …" A lump in his throat rose and fell. "Will you marry me?"

Summoning all her energy, Marcelle forced out a weak, "Yes."

Adrian's head jerked around, and his lovely eyes came into view. "Marcelle! You spoke!"

Trying to smile, she nodded.

"So, you said yes. Yes to what? That you forgive me, or that you'll marry me?"

"Both." Taking a deep breath, she again gathered her strength. "I want to ... marry you ... Adrian Masters. ... I want to ... fight at your side."

More tears fell from Adrian's chin. She turned her hand and let them drip into her palm. "This is ... my symbol. ... I hope you understand."

He pulled her close and whispered into her ear. "I understand. We will catch each others' tears and never be the reason for the shedding. Even if taking you to the healing trees in the Northlands doesn't work, even if you stay paralyzed and can never lift a sword again, I will stay at your side." He kissed her cheek. "I love you. And, by the Creator's strength, my love will last forever."

As his breath warmed her skin, the light ahead shrank and faded, its flickering steadying to a constant glow. Still in darkness, she stared at the light. It wasn't a lantern at all. It was her glow stick, lying on the floor next to her scabbard.

She pinched it and drew it close. Its glow felt warm and comforting. She had a body again, but it seemed that she had left her heart behind. Yet, it was safe. Adrian Masters carried it in his strong arms, and he would never let it fall.

SIXTEEN

MARCELLE pushed the dungeon's trapdoor open a crack. With the keys in her possession, unlocking it this time was much easier than prodding the spring with a sword. She peeked out. No one was in sight.

Lifting the door just enough to squeeze through, she climbed to ground level, then let it fall silently. Holding her cloak's hood closed over her nose and mouth, she hurried down a path that led away from the palace, supposedly a route that passed by the rear of the dungeon.

Although she had lived in the palace for years, there had never been a reason to follow this path of gravel and sand. According to the hunters, it led to the game preserve where every so often the nobles were allowed to shoot at the stags and pheasants that roamed the area. Most arrows flew harmlessly, but a few of the nobles handled a bow with skill and brought home quite a bounty for community feasts. Although tracking animals in the midst of bears and badgers sounded intriguing, women were never allowed to go. For many men, the excursions were likely an excuse to get away from their families, tell tall tales, and spit and belch without care.

As the path continued, it curved slightly to the right and descended into a forested area. Dry pine needles now covered the gravel, making a stealthy approach even more difficult. The crackling under her shoes sounded like twigs snapping. It might as well have been a series of trumpet blasts.

After another minute, the gate came into view on her right, embedded in a long earthwork rise that stretched back toward the dungeon's main entrance. Randall stood with his hands on the gate's wooden bars, his back toward her. The afternoon sun filtered through the trees and painted a mottled yellow glow on his broad shoulders.

He unlocked the gate, swung it open, and walked in. He then kicked away a stone and picked up her note. When he walked out to the light, he drew it close, his head moving back and forth as he read.

Marcelle ducked into the woods to the left of the path and hid behind a wide tree. When Randall finished reading, he squinted, apparently confused.

"Come on, Randall," Marcelle whispered to herself. "It's not that difficult."

After pushing the note into his pocket, he touched his hip. No scabbard was attached.

Marcelle drew her head back. Why would that be? He went to warrior school. He knew better than to walk around unarmed during perilous times.

Something rustled deeper in the woods. Marcelle dropped to a crouch and hid herself among a cluster of bushes. A line of seven men hustled past, all but one with a quiver on his back and a bow in hand. The seventh carried a woman in his arms. Dressed in a dirty white gown, her limbs hanging limply, she appeared to be asleep or unconscious.

The six archers spread out near the edge of the forest, raised arrows and bows, and took aim at Randall, while the seventh laid the woman near the far end of the line. He drew a sword and watched Randall from behind a tree.

Marcelle bit her lip. Should she cry out? Run to help? Yet, the archers didn't appear ready to shoot. They just stood casually with arrow to string. Maybe now that Orion's guardians were in place, he would soon arrive.

Crunching pine needles sounded from the path. Orion approached from the direction of the palace. Wearing a long, hooded cloak, he glanced from side to side as he walked, his brow deeply furrowed, making his hooked nose reach closer to his lips.

Just before the final turn toward the dungeon gate, he caught sight of one of the archers, and his face relaxed. When he reached Randall, he halted and leaned close, apparently whispering.

Randall glanced at the forest, also whispering. Then the two just stared at each other as if in optical combat. Finally, Randall cocked his head and grinned, saying something else too quiet to hear.

Orion turned, walked a few steps back on the path, and shouted, "Archers! Leave us! I am safe!"

The archers lowered their bows, thrust their arrows to their quivers, and marched back the way they had come. As they walked, they tromped heavily and brushed the foliage with intentional swipes. When the forest noise quieted, only the sword-wielding bodyguard remained, the unconscious woman still lying near his feet.

Orion walked toward the dungeon, pulled a photo gun from his cloak pocket, and stopped just out of Randall's reach. "While it is true that dragon allies are of great value on the battlefield," Orion said, aiming the gun at Randall, "they are not so helpful when absent."

Marcelle looked at the bodyguard. It seemed that Orion spoke loudly in order to allow the guard to monitor the conversation.

Maintaining a fiery stare, Randall matched Orion's volume. "What makes you think they're absent?"

Orion shifted the gun toward the open gate. "Shall I fire into the dungeon? That should blow up the only potential hiding place and likely disable any dragon allies who might be there."

Randall stepped to the side. "Feel free to shoot, but you and I both know how long it takes your gun to re-energize. I will be able to disarm you during that time." He spread out his arms. "Or you could just shoot me. The dragons will kill you before you fire another shot. You will never learn the secrets I hold, secrets that could give you control over not only Mesolantrum but all of Major Four as well."

While Orion stared into the dungeon, Randall continued. "Think of it. Viktor Orion would have the power to extend his goodwill throughout the world, granting favor to those who deserve it, the faithful followers who believe in his sacred crusades. Not only that, the great governor could extend that beneficent hand through space, take the Lost Ones into his protective arms, and bring them home to the shouts and adulation of every man, woman, and child on both worlds."

Marcelle nodded. Good show, Randall! Her student was prepared.

Orion lowered the photo gun. "What do you want me to do?"

Randall raised a fist. "Assemble our military forces. Every able man, whether active or retired, must be called to duty, including those in neighboring regions. There is a portal that will take us to a land in Dracon's northern climes, and we will be able to attack the dragon realm by surprise, rescue our people, and make sure no foul beast ever crosses to our world again."

"Why would dragons betray their own kind?"

Randall took a step closer to Orion. "A usurper has taken control there, and the deposed king wishes to restore his rule. If we help him, after we succeed, the high priest of that land will close every portal forever, and both worlds will live in peace."

His stare again locked on Randall, Orion also took a step, closing their gap to a mere arm's length. Orion extended the gun toward Randall and spoke in a tone too low to hear.

As Randall's eyes darted around, he slid his fingers under the gun and lifted it from Orion's palm.

Marcelle cringed. Orion was setting a trap, and Randall was falling for it.

"Why are you doing this?" Randall asked.

Orion pointed at himself, but his voice stayed too low to hear.

When Orion finished, Randall's eyes settled back to a fiery stare. He replied, but his voice again failed to reach Marcelle's ears.

After the two exchanged a few more words, Orion snapped his fingers. The bodyguard sheathed his sword, picked up the woman, and carried her toward the dungeon gate.

Randall reeled back and swiped a hand across his hip but found no sword hilt there.

"Easy, boy," Orion said. "I sent my archers away, but I said nothing to my personal bodyguard. Do not fear."

When the bodyguard arrived, Orion gestured toward the ground. "Lay her here, then go to your quarters. I will see myself home."

The guard laid her on the path. With a hand on his sword hilt, he bowed to Orion and marched back toward the palace. Then, when he reached a point out of their sight, he skulked into the woods and hid behind a tree, not more than twenty paces to Marcelle's right.

Orion swept an arm over the woman. "I found your mother, and I now restore her to you."

"Mother!" Randall lunged to her and knelt at her side. "Mother, wake up. It's me, Randall."

Marcelle bent low to stay out of the bodyguard's sight. Orion had set the bait. He was using an emotional hook to get Randall on his side, and his guard had stayed to ensure that the hook would be set.

Orion curled a hand and looked at his fingernails. "We gave her a mild sedative to help her rest. She will awaken soon."

"If I find out you had anything to do with her imprisonment, I'll ..." Randall rose slowly to his feet, his face and fists tight. "How did you know you needed my mother as a bargaining tool?"

"Bargaining tool?" Orion laughed. "My dear Randall, I have given her to you freely. My bodyguard merely held her in the forest until I was sure it was safe to bring her out. Lady Moulraine has been my friend since childhood, and I would never want to see any harm come to her. If you are looking for an enemy, I suggest you turn your attention to Drexel. When you told me about the note you found in his quarters, I conducted an investigation. My bodyguard found your mother bound and gagged in Bristol's quarters, and you know who held Bristol's leash. She was hungry and thirsty, but unharmed. I hope this gesture convinces you of my goodwill, at least enough to convey confidence to the dragons."

"I see your point." Randall made a cradle with his arms and lifted his mother's body. "I will talk to the dragons."

Randall carried her into the dungeon. Orion leaned to the side, watching for a moment, then turned and hurried along the path.

Marcelle glanced around. The archers were gone. She could take on the bodyguard without a problem.

Shedding her cloak, she drew her sword in the same motion, making sure to keep the blade quiet. The bodyguard emerged from his hiding place and followed Orion. Glancing in every direction, he seemed nervous. Apparently the presence of dragons had everyone on edge.

Marcelle tiptoed out of the forest. Obviously her footfalls would eventually alert the guard, but she could at least get close enough to lunge when he finally heard her sounds.

As she neared, the guard slowly withdrew his sword, his eyes trained on Orion. Marcelle gulped. The guard wasn't listening for her; he had another target in mind.

Just as the guard reared back to slice Orion's neck, Marcelle hissed, "Orion!"

He spun and ducked under the swinging blade. Charging, Marcelle thrust her sword into the bodyguard's back. As he arched his body, she pressed close and covered his mouth with her hand, stifling a shout. When he collapsed, she jerked the blade out and kept her head low, hoping the darkness would conceal her face.

His mouth dropping open, Orion stammered. "You ... you saved my life."

"It seems that conspiracies abound," she said, trying to disguise her voice. She stooped and wiped her blade on the dead man's tunic while watching Orion out of the corner of her eye. "I think you owe me."

"Of course. Of course. Anything you ask." He squinted at her. "Who are you?"

"Anything?" She rose and pointed the sword at him. "Don't make a sound, or you're dead."

He stiffened, then nodded. She guided him deep into the forest and shoved him to the ground, driving his face into the dirt. With the sword again pricking his back, she nudged his ribs with the toe of her boot. "I assume you heard about the missing dungeon prisoners."

As his cheek pressed against the ground, his visible eye rolled toward her. "Marcelle! How is it possible?"

"That I survived the execution?" She laughed. "Your schemes are falling apart, aren't they?"

"Then you *are* a sorceress! When I tell Leo—"

"I'm not a sorceress, and you're not going to tell Leo or anyone else."

"What are you going to do? Stab me in the back while I'm unarmed?"

"No." She gave the sword a gentle push. "That's something you would do."

Orion winced under the blade's sting. "I opposed you publicly, face to face, never in a dishonorable fashion."

"Dishonorable? Was it honorable to set flame to the pyre before I began speaking? Was that in keeping with the spirit of your promise?" She scanned his body. What could she use for a gag? Ah! His socks. "You were kind enough to rescind Leo's gag order, but I'm afraid I can't reciprocate. Take your boots off."

"What do you intend to do?"

She lifted the sword. "Just do it!"

"Very well." He turned over, sat up, and slid his feet out of his boots.

Marcelle pointed with her sword. "Now your socks."

"This is most unbecoming." Orion peeled down his socks—dark purple and knee-length—and flung them on the ground next to Marcelle. "Satisfied?"

"Not yet." She pressed the point of the sword under his chin. "Stand up."

Orion rose slowly, swallowing as he looked cross-eyed at the blade.

Marcelle nodded toward a nearby tree. With leafy vines hanging from head-high branches, it would be perfect. "Pull down some of those vines."

"It seems that you are inventing this scheme as you go."

She scooped up his socks. "That's what makes life exciting."

He grabbed a vine and pulled. The upper end broke loose from a high branch and reeled down to a pile at his bare feet. "Now I suppose you want me to tie myself up."

"As much as you can." She pointed the sword at the trunk. "Stand there and hold the vine up to your chest."

Scowling, he picked up the vine and stood with his back against the trunk, the vine under his armpits. She scampered to the other side, leaned her sword on the tree, and jerked the vine tight.

Orion let out a grunt. "If you intend to murder me by humiliation, you are well on your way."

"That would be too merciful." She tied a secure knot. "The next step will be a dose of justice."

"Justice?"

She stalked around the tree, keeping her eyes trained on him as she orbited, reeling out the vine and binding his arms to his side. "You kidnapped innocent children," she said as she eased into a haunting tone. "You chained them to dungeon walls and stuffed dirty rags in their mouths to keep them from crying out. Giving them barely enough food and water to survive, you used them as insurance, a way to keep your posterior in power. You are the one practicing sorcery, for you bind the hearts of the valiant with a force greater than courage—the love of parents for their offspring. Like a sorcerer, you transformed that love into shackles and emasculated fathers; you ripped the hearts out of mothers, and you made the world a living hell for souls who should be playing with dress-up dolls and clashing sticks in mock battle instead of choking on filthy rags, wallowing in their own waste, and silently crying out to the Creator asking why Daddy hasn't charged to their rescue."

The moment Orion's mouth opened to respond, she pushed his socks inside and jammed them in so deeply, he gagged. His cheeks bulged, and his face reddened. He coughed and heaved, but the socks stayed put.

Finally shifting the socks enough to breathe, he glared at her, his eyes casting obscene insults.

Marcelle sheathed her sword. "You told me that the children were well cared for. Since this is your definition of that term, I assume you won't complain." She reached up and grabbed more vines. "Now to tie you more securely."

After a few minutes, she had wound several vines around Orion and the tree, securing his arms more firmly and binding his legs. Then, brushing her hands together, she stood in front of him and crossed her arms over her chest, leaning back slightly to admire her work. "Not bad for a sorceress who was burned at the stake, don't you think?" She waved her hand. "No need to respond. It's not polite to talk with your mouth full."

She pivoted toward the dungeon. It was time to pay Randall a visit.

When she reached the forest edge, she looked at the gate leading to the maze. It was now closed, and Randall was nowhere in sight.

After glancing both ways down the path, she dragged the guard's body into the forest underbrush, then hustled to the gate and peered inside. A draft wafted into the maze and then out again, carrying with it a slight rumble—dragon respiration. They were still in there, but where had Randall gone? Obviously he had to care for his mother, and he probably wouldn't be able to find safe refuge for her in the palace. That meant a journey to a peasant commune, which would take a while. Also, dinnertime loomed. With the dragons locked up, Randall would have to find food for them. Dragons probably ate a lot, and keeping them satisfied wouldn't be an easy job, especially since extane likely increased their metabolism.

She hurried back to the woods and stood in front of Orion. "Promise to keep your voice down, and I'll relieve you of the gag."

His face bright red, he nodded.

Marcelle reached in and withdrew the damp socks. After shaking them out, she pushed the ends into her trousers pocket and let them hang there. "Better?"

His scowl returned. "As if you cared."

"I do care. I saved your life, didn't I?"

"You did, but obviously for your own purposes."

"True. I can't deny it." After retrieving her cloak and draping it over the ground, she lowered herself and sat cross-legged on the cloak's edge near the pocket that held the mirror, keys, pencil, and parchments. "Try to relax. It might be a while before Randall returns."

As she sat, she pushed her hand into the pocket and caressed the mirror's wood while gazing at the sky through the canopy above. Afternoon waned. Solarus was likely already setting. The palace's banquet room would be filling with the residents and the usual parasitic freeloaders who invited themselves to the bounty. A few seats would be conspicuously empty—her own, her father's, and the chair at the elevated table, Orion's. With the governor absent, Maelstrom would have a prime opportunity to make sure the next backside to fill that seat was his own.

As the darkness of evening settled in, Marcelle refocused on Orion. "What was Leo doing the last time you saw him?"

He glared at her. "With such maltreatment from a witch, do you expect me to reveal what I know?"

She shot to her feet, whipped out her sword, making metal ring on metal, and pressed it against his throat. "As a matter of fact, I do."

He looked down the blade, this time with less fear in his eyes. "I suspect that you will kill me whether I tell or not, so your histrionics will avail you nothing."

"Allow me, then, to deduce his actions." She slid the sword away. "After witnessing his power in the courtroom and his animosity toward you at my execution, I have been wondering about his absence since that time. Someone who publicly displays such power doesn't usually go into hiding afterwards. Why would that be?"

"He is seeking witches. Such a hunt requires stealth."

She laughed. "I know you don't believe that. He is seeking something else, isn't he? Because of your cowardly kidnappings, he found no military leaders willing to help him usurp you, but they are likely more than willing now that their loved ones have been restored. They went to him and conceived a plan to remove you from office. Leo has been scarce during recent hours because he has been plotting the assassination I saved you from. And since he secured military help in that plot, you have no hope of regaining your seat of power."

Orion stayed silent, his face hardening.

Marcelle laughed again. "Why, Governor Orion, it seems that you should be expressing more thankfulness to your deliverer!"

He turned his head and looked away. "I didn't need your deliverance. I was protected until you meddled in my affairs."

"Protected? You mean you hid behind the skirts of imprisoned little girls." She sat again, this time with her knees propped up. "My guess is that Maelstrom, or Leo, as you call him, is even now in the process of gaining control of the palace and more of the military. If I were to release you, I would be sending you to your death. It is in your best interests to cooperate with me."

With his brow bent low, he fixed his gaze on her. "What is it that you want?"

"With Captain Reed on my side, I'm sure I can get a detachment sent to the dragon world, but in order to requisition supplies—"

A rustling sound filtered through the woods, moving from left to right toward the dungeon. Marcelle jumped up, jerked the socks from her pocket, and shoved them into Orion's mouth. Grunting and blowing, he tried to expel them, but he soon gave up.

"Don't go anywhere." Marcelle followed the sound. Fortunately the noise masked her own footfalls, making stealth easy. When she reached the forest edge, Randall came into view, dragging a stag by its antlers up to the dungeon's rear entrance.

Holding a bow over his shoulder, he dropped the stag, opened the gate, and called into the maze. "Come out. I have your dinner."

After a few seconds, Arxad and Magnar emerged and stretched their wings and limbs. With the moon now casting its glow, their scales shimmered as if aflame in white and yellow.

Marcelle crept closer on hands and knees, hoping to hear. They would likely keep their voices quiet.

Randall nodded toward the stag. "I didn't have much time, so I have only this one. I hope it's enough."

"Thank you," Arxad said. "It will be sufficient."

Magnar extended his neck, bringing his head close to Randall. "I heard some of your conversation with the new governor, but you intentionally kept your voices low during much of it. What were you hiding?"

"I kept my voice down for Orion's sake. I'll tell you everything I know."

While Randall spoke, Magnar opened his maw and clamped down on the stag's midsection, crunching the bones loudly and forcing Marcelle to sneak on her belly to continue listening. Fortunately, the breeze blew from their direction. They wouldn't detect her scent. Still, even this close, most of Randall's words were garbled, as if chewed and spat out by Magnar. His final statements, however, came through clearly.

"So Orion wants to send a small number of troops to see if our claims about your planet are true. He doesn't want to leave Meso-lantrum undefended."

Magnar swallowed, spilling blood over his chin, and looked at Arxad. "You expected this offer. Is your counsel unchanged?"

With his gaze drifting toward Marcelle, Arxad nodded. "Any leader would have the same concern Governor Orion has. I urge you to take this opportunity to make peace with Darksphere's rulers and fight our common enemy under these judicious terms. There is no reason to insist on your original plan."

Marcelle closed her eyes to slits. If Arxad caught their gleam, he would know that a spy was in their midst.

"True," Magnar said. "A scouting cadre of humans will report that we have told the truth. Yet surely Taushin realizes our plan by now. He could delay his ultimate weapon until he is certain all the forces against him have arrived."

Randall raised a hand. "Hold on a minute. What ultimate weapon?"

While Magnar resumed his noisy eating, Arxad shifted his focus to Randall. "As you might expect, we would not request an army unless we anticipated great danger. Taushin hopes to unleash a weapon that will kill every human on Starlight, including invading forces from Darksphere."

"What exactly is this weapon?"

"A hovering body of light we call Exodus. Taushin hopes to use Koren the Starlighter as its pilot to spread a disease that is always fatal to humans."

Randall shook his head. "Koren wouldn't do that. At least not intentionally. She's on our side."

Magnar swallowed again, sending a huge lump down his throat. "How little you know. Starlighters are unpredictable. Cassabrie and Zena proved that. Koren now wears the dark vestments and is doing Taushin's bidding. I knew this could happen. That's why I insisted on her execution, but Arxad, in his mercy, prevented me from averting this crisis."

"Why didn't you subdue Taushin?" Randall asked. "He's blind, right?"

"Arxad hoped to keep Taushin free because he alone knew how to seal a hole in Exodus and make it rise. Implementation of that knowledge would allow the star to fill the atmosphere with pheterone, the gas you call extane. With pheterone abundant, we could release the slaves and send them home. We hoped to learn the secret for resurrecting Exodus, work out a way to implement it without spreading the disease, and then subdue Taushin before he implemented it himself. That is why we are here."

"But you didn't have a way to get here until you found the portal peg. This plan could never have worked without it."

"I didn't have a way to get here," Magnar said. "Because of a curse, I am unable to pass our barrier wall to the north or the mountains to the south. If we had been unable to find the crystal, Arxad would have guided the human army through a portal that emerges in our world in the Northlands."

Randall squinted at him. "A curse? What kind of curse?"

Arxad glanced Marcelle's way, a hint of recognition in his eyes. "In our region of Starlight," he said, "we have constructed a wall on three sides, which the slaves believe to be a way to keep them in. That is true to a point, but the wall, combined with a mountain range on our southern border, creates a barrier that keeps something out, as well. These borders have been the site of many battles, so in order to establish peace, Magnar agreed to a mutual exile for the kings of the opposing sides, and a curse is the sealing enforcement. Our king, Magnar, is unable to cross the barriers, and in exchange, our opponents are unable to enter. Not only that, the curse sent our opponents to a place of captivity we know little about, and their king has been separated from them for as long as the curse is in effect. Because of this agreement, we live at peace."

"You have opponents that could threaten dragons?" Randall let out a whistle. "What kind of creatures are they? Another dragon species, or something else?"

Magnar slapped his tail on the ground. "Enough! We will talk no more of this. It is irrelevant to the matter before us."

"Okay, okay!" Randall kept his eyes on Magnar, apparently deep in thought.

Marcelle focused on Arxad. He seemed to be staring right at her. If he knew she was watching and listening, why hadn't he alerted the others?

"It's all coming together," Randall said, nodding, "except for one thing. How could a newly hatched dragon know a secret that no one else knew?"

Arxad broke away from his stare and looked at Randall. "I wondered that for centuries. We have a prophecy that foretold his ability, but we could only guess at how he would learn something no one else knew. Not even the king of the Northlands knew. He told me so himself."

"Do you know now?" Randall asked.

"We have a theory. Zena used another Starlighter's finger to communicate with Taushin while he was yet in the egg. That Starlighter, Cassabrie, was powerful, and even in death it is clear that her body radiates the mysteries of Starlight. Through a single finger, she might have communicated to Taushin the key to sealing Exodus."

Randall shivered. "How do you know her body is powerful in death?"

Arxad looked at Magnar, apparently seeking approval.

Nodding, Magnar heaved a wave of sparks that floated upward with the heated air. "We have told him everything else."

"We also have an ultimate weapon," Arxad said. "We have preserved Cassabrie's body. If we could restore her spirit to her body, we would have the more powerful of the two Starlighters. Cassabrie would be a force Taushin could not overcome, even with Koren fully on his side."

"Even if Taushin unleashed the disease?" Randall asked. "Are Starlighters immune?"

"Koren wasn't immune, but ..."

Marcelle cringed. Arxad was again looking her way. What did he have in mind?

"*Wasn't* immune?" Randall tilted his head to the side. "How could you know that unless she contracted it? And if she contracted it, then how could it always be fatal?"

A low rumble emanated from Magnar's throat. "Take care, Arxad. The human's questions will never end until he learns everything."

"This will be the last response." Arxad shifted his focus back to Randall. "She did contract the disease, and she died, but that story is one you need not hear. For now, we should—"

"Wait a minute! You can't spring that on me without explaining it. How could Koren have died? She's alive ..." Randall squinted. "Isn't she?"

"She is alive," Arxad said, "but if I tell you that story ..."

"No!" Magnar's head wagged at the end of his swinging neck. "I draw the line there. We cannot allow the humans to know. Not yet."

Randall jabbed a finger toward Magnar. "Listen. You're asking us to fight *your* battle, for *your* kingdom. Don't tell me—"

"For the lives of *your* people," Magnar said, nearly shouting. "And I will share *my* knowledge at *my* discretion. If lacking an answer to a question keeps you from a rescue attempt, then by all means stay here with your fellow soldiers, and we dragons will do what we must to save our planet. If the lives of human slaves are lost in the effort, then so be it. I will tell them that the people of Darksphere abandoned them because of their insatiable curiosity about tangential matters."

Randall shook his bow at Magnar. "Don't play me for a fool. I've watched my father's political maneuvering all my life, and I recognize a brow-beating dodge when I see one. You're the ones who kidnapped my people and enslaved them in the first place, so don't give me that verbal excrement about curiosity. You should be thanking us that Orion didn't order an immediate invasion to wipe out your species from the face of your planet."

Magnar shot a sizzling ball of flames that flew within inches of Randall's ear. "You fool! If you knew the truth, you would drop down on your knees and beg for forgiveness! You are indebted to us for your life, especially to Arxad, so—"

"Stop!" Arxad fanned his wings and blocked both Randall's mouth and Magnar's. "This is senseless."

Magnar knocked Arxad's wing out of the way with his own. "You and I both know that he is the senseless one. He barks at the howling wind, an ignorant mongrel who knows neither the source nor the direction of the breaths that gave him life." Huffing another spark-filled snort, he shuffled toward the dungeon gate. "If you can speak sense to him, then do so, but you may not tell him about his origins. You have said too much already." He squeezed through the opening and faded into the darkness inside.

Arxad let his wings droop, uncovering Randall's mouth. Curling his neck, he brought his eyes level with Randall's. Although close enough to allow a whisper to be heard, he kept his speaking volume high, as if to make sure Marcelle could hear. "There is much you do not know, and you lack even the knowledge of why you do not know. Do not allow your curiosity to overcome your commitment. Trust me. Learning these secrets will not help you."

While Randall stared at the dungeon, apparently in deep thought again, Marcelle kept her focus on Arxad. There was no doubt about it. He knew she was there. His last speech seemed to indicate that there was nothing left to learn from eavesdropping. With Magnar gone, maybe it was a good time to talk to Randall.

She rose slowly to her feet and backed away. She was too close to approach. Randall might not like it if he discovered that she had been spying on him. Maybe sneaking back to the forest edge and making some noise from there would be a better idea.

Randall loosened his fingers around his bow. "There is one piece of information I'll need to know right away—the location of the other portal. If I am to lead Orion's scout team, I have to tell them how to prepare. A long march? Cold weather?"

As Marcelle backed away, her shoe crunched a bit of gravel on the path. She halted, cringing.

Arxad's ears rotated, as if searching for the source of a sound. He heard, but apparently Randall didn't. "Well," Arxad replied, "there is a problem. It has been so long since I passed through that portal myself, I am not certain I can find it again from this side. Forest growth has altered the landscape, so it is no longer familiar to me. In recent times, however, I sent an emissary who has informed me about the portal's location relative to landmarks you probably know."

"For example?"

Marcelle continued backing away. Soon she would reach the forest and could approach without Randall suspecting anything.

Arxad again kept his voice raised. "My emissary mentioned a gas pipeline's termination point in the forest. The portal is perhaps a ten-minute walk from there."

"Okay," Randall said. "I think I know where that is. We can get there in less than an hour. But what about the conditions where it comes out in your world?"

"Have the soldiers prepare for very cold weather, including ice and snow, then for a march of perhaps two days with a change to temperate conditions as their journey proceeds."

"That shouldn't be a problem. When should I tell Orion to have the men ready?"

"As soon as possible. Already the march from the Northlands might take more time than we have." Arxad turned toward the dungeon, but curled his neck to keep his focus on Randall. "Come for us when you are ready to depart."

"I will."

Arxad squeezed through the gateway and disappeared into the dungeon's entry corridor.

Marcelle nodded. Perfect. Arxad was gone. She strode down the path, her hand clutching the hilt of her sword. "I heard you talking about having the men ready. Maybe you should ask a woman what to do."

SEVENTEEN

RANDALL backed away a step, his eyes wide. "Marcelle?" He leaned closer. "Are you all right?"

She waved a hand. "I'm fine. Just pay attention. I have been listening to your plans. This isn't the time to play games with Orion. This is life and death. Strike hard, and strike now."

Shaking his head, Randall laughed. "I assume you have an idea to go along with that bravado."

"I do. Didn't you get my note?"

"Oh! So *you're* the M!"

"Of course." Marcelle set a hand on her hip. "Do you think any male soldier would have handwriting like that?"

"Well, I wasn't sure. It's possible that it was dictated to a female who just ran out of ink."

Marcelle rolled her eyes. "No, Randall. I just wanted to make sure no one else knows I'm here in Mesolantrum. I thought you had seen my handwriting enough times to know who wrote it."

"Okay, okay. I get the point." Randall glanced away for a moment, his face displaying a hint of shame. "You said you want more troops. What's your plan?"

"It's simple. We abandon the reconnaissance contingent idea, escort Orion directly to Starlight, and force him to order his armies to join us immediately."

"Kidnap him? Don't you know how many guards he has? Even his bodyguard has a bodyguard, and he has archers with him wherever he goes."

"Didn't you pay attention? He sent his archers and bodyguard away."

"Right. I saw that." His expression seemed to want to add "so what," but he stayed quiet.

Marcelle let out a huff. "Follow me, my friend." She marched toward the forest, trying to display a confident stride. As she walked, she focused straight ahead. Randall's footfalls were almost completely silent. Apparently he had learned to apply his training well.

She halted at the tree where Orion still stood bound and gagged. He wriggled and grunted, but the socks muffled every word.

"He's enjoying a meal of socks," Marcelle said, pointing at Orion's bare feet. "It's all I could find."

Randall gasped. "You kidnapped the governor?"

"Desperate times call for desperate measures." She winked. "Besides, have you ever known me to do things diplomatically?"

"Okay." Randall stretched out the word, obviously skeptical. "What's the next step? Authorization letters for our army? A call-to-arms appeal to the other governors?"

Marcelle pressed a thumb against her chest. "Leave both to me. We'll get the signatures now, and I'll fill in the verbiage. I already have the funds I need to get supplies for the troops. Now all we need to do is get Orion to Starlight right away so there'll be no chance for him to countermand the letters."

"If we can find the portal," Randall said. "We know its approximate location, but we still have to find it."

Marcelle picked up a long stick and began scratching a bare patch of dirt. "I know where it is. I'll draw a map."

With a desperate heave, Orion spat out the socks. "Don't listen to her! She's a witch, I tell you. A witch!"

Marcelle whipped out her sword and set the point under his chin. "If you breathe another word, you will see your tongue skewered on this blade."

His eyes flaring, Orion pressed his lips together and nodded.

Randall picked up the socks. "Governor Orion, I thought you said your witch-hunting days were over." He gave Marcelle a nod. "Let him answer, as long as he does so quietly."

She lowered the blade but kept it at the ready.

"I …" Sweat beaded on Orion's forehead. "I did give up witch hunting, but look at her. She is practically a ghost. Feel her hands. They are icy. You will see."

Randall looked at her hands. "Marcelle, do you have chills?"

She gave him a hot glare. "We don't have time to do a medical diagnosis. Let's get on with the plan."

"Feel them," Orion said, nodding rapidly. "You cannot deny your own observations. I could tell you more of what I have seen, but you likely would not believe me."

"That's enough!" Marcelle grabbed the socks from Randall and stuffed them back into Orion's mouth.

"Marcelle?" Randall reached for her. "Something really is wrong with you. Let me feel your hand."

She sidestepped his reach. "I told you I'm fine."

As he stared, she averted her eyes. How could she keep avoiding the obvious? Just display some negative body language to repel his questions? She crossed one arm over her chest and clutched her opposite bicep, tapping her foot with feigned impatience.

"The things I don't know keep piling up," Randall said, "but at least we have a plan that should work." He turned toward the palace. "Let's get moving."

"Wait!" Marcelle grabbed his sleeve.

Randall pivoted back. "What?"

"I need you to fill me in," she whispered as she glanced at Orion. "What's your story? Did you go to Starlight?"

He nodded, keeping his own voice low. "With Jason and a couple of others."

"Others? Who?"

"Do you know Elyssa and Tibalt?"

"Yes, of course. I met them both in the dungeon." Marcelle resumed her toe tapping. "So that's where they went. I supposed Drexel got them out of the dungeon. I'm surprised he kept his promise."

"Jason got them out, but it's a long story that'll have to wait. All three of them are still on Starlight, and they're all likely in trouble with the dragons."

Marcelle nodded. "And Adrian and Frederick, too."

"So let's get going and—"

She tugged his sleeve again. "Help me get Orion's signature for the letter of marque I'm having drawn up." She picked up her mourning cloak and withdrew one of the two remaining parchment pages. "We'll cut him loose, and one of us will guard him while the other gets his signature."

"Since you know the way to the portal, maybe I should get the letter drawn while you take Orion to the portal."

Marcelle shook her head. "I have dealt personally with the military commanders, so let me handle the letter while you go with Orion and the dragons. Get some warm clothes and enough supplies for a few days, and I'll be there as soon as I can with the soldiers."

"I took my mother to Jason's commune. I can probably get clothes for us there. I'm not sure if anything will fit Orion, as tall as he is, but we'll see." Randall looked toward the forest beyond the dungeon. "You said you could draw a map."

"I'd better do that before we get the signature." Marcelle withdrew the final parchment page along with the charcoal pencil. She made a twirling motion with her finger. "Turn around. I need a surface to write on."

Randall complied. "Now I'm a desk?"

"That's right." She pressed the page against his back and drew a serviceable map. Although it wasn't to scale, and it omitted details, Randall was skilled enough to follow it. "I'm done."

When he turned around, she pointed at the charcoal lines. "It's a little past the forbidden zone, but if you stay alongside Miller's Creek, you shouldn't get lost, especially since Adrian and I have both been there recently. The trail we blazed should be easy to follow."

"Maybe not so easy in the dark. By the time I get supplies, it might be midnight."

"Perfect. All the better for keeping the dragons out of sight."

"Good point. That won't be easy. Maybe it would be better just to let everyone see them so they'll believe in Dracon."

Marcelle shook her head. "We don't want panic. With Maelstrom likely having his way in the palace by now—"

"Maelstrom?"

"The new Counselor. Leo. But that's another long story. Just realize that with Orion gone, Leo probably hasn't wasted any time in taking Mesolantrum's reins. If we have panic and a potential dragon threat, the troops will be less likely to come with me."

Randall nodded. "Another good point."

"One question, though," she said, raising a finger. "Did you hear about the execution of a witch?"

His face hardening, he leaned close to her and whispered. "Definitely. Everyone wanted to go, including some slaves we rescued from Starlight. They were hoping to do whatever they could to stop the execution. It took me all morning to convince them to stay in hiding."

Marcelle kept her voice low as well. "Did you know I was the one being executed?"

"You? No." He glanced at Orion. "Why? And how did you escape?"

"I'll have to tell you later. I was just wondering why you weren't there." She tapped on an open circle at the end of the map's trail. "The portal is in the middle of a clearing, and it should be open, meaning that if you walk through it, you'll instantly be in a snow-blanketed forest. That's the Northlands. I'm sure the dragons can guide you from there."

"Got it." He took the map, folded it, and stuffed it into his tunic's inner pocket. "Let's get the signature."

Marcelle cut through the vines binding Orion and extended the parchment and pencil. "It's for your own good. If you give me control of the military, we will crush Leo when we return from Dracon. Otherwise, he'll gain control first, and you'll have no hope of stopping him."

"I had control until you came along." He snatched the pencil and page. "I'll need a writing surface."

"I found Randall's back to be a fine desk." She pushed the tip of her sword close to Orion's ear. "Just make sure your hand doesn't shake."

After signing the page, he gave it and the pencil back to Marcelle. "Take care, young lady, that you stay wary of Leo. He is more dangerous than you realize. He is a sorcerer whose power is from the Creator's enemy, and it continues to strengthen with every person's energy he absorbs. The soldiers you muster might not be enough to defeat him."

"Then why did you bring him here?" Randall asked. "I thought you wanted to rid Mesolantrum of sorcerers."

"To be sure. You see, Leo wants to rule the world, and he knows that other practitioners of sorcery would forever be hoping to steal his power, so he is obsessed with finding them and taking their power first. After he eliminated the others, I had a plan to eliminate him, but you have ruined it."

"How so? Can't we implement your plan?"

"Not with my leverage gone. Those children were the keys to keeping Mesolantrum out of his hands. At the right time, I would have restored them to their parents and blamed Leo for the kidnapping. Then the fiery wrath of fatherly indignation would have fallen on Leo's head. Now that the children are home, Leo will likely threaten them himself in order to control the military and keep his newfound power. So, in spite of all your meticulous planning, my signature will do you very little good."

"I can use it if I hurry." Marcelle rolled the page up. "Leo hasn't had time to inform everyone yet." She looked at the sky. A bank of thin clouds now veiled the moon. "You'll need a torch."

"I'll get one at Jason's," Randall said. "I know the way well enough from here to there. We'll take a path that'll keep us out of sight, and then we'll return for the dragons."

"That should work."

Randall gestured with his sword toward a narrow trail that led deeper into the woods. "Former Governor Orion, if you'll precede me, I will provide directions."

Grumbling under his breath, Orion trudged ahead on the trail.

Randall gave Marcelle a half smile as he passed, whispering, "I'm traveling with two dragons and a bizarre species yet to be named. Thanks a lot."

Marcelle smiled in return, though he probably couldn't see it. After a few seconds, the rustling of forest debris diminished, leaving only the sound of a gentle breeze in her ears. She clutched the rolled-up note. Getting this to Dunwoody remained the highest priority. She had to gather the troops as soon as possible, but one question remained that wouldn't relent. Why was Arxad watching her? Did he want to say something? Although dragons weren't trustworthy, he seemed wiser than the others. Simply learning what was on his mind couldn't hurt.

After putting the mourner's cloak on again and sliding the note into her pocket, she jogged to the forest edge and emerged onto the path. With thicker clouds moving in, the open area seemed every bit as dark as the forest. Torchlight flickered at the distant palace, but it didn't help at all.

Keeping her footfalls as quiet as possible, she crept closer. When she reached the gate, she peered inside, again listening for the sounds of dragon respiration. As before, gentle rumbles drifted past. But which dragon was closer? Arousing Magnar wouldn't be a good idea.

A low whisper glided with the rumbles. "I am glad you have come."

Marcelle gripped one of the gate's bars. "Arxad?"

Two eyes appeared, framed by a dark shape that swayed from side to side. "Yes, it is I. I assume you are wondering why I focused on you earlier without signaling my king."

She nodded. "You are very perceptive."

"That is part of my occupation." He drew so close, his hot breath caressed her cheeks. "That is why I have also discerned that there is great political turmoil here. Orion walks and speaks like a threatened man. I assume there is a potential usurper who would wrest away his power."

"Right again. But I'm afraid it's more than just potential. He might already be in control. And he might be more powerful than we can handle."

"Trust me. I understand. We have the same problem in our world." Arxad's head stopped swaying for a moment. A few sparks spewed from his nostrils and drizzled to the ground. "Perhaps your race will provide the solution to our crisis, and our race can do the same for yours."

"What do you mean?"

"We need your military presence in order to conquer a usurper, Taushin by name."

Marcelle nodded. "I overheard the story."

"I must return to my world in order to ensure that Taushin's schemes are averted, but if Magnar returns by way of the North-lands portal, he will unleash a curse that will have unpredictable consequences."

"Are you saying you want to leave him here on Major Four?"

"To help you battle your usurper. Surely he is not more power-ful than Magnar."

Marcelle tilted her head. "Why would Magnar help us? He hates humans."

"Hatred will fuel his passion. The question is whether or not we can find the proper motivation to direct and control his destruc-tive power."

"Well, if the usurper obstructs us from mounting an army that will go to Starlight, wouldn't Magnar want to help us?"

Arxad's head lifted an inch. "Is such an obstruction likely?"

"I think so. We believe Maelstrom, our usurper, hopes to use our military to strike at the heart of our kingdom so he can become king himself." She glanced past Arxad, but no other dragon was in view. "You mentioned Magnar's power, but I'm afraid Maelstrom has a lot as well. He not only can absorb energy, he is able to per-suade to an almost miraculous degree."

"Interesting. I have heard of such a creature."

"Whatever he is, he'll be able to convince the military leaders of an invented pretext for invading."

"Then you have a pretext of your own that needs no invention. It would be better for all involved if Maelstrom is empowered to obstruct your plan, thereby creating the impetus we need for Mag-nar to eliminate him."

Marcelle nodded. "I understand, but what do we do with Magnar after that?"

"By then I will have been able to arrange passage through a portal in a mining mesa in our own region. Magnar knows how to get to the location of that portal in your world."

"Since that portal leads straight into your region, can we use it for our military? Avoiding the Northlands would be helpful."

"Perhaps, but my ability to open it soon is not guaranteed. It would be better to plan on going through what we know to be open rather than risk marching to a closed door that would surely demoralize your men. They might not be willing to try a second one."

"That's true." Marcelle gazed into Arxad's sparkling eyes. They seemed so sincere, so truthful. Yet one part of the plan remained unaddressed, and it would take a dose of insincerity from Arxad to make it work. "How are you going to trick Magnar into staying here?"

Arxad blinked, momentarily shielding the sparkle. "I am uncertain if I will be able to do so, but there is one person I could use to bring about our desired purposes. She is unpredictable, so my uncertainty is warranted."

"Unpredictable?" Marcelle couldn't hold back a smile. "Let me guess. Cassabrie."

"Correct. She is supposed to monitor the portal. If she sees us and materializes there, I might be able to persuade Magnar to stay away for the time being. She is very powerful, and, although Magnar denies it, he fears her. Then while he is away, perhaps we can pass through the portal and leave him behind."

"Won't that get you in trouble with Magnar?"

"A great deal of trouble, but no more than I have endured in the past. If at the end of our conflicts he is once again king of the dragons on Starlight, his wrath will be appeased."

Marcelle lifted her sword and propped it on her shoulder. "Just remember, as long as one human slave remains on Starlight, our wrath will never be appeased. Our armies will never relent. And my blade will find Magnar's belly. They will all be set free, or else."

Arxad's head bobbed. "Our ultimate goals are the same—freedom for your people, survival for ours, and peace between our worlds."

"So be it. As a representative of the human species, I pledge to fight for your cause, to unseat your usurper."

"A pledge without condition? Even if all the human slaves have already been freed?"

She nodded. "Even if."

"In spite of the dangers presented by a possible disease in my land?"

"I heard you talking to Randall about the disease. Since my people are in danger as well, I must take that risk. It won't stop me from keeping my word." Marcelle sheathed her sword and reached between the bars. "Do dragons shake hands?"

"Ah! A human's sign of solemn agreement." Arxad's head swayed from side to side. "We do not share that symbol."

She drew her hand back. "Then how do you seal a vow?"

"For an unbreakable vow, we rip off a scale bordering our vulnerable spot and offer an exchange. Since the wound we make is raw, the new scale adheres and stays. In fact, I am wearing one of Magnar's now, and he is wearing one of mine. It is said that if we break the covenant, the scale will fall off, and we will be easy prey, but the truth is more immediate than that. As long as we possess the scale of the one with whom we have made a covenant, we are constantly reminded of it, because the scale never feels natural. Its presence prods. Its foreignness pricks body and mind. For as long as I have lived, I have never known a dragon to break such a vow."

"That is a poignant symbol, but—"

A soft grunt sounded. Then Arxad's clawed hand appeared between the bars with a body scale covering it.

Marcelle gasped. "You … you didn't have to do that!"

"Yes, I did." He extended it farther. "Take it."

She picked up the palm-sized scale. "Where should I put it?"

"It is still moist," Arxad said as he withdrew his foreleg. "It should adhere to your skin wherever you choose to place it."

Marcelle cringed. This dragon, a member of the cruel race that had enslaved and tortured her people, scourging the backs of children with razor whips, now wanted her to wear a symbol of his species. In a sense, he was asking her to become one of them, to step into his scaly hide, to put on, as it were, his draconic likeness.

She drew the scale close and studied its surface. As she tilted her hand back and forth, the scale shimmered in the failing moonlight, like a mirror coated with condensation, clear enough to provide a phantom reflection, yet warped and indistinct. With each new angle, her image bent and twisted, becoming less and less humanlike.

Turning, she looked toward the palace and its flickering torches. Within those walls sat a human—a twisted, warped human who wielded a whip of his own. Like Prescott and Orion, this dragon in human skin rested in plush comfort while others bent their backs to provide the cushions, all the while threatened with the pillory, the dungeon, or the gallows should they try to shrug off the load.

She blinked at the reflection, now almost completely dark. Maybe this was part of the answer, a visible symbol that a courageous member of each species would wear as a reminder of their stated goal. This mutual recognition could serve as a propitiatory pact, a treaty signed by the ambassadors of the warring factions.

"Marcelle," Arxad said, "your hesitation is understandable. If you wish not to—"

"No, no, that's not it. I know just the place for it." She reached under her tunic and pressed it over her left pectoral. It stung for a moment, feeling like a hundred needles pricking her skin. Then, as she lifted her fingers, the sensation eased, though it still pricked her skin. "I put it over my heart. May the heart of Arxad and mine be one in purpose, to bring justice to our worlds and to set every captive free."

Arxad's eyes shimmered. "Well spoken. I make the same vow. Your heart and mine are now one."

"But …" She touched her stomach. "But I have no scale to give you."

"My knowledge of human anatomy is fairly complete. If I could make a suggestion …"

"By all means."

"As scales protect a dragon, so do skin and hair protect a human. Yet, as I have given up part of me that protects my most vulnerable spot, you should provide something that makes you more vulnerable."

"And that is …," Marcelle prodded.

"When an attack comes, you raise a hand in defense. It is a human's first instinct." His head drew close enough for his snout to protrude between the bars. "Give me skin from your palm. It will not be an effective replacement for my scale, but it will be worthy enough to consider our vow complete."

Marcelle looked at the palm of her hand. Obviously she would have to peel enough skin to make the symbol a real sacrifice, but …

Furrowing her brow, she flexed her fingers. It wouldn't be a sacrifice at all, not with a hand that bore no real skin. It would probably regenerate on its own. In fact, telling him that she had placed his scale over her heart was misleading. Although her heart might be there, how could she be sure? It never stirred within her breast.

"Arxad, I have a problem. It's hard to explain, but this isn't my real body. I conjured it from the soil of this planet."

"Ah! You are like Cassabrie. I am familiar with how she appears in this world."

"Right. So if I gave you skin, it wouldn't be real. It would crumble to dust, and you would have no replacement for your scale."

"I see." Arxad's eyes dimmed. "It seems that I have made a hasty gesture."

"I just don't know what else to give you. They couldn't burn me at the stake, so maybe I'm not physically vulnerable at all."

"Are you emotionally vulnerable? Spiritually vulnerable?"

"Not really. My mother taught me to be strong, to not let anything …" Her words trailed away. Mother *had* made her emotionally strong, and her death had sealed that instruction forever. Even now she carried a reminder of her emotional strength.

She reached into her cloak's pocket and withdrew the mirror. Swallowing, she gripped it tightly. "I have something …" Her voice cracked. "You might find it … worthy."

"Marcelle …" Arxad's voice grew soft and gentle. "If it is worthy to you, it is worthy to me. I sense great emotional turmoil in your voice that is far more profound than words."

"It was my mother's. She called it a manna mirror. When I carry it, I remember her love, and I feel protected. If I were to lose it, I would wonder if the blessings of the Creator had departed and left me without a shield."

"Such a gift will surely suffice." Arxad's scaly hand appeared again, his claws looking sharper than before, more bestial than ever.

She lowered the mirror toward his palm but snatched it back. "It's breakable."

"Excellent. Your risk is even higher, heightening your vulnerability."

She turned it over to the mirror, then back to the manna wood. "Which side would you show, the mirror or the wooden backing?"

"Which is more appropriate?"

She rubbed her fingers along the smooth wood. "It … it has a verse from the Code on the back. It says, 'Your heart is reflected by the light you shine. How great is your light when you sacrifice all you have for those who have nothing to give.'"

"I have heard these words before. They are great wisdom."

"Yes … yes, they are." She turned it over once again. "The mirror reflects what is physical, and the verse reflects what is spiritual, so I suppose you should place it so the mirror faces outward and the verse faces inward."

"More wisdom. I will do as you suggest."

With a quick motion, she set the mirror in his grip and stepped back. When his foreleg drew away, she flexed her hand, its emptiness feeling like a great void. "I have a lot to do, so I'd better get going."

"Yes, you do."

She turned toward the path but quickly pivoted back. "When you get to Starlight, will you do something for me?"

"If it is in my power."

"Adrian's on his way to the Northlands, and he's carrying my body."

"No doubt you seek to be restored."

"Well, that wasn't what I was thinking, but do you know how to do that?"

"There is a way," Arxad said, "but it is quite dangerous. It involves ingesting a potentially deadly substance, but there is no need to go into detail. By the time you arrive, perhaps I will have a plan in place to restore you."

"Thank you." She stepped forward and grabbed the bars. "What I really need you to do is give Adrian a message. If you see him, tell him I love him and that if he meant every word, then I meant every word. He should know what that means."

"I will do more than you ask." The warm breath carrying his words seeped into her skin. "Along with my vow to do all I can to free your fellow humans, I will never rest until your spirit is reunited with your body."

"Then I will be in your debt." Marcelle backed away and placed her hand over the scale on her chest. "Until we meet again, noble dragon."

Gripping the hilt of her sword to keep it still, she turned and jogged up the path toward the palace. Although clouds still shielded the moon, enough light shone through to reveal any obstacles. When she reached the dungeon's front entrance, she stopped and set her hands on her hips. Returning to the escape tunnel would be the safest option, but safety had to yield to necessity.

She pulled her cloak's hood up and drew it low over her eyes. Since none of the guards knew of her disguise, maybe she could discover Maelstrom's whereabouts as well as whether or not he had taken control.

After covering the sword with her cloak, she marched toward the palace, its torches and ever-burning lanterns guiding her way. When she drew close to the rear steps, she slowed to a furtive pace and eyed the guard at the door, a tall, unfamiliar man. With a wall-hanging lantern casting a glow across his body, a long shadow painted the porch's floor with a dark copy of the guard's relaxed posture.

Marcelle kicked a stone. The guard's neatly trimmed mustache flinched, and he grasped a sword hilt at his hip. "Who is there?"

Clutching her cloak closed, she stopped at the bottom of the steps, her head low. "Excuse me, sir," she said, again using her younger voice. "My name is Ophelia. I am an orphan who is supposed to be adopted by Captain Reed. Do you know where I might find him?"

"Oh, yes. I heard about you." He relaxed his grip on the sword. "It's no wonder that you are unable to locate your adoptive father. The new governor has sent messengers who have been looking for him for hours."

"The new governor? You mean Orion?"

The guard smiled. "Things change quickly these days, Miss. Leo has assumed the governor's seat."

Marcelle dipped into a shallow curtsy. "Begging your pardon, sir, but I saw Governor Orion only this morning. What is the nature of his departure? And why the haste to install a new governor?"

"Now don't trouble yourself with political affairs, little lady." The guard gestured toward the door. "Come. I will take you to the infirmary. You can sleep there until we find your father."

Marcelle ascended the steps, careful to keep her face and sword concealed. The guard lifted a key from a ring attached to his belt and unlocked the door. After pulling it open and allowing Marcelle to enter, he relocked it from the inside and marched down the center hallway. "This way, please."

As they walked, Marcelle scanned the corridor. The governors' portraits had all been removed. Only bare walls with faded blue paint remained, save for the rectangular shapes of more pristine blue where the portraits once hung. "What happened to the pictures?"

"The governor wishes to purge the corruption of past administrations along with memories of the corrupters. He claims that his rule will be a new dawning of justice, equality, and openness." The corridor ended at the front lobby. After crossing the spacious room to the left, they entered another corridor, void of extane lights on the walls. Although light from the lobby illuminated the first part of the new passageway, it grew dimmer as they continued.

"Do you believe Leo?" Marcelle asked. "Were the other governors corrupt?"

He laughed. "Every guard knows not to question the governor, unless you want your neck stretched a bit, if you know what I mean."

"I'm no snitch." Marcelle cringed at the words she planned to utter next. "I'm just a girl."

"So you are." He stopped at a double doorway on the right and turned toward her. The lack of light kept his face in a dark shadow. "I will tell you this. There is one rule in government that I have never seen violated. No matter what a new leader promises, very little changes. Oh, window dressing, maybe, but the rulers always see to themselves first. They will do whatever they must to stay in power. I have never seen an exception."

"Power? Does Leo already control the army?"

"Not yet, but he will soon. He already has power the generals can't resist. They will either obey or die."

She nodded toward him. "And what about you? Will you do what Leo says?"

"Without a doubt. I've learned to lay low and mind my own business. Another governor will be along someday to replace this one. They come. They go. Just do your job, and keep the rope from biting into your neck."

Marcelle redoubled her effort to sound like a young girl. "Even if the governor tells you to do something wrong?"

The guard laughed nervously. "Listen, Ophelia, I think you're a bit young to be questioning governmental ethics. You haven't been in my position to—"

"I don't mean to judge you, sir. I'm just curious. I want to know more about guards and soldiers." She gave him another quick bend of the knee. "Do you think my new father would agree with you?"

"Captain Reed?" The guard stroked his chin. "He has more integrity than is good for him. Eventually it will prove to be his noose."

"His noose? Why do you say—"

The sound of tromping footsteps echoed from the lobby. The guard lifted a hand. "Wait here." Then, he hurried back down the corridor.

Marcelle followed, staying back several paces. When she reached the end of the hall, she peered around the corner. Maelstrom marched her way, a soldier wearing a Tarkton uniform accompanying him. Their boots clopped, and the Tark's scabbard clinked against his belt. He carried a coil of rope over his shoulder that looked darker than the rope that had bound her at the stake, though crystals embedded within glimmered in the light. "We have a spy following him," the Tark said, "so we will soon learn his plans."

The palace guard stepped in front of them. "May I help you?"

They stopped and glared. "Who are you?" the Tark asked.

"Kordeck," he replied, bowing. "I guard the rear entrance. But you need not worry about security. I locked it before leaving."

Maelstrom's face bent into a scowl. "Yes, I know. I wanted to exit that way. I don't yet have the key to that door, so I was looking for you."

Kordeck reached for his key ring. "I will be glad to open it now. If you'll just follow—"

"Are you ill?" Maelstrom asked.

Blinking, Kordeck glanced between Maelstrom and the Tark. "I feel fine. Why do you ask?"

Maelstrom nodded toward the hallway. "I thought you might have been at the infirmary."

Marcelle leaned back and flattened herself against the wall. This was getting too close for comfort.

"I was guiding an orphan there," Kordeck said. "She came to my post looking for Captain Reed, her new father."

"An orphan? Why would an orphan be lurking about the rear entrance at this time of night?"

"I didn't ask, your eminence. She was wearing an orphan's cloak, and with rules so strict regarding orphans, I didn't want to risk—"

"Your excuse is as lame as a crippled cur," Maelstrom growled. "I gave strict orders to watch for any strange female, and now one tricks you with a simple cloak."

A slapping sound echoed into the hall, followed by the Tark's shout. "You fool! Disguising herself as an orphan was the only way she could enter without showing her face, and you fell for it."

Slowly drawing her sword, Marcelle backed toward the infirmary. With every step, the hallway grew darker. Maybe a hiding place among the beds and cabinets would allow her to spring at them without warning.

"But she didn't fit the description," Kordeck said. "I saw her eyes. They didn't glow green at all."

Marcelle stopped at the door. Glow green? Since when did her eyes glow?

Kordeck's voice shook with fear. "So she couldn't be who you think she is, right?"

"She is a mesmerizing witch," Maelstrom said. "She could easily have manipulated you with her powers. That's why I ordered every undocumented girl to be detained."

"Where is she now?" the Tark asked.

Marcelle grasped the door's handle and pulled, then pushed, but it wouldn't budge.

"I was just about to unlock the infirmary for her. I told her she could sleep in there until—"

"Silence, fool!"

The snick of a blade against a scabbard followed. Marcelle retreated farther into the corridor until her back pressed against a wall. Now in complete darkness, she crouched, her sword ready. Battling three men at once might be impossible, but there seemed to be no choice.

"Go and retrieve her," Maelstrom said. "If she dissolves, you should be able to capture her with the crystalline rope. Cassabrie must not escape."

Marcelle furrowed her brow. *Cassabrie? They think I'm Cassabrie?* She nodded. Of course! They believe Marcelle is dead.

"Light the rope." Maelstrom's voice echoed in the corridor. "We need to heat up the crystals. Soon Cassabrie will suffer Marcelle's fate."

A clicking sound reverberated, then the crackle of fire. Kordeck and the Tark appeared at the end of the corridor, each with a sword drawn. The rope stretched between their hands, burning and sizzling, the slack making it look like a flaming smile. Only the ends stayed free of fire.

Marcelle clutched her hilt tightly. Between their fear of Cassabrie and their preoccupation with the burning rope, maybe she stood a chance. They probably didn't expect her to have a sword at all. Maybe she could dash past them and avoid a battle, but once she reached the lobby, what would Maelstrom do? Why wasn't he watching or lending a hand? Maybe he showed his fear of Cassabrie in ways beyond sending his lackeys into battle for him. The fact that he turned pale in the Starlighter's presence might indicate something more than mere fright. His own fear might be her best weapon.

As the two swordsmen drew closer, lighting up the corridor, Marcelle altered her voice to a ghostly moan, loud enough for anyone in the lobby to hear. "Leo, beware! The last time we met, I dissolved and left you unharmed. Do not test me again, or the consequences will be dire."

Kordeck glanced back for a moment, his legs trembling. Marcelle leaped up and charged. Dropping to her backside, she slid under the rope and rode her momentum to vault back to her feet. As she leaped again to run, her cloak caught, snapping her body back. She fell to her bottom, spun on her tailbone, and looked at the guards.

The Tark, standing on the edge of her cloak, shouted, "Throw it!" He and Kordeck tossed the flaming rope toward her. With a quick backwards somersault, she jerked free of the Tark's foot, flipped away from the rope before it could land, and fell on her stomach. The rope slid across the floor and stopped inches from her face. Heat flashed across her cheeks, and the melting sensation from the burning stake returned.

"No!" As she pushed against the floor to back away, the Tark chopped down at her with his blade. Like a rolling log, she whirled toward him. When the blade smacked against the floor, she hacked at his ankle with her own sword, slicing to the bone, then rammed the blade up into his chest.

As he stumbled backwards, she whipped the sword out and whirled just in time to block Kordeck's blade. His momentum carried him over her body, his legs straddling her as he passed. With an overhead thrust, she shoved her blade into his belly, then jerked it out, ducking to the side to avoid the blood.

She rose slowly to her feet and stared at the carnage. In the glow of the burning rope, two men lay motionless, barely visible in the dim corridor. Normally after a battle, her heart would be pounding and her chest heaving. Now she stood without feeling, numb to the surroundings—death—senseless, avoidable death. But for some reason, it didn't matter, not a whit.

Marcelle touched her tunic where Arxad's scale lay underneath. Where had the callousness come from? Had witnessing so much cruelty in a few short days desensitized her to a coldness that matched her frigid skin? Or had the union with a dragon made her see the human tyrants and their guardians for the vermin-like predators that they were?

Closing her eyes, she tried to summon an appropriate emotion, just a hint of regret for the loss of life, but nothing arose. She had become a heartless, bloodless, tearless monster. Too much tragedy had squeezed her heart dry.

She snatched up an end of the rope and dragged it with her. Ultimately, Maelstrom was to blame. Even if he had stayed to witness the battle, he was probably long gone now. The coward sent surrogates to bleed while he kept his silk and satin spotless.

After leaving the corridor, she stopped in the lobby and looked around. The glow of wall-mounted extane lights reflected on the pristine marble tiles, but no shadow of Maelstrom interrupted the sanitized shine.

She slid her sword away and stamped out the rope's flames. With each press of her shoe, the fibers popped and sizzled. If only she could do the same to the foul usurper, but she had to let him flee. As Arxad advised, it would be better to let Maelstrom have his way for now so that Magnar would be motivated to destroy him.

She picked up the charred rope and ran her fingers along the hot, sticky fibers. All but the ends had been doused with some kind of fuel to make the rope burn easily, and much of the fuel remained. Since Maelstrom used this rope for hanging, for tying her to the stake, and for attempting to capture Cassabrie, it was clearly his favored device. Maybe using it against him would create a lovely irony.

Marcelle wrapped the rope around her waist and tied it in place. Then, closing her eyes, she let her muscles relax. Patience. The plan required time and trust. Somehow Maelstrom would meet his end, even if it took an enemy dragon and a dragon sympathizer to do the job.

EIGHTEEN

ADRIAN set the cart down under the boughs of a tall tree. Resting comfortably curled in the cart's nest of straw, Marcelle could continue sleeping under the deer-skin while he and his fellow travelers rested. The darkness of the night hours had provided cover for travel, but with dawn coming soon, it made sense to stop at a sheltered spot. The tree's low limbs and dense green foliage would block the rising sun quite well, and Trisarian, now drifting toward the western horizon, provided enough light to allow them to prepare a campsite.

Training his eyes and ears on the surrounding forest, he surveyed the landscape. A stream they had followed ran about thirty paces to the east, and beyond that, a meadow stretched out as far as the eye could see. To the west, the forest grew darker and denser, likely continuing for miles in that direction. A bird flitted from branch to branch, but no other sounds disturbed the serenity of the closely packed woods.

During the night, something had lurked behind them nearly every step of the way, something far stealthier than the cat in the swamp. No matter how many times he stopped and looked back, the subtle noises instantly evaporated. The crunching of forest debris was too consistent to be caused by the wind. An echo of their own footsteps? Maybe. In any case, they had to be on guard.

Shellinda plopped down next to Marcelle's cart, crinkling a carpet of fallen leaves, and set a hand on its frame. Now clothed in double layers, beads of sweat dotted her upper lip. "I don't smell anything. Do you?"

Adrian shook his head. "I think she's clean. She hasn't eaten anything, and I couldn't get her to take more than a swallow or two of water." He slid his flask's strap from his shoulder and took a long drink from its spouted end. Carrying Marcelle over such a long distance had drained his body of energy and hydration.

"She's probably comfortable," Regina said, her eyes closed as she leaned against the tree. Thick, wool-like material covered her arms and legs, and stockings and sandals dressed her feet. "Being asleep all the time, she probably doesn't need much."

Clutching the hilt of a sword in a hip scabbard, Wallace strode up to Adrian. Wearing a thicker tunic and trousers, his slavery-toned muscles seemed to bulge all the more. "You rest first while I keep watch."

Adrian raised a pair of fingers. "Two hours. Then you can have two hours. After that we'll see if it's safe to travel in the daylight." He turned to Shellinda. "Will four hours of sleep be enough for you girls?"

Shellinda nodded. "I slept at the cabin. I'm fine."

"Me, too," Regina said. "I'm not sleepy at all."

"Regina and I will take Marcelle to the stream and check her clothes," Shellinda said. "And we can fill our flasks."

Adrian pointed at the sword in Wallace's grip. "Can you make the next mark for Jason?"

"Sure." Wallace glanced at Solarus. "I figured out your system."

"Good." Adrian sat next to Shellinda at the tree and gave her his flask. "It should be safe if you go together. The stream's not far."

"I can hear it." She slid the strap over her shoulder. "We'll be back in a few minutes."

After the girls carted Marcelle away, Adrian closed his eyes and imagined Wallace and the girls taking care of the details. Wallace needed to find a tree near the stream that Jason would be likely to see should he be traveling between the Northlands and the Southlands. There Wallace would etch a symbol in the bark on the north and south sides, indicating the angle of Solarus in the sky as well as the number of days since the two of them parted company on Major Four. Maybe letting Jason know where he was would help somehow, even just to provide a boost that his brother was still alive and thinking about him. And maybe, just maybe, Jason could use the symbols to bring about a reunion between them, but that would take a miracle.

His arms aching, Adrian let them fall limp. Dizziness took hold within seconds. Still marching through the underground tunnel in his mind, his eyes throbbed with every step as he relived the recent journey. Because a torch he had made lost its flame early on, they were forced to journey through darkness once again.

Heaving a sigh, he pushed away the pain. Sleep would come soon. It had to. An exhausted warrior couldn't protect himself, much less those who depended on him. Marcelle needed him. The children needed him. And they still had a long way to go.

He drew a mental map—the route he had taken from the Northlands to the barrier wall. Although only a few days had passed, that journey seemed so long ago. Since much of it had flown by, either atop a raft or in the clutches of a dragon, it seemed impossible to tell how long it would take to arrive in the Northlands from this point. They had recently passed the waterfall, so they were perhaps a sixth of the way there, maybe less.

With so much at stake, traveling during the day was essential, in spite of the risk of being spotted. It seemed a small risk now. They hadn't sighted a dragon since their exit from the underground stream just north of the barrier wall. Still, caution had to prevail. It would take only one dragon to ruin their plans.

Adrian fell into a pattern of dozing and being startled awake by various sounds—Wallace's feet pressing down the leaves, an occasional owl-like hoot somewhere above, and the flutter of wings that, in the midst of his sporadic dreams, grew draconic in volume and fury. Finally, a girlish whisper brushed his ear.

"Adrian. You have to come and see this."

He opened his eyes. Shellinda leaned close, nearly nose to nose. "Come," she said, taking his hand. "It might go away."

Adrian shot to his feet and, with Wallace trailing, followed Shellinda's guiding hand toward the stream. When they arrived, Regina stood at the water's edge, facing the field on the other side. A spherical object hovered above the grass. It appeared to be quite large, but the darkness made its exact size hard to determine.

He glanced at the cart, now sitting a few steps from the stream with its front wheel pointing toward the forest. Marcelle rested within, her hair wet, apparently freshly washed. As he crouched next to Regina, Shellinda pressed close from his other side. "What do you think it is?" she whispered.

"I have no idea."

Her eyes closed, Regina breathed out, "Exodus."

"Exodus," Adrian repeated. "Cassabrie mentioned that name."

With her eyes still closed, she spoke in an eerie whisper. "It's a star. So bright. So lovely."

Adrian gazed at her face, illuminated by Trisarian's pale yellow glow. "It's not bright at all. If not for the moon, I wouldn't be able to see it."

"Oh, but it *is* bright, and it's speaking to me. That's how I know its name."

"Can you answer?" Adrian asked. "Can you ask why it's here?"

"I already tried. I don't think she can hear me from this far away."

"She? Exodus is female?"

Regina shook her head. "Exodus is the star. The girl is inside. She is a Starlighter."

"A Starlighter? Is her name Cassabrie?"

"She hasn't said her name. I don't think she's said anything out loud at all. Words are coming into my mind. I don't hear them with my ears."

Shellinda pointed. "Look! It's glowing."

A white aura formed around the sphere, making its size and position clearer. Hovering about twenty feet above the ground, it appeared to be ten to fifteen paces in diameter. Its semitransparent skin, radiant and pulsing, allowed a view of the inside. A girl stood within, her arms spread out, as if stretching after a long nap. Then, the sphere's light blinked off.

Adrian blinked as well, trying to refocus on the darkened star. It lifted higher and began drifting toward the barrier wall. Soon, it floated out of sight.

"Exodus is Starlight's guiding star," Regina whispered in monotone, her eyes still closed. "It tells the tales of this world so that Starlighters can retell them to the inhabitants. It was lost, buried, forgotten. Now it lives again."

Adrian touched her shoulder. "Those are some big words! Is Exodus telling you that right now?"

"A minute ago." She hugged his arm and pulled him closer. "Adrian, I'm scared."

He gathered her into his arms and whispered, "Why?"

As she hugged him, her words came out in spasms. "That girl. ... I'm scared for her."

"Is she in danger?"

"Exodus talked about a terrible sickness. I think the girl has it. She'll die if she doesn't get help."

"Do you know where she's going?"

Regina shook her head. "Exodus didn't say."

As he slowly released her, he straightened and looked back at Wallace. Standing at the forest's edge, the boy stared at the field, his one eye unblinking. A tear glistened on his cheek, and the sword dangled loosely in his grip.

"Are you all right?" Adrian asked.

Wallace barely moved his lips. "Elyssa told me about Exodus and the disease."

"Then fill us in."

"It'll take a while." Focusing on the ground, Wallace walked toward the stream, his legs brushing a section of tall grass along the way. "I need a drink first."

"That's fine," Adrian said. "You can tell the story when we're settled under the trees again."

Wallace stooped at the stream's edge. "Hey! Take a look at this."

"What?" Adrian hurried to join him.

"Look at how it leans," Wallace said, nodding at the surrounding grass. "Do you think there was a flood?"

Crouching next to him, Adrian brushed his hand along the blade tips. Every one bent as if overwhelmed by a fast-moving stream. "There's no doubt about it. The stream must have swelled in a torrential downpour."

"There's one problem." Wallace pointed upstream. "It's bending the wrong way."

Adrian compared the stream's flow to the angle of the grass. If floodwaters had rushed through, the grass would be pointing the opposite way.

"Could the stream have switched directions?" Wallace asked.

"I don't see how that's possible." Adrian smiled. "Unless the ground shifts its angle once in a while."

"Then how would you explain it?"

Adrian scanned both banks. Every patch of grass bent the same way, ruling out any theory that this particular patch had been sat upon by an animal. "I'm not sure what to think." He scooted to a section of damp soil, looking for more clues. Although still dim, the muddy bank revealed a set of shallow divots. "Now this is interesting."

"What?" Wallace shifted over and stooped next to him.

"Tracks of some kind." He scanned farther upstream. With the earliest rays of dawn barely easing over the horizon, the impressions weren't crystal clear, but their shapes and configurations were apparent—paw prints in a line parallel to the water. They appeared to be from a dog, though bigger than any from Major Four. "Do you have wolves here?" he asked, keeping his voice low.

Wallace looked up, his eye widening. "The dragons tell us about wolves. Supposedly they hunt in packs, and they'll eat humans, so the dragons chase them away, but I've never seen one."

Adrian mentally drew the wolf that could make such prints, a hefty creature almost twice the size of those at home. Unless this species walked single file, there was only one wolf, two at the most. He and Wallace could probably dispatch them, but if there were more, they would be hard-pressed to fight while protecting the girls. They couldn't afford to lower their vigilance. "I hope you're not too tired."

"Uh …" Wallace straightened his sloping shoulders. "I'm okay. Why?"

"We need to keep moving."

Wallace glanced at Shellinda and Regina. Both leaned over Marcelle's cart, fussing with her hair. "You think the wolves are close?" he whispered, even more quietly than before.

Nodding, Adrian raised his voice. "The girls said they aren't tired, so we might as well keep moving. If we stay close to the trees, we can get under cover if we see a dragon."

Wallace gave Adrian the sword and scabbard and walked casually toward the cart. "I'll take Marcelle. I can tell my story while I'm pushing."

After they gathered their flasks, Wallace marched ahead with Shellinda touching one side of the cart and Regina the other.

Staying within a few steps of the stream, he pushed the cart over roots, divots, and rises. Adrian trailed the procession, watching for more tracks at the water's edge. At times, the oversized paw prints disappeared, perhaps signaling the wolves' entry into the stream, but they always reappeared again, freshly pressed tracks blazing the trail. They were somewhere ahead and probably not very far. Since they were clearly not in pursuit, maybe a bit of noise would frighten them should they draw near.

"Go ahead and start your story," Adrian called, "and speak up so I can hear you from back here. The water's pretty noisy."

Keeping his focus straight ahead, Wallace nodded. "It's like this. At one time, Exodus floated around in the sky. Everyone called it a star, but it's smaller than a real star, and it's hot, but not so hot that it'll burn you when you're close. Anyway, the star emitted pheterone, a gas that dragons need to survive, so they loved it. Some even worshiped it. Humans hated Exodus, because they couldn't see any purpose for a star that made them sweat more than usual, so they decided to try to get rid of it."

Wallace looked at the sky. "They flew up to Exodus on a dragon and pierced it with a spear. It spewed vapor that spread out everywhere, and it shot away out of sight. With Exodus gone, there wasn't enough pheterone anymore, so the dragons were in danger, and that white vapor carried a disease that affected only the humans.

"It caused terrible sores, and the sores spread, like the disease was eating them alive. Anyone who caught it died in just a few days. Some of the kids seemed to be immune for a while, and some of the smarter humans tried to figure out why.

"Elyssa said something about ..." Wallace glanced upward again. "Genetics, I think."

"Sure," Adrian said. "We know all about genetics at home. Go on."

"Anyway, they couldn't find a cure, and every human died." Wallace shrugged. "Elyssa wasn't clear about the rest of the story, but she thinks the dragons preserved the genetics of the humans and started a new population on another world."

"Major Four?"

Wallace glanced back. "We call it Darksphere."

"Yes, I know."

"One more thing," Wallace continued. "Elyssa said someone would try to bring Exodus back, and if that happens without healing its wound, it will spread the disease again, and all the humans on Starlight will die, just like before. Only Elyssa is protected. Only she can seal it without getting the disease."

"So that's what Exodus meant last night," Regina said, still clutching the cart. "I heard it say that it was healed."

"By the girl inside?" Adrian asked.

She nodded. "I think so."

"So if that girl is sick ..." Adrian pointed toward the field across the stream. "She must not be Elyssa."

Regina cocked her head. "Elyssa is from your world, right?"

"Right," Adrian said. "She's a friend of my younger brother."

Regina touched herself on the chest. "The girl inside Exodus is a Starlighter from my world."

"Maybe she *is* Cassabrie." Adrian said.

"Or Koren," Wallace offered.

Regina dipped her head low. "I'm sorry. I didn't know how to ask her name."

Adrian hustled past Wallace and walked at Regina's side. "That's okay." He touched her shoulder with a gentle hand. "You've given us a lot of information."

"But what can we do with the information?" Wallace asked. "We don't know where Exodus went."

Adrian propped the sword on his shoulder. "And even if we did know, what could we do? Since the wound's been sealed, she might not be contagious while inside the star, so maybe there's no danger, no one to warn."

"So we keep marching northward." Wallace pushed the cart over a protruding root, careful to keep it from bumping too hard. "How long do you think it will take?"

"All day. Or longer." Adrian glanced at the paw prints. More wolves had joined the pack, at least five all together. "Let me know when you want me to take the cart."

"I'm fine. No offense, but I've probably pushed more heavy carts than you have, and I know you're better with that sword."

Adrian smiled and slowly dropped back to the trailing position. As he kept a wary eye on the tracks, he took a deep breath. A sweet fragrance filtered in, a blend of wild perfumes. Grass pollen incited a slight itch in his nostrils, but no hint of wolves or any other beast joined with the odors. Sunlight now poured over the field on the right, highlighting the flowers he and Cassabrie had enjoyed during their journey southward. Blossoms of red, purple, and yellow waved in the breeze, cooler than in the Southlands, a strangely contrasting backdrop to the dark uncertainty that lay ahead.

Soon, they would likely come upon wolves, and later, if they survived, they hoped to meet the white dragon, but would that encounter be just as troubling? Might he have no solution to the mystery that plagued Marcelle? Could he explain the Exodus puzzle and the disease it might be carrying?

"Wallace, what do you know about the white dragon?" he asked.

Wallace gave another light shrug. "I've heard stories about it. Most of us think it's a myth."

"He's no myth. A mystery, to be sure, but not a myth. I've seen him."

"Then what I've heard might not do you much good."

"Go ahead. I'll take it for what it's worth."

Wallace guided the cart closer to the stream, dodging a limb bent nearly to the ground. "Some say he's trapped in the Northlands because he's a tyrant. The Creator banished him to a land of ice and snow to keep him from conquering the world. He's a deceiver who'll do anything to get out."

"What could someone do to help him escape?"

"I never heard. Even if the story's true, I doubt anyone knows how he could get out. Until you came along, no one's ever been to the Northlands and come back to tell about it. People just make things up."

"You're probably right." As Adrian marched on in silence, an image of Beth came to mind. Impaled and trapped, surely she had motivation to deceive, but so did Alaph. Which one was telling the truth? Alaph had helped Jason heal their father, but could that be part of the deception? Alaph admitted that those who followed him had given in to his influence, so he obviously had some kind of mesmerizing power.

Letting out a silent sigh, Adrian looked to the north. Soon they would all learn the truth, whether from Alaph's actions or, if Drexel succeeded, the actions of the other three white dragons. It seemed that all of Starlight's history was about to collide.

✳   ✳   ✳   ✳   ✳   ✳

Marcelle sat in front of the lantern, watching its flickering flame as it cast a wavering light around the archives escape tunnel. The children she and Captain Reed had rescued from the dungeon lay sleeping in various poses on the floor, while Dunwoody sat leaning against the trunk, his head bobbing and his eyelids batting as he fought sleep. Somewhere in the palace, Maelstrom was likely searching for her, still convinced that Cassabrie lurked, perhaps also convinced that the spirit of Marcelle was trapped within his rope's crystals. Maybe he had collected the crystalline remains in the execution embers and embedded them in the new rope. If so,

351

he was probably furious that he no longer had them. Maybe his obsession with finding her would preoccupy him for a while and keep him from meddling with the military.

Blinking at the lantern's wavering flame, she brought her mind back to the present. All the pieces of the plan were now in place. Captain Reed had the letter of marque and was rounding up the troops, careful to watch for Maelstrom's loyalists. Father, disguised as an old general, worked through the night buying food and warm clothes, securing weapons, and packing provisions.

By now, Randall had already passed through the portal with Orion and Arxad. If Arxad's plan worked, only Magnar remained on Major Four. With his foul temper, who could tell what rage he was already displaying? Would he stay near the portal, waiting for the troops to arrive? Probably. He wouldn't want to miss the toppling of Starlight's usurper.

She laid a hand gently over the scale attached to her chest. It stung, a constant reminder of her alliance with Arxad, and, by association, with Magnar. No matter how ornery and antagonistic he became, she had to stay patient and figure out how to win him over. At the end of the day, he might be the key to winning the war.

She looked at an hourglass Dunwoody had set near his foot. The last grains of sand at the top filtered through the pinched throat and settled on the pile. Dawn had arrived. If Reed followed the schedule, the three scouts he assigned to check the portal for Magnar's presence would be waiting at the point where the pipeline ended in the forest, and they needed her to lead the way to the portal. Dunwoody had already shown her a map of the gas lines. Since it forked only twice, it would be easy to follow the pipe to her destination.

She shifted her gaze to Dunwoody. The old professor had fallen asleep, his chin now touching his chest. She rose and shook his shoulder gently. "I have to go."

He jerked up and glanced at the hourglass. "Oh! Yes! By all means!"

Grabbing his wrist, she helped him to his feet. He brushed off the seat of his pants and looked at the hole leading to the pipeline. "I dreamed about you flying on Magnar. I have no idea what he really looks like, but it was a splendid sight. Would you describe him so I can see how accurate my dream was?"

"Although I despise him," Marcelle said, "I have to admit that he is magnificent in appearance—shimmering reddish scales, sleek muscular body, and radiant eyes that would make most cower just by staring at them."

"Interesting. In my dream, he was two-toned, some green and some brown, close to the coloring of a toad."

Marcelle laughed. "I suggest that you not mention your description to Magnar if you ever meet him."

"Of course. It is not wise to offend someone who can set your hair on fire." Dunwoody looked toward the access panel leading to the archives room. "How do you plan to use Magnar to topple Leo?"

"The hardest part will be to convince Magnar to come with me. Getting left behind probably wounded his pride, so he likely won't be ready to listen to a woman's advice." She looked up, imagining the palace's layout above. "Maybe I could appeal to his anger and desire to destroy. The front doorway construction is wood and glass. I'm sure he could break through and create a huge mess."

"True, but the palace is not a favorable place for a dragon invasion. Once inside, where would you and a dragon go? Flying would be difficult, if not impossible."

"Do you have a suggestion?"

Dunwoody propped his chin on his hand. "I was thinking that you could attack the Enforcement Zone and destroy the gallows and pillory. At the very least, you will have ruined symbols of injustice in Mesolantrum, and you would be out in the open, which would be a perfect environment for Magnar. Surely the commotion would bring Leo and his loyalists out for battle."

"His thugs, you mean." Marcelle mentally replayed Maelstrom's absorption of Philip's energy. He was bold when in control of a situation, but when he faced someone he had no power over, he seemed almost cowardly. "I'm not confident that Leo will show up. He seems to run like a rabbit when the odds are against him."

"Then what will you do?"

"Your idea is the best one I've got. We'll attack the Enforcement Zone. If we can at least get rid of his armed supporters, we'll have the upper hand."

"I will get a message to Captain Reed to let him know what you're doing, and I will find another refuge for these children. I fear that this one is too porous." Dunwoody turned to the trunk. "There is something here you should take with you."

"The eggshells?"

"No. They are far too fragile, and I see no benefit." He lifted the lid. "Did you notice the inner compartment?"

She nodded. "It needed a key."

"I have it." He withdrew a key from his pocket and reached into the trunk. After turning the lock, he opened a flap-like door, no wider than two fingers. On a tiny shelf inside a shallow hole lay a small leather bag tied at the top with drawstrings. He took it out and dangled it in front of her.

She squinted at the bag, but it appeared to be nothing more than a tobacco pouch. "What is it?"

"I had a good deal of time to study the dragon's journal, and now I know what this is for." He laid it in her palm. "Inside, you will find a metal box, and within the box you will find a shining sphere about the size of my thumb knuckle."

As she reached to untie the bag, he batted her hand away. "Take care. You must not touch it until the proper time. It is beastly hot and will burn your skin."

354

She enclosed the bag in her hand. "What is the proper time?"

"When you attempt to reunite with your body. It is called a stardrop. The dragon scribe said that it heals, so I hope that it will repair whatever damage your real body has suffered."

"But if it's so hot, won't it burn my insides?"

"My thoughts exactly. I suggest that you find the dragon and inquire further."

She pushed the bag into her tunic's pocket. "I will. The dragon scribe and I have a lot to talk about."

As Dunwoody gazed at her, his eyes glistened. "My dear Marcelle, I have a confession to make."

"You do?" She slid her hand into his. "What is it?"

"Ever since ..." He cleared his throat, strengthening his voice. "Ever since the day you walked through my classroom door, I have held a special fondness for you. You entered as a scared and lonely peasant who had recently stepped into nobility. You disguised your fear and grief with bravado. You masked your vulnerability with confidence. You put on armor of steel to protect your heart of flesh. And as a result, you became lonelier still.

"In spite of the masks you wore during this solitary journey, you slowly grew into that courage, your muscles conforming to your inner strength, your skills matching your daydreams. Although I sat as a hermit in the archives, I watched you grow through official reports of your tournament victories, through your student records, and through your father's occasional visits to my hermitage. More than one video tube featuring you has passed through my hands, so I was able to view you from afar, a lonely little girl blossoming into a strong, confident young woman."

His lips trembling, he forced a smile. "Hear my parting counsel, Marcelle Stafford. Few are they who are willing to penetrate the protective shell you have created. They are not enamored with your muscles, your skill with a sword, your tournament victories. They love the lonely little girl still residing within and the woman she has become, the Marcelle without a mask."

He clenched his fists. "Hold these people close to your heart. They are more precious than jewels. They are the ones who will abide with you forever, whether you gain a crown of victory or suffer the shame of defeat. Your real friends will never forsake you."

Marcelle threw her arms around him and pulled him close. Biting her lip, she sobbed within, though no tears flowed. The warmth of his body seeped into her skin, casting off some of the chill and easing the spasms.

She drew back and looked into his tear-filled eyes. "Love has stripped away my shell—your love, Adrian's, and even the strange love of a mysterious Starlighter. And I will be forever grateful for your patience with this mule-headed sword maiden who didn't know when to lower her shield and put away her sword."

Dunwoody reached behind her cloak, drew out her sword, and pressed the hilt into her hand. "And now is not that time, dear Marcelle. Now is the time to become the warrior the Creator made you to be. It is time to fight! It is time to sever the oppressive hands and claws of tyrants. It is time to break the shackles of slavery and lead the liberated to lands of peace that you have cleansed with fire." He clasped her wrist firmly. "Go now. With the Creator at your side, no dragon or dark Starlighter will be able to stop you."

She kissed him on the cheek, then, without another word, crawled through the hole in the rubble and into the pipeline tunnel. She withdrew a glow stick from her tunic pocket. After shaking it, she held it out in front, letting its yellow radiance wash over the dirt walls and floors as well as the waist-high pipeline to her left. As before, extane coated her tongue, a reminder of the task ahead. Magnar awaited, a king of the dragons who had likely been energized by the gas. Harnessing that power and turning him into a willing helper would be far from easy.

With a purposeful stride, she marched forward. Although puddles occasionally dampened the floor, and a rat or two scurried past, the journey offered no real obstacles, just time to ponder the past few event-filled days. Less than a week ago, her only concern was facing Adrian in the tournament finals. Would he fight? If so, could she hold her own against him? Although he had been chosen as Prescott's bodyguard, no one really knew how good this peasant was with a sword. All she knew was that he was taller, more muscular, and faster. He had won the earlier rounds with ease, and even then he seemed to be holding back, as if not wanting to embarrass his opponents. The gentle warrior knew how to handle a hilt and a heart.

Since that day, her world had exploded. The laurel crown had withered into a peacock's defrocked plumage, and her rivalry with Adrian had been exposed as a silly, pebble-slinging contest. The real world had slapped her in the face, dislodging the mask that had blinded her to the ugliness of the slavery in her midst. And now she wielded a sword in a tournament that crowned no victor and awarded no accolades to the one left standing. This was a battle whose champions fought on bended knee, servants to those shackled in chains.

As she neared the pipeline's termination point, a shaft of daylight appeared in the distance. Apparently the scouts had followed instructions to dig an opening to allow her exit from the tunnel.

When she arrived at the hole, she touched a valve on the pipe and looked up. It seemed quiet on the surface. Maybe the scouts were resting. After all, it had probably taken quite a while to dig a hole so large and deep.

A crunching sound reached her ears, but not from above. It seemed to come from somewhere in the tunnel. She stepped back into the darkness and peered into the recesses, waiting for her eyes to adjust. No more sounds emanated. Could it have been a rat? The last time she guessed a rat as the cause of an unexpected noise, she lost the opportunity to rescue the children in the dungeon. But what could she do? Darkness favored a hidden assailant. It didn't make sense to stay or to search for the source of the sound.

She climbed to the top of the pipeline and vaulted up through the newly dug hole. Now standing in the center of a forest clearing, she looked around. Picks and shovels lay on the ground in haphazard array, but no diggers showed their faces. Trees stood twenty paces in any direction, most at least sixty feet tall and so densely packed, the scouts could be lounging anywhere among them.

She looked at the dirt, still somewhat damp from the downpour a few days ago. Footprints gave evidence of all three scouts. Scuff and sliding marks led from a shovel to a dark space between two trees.

A low growl sounded from the gap. Marcelle whipped out her sword and set her feet in a battle stance. She peered into the trees, but nothing came to light. "Magnar?" she called.

Her voice bounced back, weak and thin.

"Magnar," she called again, raising her voice, "you've made your presence known. What do you want?"

The growl returned, this time forming words. "I want passage to Starlight."

She stared into the gap. Draconic eyes appeared along with a dark shadow behind them. "What did you do with our scouts?"

"They are unharmed, and they will remain so as long as you cooperate with me."

Marcelle kicked the shovel toward him. "I am not the keeper of the portal. What makes you think that I can grant you passage?"

"You have traveled to my world and returned to yours. It is clear that you are familiar with the means to do so."

Marcelle nodded. Magnar was no fool. Trying to outwit him might be a waste of time. She looked again at the discarded tools. This dragon had captured three soldiers bearing weapons. He was formidable indeed. Still, perhaps he had a weakness other than the soft spot in his underbelly. "Where is Arxad? Why aren't you two together?"

The growl deepened. "That is not your concern. Conduct me back to Starlight, and all will be well for you and your fellow humans. Otherwise, I will kill you all and find my own way."

She set a fist on her hip. "Well, if Arxad doesn't trust you enough to bring you with him to Starlight, why should I? You might kill me as soon as I take you there."

"I might kill you now and wait for your army to arrive. Those who have already passed through will make sure the portal is open for their soldiers." A flash of fire erupted from Magnar's snout, temporarily illuminating his scaly head. "If you want to save your life, I suggest that you decide to trust me."

"The army will not enter Starlight except by my command, and I know how badly you need them there." She pointed her sword at him. "So unless you wish to find a cave here in our world where you can retire from your kingly rule, you'd better do what I say."

A ball of flames erupted and shot past her. "Foolish human! Do not play games with me! I am not a simpleton who is ignorant of deceptive rhetoric!"

Marcelle forced her facial muscles to stay relaxed. In spite of his bluster, Magnar stood in a poor negotiating position. She held the key to the portal, and he knew it.

A stinging pain radiated from her chest and spread to her arms. The scale seemed to dig into her skin, an odd sensation considering that she was little more than a shell of dirt. Maybe since the dragon scale came from Starlight, it could somehow incite a pain response. The same might be true of the truth-detecting crystals.

Her covenant with Arxad again came to mind. She had to honor her word and search for peace with this cantankerous dragon. "I apologize for my inflammatory posturing, and I will respect your wisdom and intelligence, rightful king of Starlight. We will honor your request to send an army to crush the usurper in your midst. I ask, however, that you do the same for us. A madman has seized control of Mesolantrum, and our ability to send an army to Starlight has been compromised by his seizing of power. I need you to depose him for us. That should be a simple task."

"If it is a simple task, why can you not take care of it yourself?"

"I said simple, not easy. The complexity is low, but the difficulty is high. Maelstrom is a Starlighter who can absorb power from his opponents, but dragon fire can destroy him. So for a dragon such as yourself, it should be a simple matter. Blast him with fire and be done with it."

"You know so little." The sharpness in Magnar's words faded. "A male Starlighter has not been seen in our world in centuries, and I have never seen one myself. We have only legends, but they are dark tales. His power enabled the humans to enslave dragons in the first place."

"All the more reason to help us." Marcelle propped the sword against her shoulder. "Don't think Maelstrom will stop at conquering my world. As long as he knows there is a portal to yours and a way for his slaves to escape, he will soon be knocking on your door with an unfriendly army."

"Your point is sound, but one fact of history has escaped your reasoning. Whenever a despot is removed, if there is no preserving force in the land, another despot will take his place. If I help you depose Maelstrom and then leave with your army, you will return to find a new slave master, perhaps one even crueler and more powerful. Peace must be established through constant vigilance by a firm, benevolent monarch. That is how I maintained my rule for so long."

Marcelle shook with rage. "Benevolent! How dare you! Your whips and chains have scarred my people and—"

"*Your* people!" Magnar roared, his head now protruding from the trees. "Your people cruelly enslaved mine. I am benevolent to dragons and dragons alone, and I will not be cowed by your insolent anger. Either do what I say or ..." His eyes suddenly grew wide.

"Or what?"

Magnar spat out a fireball, then jerked his head back into hiding. The fireball zipped past Marcelle's ear. A scream erupted behind her. She spun, swinging the sword with her momentum. Her blade crashed against another. A tall, muscular soldier in a Tarkton uniform stood at the other end of the opposing sword. With their blades locked, she backpedaled and allowed him to advance, giving her a better view of the hole to the pipeline. A man knelt at the edge engulfed in flames, while others poured out of the opening one by one, each with a glow stick attached to his orange-and-black sleeve.

With a powerful leap, she flipped backwards, kicking at her opponent's wrist as she sailed. When she landed on her feet again, the Tark scrambled on the ground for his sword while at least ten other Tarkton soldiers faced her, all with swords drawn.

A graying man wearing officer's stripes stepped to the front of the line, a sword in hand—a dark-bladed viper. "Drop your weapon," he ordered.

Marcelle stood with the soldiers between her and the pipeline, her back to Magnar's hiding place. They had to be wondering where the fire came from. Would the unpredictable dragon do anything more to help her?

She lowered the sword's tip to the ground. "Why should I drop it? Aren't you here to go to Dracon to battle the dragons and set the slaves free?"

"That expedition has been canceled." The officer pointed the black blade at her. "Captain Reed is in custody, as is your father. If you refuse to surrender, they will be killed."

Hiding a swallow, Marcelle sidestepped. With each shift of position, the soldiers facing her shifted as well. They seemed frightened, perhaps hearing about her prowess, or, more likely, hearing rumors about her sorcery. "What do you want me to do? Go back through the pipeline to the palace?"

"That's the shortest route to the dungeon," the officer said, "which is where you'll be staying for a very long time. Since we can't seem to burn a sorceress, we'll see if Leo's crystalline rope will hold you."

She continued her slow sideways walk. "How did you figure out where I was going? Leo doesn't even know I'm alive."

"Captain Reed told your plan to an officer who was more devoted to Leo than to him. It was an easy matter to follow you from the false wall in the dungeon's lower level." The Tark's angular face hardened. "It seems that the captain's disloyalty to Governor Leo has returned to him."

Now at a ninety-degree angle with respect to the pipeline hole and the forest, she glanced at the trees where Magnar hid, but he wasn't in sight. "Speaking of loyalty, as an officer of Tarkton, sworn to uphold our good king's principles, surely you don't support aiding a usurper. Leo doesn't have the king's best interests in mind."

"Sometimes we have to sacrifice principle for the greater good." He stepped closer and pressed the viper's point against the tip of her nose. With his arm extended, three square patches, two gold and one silver, were easy to see. "I will not be lectured by a sorceress. Leo warned me about your beguiling ways."

"Is that so?" Unblinking, she met his gaze, using the blade to lock their stares. "While we're on the topic of loyalty, have you wondered why Leo sent you on this mission instead of going himself?"

As his brow bent, he lowered the sword. "Just get into the hole."

Walking more quickly, she sidestepped over the smoldering body and set her heels at the edge of the hole. "Aren't you wondering how your fellow soldier ignited so easily?"

"No one is surprised by what a sorceress can do." The officer and the other Tarks now faced her with their backs to Magnar's refuge. "If you try it again, we have enough of us here to remove your head, and I swear to do so even while in flames."

Magnar slowly emerged from between two trees and unfurled his wings, completely silent in his movements.

"Remove my head?" She counted the stripes on the officer's sleeve. "Are you a captain, and yet you believe such superstition? Do you really think I have the power to create fire?"

He pointed at the smoking body with his sword. "How else would you explain this?"

Magnar, now in full flight, hurtled toward them, his mouth opening and a firestorm pouring forth.

"You're about to find out." She stepped back and dropped into the hole. When her feet struck bottom, she looked up. A torrent of flames shot over the opening, some tongues dipping into the tunnel. Screams erupted. The extane-drenched air sparked and sizzled. Sparks landed on her clothes, but she batted them away before they could catch.

After a few seconds, the fire died away. The screams ebbed to gasps and grunts. Marcelle climbed to the top of the pipe again and leaped out. Burning bodies lined the edge of the hole. Smoke drifted her way, carrying the foul stench of roasting flesh. Magnar sat on his haunches, his brow low and his eyes aflame.

She bowed her head. "Thank you."

"Trust me," Magnar said, a hint of a smile forming, "burning those fools was my pleasure."

Marcelle looked toward the palace. "Now we have to set our officers free."

"We?"

"Of course." She waved her sword at him. "Do you think I can invade the palace and subdue the usurper and his supporters by myself?"

Magnar swung his neck, aiming his eyes away. "I have lost my patience with the human chattel. It is clear that they cannot be trusted to stand with us. Even if an army were to join our cause, they might turn against us after the battle is won."

Her fists tight, Marcelle strode around until she could face him again. "*I'm* standing with you. Don't you trust me?"

He drilled his scowling stare into her. "Why should I? You are standing with me only to acquire something for yourself. Once you use me to unseat your usurper and raise your army to set your fellow humans free, you will have no incentive to help me and my cause any longer. Without self-motivation, humans cannot be trusted to do anything."

"That shows how little you know about humans." She pulled her collar down, stretching it enough to expose a portion of Arxad's scale. "Do you know what this is?"

Magnar drew his head close to her chest and sniffed. "Arxad's?"

She released the collar, letting it snap back in place. "I made a covenant. I pledged to help unseat your usurper no matter what."

Magnar's scowl wilted. "I assume that it is painful."

"Enough to remind me of my promise. I am glad to endure it."

Closing his eyes, Magnar bowed his head. "Very well. I agree to help you."

Marcelle reached out to caress his cheek, but quickly jerked away. No use pushing his acquiescence beyond his boundaries. "Thank you, Magnar. I am very grateful."

He opened his eyes, revealing reddish pupils that pulsed like a beating heart. "What do you suggest that we do?"

She scanned the forest. "First, where are the scouts?"

"Hiding somewhere behind where I sat a moment ago. They are still nearby. I can smell them. I assume their loyalty was sufficient to keep them from fleeing."

Marcelle cupped her hands around her mouth and shouted. "Scouts! Hear me!"

Within seconds, a soldier in a Mesolantrum uniform strode into the clearing and bowed. "I apologize, Marcelle. The dragon—"

"Never mind. Just listen. I will lead you to the portal, and you can report to Randall that we will return with troops as soon as possible. Understood?"

The scout nodded. "Understood."

Thrusting her sword into its scabbard, Marcelle turned to Magnar. "After we lead the scouts to the portal, take me to the palace. We will strike directly."

"Take you? If I fly with you in my claws—"

"Not in your claws." Marcelle ran to Magnar's rear flank, leaped to the base of his tail, and climbed up toward his head, grabbing the protruding spines along the way to keep her balance. When she reached his neck, she sat down behind a spine and patted his scales. "I'm ready!" she called.

Magnar's neck bent, swinging his head around. "Get off me immediately! I will not have a human riding on my back!"

"Stop arguing and get going! We have to hurry!"

A fierce growl burned in the air. "Beware, human. You are testing my limits. I can find a way to succeed without you."

"No, you can't. The fact that you came here proves it." She nudged him with a heel. "Let's go."

"You are more annoying than a swarm of hornets." His voice settled to a rumble. "Have you ever flown atop a dragon before?"

"Never. But I'll bet you're just a gentle, fire-breathing pony."

Magnar's growl returned, now a low simmer. "If you continue your insults, you will eventually regret your words." He extended his wings and leaped into the air.

Marcelle gripped the spine and hung on. As he ascended, her backside pressed against his scales, and her entire body bent low. Extending a finger, she shouted. "The portal is that way!"

"I am aware of its location. My faithful brother made sure I was locked out." He straightened and headed in that direction.

Below, the three scouts ran through the forest in Magnar's shadow, glancing up every few seconds. When they arrived in the portal clearing, Magnar landed on the grass near the edge in a graceful slide. Marcelle dismounted, spun, and touched Magnar's foreleg. "You'd better take to the sky again. We don't want you to scare anyone on the other side of the portal. Come back in three minutes."

"I advise you to pose future commands as requests. At least then you will not appear to be so arrogant."

She offered a sly wink. "I will try to lower my arrogance level."

As he took off again, she ran to the center of the clearing. While the three scouts waited at the forest edge, she pushed her head through the portal and looked around. Edison Masters knelt at the line of crystalline pegs with his hand wrapped around the central one. Orion stood to his right and farther back, shivering and pulling his cloak close to his body as he watched. Although snow covered the ground with a thick white blanket, a mixture of rain and snow fell from the sky.

Marcelle blinked at the icy precipitation. How strange! During her previous visit, it seemed far too cold for anything but snow. And why was Adrian's father here? Where was Randall?

"Let's go," Edison said as he rose to his feet. "It won't hurt to check once more."

"For the twentieth time." Orion again wrapped his cloak closer to his body and sauntered toward the portal. "At least it's warmer over there."

Marcelle pushed an arm through, but it was misty and semi-transparent. When she pulled back, her vision fogged for a moment. A swirl of soil rose from the ground and filled in her arm. As her eyesight cleared, it seemed apparent that the soil refashioned her face as well.

Edison and Orion walked through the portal, nearly bumping into her as they passed.

"Welcome!" Marcelle said with a bow.

Edison extended his arms. "Wonderful to see you!"

After sharing a brief hug, Marcelle drew back. "Where's Randall?"

"It's a long story. You see—"

"Probably too long." She gestured toward the scouts. "Listen, I don't have much time. These three are going to the palace to lead our army here. I also have to go there to … well … do a bit more persuading, but I'll be back."

"How long until the soldiers arrive?" Edison asked.

"I have no way of knowing. Just stay ready to open the portal and assume it could be at any time."

Orion took a step closer and bent his tall body toward her ear. "Does your persuading have anything to do with a certain Counselor from Tarkton?"

She raised an eyebrow. "You haven't told anyone?"

"I cannot tell that which I do not know," he replied in a monotone whisper. "Speculation is futile."

She drew back and raised her voice. "I really don't have time to explain what's going on. We all have to hurry."

"Very well." Orion pulled his cloak's hood over his head and looked at Edison. "I assume we should return with the news."

"Definitely." Edison clasped Marcelle's shoulder. "By your appearance and your whispers with Orion, I get the impression that there is much you are hiding, but I trust you. I hope to see you again very soon."

She grabbed his wrist and pulled his hand down into hers. "Have you seen Adrian lately?"

After flinching for a moment, he shook his head sadly. "I was going to ask you the same question, but since you're in a hurry—"

"I *am* in a hurry. Just be watching for him. I think he's heading north."

"I will be sure to do so." Edison turned and walked through the portal, disappearing as he passed the boundary.

Orion walked that way as well but paused. "Leo has a weakness."

"I know. Dragon fire."

"I am not aware of that one, but I have heard that his greatest weapon is his greatest fear. That riddle has puzzled me for quite some time, but if you can decipher it, perhaps it will help you." Hugging himself tightly, he walked through the portal and vanished.

Seconds later, Magnar flew down and landed near the edge of the clearing. After sending the scouts away, Marcelle climbed on again, and the two lifted off. Soon, they were flying over the tree-tops, the palace's dome in view. Instead of the hour or more it took to walk to the end of the pipeline, the return journey would take only minutes.

With a hefty breeze blowing her hair back, she hunkered lower. Maelstrom had better watch out. She and her fire-breathing pony were on their way.

NINETEEN

ADRIAN set the cart's handles down. His arms ached. Sweat dampened his clothes. Ever since he took over the cart duty from Wallace, the drier ground seemed to get rougher and the wetter ground stickier. Pushing the wheel through all the obstacles was becoming too much to bear.

Behind him, Shellinda and Regina walked hand in hand, deep furrows in their brows as they shuffled along over roots and ridges. Wallace trailed them by several steps, the sword dragging at his feet, the empty scabbard beating his thigh, and his head hanging low. When they traded cart for sword a few hours earlier, he was tired, but now he seemed ready to collapse.

When they caught up, Adrian gathered them around. "Listen, I know I said we have to keep going, but I think it's time we took a good, long rest."

"But what about the ..." Wallace nodded at the stream. "You know what."

"The water?" Adrian winked. "Don't worry. We won't sleep close to the stream. The noise won't wake us up."

Wallace nodded, apparently figuring out the message. Since the wolves never strayed from the water's edge, maybe sleeping out of smelling range would increase everyone's safety.

"I'm all itchy," Regina said as she scratched her arm. "But I didn't feel any bugs biting me."

Adrian took her hand and pushed her sleeve up to her elbow. A rash covered her skin. "Do you have poison ivy in this world? It's a plant that causes a rash if you touch it."

She shrugged. "We hardly had any plants at all in the camp."

"I've never heard of it," Wallace said. "I'm itchy, too. On my back and ankles."

Shellinda raised her hand. "No itches for me. Maybe it's just 'cause we're so dirty."

Adrian scanned each face, all looking up at him. Were they wondering about the disease Wallace talked about? Although the rash couldn't be denied, there was no need speculating beyond Shellinda's more likely guess. They were all dirty, and Regina's newly healed skin might be more sensitive to forest allergens. But what about Wallace? He seemed as healthy as a horse.

He pulled the flask strap from his shoulder. "Let's all wash. We can fill our flasks and then get a nap." He waded into the stream. The cool water felt wonderful as it passed across his aching feet. Since his own skin didn't itch, there was no need to do more than splash his face and wash his hands.

As Shellinda and Regina joined him, smiles returned to their faces. "Oh!" Regina called. "It feels so good!"

Wallace waved from the cart. "I'll stay with Marcelle until you get out. I can wash later."

While the girls splashed around and scrubbed their exposed skin, Adrian waded to the far side of the stream and checked the bank for wolf prints. The grass grew thicker here, too thick to reveal any tracks even if a parade of wolves passed through. Yet, something unusual appeared, a wooden object lying in the midst of the tallest grass.

He trudged out of the water, up the bank, and into the hip-high blades. A raft lay nestled there, as if intentionally hidden. He grabbed a vine that held the saplings together and hauled the raft down to the shoreline. As he studied the construction, the girls stopped splashing.

"What is it?" Shellinda asked.

"A raft."

"Too bad we can't ride it north," Wallace called from the opposite bank. "We could sleep while the water did all the work."

Adrian touched a notch in the wood. This was the cut he had made with the hatchet when he was escaping the vog. This was his raft, the same one he had constructed during his southward journey, but after being captured by a dragon, he watched from above while it floated toward the waterfall. It had lodged on the bank just before going over the cliff, but it wasn't there when they passed by that point earlier. Yet, here it was now. Why would anyone drag it this far upstream?

A growl rumbled from the high grass. Adrian scanned the area, sniffing the air, but with the wind blowing from behind, no scent reached his nose. Something lurked, probably close.

Waving a hand, he backed into the water. "Girls!" he hissed. "Get out of the water! Go to Wallace!"

As Adrian kept his stare on the grass, new splashes erupted behind him, then Wallace's voice. "Want me to bring your sword?"

"Yes." Still backing up, Adrian stretched out his arm and opened his hand. Within seconds, the sword's hilt pressed against his palm. "Stay with Marcelle and the girls."

Two eyes appeared, framed by a wolflike head with its ears pinned back. The wolf emerged slowly from the grass and stalked into the water, crouching low. As its lips curled, revealing rows of sharp teeth, a new growl emanated. As big as the smaller bears on Major Four, it was a formidable beast indeed.

Adrian backed up the sloping bank and out of the water. He swung his sword, hoping to frighten the wolf away, but it continued its slow prowl.

"He's not scaring easy," Wallace said.

"I know. That means he's probably not alone." Even as Adrian spoke the words, two more wolves appeared at the edge of the grass, then a fourth.

Adrian looked back. Gasping, Shellinda crouched behind the cart's front wheel and pulled Regina down with her. Marcelle, still covered by the deerskin, lay in the cart, out of Adrian's view.

Wallace stepped up to Adrian's side, a hefty branch in his grip. "Just tell me what to do."

"We protect the girls." Adrian grasped Wallace's shoulder. "Nothing else matters."

"Should I wheel the cart into the woods?"

Adrian shook his head. "Wolf packs try to isolate the most vulnerable. Our only chance is to stay together."

More wolves emerged from the grass, now ten in all. After crossing the stream, four circled around Adrian and the others, two to the left and two to the right, while six approached directly from the stream, all with their bodies low and their hackles raised.

"Guard the other side of the cart," Adrian said, motioning with an arm. "Shout if you need help."

"Don't worry. I will." Wallace scrambled around to the cart's front wheel and stood within a step of the two shivering girls, his back to the cart. Gripping his branch with both hands, he called, "I'm ready."

"Hold your ground. I'm going to strike first." Adrian leaped toward the six and swung at the neck of the lead wolf. It ducked but not far enough to avoid the blade. Adrian cut into the wolf's skull and slammed its entire body to the ground.

The other wolves leaped at him as one. He whirled like a top, slashing the sword in every direction. Jaws clamped on his leg. Another set latched on to his left bicep. His blade sliced and hacked bones and flesh. Blood spewed across his face and chest.

Pain tore across his body, every nerve screaming as his own flesh ripped in various gashes from his shoulders to his knees.

"Adrian!" Wallace shouted. "Help!"

Adrian crouched under the weight of two wolves, then heaved upward, his arms extended. The wolves flew away, the teeth of one ripping a sleeve. He leaped over a wolf carcass and stormed to the other side of the cart. Wallace hunched his body under two snapping wolves, two other wolves lying dead nearby with his branch on top, broken in half.

With a powerful jab, Adrian shoved the sword through both wolves at once and heaved them off Wallace. As he withdrew the blade, the two other wolves he had thrown off earlier leaped over the cart and attacked. He slashed at one, cutting into its ribs, but the second landed on Regina, latched its jaws around her upper arm, and dragged her toward the stream.

Thrashing wildly, she screamed, "Adrian!"

"No!" Adrian leaped for her but fell short. He looked back. A dead wolf's teeth were still snagged in his trousers cuff. With a wild swipe, he sliced the wolf's snout, dislodging the teeth. Just as he shot up to leap again, another wolf jumped into the cart and tipped it over, spilling Marcelle.

Adrian rammed the sword into the wolf's skull and pinned it to the ground. As he tried to dislodge the blade, the final living wolf continued dragging Regina away, now within a few steps of the water. Although she continued to thrash and wail, its jaws stayed tight around her arm.

Wallace lay unconscious on the other side of the cart. Shellinda vaulted from her crouch and dashed toward Regina. "I'll help you!"

Adrian grabbed Shellinda and jerked her down. "No! Stay put!" Letting go of the sword, he climbed to his feet and lumbered toward the slowly fleeing wolf. Blood dripped in front of his eyes, and his knees threatened to buckle at every step. When he drew close, he lunged and grabbed the wolf's snout. Using all his remaining strength, he pulled the jaws apart, threw the wolf to the ground, and wrapped his fingers around its throat. Then, strangling it, he banged its head against the ground again and again until its eyes closed and its body fell limp.

He shifted to Regina. She lay still, her limbs splayed as blood spurted through a tear in her sleeve. He pressed a palm over the wound and felt for a fracture. The bone seemed to be intact. "Shellinda!" he shouted, looking back. "Is Wallace alive?"

Trembling violently, Shellinda crawled to Wallace and set her ear against his chest. "He's alive!" she whimpered.

"Pour your flask over his face. If he's able, help him up. We need to get on the raft. We're heading south on the stream. I think the wolf severed an artery. Regina will bleed to death if we don't find help soon."

She untied the top of her flask. "Who will help us?"

"We have to go to the underground stream, and if the water there doesn't work, we'll beg the barrier wall dragons for something to stitch her cut."

She began pouring water on Wallace's face. "What about the healing trees?"

"They're in the Northlands. I'd have to carry her, so it would take another day to get there. Our only hope is that water. We'll get out at the falls and hike from there. It's not far from that point."

Wallace sat up, shaking his head. Droplets flew left and right as he struggled to his feet.

"Wallace!" Adrian yelled. "You and Shellinda get Marcelle to the raft. I'll carry Regina."

Reeling back and forth like a drunkard, Wallace staggered to Marcelle, knocking the sword loose from the wolf's head. While he and Shellinda gathered her into the cart, Adrian scooped Regina into his arms and carried her to the river. With blood still dripping across his field of vision and down to her tunic, and pain still throttling his senses, the raft at the opposite side of the stream seemed veiled by a hazy, red-tinted curtain. The entire scene rocked from side to side as if teetering on a ledge.

When he reached the stream, he dragged his feet through the rushing, hip-deep current. Now the water felt like icy daggers knifing at his leg wounds, worse than the teeth that had ripped his flesh.

Trudging on, he made it to the other side and laid Regina on the raft. As he ripped away his torn sleeve to make a bandage, he looked back. While Shellinda carried Adrian's sword, Wallace pushed the cart into the stream, but they stopped before reaching the middle of the bed. An aura of light washed across their faces, illuminating their wide-eyed stares.

From beyond the grass, a bright sphere floated their way, much like the one they saw the night before, but now its radiance stayed consistent, a miniature star that outshone Solarus. A female form within spread out her arms, displaying a blue cloak. Red hair streamed over her shoulders, and her green eyes sparkled. With her hands splayed, a missing finger on each was obvious.

"Cassabrie?" Adrian called. "Is that you?"

As the star hovered closer, she cried out, "Oh, Adrian! We need to get help right away!"

He pressed a patch of cloth over Regina's wound and tied it in place. "Unless you have a needle and thread, we're going to ride to the waterfall and walk to this healing spring I found, and if that doesn't help, maybe the dragons at the barrier wall—"

"Those dragons won't help you. There is only one dragon who will."

"If you mean the king of the Northlands, I'm not so sure about that, but if you know of a way to get there in a hurry, I'm listening." Keeping a hand on Regina's arm, he pulled the raft into the water, altering to an abrupt tone. "But if you don't, we have to be on our way."

While Shellinda and Wallace shifted Marcelle to the raft, the star floated closer. "I get the impression, Adrian, that you lack faith in me. Is it because of how I manipulated you?"

"For lack of a better word, I guess *manipulated* will do." With the other four settled on the raft, Wallace with the sword now in its scabbard, Adrian climbed on. As the raft sank lower, water sloshed over the bundled saplings. It stayed afloat, but just barely. The raft slowly accelerated, its bottom scraping the bed at times.

Adrian took Regina into his arms and pressed against the bandage, trying to slow the bleeding. Wallace and Shellinda each set a hand on Marcelle as she lay tightly curled on her side. She continued staring blankly, seemingly unaware of the danger. With cart, bedding, and deerskin gone, she shivered in the misty air.

Standing on the interior floor of the star, Cassabrie floated behind them. "Adrian, what can I do to restore your faith in me?"

As she closed in, warming his skin with the star's radiance, he focused on her emerald eyes. "Look, Cassabrie, I understand what you did. You helped me figure things out about Marcelle and me. But you did manipulate me with your mesmerizing charm or whatever you want to call it. And I suppose that you somehow regained your body in this world, even though you claimed that you were nothing but a spirit here. Right now, I don't have time to think about why else I'm skeptical. If you want to help me, then great. Do it. Otherwise, let me figure out how to save this girl's life."

"I will do what I can." Accelerating, Exodus lifted over their heads and flew downstream. When it reached a point about a hundred paces away, it settled into the water and brightened, as if energized by the contact. Steam flew upwards in billowing plumes. The water between the star and the raft piled into a rolling wall, repelled by the star's presence.

As Adrian and company floated downstream, Cassabrie and Exodus drifted upstream, driving the water toward them. Within seconds, the two forces would collide.

"Hang on!" Adrian shouted, hugging Regina closer.

Wallace pulled Shellinda down, threw himself over her and Marcelle, and grabbed a vine. When the raft met Cassabrie's wave, the front lifted, tipping the floor at a precarious angle. Wallace began sliding toward the back, dragging Marcelle and Shellinda with him. The vine snapped. Adrian lunged, turning to his side and holding to Regina as he latched on to Wallace's wrist. The raft bobbed and pitched wildly. Like violent sea waves, water cascaded over their bodies, soaking them as it tried to sweep them from the deck.

Finally, the raft settled to an even keel. Adrian let go of Wallace and settled to a sitting position, a mixture of water and blood dripping from his hair. Regina curled into his lap, shivering. Wallace sat up and helped Shellinda rise. As always, Marcelle lay quietly, oblivious to everything.

About ten paces behind, Exodus drove the water upstream, leaving only narrow rivulets trickling southward underneath the raft. Ahead, the entire river had reversed direction, as if anticipating the coming force. It picked up the cart they had left behind and drove it forward until it washed to the side and tumbled into high grass.

Heaving deep breaths, Adrian called out, sputtering, "What ... how ... how did you do that?"

"Did you not read the signs?" Cassabrie asked. "Marcelle told me that you notice everything."

"What signs? What do you mean?"

"Signs that this stream has reversed course in the past. I saw the bent grass blades myself. Didn't you?"

Adrian nodded. "I saw them, but I thought there must be another reason. A stream couldn't just—"

"Ah! Then you came up with an alternative—a simpler, more logical explanation. What was it?"

"Well … no." With the star bathing everyone in warmth, Regina's shivers ceased, but her breathing became erratic. Sweat blended with the water on Adrian's face, stinging the cuts and scrapes. "It doesn't really matter what I thought. Let's just keep going."

"Very well, Adrian, but the king is likely to ask you similar questions, and he will not be so easily persuaded to drop the subject."

"But what's the point? To make me look like a fool for being surprised about a stream that reverses course? Anyone would be surprised."

"Do your companions share your reaction?" Cassabrie asked.

Wallace nodded vigorously. "*Surprised* doesn't even come close, and I thought I'd seen everything."

Tears coursing down her cheeks, Shellinda laid her head on Marcelle's chest. "I'm not saying. I just want everyone to be all right."

Cassabrie spread out her arms. "You don't understand. I'm not admonishing you, nor would the king. I am simply trying to prepare you for a future event that exceeds this one in wonder and importance. But if you're not prepared to believe in advance of the event, then it won't benefit you. This stream's reversal is hastening your rescue even without your faith, but the one about which I speak will leave you without hope if your hearts are not ready."

"So will we get a sign?" Adrian asked. "Something like the bent grass?"

"If the sign is revealed in advance, then faith will be void. Yet, I will provide a quote from the Code, which you likely already know." Cassabrie folded her hands as if in prayer. "To those without faith, the cure to their ills appears as poison, a scalding star that sets aflame, for they see only with their eyes. They understand not that the wounds of the human heart are incurable. The heart of man must die in order to be renewed, for that which is planted cannot rise unless its shell is first shattered and cast off."

As the raft rushed onward, sending a fine spray over his face, Adrian let the words settle. They were somewhat familiar, perhaps uttered in a Cathedral sermon long ago. When he sat with his family in the peasants' section near the back, he often paid no attention, preferring to daydream while he pretended to listen. Still, much of the Code had penetrated his meandering mind, even if he hadn't intentionally allowed it. When Prescott later banned the Code from all but the Cathedral officials, the words suddenly became more precious, and a rabid study of hidden fragments was more of a refresher than a new revelation, proving that he had listened more intently than he had thought.

"A scalding star that sets aflame," he murmured. How strange that the Code would mention a star, seeing that a terrestrial star now referred to that passage as part of a riddle. These two worlds seemed so vastly different, yet they were somehow linked by an ancient connection, a binding tie, mysterious and hidden from sight.

Regina twitched. Her eyes opened. Although glazed, they seemed to focus on Adrian's face. "Are you going with me?" she asked.

"Of course. I won't leave you. Not for a moment."

"But you can't go with me unless you—" Her back arched, and her mouth locked open. Her eyes clenching shut, she wailed in agony.

"Regina!" Adrian shouted. "What's wrong?"

Cassabrie called out, "I was afraid of this. I'm going to push you to shore."

With a spin of her cloak, the star turned, and the current shoved the raft onto an alluvial beach. Adrian jumped up and laid

Regina in the soft meadow beyond the sand. Surrounded by red and blue flowers, her stiff body relaxed. Blood had soaked her bandage, but the hemorrhaging had slowed to a minor trickle. The cooler winds of the north cut through their damp clothes, raising shivers from every passenger. "The cut's sealed!" Adrian yelled. "What could be wrong with her?"

Exodus floated closer, again providing warmth. "Check her abdomen. That's the surest sign."

"Surest sign of what?" He lifted her tunic, exposing her stomach. Ulcerated lesions covered her skin. "Oh, dear Creator! What is it?"

"A disease," Cassabrie said calmly.

"The disease Exodus carries?" He scooped Regina into his arms and held her close. "Did you infect Regina?"

"I don't have the disease. It was released in the dragon village and has spread throughout that area. I assume you were close enough to contract it. It's possible that you all have it at one stage or another."

"How do you know you don't have it?" As Regina convulsed again, he rocked back and forth with her. "How do you know you're not spreading the disease now?"

"I am immune, and Exodus is sealed. It cannot expose anyone to the disease unless it leaks." She pulled a short, paper-covered cylinder from under her cloak. "I am now taking the star to the Northlands to aid your soldiers and ponder a potential cure for the disease, but there is no time to explain further. We have to help Regina."

Adrian laid Regina down and ripped her tunic, again exposing the sores—bleeding, oozing boils that had spread toward her chest. Her body lay still, though she breathed easily.

"For some reason it's spreading through her body quickly," Cassabrie said.

"She's weaker than us. Her immune system can't handle much." He touched the edge of one of the sores. "I don't think she'll make it to the Northlands."

"You're right. That's why I brought you to shore." Cassabrie drifted closer. "You saw what Jason did to heal your father."

Adrian nodded. "He brought a stardrop from Exodus, but we don't have a healing tree."

"The healing trees won't cure this disease. We have to take a more direct approach. Regina must swallow a stardrop."

"Swallow it? But won't that burn—"

"Ohhh!" Regina's body bent again, this time twisting with the spasm, though her wail was more subdued, as if breathing had become a hopeless chore.

"Scoop radiance from the star's skin, Adrian! She's dying!"

He hustled toward Cassabrie, shielding his eyes with his hand. Although the heat felt soothing at first, it soon became a scalding barrage of stinging fire. He formed his hand into a ladle and dug into the star's membrane. Like glittering sand, tiny crystals flaked away and fell into his palm.

He took a step back, letting the crystals settle to the center. They bit painfully into his skin. "What now?"

"Pierce Exodus with your sword, just an inch or so. Have no fear of a leak. You are already exposed, and I will seal the wound immediately."

Wallace ran up and set the hilt in Adrian's hand. With the hot crystals still burning his palm, Adrian pricked Exodus with the blade and gently eased it in. When the tip emerged on the other side, Cassabrie pressed her finger against it until she bled enough to coat most of the tip.

"Pull it out now and mix my blood into the crystals. It's the only way to cure the disease."

Adrian withdrew the sword. As the tip passed through the membrane, Cassabrie's blood sizzled. She pushed a finger through the hole, scooped a dab of crystals onto the tip, and drew it back in. From inside, she rubbed them over the cut, instantly closing it.

Adrian wiped the blade's tip over the crystals in his palm. As the blood seeped in, the sizzling heightened, and the crystals turned scarlet and began to shrink.

"Compress it," Cassabrie said, "just as if you were forming dough into a ball. But don't drop it or let it touch anything but skin, or it will dissolve."

Adrian laid the sword down, pressed his hands together, and began rolling the crystals. With every rotation, the ball grew hotter and hotter. After a few seconds, smoke rose from his hands, and the odor of burning flesh assaulted his nose. He blew through the gaps between his palms, but the air did nothing to ease the torture.

Finally, he opened his hand. A shining ball sat on his palm, singed flesh surrounding it and smoke curling up from the wound.

"Now tell Regina that this is the cure," Cassabrie said, her voice calm. "Ask her if she wants to swallow it. You must warn her, however, that it will burn terribly. She must make the choice herself."

Gritting his teeth at the burning pain, Adrian shook his head. "There has to be another way. This will kill her."

"I cannot deny it. In her weakened state, it might kill her. Yet, it's her only hope. She'll be dead in moments if she doesn't take it."

Adrian sighed. "I guess you're right." He hurried back, sat next to the raft, and pulled Regina into his lap. "Regina," he called in an urgent whisper, "I need you to listen to me."

She blinked her eyes open, revealing her familiar glazed orbs. "I ... I'm listening."

"You have the disease Exodus carries, and you'll die if you don't take this pill I have."

"A pill? What's a pill?"

"It's something that's small enough to swallow, and it heals your body, but this one is very hot." He pinched the stardrop, instantly scalding his fingertips, and drew it toward her mouth. "I'm putting it close to your lips so you'll feel how hot it is. You have to tell me if you want to risk it. You're so weak, you might die anyway, but if you don't take it, the disease will kill you."

As he inched the stardrop toward her lips, her face twisted. "It *is* hot!"

He pulled it back and let it settle in his palm. His skin continued sizzling, and smoke continued to rise. "Will you take it?"

"Will it make me see?" she asked.

Adrian looked at Exodus, now about ten paces away.

"I wish I could tell you, Adrian," Cassabrie said, "but I simply don't know. I have been told that it can cure the disease. I have no more information than that."

Regina closed her eyes tightly, furrowing her brow.

"Regina? Did you decide?"

"Shhh. I'm asking the Creator what to do. I want to see again, so I'm asking him."

"Okay, I'll—"

"Augh!" Her eyes and mouth shot open wide. Her body bent into another convulsion. Clutching Adrian's arm, she cried out in a stuttering wail. "Give ... it ... to ... me!"

Holding his breath, he pushed the stardrop deep into her mouth and closed her jaws. Her eyes widened further, and her cheeks flushed red. Closing her eyes tightly again, she swallowed.

For several seconds, no one moved. All was silent. Then, Regina's skin grew hot. The ulcers on her stomach, still exposed by the torn tunic, began to bubble and sizzle. The outer edges receded, instantly replaced by healthy skin.

Regina smiled, her eyes still closed as she whispered, "I feel much better."

"Whew!" Adrian swiveled toward Cassabrie. "You did it! The stardrop worked!"

"Yes, I see that." Cassabrie neither smiled nor frowned. "That confirms what I must do for all of Starlight."

"What do you mean? What must you—"

"Adrian?" Regina called.

He turned back to her. "Yes?"

She blinked rapidly. "I still can't see."

"Well, the stardrop wasn't supposed to—"

"But …" Her voice took on a lamenting tone. "But the Creator said it would work. He said I would be able to see."

"The Creator spoke to you?"

She nodded. "Not like you speak to me. I saw him in my mind. I heard his voice inside me."

"She is a Starlighter," Cassabrie said. "I can recognize my own kind. Exodus has provided the Creator's words to her gifted senses."

"But if the Creator said she would be able to see, then why—"

"Help!" Regina stiffened in his arms. Her eyes rolled up, exposing only the whites. Clutching Adrian's tunic, she let out a long, wordless wail. Then, she fell limp.

Adrian touched her cheek. "Regina?"

Wallace and Shellinda crept closer. "Is she all right?" Shellinda asked.

"I think so. The sores are gone." Adrian pushed an eyelid up. Her eye stared straight at him, still glazed, still blind. "Regina, can you hear me?"

"I don't think she's breathing," Wallace said. "Check her heart."

"She's just resting. The stream's too loud to hear her." As Adrian shifted her to the raft, his arms shook violently. "The stardrop's power must have sapped her strength."

Wallace set his ear on Regina's chest. "I don't hear anything. No heartbeat at all."

As Adrian looked at him, his throat tightened. He couldn't say a word. Shellinda slid a hand into his and whispered, "You did the best you could."

He turned to Cassabrie. With her chin resting in her hand, she seemed puzzled, but she stayed silent.

Adrian touched Wallace's head. "Let me." When Wallace moved out of the way, Adrian laid his cheek on Regina's chest and listened, tuning out the surrounding noises. Her frail chest stayed motionless, and her heart made no sound.

As he rose and looked at Cassabrie, he swallowed hard, loosening his throat. "If the stardrop cured the disease, why did she die?"

"I have a suspicion." Cassabrie tapped her foot on the star's floor. "I wonder."

Adrian laughed nervously. "It's some kind of Starlighter trance, right? She can stop her heart and—"

"No," Cassabrie said. "Don't let your grief fabricate a myth. Something else is happening."

As tears trickled down his cheeks, Adrian's voice took on a tremor. "Then what *is* happening?"

"Stand back!" Cassabrie ordered. "Everyone move away! Immediately! I need room."

Adrian scooped Marcelle up and guided Wallace and Shellinda to a spot several paces from the raft. After laying Marcelle down, he looked back, a hand again shielding his eyes. "What are you going to do?"

Cassabrie guided Exodus directly over Regina and lowered the bottom of the sphere to a point less than a foot above the raft. As the star's radiance washed across her, her body bent into a new convulsion, this one more violent than the others.

Shellinda clapped her hands. "She's alive!"

"In a manner of speaking." Cassabrie lowered herself to her knees and looked down through the star's transparent skin. "You have to, Regina. It's the only way."

Regina panted, her scalded tongue protruding with each breath. "I want ... to see! ... I want ... to be healed ... by the trees!"

"Come with me, my dear Starlighter. I will show you complete healing. You will see in ways you cannot imagine, and you will be able to help Adrian and Marcelle in ways you never could before."

Adrian took a step closer. "Cassabrie! What are you doing?"

"Stand back, Adrian," she commanded, lifting a hand. "There is nothing you can do to help her."

Adrian bit his lip hard. Cassabrie knew everything about Starlighters, and he knew nothing. He had no choice but to let her take over.

Cassabrie set a palm against the star's floor. "Now, Regina! You must hurry, or it will be too late!"

His arms trembling, Adrian called out, "Regina! It's okay, sweetheart! Do what she says. You can trust her." Even as he uttered the words, doubt rolled in. Although Cassabrie's plans had worked out before, it seemed that her ideas always balanced on a thread. The slightest mishap could mean tragedy.

A sparkling aura formed around Regina. Like an animated glove, the aura moved as her tortured body convulsed. Then, like a marionette dropped by its master, she fell to the raft, once again limp.

Adrian took a hard step toward her, but Wallace held him back. "Wait!" Wallace said, pointing. "Look!"

The sparkling glove lifted away from the limp form, a perfect replica of Regina, though silvery white and radiant. As she rose, Exodus lifted to give her room. She turned toward Adrian. Flashing a big smile, she shouted, "I can see!"

Adrian spread out his arms and rushed toward her, but Cassabrie raised a halting hand. "No!"

He stopped within a few paces. "What's wrong?"

"She is in an intermediate stage and is unstable. I have to take her to the Northlands where Alaph will complete her transition. By the time you arrive, she should be ready to interact with you."

"Can she be reunited with her body?"

"It is possible. The same kind of process tore Marcelle from her body, and the energy she absorbed has kept her intact, but it won't last much longer. Her will to stay alive has been a preserving influence as she has maintained a connection, but this won't happen with Regina. Her body will soon deteriorate."

"Why?"

"She wants to see," Cassabrie said, passion spiking in her tone. "She wants to leave her blind shell behind. The Creator has seen fit to allow her departure, so you will have to accept the loss."

Adrian nodded. Again, what could he say? Cassabrie knew so much more than he did. He lifted a trembling hand and waved. "I will see you soon, Regina."

Her smile grew even wider. "And I'll see you, too, Adrian Masters!"

Cassabrie stayed on her knees with her palm on the star's floor. "Now set your hand against mine, and we'll be on our way."

Regina pressed her palm against Exodus, matching Cassabrie's outline. The star began to rise, and Regina rose with it. As it lifted higher, Cassabrie looked down, her gaze focused on Adrian. "I also hope to see you again, my love, but I don't think I will until we are both eternal spirits. I will never forget our time together. I hope your memories of me will someday be stripped of distrust."

She turned toward the north, her head low. Then Exodus and Regina's radiant spirit sailed away.

"She's gone!" Shellinda took Adrian's hand and pressed it against her chest. "They're both gone!"

"Yes ... they are." Adrian gazed at Regina's body as it lay motionless on the raft. The rip in her tunic still displayed her pink, healthy skin. Cassabrie's stardrop had expelled the disease, but that wasn't enough. Regina prayed for sight, and the Creator granted her request.

He turned again to Shellinda. Her arms and face were still clear. "Wallace, check your skin."

Wallace lifted his shirt. A pink rash covered his flat stomach. "It doesn't look good, does it?"

"Better than Regina's rash." Adrian checked his own abdomen. His skin appeared to be normal. "Maybe since we're stronger, we can make it to the Northlands."

Shellinda dropped to her knees next to Marcelle and lifted her shirt, exposing her rippled abdomen and perfectly healthy skin. "Will Cassabrie make stardrops for everyone?" Shellinda asked.

Adrian took in a long breath. "I have no idea. She seems to have a plan, and she left in a hurry to carry it out, so I guess we'll just have to trust her."

Wallace pinched Adrian's sleeve. "I don't see how we're going to keep up with them." With a tear trickling from his eye, he set the sword's hilt in Adrian's hand. "The river's going in its normal direction again."

Adrian nodded at the raft. "The two of you can drag the raft to the river. Let's send it downstream so it'll go over the falls. It has infected blood on it."

While Wallace and Shellinda obeyed, Adrian scanned the area. From the north, gray clouds drifted closer, portending rain or perhaps snow. He stooped next to Marcelle and felt her clothes, dry now due to the presence of the star. "It's not much farther," he whispered. "I can already feel a cooler wind. I'll do my best to keep you warm."

Soon, Wallace ran to his side, Shellinda trailing. "We don't have a cart," Wallace said. "I can carry Marcelle for a while."

Smiling in spite of the burns in his palms, Adrian rose and set a hand on Wallace's shoulder. "Since she and I aren't showing any symptoms, I'd better carry her. But first ..." He stabbed the ground with the sword. "We have a little girl to bury."

TWENTY

"FLY lower," Marcelle shouted, "or the guards will see you!"

Magnar beat his wings, staying high above the treetops. "Do you think I fear a few human soldiers? I will make them into torches before they can draw an arrow."

"It's not about fear. It's about stealth. We don't want Maelstrom to know we're coming until we arrive."

His neck bent, bringing his head close. "I have heard your warnings about his power too many times. If we burst into his abode, we will attack with speed and flames. He will not have time to prepare."

"No! You won't be able to fly once you're inside the palace. It's not big and roomy like the Zodiac. You could be trapped."

"Then what is our target?"

"It's called the Enforcement Zone. It's near the back. I'll point it out when we get there."

As they closed in on the palace, Evan came into view, again guarding the front gate. He pointed toward the sky and shouted, but his voice was too weak to be heard above the sounds of Magnar's wings and the whipping wind. He ran toward the front door, slipping once along the way.

"Do you see that man with the ponytail?" Marcelle called.

"Ponytail? I see no tail on any man."

"His hair. It's tied in the back. That's a ponytail."

Magnar's face aimed toward the fleeing guard. "I see him."

"He's going in the front door to sound an alarm. Fly to the opposite side. Hurry!"

Magnar swung to the right and circled around the huge marble-coated building. Soon a rectangle of red stones and surrounding green shrubs came into view. From the air, the Enforcement Zone looked like a child's playground, a crudely painted foundation with wooden structures small enough for little ones to climb and swing upon—the burning stake, now clear of embers and ashes; the gallows, still void of a hangman's noose; and three pillories bearing holes void of captive victims. As small and harmless as the devices seemed from the air, they were as deadly as adders.

"See the platform with the wooden arm over it?" Marcelle shouted.

"I do."

"That's your first target. Destroy it, then land, and I'll tell you … I mean, I'll make my next request."

Magnar's neck bent toward her again. "Is it acceptable to destroy everything in sight?"

Marcelle nodded. "That sounds good to me."

"Then be prepared for a rough ride." He straightened his neck, pulled his wings in halfway, and angled into a dive.

After checking the sword at her hip, Marcelle clutched the spine, lowered her head, and stayed quiet. Magnar needed to attack with swiftness and efficiency, thereby striking fear into the hearts of any witnesses. He had proven himself to be an exquisite and powerful flying machine, and his perfectly executed attack on the Tarkton soldiers gave evidence of his intellect, so he probably needed no further instructions.

As he descended, Magnar blew a barrage of flames at the gallows' support beam, setting it ablaze. He followed with a ball of fire that splashed across the platform and spilled over the sides, like flaming soup overflowing its pot.

Zooming down, he crashed through the weakened support arm and sent it flying across the yard. Fiery wooden shards flew in every direction. Sparks and splinters rained on Marcelle's hair and tunic, but she quickly brushed them away.

Magnar landed on the run, his wings beating madly. His neck snapping like a viper's, he shot a fireball at one of the three pillories, then shifted to the next and the next. Each flaming sphere seemed bigger and brighter than the one before.

Shouts erupted from the palace. A bell gonged. Yet, no one ran from the rear entry.

The dungeon trapdoor flew open. Soldiers dressed in Tarkton uniforms spilled out. Carrying spears and bows, they formed a line at least twenty men across. Several shot arrows that clinked off Magnar's armor, and one threw a spear that glanced off his scales and fell harmlessly to the ground. Then, shouting at the top of their lungs, they charged.

Magnar swung his tail, knocking five men off their feet. With another viper strike, he launched a wave of fire that rolled over three bowmen and engulfed them in flames.

As the one-sided battle continued, Marcelle flattened herself on Magnar's back and watched the soldiers continue their futile attempts. It didn't make sense. Why were there so many waiting in the dungeon? Why were they armed and ready when she and Magnar arrived? And why were they lobbing harmless projectiles that couldn't possibly injure an armored beast of his size? Even if they were trying to tire him out, it would take hundreds of soldiers to drain his energy.

"Drain his energy?" She scanned the Enforcement Zone. At the far end, shielding himself behind the burning stake, Maelstrom extended an arm, his palm out and his eyes fixed on the rampaging dragon.

"Magnar!" she shouted, pointing. "Look that way! Blast him!"

Still spewing flames, Magnar showed no sign of heeding her call. Between his own roars and the shouts of the soldiers, he probably didn't hear.

With the rain of arrows and spears diminishing as the Tarks burned, Marcelle slid down Magnar's scales and sprinted toward the stake. As she neared, she slowed to draw her sword.

Maelstrom heaved the stake out of the ground and hurled it at Marcelle's feet. She leaped but misjudged its speed. Her toe caught on the rolling stake's side, sending her flying headlong. She landed on her stomach and slid across the red stones, ripping her tunic. Arxad's scale pressed painfully against her chest.

She flipped to her back, jumped up, and set her feet in battle stance. Maelstrom stalked slowly toward her, his own sword drawn and his red hair hanging at an angle across his eyes.

"It is time we finished our battle," he said with a nonchalant air. "You don't have Orion to help you now."

Marcelle studied his face and posture. Even after pulling up that heavy stake and throwing it, he showed no reaction to the effort. He neither sweated nor breathed heavily, even in the sun-drenched humidity. The dragon's power had made him strong, indeed.

She glanced at Magnar. He lay on his side, his neck reeled out over the red stones and his head motionless. Although he had been drained of energy, every soldier lay broken or burning around him, so he was safe for the time being. Three Tarks sprawled close by, their burning clothes warming her chilled skin. The stake had rolled next to one of the bodies, and it, too, burned with the dragon's fire.

Maelstrom lunged with his sword. Marcelle jumped to the side and swung her blade at his throat. As fast as lightning, he blocked her stroke. Then, with a powerful twist of his wrist, he wrenched her sword from her grasp and slung it away.

As he drew back his sword to strike again, Marcelle dove for hers, scooping it up as she slid. She jumped to her feet and backed away, resisting the urge to flinch. Such power and speed! How could she possibly defeat him?

Maelstrom continued a slow march, his sword pointed at her. "You seem surprised. Did you really think you could defeat me in a fair fight?"

"Fair?" Marcelle scanned the flaming debris, then the palace's rear door. Someone skulked out, but his cloak and hood hid his identity. "You call this ambush fair?"

"Ambush?" He stopped and pointed the sword at Magnar. "I was merely protecting my domain from this beast."

Marcelle stopped as well. Her shoe crunched on something. With a quick glance down, she spotted a rope fragment, part of the remains of the execution. "How did you know we were coming?"

"The torture of his sister did wonders to loosen the captain's lips."

Marcelle scowled but held back the insult that begged to be shouted. "Where is he now?"

"Reed is in custody along with all the disloyal officers and your father."

Marcelle nodded. He didn't mention Professor Dunwoody. Apparently he hadn't been apprehended. "What are you going to do with them?"

"I see no need to tell you. The only reason I have deigned to provide any information is so that I can issue an ultimatum."

"And that is?"

"Watch and see." He clapped his hands and turned toward the dungeon entrance.

Bryan Davis

Marcelle spun that way. Her father climbed slowly out, followed by a Tark with a dagger at his back. The Tark also carried a pair of fireplace tongs. She swallowed back another shout. She had to stay calm. Defeating this madman would require a clear head.

"With the dragon's energy coursing within me," Maelstrom continued, "I have the power to slice you into pieces, but you would merely crumble, and your spirit would escape, just as Cassabrie's did when I tried to capture her. Yet, with your father's life as leverage, I can ensure that your destruction is complete." He opened his left hand, displaying a crystal in his palm. "This is the same kind of crystal that I embedded in the rope. When it is heated, it absorbs the spirit of a bodiless witch. My plan was to return to the stake and collect the crystals that absorbed you, but it seems that I waited too long, and my delay allowed you to escape. Now, if you want your father to live, we will reenact the execution without the usual pageantry. You will hold this crystal and set yourself aflame with one of the many sources of fire here. Once you are absorbed, you will be trapped and out of my way. Then I will release your father."

"Two questions," Marcelle said, raising a pair of fingers. "First, how do you plan to keep me in the crystal? It will eventually cool off."

Maelstrom's lips bent into a twisted smile. "You will be a decoration in my fireplace, a jewel in the midst of perpetual flames. As I sit and enjoy the warmth, I will know that you are suffering inside, tormented day after day in a crystalline prison. My hope is that you will be able to look out into my quarters and watch me enjoy the fruits of my labors. The more you suffer, the more I will relish the pleasure."

"So you're a greedy, sadistic narcissist. I get that." With another furtive glance, she spotted the cloaked skulker as he circled the Enforcement Zone, apparently undetected by the Tark holding her father. "But how do I know you'll let my father live?"

96

"Watch as I speak." Maelstrom took a step closer and spoke toward the crystal. "If Marcelle Stafford sacrifices herself in flames and is absorbed, I will release her father and allow him to live in comfort for all his natural days."

Marcelle eyed the crystal. It shone brightly without a shade of gray.

"You see?" He nodded at his palm. "Perfectly clear."

Scowling, she spoke toward his palm. "Leo is a wise, benevolent man." The crystal instantly turned black.

As it slowly regained its clarity, Maelstrom shook his head. "Your attempts at humor are quite entertaining."

Maelstrom quickly closed his fingers around the crystal, but Marcelle caught a glimpse of it before it disappeared. It had stayed clear in spite of his obvious lie. Did a male Starlighter have the ability to lie without detection?

She laid her sword down and extended her hand. "Give it to me. I will set myself on fire."

Bending his brow into a skeptical arch, he opened his hand again, revealing the crystal, still as clear as ever. "You're telling the truth."

"Of course I am." She snatched it out of his hand. "I'll do anything to save my father." She stealthily glanced again at the cloaked man. He had made his way around to the side. With an arrow set to a bow, he crouched behind a shrub. The Tark was easily in range of an expert archer, but who could tell if this man had enough skill? Even if not, her plan had to proceed.

She pointed at the burning stake, which lay only three paces to her left. "That source of fire should suffice."

"I assume so. Just get on with it before the dragon recovers."

As she stepped toward the stake, she glanced once again at the archer. He raised the bow and stretched the string. He was ready.

"Marcelle!" her father called. "No!"

She swiveled toward him and gave him a weak smile. "Trust me, Daddy. It's the only way."

He shook his head hard. "I am old. It's better that you live and I die. Fight him! I know you can defeat the likes of him."

She let her smile wilt. "Thank you, but there is too much for you to do. You will see." She knelt next to the stake, grimacing at the heat, laid herself over the burning wood, and hugged it with both arms. Heat raged from head to toe. Pain ripped through every nerve. It seemed that her core had exploded into a furnace.

Now fully ablaze, she rose to her feet, took off the rope she had tied to her waist, and charged at Maelstrom.

Gasping, he staggered backwards. He raised an arm, but Marcelle threw a loop of the rope around him, tied a hard knot in front, and shoved him to the ground.

The thwack of a bow sounded, then a man's scream of anguish. Marcelle spun in place. The Tark had fallen, an arrow protruding from his neck. The cloaked man ran out of hiding. His hood blew back, revealing Professor Dunwoody's aged head.

"Water!" her father shouted. "We need water for Marcelle!"

Professor Dunwoody ran toward her, waving his arms. "Marcelle! Roll on the ground!"

Her father leaped at her with outstretched arms, but she dodged and staggered toward Dunwoody. Everything in her view elevated, as if her lower body crumbled with each step. She held out her fist and gasped, "Keep the crystal!" Her hand dissolved. The crystal tumbled to the ground and seemed to zoom toward her. Then, sheer whiteness overwhelmed her senses.

*　　　*　　　*　　　*　　　*　　　*

Marcelle rode up and down, bobbing like a raft on a river. She opened her eyes and looked around. Once again, a boy walked in front of them with a girl at his side, but the other child was no longer there. A stream bubbled somewhere to the left, and the two children whispered to one another, though their words were indistinct.

Marcelle flexed her fingers around Adrian's wrist. As before, he carried her, but this time out in the open instead of in a dark tunnel. Clouds raced across the sky, and a cold breeze brought a chilling shiver.

"I'm sorry, Marcelle," Adrian said. "I know it's cold, but we lost the deerskin along the way. When we get to the Northlands castle, we'll find a soft bed and warm blankets."

Marcelle gazed at his profile. Sweat trickled from his temple to his jaw, drawing a line down his dirty, bloodstained face. Solarus shone across his beard growth, thick in spots, nearly bare in others. Cuts and scratches marred his cheek and chin, and a bruise dressed his jaw in purple. Every mark, though likely painful, was beautiful to behold. This man was truly heroic, a warrior with a heart of gold.

As Adrian's arm tightened around her thighs, she luxuriated in his embrace. It felt so warm and good. Taking in a deep breath, she forced out, "The Northlands?"

He nodded. "It's not far. That's why it's getting so cold."

"Your father ... is there. ... Waiting ... for you."

He looked at her and smiled. "It's good to hear your voice again."

She frowned. "Look ... for him."

"My father?" He glanced ahead before continuing. "Sure, I'll look for him. I saw him get healed there. I'll tell you all about it when you recover."

Marcelle blinked. Recover? Had she returned fully to her body somehow? What had happened on Major Four?

Fire blazed in her mind, then the image of Maelstrom's burning body. Had she succeeded? Did Professor Dunwoody keep the crystal, and could she emerge from it when it cooled? And did he and Daddy escape?

After taking another breath, she reached for more words. "Have to … go back. … When it's cool. … Get the soldiers."

"When it's cool?" Adrian laid her on the ground and knelt beside her. The boy and girl stopped and sat in the flower-filled meadow, both with slack shoulders and drooping heads.

After wiping sweat from his brow, Adrian took Marcelle's hand and rubbed her fingers. "You're already cold. You need to warm up, not cool down."

She groped with her free hand, using her fingers to climb his tunic until they reached his face. She caressed his cheek and looked into his eyes. "Thank you … for taking care of me."

He returned the caress. "I would do anything for you. Just relax and concentrate on getting better."

"Can't … relax. … Too much … to do."

"I've heard. You've been talking about being home on Major Four, something about traveling there in spirit. I don't know if you're just dreaming or not, but no matter what happens—"

"Shhh." She moved her fingers to his lips. "Just tell me … one thing."

He lowered his head closer. "What's that?"

"Did you … mean it? … Or was I … dreaming?"

"Mean what?"

"Your question." Closing her eyes for a moment, she took in a deep breath and summoned her reserves. "You asked me to marry you."

"Oh, Marcelle!" He took her hand again and ran his knuckles across her cheek. "If it will help, I'll ask again."

She pressed a fingertip over his lips. "Wait. … Wait until … I return … from Major Four." Exhaling, she closed her eyes. The darkness behind her lids transformed from gray to black, and it seemed to fly away, replaced by vague light and color. The sound of the nearby stream faded, and only a soft echo reached her ears.

"Hurry back, my love. I will be waiting."

Marcelle opened her eyes. A dresser stood to her right, familiar, yet somehow out of place. She lay in a bed, soft and warm. It, too, seemed familiar. Had Adrian already brought her to the Northlands and laid her in a bed as he had promised?

She sat up and dangled her legs over the side. No. This was her own room, the one attached to her father's. The last time she was here, it had been ransacked, but now everything had been picked up and put in order.

With a quick slide, she dropped to the floor. Her shoes were still on, as were the same trousers and tunic she had been wearing on Major Four, though no longer ripped by her fall in the Enforcement Zone. A chill swept across her skin, forcing her into a hard shiver. Yes, she was back in her bloodless form, a spirit wrapped in a cold shell of dust.

She turned to the bed. A crystal lay in the sheet folds. She snatched it up and drew it close. It appeared to be the same one she had taken from Maelstrom or at least one very similar to it.

Male voices drifted in from the adjoining room. She stepped close and peeked around the corner. Her father, Professor Dunwoody, and Captain Reed sat in high-backed leather chairs—Father facing away with his chair close to the bed, and Dunwoody and Reed facing him, their backs to his desk. Beyond all three of them, flames crackled in a fireplace. The logs appeared to be newly set, barely scorched at all. To her right, her sword and scabbard lay perfectly aligned on the neatly made bed.

She leaned in, then drew back. Hearing their conversation might be beneficial. Perhaps they would be more unguarded in her absence.

"It was dragon fire," Dunwoody said, pointing at a book on his lap. "Arxad said he and the crystals could be destroyed with it, so I don't think Leo is in one of the surviving crystals at all. He has been destroyed. Magnar's flames were the source for every blaze, so it was dragon fire that burned the stake. Marcelle took on those flames and transferred them to Leo. Earlier, I expressed my doubts to her that dragon fire differs from any other, but it seems that it carries a unique quality I cannot explain."

"Your theory has merit," her father said. "Still …" He slid his chair to the side, grabbed a poker from a rack, and stoked the logs in the fireplace. "I should like to keep this fire going. If our former governor is indeed trapped inside one of the crystals, I want to make sure he stays there."

"How many crystals did you throw in?" Dunwoody asked.

Father raised three fingers. "The rope was incinerated, as were most of the crystals. They were no more than shining dust for the most part."

Captain Reed withdrew a folded parchment and spread it out on his lap. "Will the new governor sign the order to invade Dracon?"

"With pleasure." Father leaned toward his desk, plucked a pen from an inkwell, and took the parchment. "I assume you found the funds to be satisfactory."

"Indeed. We will be well supplied."

Father signed the bottom of the parchment. "And the recruits?"

"Six hundred strong and climbing. It seems that Marcelle's speech had much more of an effect than we realized."

"Freedom," Dunwoody said. "When oppression is lifted, courage soars. Of course, the greatest heroes rise against despots even in the midst of tyranny, but we will not condemn those who are newly born heroes. We all had to start somewhere."

Captain Reed nodded sadly. "You speak this truth to my shame. I gave away much information when my sister faced brutality."

Dunwoody pointed a gnarled finger at him. "You judge yourself too harshly. You cared for someone else, not yourself. I was too frightened to pick up the crystals at the burning stake. I feared Leo. I put my own hide before Marcelle's life and hid under the gallows like a whipped dog. I have the greater shame."

"And I," Father said, raising his hand, "resisted Marcelle's efforts to journey to Dracon. I was more concerned about appearances and our family's reputation. My heart was broken by tragedy, to be sure, but that is no excuse to harden it to the cries of children who needed her sword."

Professor Dunwoody lowered his head, nodding. "So there is only one hero among us, the only one willing to sacrifice herself without question, without regard for herself or her reputation."

"Marcelle!" Her father rose to his feet. "I didn't see you there!"

Dunwoody and Captain Reed rose as well. "Excellent!" Dunwoody said with a grin as he laid the book on his chair. "It worked. The crystal cooled, and you emerged in the comfort of your own bed, just as I had hoped."

Walking in, Marcelle held out the crystal in her palm. "But if dragon fire destroys these crystals, how did this one survive?"

"Oh, yes!" Dunwoody stooped and retrieved a palm-sized leather bag from under his chair. As he walked toward Marcelle, he untied the drawstrings at the top and withdrew the scale Arxad had given her. "This covered it," he said as he laid the scale over the crystal. "If not for this protective shield, perhaps you and it would have been destroyed."

Marcelle stared at the scale. Her covenant with Arxad had saved her spirit from death. A dragon's sacrifice, a dragon's love, had preserved a human life.

"Oh!" Marcelle looked at the window, but the drapes blocked her view. "Where is Magnar? Is he all right?"

"See for yourself." Father slid between the bed and the wall and pulled a drape to the side. "He is as bad tempered as ever, but I think Captain Reed has found the perfect job for him."

The scale and crystal still in hand, Marcelle jumped on the bed, knocking the scabbard into a spin, and slid to the opposite edge. Outside, Magnar stood in the Enforcement Zone, the area now wiped clean of debris. Lined up in dozens of rows, hundreds of men faced him as he spoke, his head swaying from side to side.

"He is providing them with the history of Starlight," Father explained, "and informing them of what they will face when they arrive. He has already briefed us, and Captain Reed thought it fitting that the soldiers be aware of what they risk."

Marcelle pulled the other drape to the side and watched the expressive dragon. With every swing of his head, sparks and smoke flew from his nostrils, making the men in the front row lean back. "Did Magnar mention the disease?"

"What disease?" Father asked.

"Magnar and Arxad talked to Randall about it." Marcelle turned toward Dunwoody. "It's the same disease they were protecting the humans from when they sent the embryos here inside the eggs."

"Embryos? Eggs?" Father squinted at her. "What are you talking about?"

Dunwoody grabbed the book from his chair. "She's talking about a disease that killed every human on Dracon!" He lifted his brow. "Is it spreading there?"

"Not that I know of," Marcelle said, "but the dragons thought it could happen. They have a usurper on their world who might unleash it." She looked out the window again. Magnar spread his wings as if ready to fly while an officer marched the troops out of the Enforcement Zone. "I think it's time to go. We can tell Father and Captain Reed about the disease on our way to meet Magnar, and we'll have to discuss how to protect our soldiers in case it's been unleashed."

Professor Dunwoody rubbed a finger along the journal's cover. "If this book is true, no amount of protection will halt the disease. We will have to let the men know the risks."

"That might decrease our numbers," Captain Reed said.

Marcelle tucked the scale and crystal into the bag and tied it to her belt. "Tell them anyway." As she strode to the door, she grabbed the scabbard and sword from the bed and sheathed the blade. "I prefer sixty valiant men over six hundred with weak spines. We might face dangers far worse than a disease."

Dunwoody laughed. "Marcelle, you might scare away more men than a dragon or a disease ever could. In the company of your courage, their own courage will feel like fear."

"My men will be inspired." Captain Reed bowed toward her. "And I am inspired as well."

"Mutual respect won't defeat a dragon." Marcelle fastened the scabbard to her belt and opened the door. "Lead the way."

"I prefer you at my side." Captain Reed marched to the door, stopped next to her, and guided her against the wall. "I think the new governor should precede us, don't you?"

Marcelle grinned. "By all means."

"Then, Governor Stafford, if you will." Captain Reed swept his arm toward the doorway. "A good bodyguard always walks behind his governor."

"Come, Issachar," Dunwoody said as he hurried from the room, "we still have to prepare notification to the king. He will want to know that we followed all the rules of succession before he officially designates you as governor."

"Very well." Father walked in his wake but stopped in front of Marcelle. He took her hand and kissed her tenderly on the forehead. When he drew back, tears welled in his eyes. "I was wrong, my dear, very wrong. If you want to wear trousers and carry a warrior's weapons, I will learn to accept it. I never should have tried to discourage you from being a mistress of the sword. I wanted to mold you in the image of your mother, and that was a great mistake. I hope you will forgive me."

"Oh, Daddy!" She threw her arms around his waist and pulled him close, her cheek on his shoulder. "Of course I forgive you! I forgive you with all my heart!"

He patted her on the back. "I wish your mother were here to—"

"Mother!" She jerked away. "I found him!"

"Found him? Who?"

She grabbed his wrists. "The man who killed Mother! It was Drexel!"

"Drexel? How do you know?"

"I have so much to tell you and so little time." She hooked her arm around his and walked with him out the door. "But first, I want to ask you a favor. Can you look into getting something made for me?"

"Certainly. A new sword? A shield? I will ask the royal black-smith to—"

"No." She stopped and faced him. Letting a smile break through, she looked into his eyes. "Ask the royal seamstress. I think she already knows my size. I need a bridal gown."

TWENTY-ONE

FREDERICK skulked toward the line of trees, his body bent low and a sword at his side. Hacking and grunting sounded from within the glade, masking his approach. As he drew within a few steps, the noises suddenly ceased. He froze in place, listening.

"Finally!" someone said.

Walking on tiptoes, Frederick edged closer and peered between two trunks. Near the center of the glade, Drexel dropped an axe and fell to his seat in the midst of piles and piles of broken branches. He looked up. "I hope you're satisfied! After endless hours of backbreaking work, you're finally free!"

Frederick followed Drexel's line of sight. Three dragons sat on sawed-off limbs, one at the south side of the ring of trees, one to the east, and one to the west, looking like huge snowy owls perched on the edge of a roof. Their heads moving all around, they appeared to be inspecting the holes where the branches had once impaled their bodies. With so many branches missing, light pouring through the gaps between the trunks made the glade brighter than usual.

"What are you waiting for?" Drexel shouted. "You're free!"

One of the dragons shifted, as if ready to reply. Frederick studied its face. This was Beth, one of the females. He had talked to her once several weeks ago while exploring the trees. Lowering his head, Frederick squeezed between the trunks. Secretly listening in on their conversation might be of great benefit.

Once inside the glade, he crawled closer, using the fallen branches as shields. When he drew within a few paces, he sat in the shadow of one of the piles and leaned around the edge, his sword in his lap and his grip tight on the hilt.

"We are free," Beth said, a groan underlying her rasping voice as she balanced on the southern limb, "but we are not healed. We will not be able to leave this place until we are well enough to fly."

Drexel spread out his arms. "How long will that take?"

"You are eager, human, far too eager. The Code instructs us to be patient. Only the patient heart is rewarded with its desires."

Drexel let out a huff. "How dare you lecture me about patience! I have worked like a slave to set you free. I could have left you here and taken my chances with the portal."

"And your faith in us will be rewarded, as I swore to you. Once we punish the dragons of the Southlands and restore our rightful rule over Starlight, we will send you back to your world with the power you need to rule."

"Will you now reveal that secret power to me?"

Frederick slid a bit closer. The answer to Drexel's question might be too crucial to miss.

Beth bent her neck toward the dragon on the eastern limb. "Tell him, Gamal. You are the prophet among us."

Gamal extended his neck and stared at Drexel, his eyes shining blue. "There is a prophecy that the world of Starlight can have only three Starlighters at one time. As we speak, we have two in the world, girls by the name of Cassabrie and Koren. A third Starlighter, who once inhabited Exodus, has left this world, which allowed for the coming of another." He looked at the dragon on the western limb. "Dalath, what was the name of the departing Starlighter?"

"Brinella, a girl who lived for centuries within the great star." Dalath stretched out her wings and glided to the ground next to Drexel. "And we also had Zena before Koren was born, but she abandoned that station long ago. When she turned away from the Starlighter's calling, her red hair and green eyes both darkened to pitch."

"Correct." Gamal flew down and joined Dalath. "And when Brinella departed to be with the Creator, a new third Starlighter arose, but her light was quickly snuffed out only moments ago."

Frederick scooted to his original spot behind a pile of branches. These dragons were within striking distance, too close for comfort.

"How do you know about the Starlighters?" Drexel asked. "You've been here for years. Decades."

"Centuries," Gamal said. "My responsibility as one of the four Benefile is to monitor the Starlighters. Even from captivity, I watched them come into existence, and I observe their actions. Now that I am free, I will bestow the power of a Starlighter on a new candidate."

Drexel picked up a sword at his feet and held it loosely. "Someone who will help me take control of my world?"

"No." Gamal thrust his head toward Drexel, stopping within inches of his face. "You will be a Starlighter."

"Me?" Trembling, Drexel backed away a step. "How? You named only females, and I have neither red hair nor green eyes. Can a male even be a Starlighter?"

"Most certainly." Gamal withdrew his head. "A male Starlighter is powerful, indeed. The hair and eye color are merely the characteristics with which a natural Starlighter is born. If I endow you with such power, you will take on these physical traits. And it will likely be to your advantage if your appearance changes."

"Yes." Drexel rubbed his mustache. "I could also alter my facial hair."

Beth flew down from her perch and landed behind Drexel, making a ring of three white dragons around him. "As the third Starlighter," she said with a purring voice as ice pellets drizzled from her mouth, "you will be empowered to defeat all your enemies, and we will teach you what you need to know."

"I understand the history concerning a Starlighter's power on this world." Drexel glanced from dragon to dragon, his voice jittery. "But how do you know it will be available on my world?"

Beth shuffled closer, snaked her neck around his from behind, and looped back until she stared into his eyes. "We have sent a male Starlighter there in the past." She hummed her words, as if singing a lullaby. "A traveler such as yourself came here, an escaped slave seeking refuge. We struck a similar bargain, yet Gamal made the mistake of endowing him with power and informing him of the portal's location and use before he set us free. Traitor that he was, he broke his vow. He climbed these trees into the Northlands castle and went through the portal. Once he emerged in your world, instead of pitying his own kind and trying to help his fellow slaves, he abandoned them and determined to use his power to take control of Darksphere. He replaced a prince's son and plotted a takeover."

His arms stiff against his sides, Drexel swallowed. "A prince's son? Which one?"

"Prince Bernard," Gamal said, "though I heard the name only in passing. I see many of the Starlighters' activities, but not all."

Beth uncoiled her neck and drew back. "And now that Gamal is free, he will be able to see more."

"Prince Bernard's son." Drexel tapped his chin with a finger. "That must be Leo."

"You are correct," Gamal said.

Frederick blinked. Leo? Marcelle mentioned him. Maybe she really *was* a spirit on Major Four after all.

"I know of Leo," Drexel said, "but we have never met. What has been his progress?"

"He progressed quite well until recent events proved to be his undoing. He made a critical mistake, and he is now unable to fulfill his desires."

"What can I do to avoid his mistake?"

Beth's tail caressed Drexel's cheek. "You have already avoided it. You set us free."

"You see," Gamal continued, more ice spewing as he spoke, "when Leo climbed the trees, he became a bodiless spirit, so when he entered your world, he had to take on a false body that was cold and pale and had neither blood nor a heartbeat. Of course, people would notice these unusual characteristics, but he learned that he could chew a substance that provided warmth and infused his skin with a fluid similar to blood. This gave him the color he needed to blend in. I have not the desire to provide the rest of his strategy or give account of his failures, but if he had set us free, we would have led him to the portal on another path. He would have been even more powerful on Darksphere, and he would have avoided destruction. Because of your faithfulness, the better path is the one that awaits you."

Drexel gave a brief, shallow bow. "Fine. I am grateful. So what do I do now?"

"First," Beth said, "you must restore the spring so that we can bathe in it for healing. In order to help you, we must be fully healed."

Drexel glanced at the hole that once served as the spring's exit. "I've been down there already. The opening is too wide to plug, but I can try to collapse the ground so you can access the river. That might take quite a bit of time."

Dalath bobbed her head. "Since we must wait for the curse to lift, we have time. We cannot leave this circle of trees until then."

"Wait for the curse to lift?" Drexel pushed the sword's blade into the ground. "When will that take place? How do you even know that it *will* take place?"

"Patience, my human ally," Gamal said. "I am monitoring another Starlighter in your world, and she is coming here very soon. Because of her mode of transport, she will break the curse for us. This will come to pass in mere hours, perhaps two or three."

"Another Starlighter? But if she comes here, she will be the third Starlighter in this world. What will become of me?"

"Since her body is similar to Leo's, her powers are weak and fleeting. I will endow you now, and she will lose her power when she arrives. Then, when we are healed, we will take you to the Northlands and send you to your world. There you will no longer need our help, as you will learn in a moment."

"Excellent." Drexel spread out an arm. "What do I have to do?"

Frederick tightened his grip on the hilt of his sword. Letting Drexel become a Starlighter could be disastrous. But what should he do? Attack? These dragons didn't seem able to breathe fire, and their wounded state might give him an advantage. At the very least, he had to dispatch Drexel. The vile murderer would kill again, and he was more vulnerable now than he would ever be in the future, especially after he became a Starlighter. Talking to the dragons probably wouldn't help, not after he balked at freeing them.

"Just stand where you are," Gamal said. "Look into my eyes and allow my mind to penetrate yours."

Frederick leaped up and charged past the pile of branches, his sword raised as he aimed for Drexel's neck. Beth reared her head back and shot a barrage of ice that slammed Frederick in the face and chest and splattered all around. He flew backwards and landed on his bottom, sliding on the ice. By the time he stopped, all three dragons had encircled him, their heads cocked back as if ready to shoot more ice.

The ice crunching with every movement, Frederick struggled against the frosty coating, but the cold knifed into his muscles, making them weak and heavy.

"This is Frederick," Beth said. "We have had a conversation in the past. He made some attempts to set us free, but the level of his faith in us matched his feeble efforts. He preferred to keep the healing waters available for himself."

As Drexel joined the ring, Frederick gestured toward him with his eyes, unable to move any limbs. His lips nearly frozen, he spoke through chattering teeth. "Don't trust ... that evil fiend. ... He murders children. ... He slit the throat ... of a young boy named Zeb."

Beth glared at Drexel. "Is this so?"

"Of course not!" Drexel pointed his sword at Frederick. "He is a liar. He would do anything to save himself. His decision to keep the spring flowing should be enough to prove that."

Frederick looked at Gamal. "You monitor Starlighters. ... Ask one to ... tell the tale. ... You will see."

"A convenient excuse," Drexel said. "An appeal to someone who isn't here."

Beth extended her neck. Her head hovered close to Frederick's face. "Did you witness this killing of a child?"

Frederick tried to shake his head, but his neck was too stiff. "I did not."

"Then why do you make this accusation?"

"He has ... killed others. ... He kidnapped the child who ... unblocked the river. ... There are witnesses."

Drexel laughed. "Such inventions! I told you about Sarah. She went with me voluntarily, and Frederick's own brother took her with him, safe and sound after she completed her heroic task."

"Find a Starlighter," Frederick said, his teeth still chattering. "Have her ... tell the tale. ... Drexel won't ... want you to see it."

Beth swung her head toward Gamal. "In order to follow the law, we cannot kill this one until we verify his story or Drexel's."

"I agree," Gamal said. "Since Frederick is the one who attacked, we will freeze him for now and seek a Starlighter."

The dragons reared back their heads and spewed rivers of ice at Frederick. As all the world turned frosty white, he breathed out a desperate whisper. "Creator, watch over the children." Then both body and mind went numb.

＊　　　＊　　　＊　　　＊　　　＊　　　＊

Walking hand in hand with her father, Professor Dunwoody on her other side, Marcelle scanned the landscape. Their path of stone ended at a grassy field ahead with a forest at the opposite border, perhaps half a mile away. About four hundred men had gathered, a smaller army than they had first counted. Captain Reed had warned the soldiers about a possible disease, and he had encouraged those with young children or no one else to support their families to stay home. Some heeded the warning; most did not.

A crowd of well-wishers had just departed—parents, children, brothers, and sisters—leaving the soldiers to prepare without distraction. As an officer led the men in rousing chants, they beat their swords against their shields and waved their spears and bows, making an enormous racket that reverberated throughout the area.

Marcelle smiled. These were good men, enthusiastic and brave. They would do just fine. Her thoughts drifted to another good man—Gregor. He sacrificed so much. His courage and passion to save her from the pyre, as well as to liberate the slaves on Dracon, would never be forgotten, not if she could help it.

Near the middle of the line of troops, Captain Reed strode out and marched toward them. He would arrive in moments. Marcelle stopped at the end of the path and looked back at the palace, now a few miles away. It looked different—brighter, more vibrant, somehow happier. A good man sat in the seat of power, yet not a ruler, a servant, someone who would seek the best interests of the people.

She squeezed her daddy's hand. He returned it with a gentle squeeze of his own. Although her fingers were probably freezing, he didn't seem to mind. He was willing to suffer, and suffering had fashioned him into the man he was now—a widower, a former peasant, a noble who didn't fit in. Yet, he sympathized with peasants and nobles alike—with the peasants, because he once shared their poverty, rejoiced in their humble delights, and ignorantly mumbled along with their prejudiced grumblings against the noble class; with the nobles, because he mingled with the posh and participated in their luxuries, endured their shallow social gatherings, and gently countered the wagging tongues that poured disdain on those who wore canvas and gunny instead of silk and satin.

They turned to face the troops again just as Captain Reed arrived. "Did you speak to Magnar?" he asked.

Marcelle nodded. "We agreed that while you're marching the troops to the Northlands portal, I'll fly with him to the portal that leads to the Southlands mining mesa. If Arxad hasn't opened it yet, we will wait until he does."

Reed pointed at himself. "I assume you want me to remind Arxad about that duty."

Nodding again, she looked in the direction of the Elbon River. The portal lay somewhere out there. Fortunately, Magnar knew exactly where it was. "We'll wait as long as one day. Magnar would agree to no more. Then we'll go to the Northlands portal."

"That's a good idea. I see no reason to push a dragon beyond his limits."

Captain Reed straightened his body and gave Marcelle a crisp Mesolantrum salute, a right arm snapped across his chest, ending with a fist thump.

She returned the salute, but her fist struck the dragon scale she had returned to her chest. Biting her lip, she refused to acknowledge the pain. It would ruin the moment. "I'm looking forward to fighting alongside you, Captain."

"And I, you." Captain Reed turned an about-face and strode toward his soldiers.

Marcelle watched his masculine gait, so much like Adrian's—strong, confident, no hint of pretense. When he joined the troops, he shouted a command that sounded more like a guttural grunt than a word. Still, the soldiers understood. With great energy, they turned as a unit and marched into the forest in a two-by-two column.

As soon as the soldiers cleared the field, Magnar flew down and alighted at the spot where Captain Reed had shouted the marching order. With a mighty beat of his wings, he settled on his haunches and waited. It seemed that he desired as little interaction with humans as possible.

Marcelle turned to her father and Professor Dunwoody. The professor extended his hand. "Marcelle," he said with a formal tone, "it has been a pleasure getting to know you again. Of all my former students—"

She grasped his hand, pulled him close, and kissed him on the cheek, following with a whisper. "Thank you for everything. You are not just my teacher; you are my friend, my mentor, and my hero."

When she drew back, he shook her hand with both of his, his eyes misting. "Thank you, my dear. I will look forward to shaking your warm hands when you return."

Marcelle reached around her daddy's waist and embraced him tightly. With her cheek again on his shoulder and his loving arms wrapping her from side to side, his warmth seeped into her frigid skin, raising memories of a hundred similar hugs from years gone by. "I'll be back as soon as I can, Daddy." She pressed even closer. "And we'll have the biggest celebration Mesolantrum has ever seen."

He drew back, smiling broadly. "A wedding festival?"

"Definitely. If my visions were true, that is." She narrowed her eyes. "But who will perform the ceremony? I know you don't trust the Cathedral priests."

He touched her nose. "Now never you mind. I am concocting an idea that should be satisfactory to us all."

"A priest from out of town, I'll bet. Knowing you, it's probably one of the older priests nobody around here respects."

"Yes, yes. You're just too smart for me." He glanced over her and nodded toward Magnar. "You'd better get going. We wouldn't want to keep a dragon waiting. When you return, the seamstress should have your gown ready. Even if your visions weren't real, at least you'll have it for the man who is smart enough to ask for your hand."

"They're real." She leaped to tiptoes and kissed him on the cheek, then turned and ran. "I'll be back with Adrian!" she shouted. "But don't show him the gown!"

When she arrived in the field, she leaped up Magnar's side and settled on his back near the base of his neck, again clutching a spine in front. She withdrew the stardrop pouch from her pocket and attached it and her scabbard harness to the spine. When they returned to Dracon, these would fall off her spirit body.

Reaching ahead, she patted his scales. "Is my fire-breathing pony ready to go to war?"

Magnar whipped his neck around and glared at her. "Beware, wench. Do not take my position as your mount as a symbol of servility, and do not confuse your newfound familiarity with me as an invitation to friendly intimacy. I am *not* your friend."

"Okay, okay." Suppressing a smile, she pulled down her collar, exposing Arxad's scale. "Then be my warrior comrade. We're in this together."

"For my brother's sake ..." As a plume of smoke rose from his nostrils, he nodded. "I can do that."

Magnar beat his wings and leaped into the air, accelerating upward at a fierce angle. With every stroke of his wings, his body bounced. Marcelle hung on tightly. This pony had never bucked so hard before. "What's your problem?" she yelled.

When he leveled out, he bent his neck and faced her. "If you are unable to fly like a warrior, then I will set you down at the safe place of your choice."

She pointed at him. "You don't fool me, Magnar. You probably push your fellow dragons around with your bullying ways, but you should know by now that I'm not as pliable."

"You are as pliable as granite. Your head is certainly that hard." As Magnar looked down, she followed his line of sight. The troops came into view, alternately appearing and disappearing under the forest canopy as he sailed over them.

"Why are you following the soldiers?" Marcelle pointed to the left. "Isn't the mesa portal that way?"

"It is. Since I am unable to fool you, as you say, I will tell you that I have no plans to go there and wait. I will pass through the Northlands portal and fight for my kingdom immediately. I will not leave your brave soldiers to fight without a dragon leader."

"Arxad is there. He will lead them until you arrive."

"He is a priest, a peacemaker. They need a war dragon."

"What about the curse?" Marcelle asked. "Arxad seemed concerned about that."

"The curse needs to be broken. My species must face reality and endure the hardships that come because of the choices we have made, whether good or bad. Surely a warrior such as yourself can understand that principle."

"I can understand, but—"

"There is no need to counter. You are powerless to stop me, so either take my advice to land somewhere safe, or take courage and ride with me to a dangerous adventure. I detect that you have the heart of a warrior. I suggest that you act like one."

Magnar straightened his neck and continued flying above the soldiers. Marcelle relaxed her grip and watched the scenery pass underneath. What else could she do? This dragon had made up his mind, and arguing wouldn't do any good. He was as stubborn as ... well ... as stubborn as she was.

Taking a deep breath, she looked straight into the wind, her hair blowing back and her muscles taut. "Better get ready, Adrian. Here we come!"

The **Dragons in our Midst®** and **Oracles of Fire®** collection
by **Bryan Davis**:

RAISING DRAGONS

ISBN-13: 978-089957170-6

The journey begins! Two teens learn of their dragon heritage and flee a deadly slayer who has stalked their ancestors.

THE CANDLESTONE

ISBN-13: 978-089957171-3

Time is running out for Billy as he tries to rescue Bonnie from the Candlestone, a prison that saps their energy.

CIRCLES OF SEVEN

ISBN-13: 978-089957172-0

Billy's final test lies in the heart of Hades, seven circles where he and Bonnie must rescue prisoners and face great dangers.

TEARS OF A DRAGON

ISBN-13: 978-089957173-7

The sorceress Morgan springs a trap designed to enslave the world, and only Billy, Bonnie, and the dragons can stop her.

EYE OF THE ORACLE

ISBN-13: 978-089957870-5

The prequel to *Raising Dragons.* Beginning just before the great flood, this action-packed story relates the tales of the dragons.

ENOCH'S GHOST

ISBN-13: 978-089957871-2

Walter and Ashley travel to worlds where only the power of love and sacrifice can stop the greatest of catastrophes.

LAST OF THE NEPHILIM

ISBN-13: 978-089957872-9

Giants come to Second Eden to prepare for battle against the villagers. Only Dragons and a great sacrifice can stop them.

THE BONES OF MAKAIDOS

ISBN-13: 978-089957874-3

Billy and Bonnie return to help the dragons fight the forces that threaten Heaven itself.

Published by Living Ink Books, an imprint of AMG Publishers
www.livinginkbooks.com ✦ www.amgpublishers.com ✦ 800-266-4977

Now Available from Living Ink Books

Now Available from Living Ink Books

MASTERS & SLAYERS

(BOOK 1 IN THE <u>TALES OF STARLIGHT</u> SERIES)

Bryan Davis

Expert swordsman Adrian Masters attempts a dangerous journey to another world to rescue human captives who have been enslaved there by dragons. He is accompanied by Marcelle, a sword maiden of amazing skill whose ideas about how the operation should be carried out conflict with his own. Since the slaves have been in bonds for generations, they have no memory of their origins, making them reluctant to believe the two would-be rescuers, and, of course, the dragons will crush any attempt to emancipate the slaves. Set on two worlds separated by a mystical portal, Masters and Slayers is packed with action, mystery, and emotional turmoil, a tale of heart and life that is sure to inspire.

Now Available from Living Ink Books

PRECISELY TERMINATED

(BOOK 1 IN THE CANTRAL CHRONICLES SERIES)

Amanda L. Davis

It is 800 years in the future, and the world is being oppressed by the ruling class. Millions of slaves toil under the Nobles' oppressive thumb, but because of microchips implanted in their skulls at birth, there can be no uprising. Monica, a young slave girl, escaped the chip implantation process. She is able to infiltrate the Nobles' security and travel where no one else is able, but can one girl free the world?

Precisely Terminated is the debut dystopian fantasy novel by Amanda L. Davis, daughter of bestselling inspirational fantasy author, Bryan Davis.

For purchasing information visit

www.LivingInkBooks.com

or call 800-266-4977

LIVING
INK
BOOKS™
Writing Worth Reading™

Now Available from Living Ink Books

SWORDS OF THE SIX

(BOOK 1 IN THE SWORD OF THE DRAGON SERIES)

Scott Appleton

ISBN-13: 978-0-89957-860-6

Betrayed in ancient times by his choice warriors, the dragon prophet sets a plan in motion to bring the traitors to justice. On thousand years later, he hatches human daughters from eggs and arms them with the traitors' swords. Either the traitors will repent, or justice will be served.